King’s Ransom

King's Ransom

Mary Daheim

Seattle, WA

Camel Press
PO Box 70515
Seattle, WA 98127

For more information go to: www.camelpress.com
www.marydaheimauthor.com

Cover design by Sabrina Sun

King's Ransom
Originally published by Harlequin Historicals, 1990

ISBN: 978-1-60381-367-9 (Trade Paper)
ISBN: 978-1-60381-368-6 (eBook)

Library of Congress Control Number: 2016930247

Printed in the United States of America

Dear Reader,

I'VE BEEN FASCINATED BY THE sixteenth century since I was in my early teens. The Renaissance, New World discoveries, colorful, charismatic leaders, social, political and religious changes—all very exciting. I remained intrigued with the 1500s for decades. When I got serious about writing books, I set three of my first four historical romances in that period. (The fourth was an American Civil War story at the behest of my agent because, he explained, "They always sell well.") And never mind that I'd never intended to write a romance novel. But my agent had already intervened after he read the first manuscript: "Old-fashioned historical books are out—romance is in. Spice it up." So I did.

But by the fifth book, I felt I was in a 1500s rut. I needed to expand my writing horizons and my knowledge of history. I took the logical step and set what would become *King's Ransom* in the middle of the seventeenth century. Of course that meant doing research. Lots of research, because I can't write a book about a time or a place without feeling as if I'd be at home in that setting and that era.

Does that sound fanciful? Maybe. But it works for me. I hope it works for you, too, when you meet Puritan Honor Dale and Royalist Captain Hood. They find themselves at odds when it comes to politics, but like-minded when it comes to love.

That's another thing I learned about the seventeenth century: The heart knows no time or place. And though I don't know about you, I find that very reassuring.

–Mary Daheim

Chapter One

THE SINGLE PEARL IN MISTRESS Honor Dale's engagement ring was the size of a sparrow egg. It thrust up against her kid-skin glove like a giant wart, making Honor's slender hand look deformed. Perhaps she shouldn't have worn the ring on her journey to London, but hiding it away in the lining of her cloak with her other jewels would have seemed like an affront to Sir Tyler Vail. Unfortunately, her fiancé wouldn't be meeting the Oxford stage, as he was too involved in his investments on the Royal Exchange. Still, Honor wouldn't have felt right about arriving in London for her wedding without her engagement ring firmly affixed to her finger.

Glancing up from under thick golden lashes, she thought that the prim-faced couple opposite her were staring at her left hand with indiscreet curiosity. Next to her on the flat, hard coach seat, a stout country doctor known as Kennel of Kenilworth swayed from side to side like a ship foundering in a storm.

"Whoever coined the term 'flying coaches' must never have ventured more than a few yards from his own cozy hearth," the doctor grumbled as he bounced first against Honor and then into the unyielding side of the clattering conveyance.

"It certainly bears no resemblance to a winged creature," observed the prim-faced woman, whose lank gray hair dangled from under a starched white cap.

Though Honor offered no comment, she silently agreed. Doing her best to ignore the bumpy road, she concentrated instead on the passing views of grass downlands, scrub and beech woods. The coach groaned round a bend like a clumsy cow giving birth on a tightrope. Leaning forward, Honor braced herself with one hand. When she had boarded the coach at Oxford, she had been told that the journey could be made in a single day. However, it was now almost noon, with the sun high over the Chiltern Hills, and they were still a good twenty miles from their midday resting place at High Wycombe. Up ahead, the six ill-matched horses were laboring over a narrow stone bridge. The driver urged them on with a desultory flick of his whip as a half-dozen crows took flight from a hedgerow that lined the road just beyond the bridge.

Five hours already spent on the road, Honor calculated, trying to resettle herself into a more comfortable position beside the obese doctor, who wheezed raspingly with every breath he took. At this rate, they wouldn't arrive in London until well past the supper hour. Should she go straight to Uncle Oliver's apartments in Whitehall? At least the Cromwells were expecting her. Anxiously, Honor fidgeted with the black ribbons of her mourning gown's skirts and felt along the edge of her cloak to make sure her jewels were still in place. She didn't really mind confronting Uncle Oliver. Despite his stern, fearsome reputation as England's Lord Protector, he had never daunted her. Even as a child, she had found her uncle affectionate, with a surprisingly puckish sense of humor.

The coach was lurching more than ever as the road continued to wind up through the Chiltern Hills. The prim couple, Master and Mistress Cosgrove by name, now wore expressions of alarm. "I say," Master Cosgrove remarked as the coach bowed and dipped over a particularly deep rut, "it might have been wise to travel by horseback."

Dr. Kennel snorted with a hint of pleasure at his companions' pain. "Sensible, for most people, but I prefer being out of the elements. Wouldn't do to call on my patients with a case of the croup."

To Honor, it sounded as if Kennel already suffered from the disease. Letting her deceptively innocent brown eyes sweep discreetly over the doctor's immense bulk, she wondered if he had long ago given up trying to find a horse strong enough to carry him from Oxford to London. She wasn't quite so sure why she had decided to go by coach, however. At the time the arrangements were so hastily made, poor Aunt Lucy's steward had insisted that it wouldn't be proper for a nineteen-year-old maid in mourning to go racketing about the English countryside on a horse. What, a scandalized Master Ormsby had demanded, would Lady Lucy have thought? Very little, if at all, Honor had assured herself, since the woman had been dead for more than a month. But Honor had no intention of disparaging her aunt's memory. For all of Lucy Dale Ashford's fussy, bothersome attention to detail and propriety, she had been a kind, if scatterwitted, surrogate parent to Honor these past ten years.

A jolt brought Honor back to the present. The coach seemed to stand on end, dumping her in the lap of the bovine physician. Honor struggled to right herself but was vexingly aware that Kennel seemed to be enjoying himself immensely.

"Aha!" he wheezed, preening at the sensation of Honor's lithesome young body pressed against his. "There are some advantages to coach travel after all, eh?"

Honor pushed her feet against the far wall to give herself leverage, then managed to sit up straight once more. Across from her, the hapless Cosgroves were doing their awkward best to disentangle themselves from each other. "I say," gasped Master Cosgrove, peering over his wife's shoulder out the window, "I believe we've lost a wheel."

"Damme," cursed the doctor, hoping to catch a glimpse of Honor's ankles but disappointed when he saw she wore boots. "We won't make London by dark."

Honor tried not to let her own agitation show. At least it was July, with daylight well into the evening. For the first time, she wished she had taken Master Ormsby's advice and brought along Yetta Ward, her aunt's dim-witted ladies' maid. But Yetta's incessant bungling, coupled with her obstinate refusal to accept responsibility for her errors, drove Honor to distraction. Besides, Tyler had a houseful of servants. Honor could pick and choose among them after the wedding.

The driver was in the doorway, requesting his passengers to get out of the coach while he and his footman put the wheel back on. Dr. Kennel grumbled, the Cosgroves muttered, but Honor retained her composure, pausing only to make sure that the lining of her cloak was still intact. Her greatest fear was that she might somehow lose her jewels. They alone made up her dowry now that her feckless brother, Palmer, had run through the inheritance meant for them both. Even that had been meager enough, considering the terrible losses suffered by the Dales in the late Civil War. If Aunt Lucy had not died so suddenly, she might have remade her will instead of leaving her comfortable estate to her two well-married daughters. For the hundredth time since her aunt's demise, Honor blessed Sir Tyler Vail not only for falling in love with her but also for being so considerate in allowing their marriage to be moved up by three months. It was quite possible that her cousins might sell Aunt Lucy's fine country house at Whitehorse Hill immediately, leaving Honor with no place to go.

Drifting away from the others, Honor sat down under the shade of a dense beech tree. Except for a few fallen leaves, the ground was all but bare of undergrowth. Holding on to her brimmed black hat, Honor gazed upward, barely able to see the blue sky beyond the trees. Only the grunts of the coachmen and the clatter of axle and wheel disturbed the quiet world of the Chilterns. Honor was suddenly aware of being not only hungry but sleepy, as well. The jolting coach ride was far more fatiguing than she could have imagined.

Slipping down still farther against the tree trunk, she closed her eyes and let her body go slack. Moments later she had nodded off. In her dream, Sir Tyler Vail, his ash-blond hair ruffled by the summer breeze and his fine patrician features molded into a charming smile, stood in the doorway of his elegant home in the Strand. He held out his arms to welcome her and Honor ran to meet him. She opened her mouth to call out a greeting, but no sound came. Honor woke with a start and saw not Sir Tyler Vail but a square-set man wearing a big cloak and a mask.

"Such a pretty maid hiding by the tree!" The man revealed uneven teeth in a startling smile. "Over here, my captain!"

Honor peered around the man, focusing her eyes with effort. Three other cloaked men stood with pistols leveled at the coachmen, the Cosgroves and Dr. Kennel. The physician appeared to be blustering while the Cosgroves veered between terror and indignation. It was only when Honor saw Mistress Cosgrove reluctantly hand over her wedding ring that the truth hit home: these were highwaymen, the scourge of the English traveler.

"Damn and blast," Honor muttered in dismay. Transfixed by a rising sense of danger, she sat as if rooted to the tree, her hands clasping her knees. Surreptitiously she glanced at the shiny black creases of her riding boots. How desperate was her situation? She wasn't sure; certainly no one could guess where her jewels were hidden. Honor's eyes shifted to see the tallest of the bandits moving leisurely in her direction. With his unhurried air and easy grace, he might have been mistaken for an idle stroller, out to enjoy the peaceful beauty of the Chiltern Hills.

But the all-enveloping black cape and mask told a different, more menacing story. A broad-brimmed hat sat aslant on his head while he casually palmed a gleaming pistol. The eyes that gazed from behind the mask were lively, yet their color was uncertain. Gray, perhaps, or hazel. The hat's big brim kept his face in virtual shadow.

"Enchanting." He uttered the word low, with genuine admiration. "'Tis a pity to rob such a fair maid." He took another three steps, moving with that effortless grace. The nimble eyes seemed to dart everywhere at once, taking in everything, missing nothing. Yet at the same time they conveyed intensity and a probing quality that seemed to hold Honor's own gaze hostage.

She jumped when he stretched out a gloved hand, the other keeping the pistol pointed toward the ground. "Allow me, milady," he said as graciously as if they had met at a masque in a fashionable London mansion. "I mean you no harm and note from your doleful attire that condolences are in order." Reaching out to take Honor's right hand, he gently but firmly pulled her to her feet. "Forgive my audacity, but I must request your jewels and your money." Still holding on to her right hand, he tipped his head to one side, revealing the suggestion of a sharply etched profile. "It's not for myself that I ask," he went on with an air of self-mockery, "but for my master." That unsettling gaze traveled up and down Honor's slender, yet rounded young body, taking in the details of the gilt-fair hair, the wide, full mouth, the great, dark eyes. His appraisal was thorough but stopped far short of being vulgar. "Well?"

Honor was surprised to find no resistance when she tried to free her hand. Quickly she covered the left with the right, lest those all-seeing eyes should notice the bulge of the engagement ring. "Your master? Who is your master?" Something inside Honor recoiled, as if the highwayman had rung a bell warning of plague.

At the roadside, the square-set man had joined the other two thieves where they stood guard over the rest of the travelers. All eyes were turned on Honor and her confrontation with the highwayman.

"My master is your master, as well," the masked bandit replied evenly. "Someday, God willing, he shall be a gracious lord to us all."

Honor's slim body went rigid. She knew he was speaking of Charles Stuart, he who would be Charles II, King of England, save for the intervention of Oliver Cromwell. Honor's Uncle Oliver, the Puritan leader, had first toppled the crown from Charles I's head; then he had severed the King's head from his body Honor trembled with hatred for all that was royal. Not only was the man who stood so casually before her a thief, he was a King's man, as well. In Honor's mind, it was a far greater crime to support Charles Stuart than to steal.

The tall man's strange eyes had narrowed almost imperceptibly. "Well? Your politics are no concern to me, but your valuables are. Clearly, you are too fine a lady to be traveling from Oxford to London without funds." Gazing up into the dense foliage of the beech trees, he frowned. " 'Tis after noon. We could wait out the day if you wish." To prove his point, he dropped down onto the leaf-strewn ground to lie on his back with his fingers locked behind his head. The pistol rested on his chest, the broad-brimmed hat was tipped over his face, and one booted leg was propped up by the other.

Honor again glanced at her boots, then at the highwayman's companions. They were armed, of course, and well in control of the situation. Her brain was ajumble with a hundred thoughts, all pointing at one single, awful purpose. This was the moment for which she had waited so long. This was the first opportunity she'd been given to carry out the vow she'd made a decade ago. This was her chance for atonement. After years of rage and sorrow, she could now fulfill that fearsome fantasy that had haunted and bedeviled her for so long.

Mistress Cosgrove's shrill voice ripped into Honor's terrible reverie. "Oh, give him whatever you have, you silly girl! We wish to be on our way!"

With a lazy flip of his fingers, the bandit nudged back the brim of his hat and offered Honor an encouraging grin. "She's right, you know. There's nothing more precious than time."

Honor was as angered by the highwayman's nonchalance as by Mistress Cosgrove's betrayal. Even if she hadn't had other, more compelling reasons for thwarting the bandits, Honor would have found her prunelike traveling companion's attitude galling. The woman wore no jewels except her wedding ring; her attire, along with her husband's, was of the strictest Puritan simplicity. Whatever money they carried probably did not represent their life savings. Well and good for Mistress Cosgrove, thought Honor savagely, but in her own case, whatever future lay before her was stitched into the lining of her cloak.

Except, argued the voice of reason, that was not quite the truth. Tyler Vail needed no baubles, however costly, to augment his personal wealth. But Honor would never forgive herself for letting some cheeky Royalist scum make off with her only financial resources. And whether Tyler needed her dowry or not, Honor was well aware that only the most pathetic, impecunious maidens came to their bridal beds without a marriage portion. Indeed, most who were not so endowed never got as far as the banns.

As Honor marshaled her emotions and her thoughts, she decided that a clever ploy might save the day. It would also give her time to consider the best way of doing what she knew had to be done. With a great show of reluctance, she reached into a deep pocket of her cape to extract a small brocade purse. In it was the money Master Ormsby had sent along to pay for her expenses on the trip to London. Regarding the highwayman with a rueful look, Honor opened the purse and revealed its contents.

Rising to his feet with that deceptive grace, the man glanced at the purse and then back at Honor. From what she could see of his expression, he was clearly skeptical. The omniscient eyes once again studied her from head to foot.

"You will have your little jest, mistress, but I'm not keen on being made the fool," he said, reaching out to flick the folds of her cloak. "Your fine lamb's wool hangs awkwardly, as if sewn by a blind man." As Honor stiffened and involuntarily moved a step backward, he snatched at the fabric, shaking it experimentally. Despite the care with which the jewels had been set inside the lining, a slight tinkle sounded. Honor's hand flew to her breast, as if her virtue, along with her dowry, were at stake.

"Please, mistress," the highwayman requested quietly, " 'tis a warm July day. You shan't need the cloak and I shall see that it's returned later. I'd not insist if my cause was not so worthy and my master so in need. Come now, be a good lass."

Despite the virile voice and the hypnotic eyes, the highwayman had chosen the wrong approach. Honor set her face in stark defiance. Heedless of the pistol he held and the determination in his stance, she wrenched the cape from her shoulders, fastenings and all, then whipped it smartly in his face. Clutching at his broad-brimmed hat, the highwayman momentarily lost his balance. Honor whirled about and ran, the cape still grasped tightly in her hands. She knew she couldn't escape, but she refused to give him an easy victory. Mistress Cosgrove's incredulous cry and Dr. Kennel's outraged grunt followed her. It came as no surprise when within thirty yards the highwayman caught up with her. As one arm seized Honor by the shoulders, the other hand pressed the muzzle of his gun against her side.

"Silly chit!" the bandit muttered, dragging her back through the beech trees. Honor's boots bumped along the ground. She was almost as humiliated as she was furious. His fingers dug into her ribs, his forearm was crushed against her torso just under her breasts. She felt as though she could hardly breathe.

The highwayman slung her up against a slender beech and held his pistol a scant inch from her bodice. The long, gleaming barrel loomed at her, a menacing reminder of danger. But it was not the hand that held the gun that frightened her as much as the hand that touched her body.

Almost as disconcerting were those strange, clever eyes, in which she could read no intentions, only evidence of an agile mind. As if teasing a baby with a sweet, the highwayman brushed Honor's cheek with the pistol's chill steel. She looked down at her gloved fingers, which still clung desperately to the fawn-colored fabric. "Swine! I pray you'll rot in hell!" Honor snarled, and thrust the garment at her adversary.

He trapped the cape between his forearm and chest but kept gun—and hand—in place. Those strange eyes glittered, perhaps with anger, perhaps with some other emotion Honor was in no frame of mind to understand. With a quick gesture, she turned her left hand palm up, hoping he had not seen the outline of the huge pearl under the glove.

But he had. That shrewd gaze missed little. Tossing the cape to one of his henchmen, the bandit indicated her finger. "I'll take the ring, too. What is it, a chunk of coal?"

Honor's dark eyes raked his face as she stripped off the glove. It was awkward trying to remove the ring without letting her body come into even more intimate contact with his hand. But even as she twisted the gold around her finger, the highwayman shook his head.

"Never mind, mistress. It's not coal, but it's well-nigh as worthless. My master already has a surfeit of sentiment. He needs what can be turned into cold, hard coinage, not poor, useless imitations."

Honor gaped at the man, then at the ring. The man was calling Tyler Vail's betrothal gift a fake! The highwayman couldn't tell a pearl from a pebble. But it was hardly a point she cared to argue.

"Dross and gloss," intoned the bandit, leaning even nearer, "is what you'd give me. A jewel for a fool, a sham for my dame." The words were idle even as he raised his hand to tip up her chin. "What else would you give a poor beggar?"

Honor felt paralyzed. Her glance darted toward the others, but robbers and victims alike were at a discreet distance while the highwayman stood in such a way that his tall body and flowing cloak virtually hid her from view. High above them, a rowdy blue jay's harsh call seemed to mock her dilemma. Honor made a feeble effort to push the highwayman away.

"Who are you?" he asked, ignoring her struggles. "The pearl may be a fraud, but I'll wager that the gems in your cloak are not. Tell me your name, fair mistress."

She wanted to deny his words, to defy his will, but his mouth came down on hers in a confident, yet exploring, manner, as if he were tasting an exotic new delicacy. Honor's mind rebelled violently against his brazen liberty, yet some alien part of her welcomed the touch of his lips. Ridiculous, of course, but wasn't the spirit said to be strong while the flesh was weak? Honor trembled as she felt his kiss grow deeper. And then, with unexpected abruptness, he pulled back and assumed a speculative expression.

"You would rebuff me—if you could." He spoke in almost a whisper. "But whatever your name, I'll find you. Even England isn't large enough to let me lose you." Stepping back another pace or two, he made as if to tip his hat. "You have my word on it," he said lightly, though for the first time she sensed an underlying seriousness to the man.

He turned away, her cloak flung over his arm and the pistol still cradled in his hand. The other thieves had the horses ready and seemed anxious to be off. Though the square-set man kept his weapon trained on the travelers by the roadside, he and his companions were already in the saddle. Honor stood alone under the beech tree, apparently forgotten by the others but still distraught. Involuntarily, she put a hand to her mouth; she could swear the highwayman's kiss lingered. As the long cape billowed out behind him, he raised the pistol on high. "For King Charles! Long live the King!"

The ringing words jolted Honor from her stupor. From out of the past, other voices echoed with the same fervent cry. Oblivious to all but her memories, Honor grappled with skirts and petticoats, delving into her right boot. To her dismay, her hands were shaking. Impossible, she told herself sternly. She must be as steady as the noonday sun. By sheer force of will, she quieted the trembling and carefully took out the small, silver-chased pistol. Raising it with both hands, she pointed the barrel at the highwayman's back. Slowly, she pressed the flintlock to ignite the priming, then tightened her finger around the trigger. Her intended victim was no farther than thirty feet away. She had practiced diligently for years; it would be an easy shot. In the next second she would send the hated Royalist thief straight to hell. Honor gritted her teeth as she anticipated the pistol's sharp report.

The breeze sighed through the beeches, a woodpecker thrummed in the distance. Mistress Cosgrove was already arguing waspishly with her husband and the doctor. The highwayman swung up easily onto his horse and cantered down the road with his followers. Honor had frozen like a stone pillar.

Even then, in her haze of shock, she was grateful that no one else had noticed her futile gesture. Her hands shook once again as she lowered the gun and slipped it back inside her boot. The coachmen were back at work, putting the finishing touches on the broken wheel. Mistress Cosgrove and Dr. Kennel were still engaged in heated disputation, but Master Cosgrove was giving unasked-for advice to the driver. The bandits had completely disappeared from view.

Honor stayed by the tree, fighting down a terrible urge to cry. Ten years ago she had sworn a sacred oath to avenge the death of her parents. As she had cringed behind a tapestry at Dale Manor, she had not been able to tear her eyes from the nightmare that was taking place there in the long gallery of her ancestral home. The King's Men had hacked her Puritan mother and father to pieces. The memory was as vivid as if it had happened yesterday; she could never forget—or forgive. Ever since that horrible, deadly August morning, she had sworn to avenge herself upon the first Royalist she met. But with the Crown's adherents run to ground by Oliver Cromwell, she had never encountered an admitted follower of King Charles. Until now.

And she had failed to keep the promise she'd made on her parents' souls. Honor hated herself even more than she hated the highwayman and all his kind.

Chapter Two

In the past few years, Honor had heard many tales about how London was being held a grim hostage to Oliver Cromwell. Yet the city seemed not unlike the noisy, smoky, foul-smelling, bustling capital that Honor remembered from her visits as a child. It was true that people generally dressed more somberly, that there was an absence of out-of-work citizens shouting anti-Royalist slogans and that no sounds of music hung on the coal-clogged air. Yet the alleged gloomy pall spawned by Puritanism rested far more lightly on London than the gossips had reported.

Even though self-professed Royalists didn't frequent Whitehorse Manor, many of the visitors there had been critical of Cromwell. "Old Noll," as he was nicknamed, generated much respect but little love. As for Aunt Lucy, her family connections kept her in the Puritan camp, but she had no serious appetite for politics. "And if I did," she once had replied in mild exasperation to an ardent Roundhead who had pressed her on the point, "who would care? I'm but a poor widow, living quietly in the country with more opinions about gardening than governing."

The self-deprecating retort had not been precisely true: Lady Lucy was neither poor nor unopinionated. Her problem, however, was that she could always see at least a dozen reasons why one thing might be so—and another dozen why it might not. It had been a grievous wrong to execute King Charles; conversely, he'd been too highhanded and autocratic. It wasn't right for subjects to rise up against their sovereign; yet if a ruler should impose his unjust will on his people, something must be done to stop him. Cousin Oliver was quite correct in refusing the crown; yet he must somehow maintain continuity and tradition, which seemed unlikely under the Commonwealth he had proclaimed.

And so it went with Lady Lucy, until Honor had begun to wonder how her aunt had ever come to the point of accepting Sir Harry Ashford's marriage proposal. It was hardly surprising that Lucy hadn't wed until she was almost thirty. No doubt she had dithered for years, keeping poor Harry dangling. Honor recalled her uncle as a soft-spoken, shadowy figure, and in retrospect she knew he must have been a very patient man.

But that was in the past, and now Honor considered the present as the ramshackle open carriage clattered over the cobbles toward Whitehall. The Oxford coach hadn't arrived in the city until after dark. Deprived of her cloak, Honor shivered as a breeze picked up off the Thames. At least the wretched highwayman hadn't taken her brocade purse with its precious cache of coins. Whether he had disdained her money as an unworthy offering or had merely forgotten about it in his quest for her jewels, Honor wasn't sure, but she supposed she ought to be grateful. Without funds, it would have been all but impossible to secure a carriage. And now they were approaching Whitehall Palace, its rambling hodgepodge of roofs and chimneys barely visible against the night sky.

Anxiously, Honor wondered if her uncle had already gone to bed or if he would still be toiling away under the burden of English government. She very much wanted the assurance that despite the robbery along the road, all would be well, as she was filled with self-loathing for what she could only call cowardice. The pistol had been tooled for her in Mons, specially ordered from Flanders along with three others for the female inhabitants of Whitehorse Hill. There were too many displaced and desperate people roaming about since the Civil War, Aunt Lucy had declared with unusual firmness. She intended to be prepared for the worst. It had never happened, but ownership, as well as mastery, of the pistol had given Honor the means to someday avenge her parents. Or so she had hoped.

She still had no idea of her intended victim's identity. The coachman, for whom thievery was an occupational hazard, insisted that he had never before encountered this particular band of rogues. Dr. Kennel, however, was used to traveling routes farther north and had thrown out several possibilities, including Black Jack Revere, Bully Phelps and Ben the Brigand. Somehow, none of the names seemed to fit as far as Honor was concerned. The thief's henchman had called him "captain." Perhaps the others hadn't caught that, but Honor made a habit of paying attention to her surroundings.

For now, however, her powers of observation were focused on the torch-lit palace. As she descended from the carriage, Honor noted with surprise that there was more than a hint of royal trappings about Whitehall. Cromwell's guardsmen were not dressed in the scarlet and gold of King Charles's time, but they were equally well attired in handsome silver and gray. As she introduced herself, one of the guards nodded soberly, though his eye rested over-long on Honor's curving body and mass of golden hair. Moments later she was being escorted through a labyrinth of corridors until they finally reached Cromwell's private apartments. The Lord Protector, explained the man in accents that evoked the west country, had stayed up late, studying the most recent reports from Dunkirk, where Anglo-French troops had defeated the Spanish.

Honor remembered her uncle as kind and humorous, sturdily built, with a ruddy complexion and a large, bulbous nose. Only his eyes had truly commanded attention: they were faintly hooded, gray, flecked with green and possessed of a remarkable expressiveness. Facing him for the first time in ten years, she felt a sudden shock. Of course he had seemed like a big man when she was a child, but though she was scarcely of average height, Uncle Oliver was only a few inches taller. His once muscular body seemed to have shrunk under the plain black evening robe, the chestnut hair was streaked with gray even as it receded from the high dome of his forehead, and the veins that crisscrossed his nose stood out like pen marks, while a trio of warts marked his left eye, his brow, and his nether lip. Yet it was his eyes that struck Honor as most altered by life. A decade ago, before sending Charles I to the block, before the Irish sieges, before dissolving the Rump Parliament, before assuming the reins of England as Lord Protector, Oliver Cromwell had possessed a gaze of mercurial quality—a flash of fun, a plunge into despair, a spark of temper, a glimmer of insight. Now those eyes were startlingly static, conveying only melancholy. Despite his unprecedented triumphs and his firm hand on England's neck, Honor had the feeling that the years had not been kind to Cromwell.

He had taken her hand, raising her gently to her feet, insisting that formalities must be ignored between kinfolk. Pulling out a high-backed armless chair for her, Cromwell seated himself in its mate and praised God for their reunion while at the same time rebuking himself for not having sent someone to escort her from Whitehorse Hill. "God grants us many blessings, yet we squander the most precious gift of all, which is Time." His usual bluff manner had turned faintly wistful.

Judging from the litter of papers on her uncle's desk, Honor doubted that Cromwell frittered away his days any more recklessly than his other blessings. "Pray absolve yourself of blame, good Uncle," Honor insisted, though she was not yet ready to amplify on her journey to London. Nor was she able to dismiss his concerns with her usual self-confidence. The pistol, which ordinarily would have given her a sense of security, had proved as useless as a toy. But Honor couldn't blame the gun; she was the one who had failed so miserably.

Cromwell, however, had moved on to other topics, expressing his sympathy over Lady Lucy's death but pointing out the goodness of Divine Providence in dictating Honor's betrothal to Sir Tyler Vail. "An accomplished man, an excellent prospect," he declared, picking up his pipe and filling it with coarse brown tobacco. "Romantic love is often a curse, yet husband and wife should find each other agreeable for purposes of domestic harmony. The Lord has smiled on you with this match."

Honor tried to assume an appropriately grateful expression, but wondered why, if the Lord had been so kindly disposed toward her in the matter of Sir Tyler Vail, He had reversed Himself by sending a Royalist highwayman to plague her. It seemed to Honor that most people's image of God shaped Him into a baffling, even capricious figure. But, she supposed, if anyone was on intimate terms with the Almighty, it had to be Oliver Cromwell.

"Tyler and I have been most fortunate to find each other." Despite the Puritan belief that romance was a shaky foundation for marriage and that passion could undermine wedded bliss, Honor couldn't imagine making a match without love. Fate, if not God, had been kind in sending Tyler Vail to Whitehorse Hill. They had met by accident when Tyler's horse had thrown him while he was hawking with Aunt Lucy's neighbors at Uffington. Disheveled and limping, he had made his painful way over a mile and a half to the gates of Whitehorse Manor. There, in the shadow of the mysterious outline of the white horse etched by long-forgotten hands against the downs, the two had met. Honor was quite taken by the patrician charms of Sir Tyler, and he was likewise enchanted with her pert features, the gilded blond hair, the contrast of the huge dark eyes, the wide, brilliant smile. Aunt Lucy praised her sensibilities; Tyler called her unaffected. Either way, Honor's forthright common sense was one of her most winning qualities.

At the end of March, Tyler had dared to ask for a kiss. Honor made a show of shy reluctance, but in fact, having passed her eighteenth birthday unkissed, she found herself impatient for the feel of his lips on hers. To her surprise, the embrace brought no stirring of the senses, no thrill along the spine, no sudden beating of the heart. Honor had been disappointed. Hadn't her cousins, her friends, even the more garrulous serving girls, all extolled kissing as the pinnacle of romantic excitement? Perhaps the Puritans were right in disparaging passion. Maybe it was only a myth, left over from the bawdy Elizabethans of the previous century.

Still, Honor did not give up all hope of being swept off her feet and transported by the rapture of marital bliss. When he asked for her hand in marriage, she came to the conclusion that Tyler, being a gallant gentleman who had been raised as strictly as she, had purposely refrained from provoking unseemly passions. Once they were man and wife, everything would be different.

Naturally, Aunt Lucy hadn't been able to give Tyler a definite answer to his request for Honor in holy matrimony. On the one hand, it would be splendid for her niece to be married and settled. But on the other, Tyler Vail was a good twelve years older, which meant he'd be very set in his ways. Sir Harry, God rest his soul, had been like that, and hadn't it been a trial to get him to change.

So Sir Tyler had rushed off to London to plead his case before Honor's senior male relative. Cromwell knew Tyler only in a vague sort of way but understood him to be a staunch supporter of the Protectorate. A marriage contract had been drawn up under Cromwell's supervision with the wedding date set for Christmastide.

But Lady Lucy's death had changed those plans. At Cromwell's urging, Sir Tyler had agreed to move the nuptials up to the first of October. With a sigh of relief, the Protector had turned his mind away from the problems of orphaned nieces to the more pressing demands of waging war and making peace.

But at the moment, Cromwell was once again ensnared in family matters. He was quick to assure Honor that she could stay at Whitehall until the wedding took place, and that his wife, Elizabeth, would help put the trousseau together. Assuming his words would please Honor, he was surprised to see her exhibit a considerable amount of dismay.

"What is it, my dear?" he inquired with concern. "Would you rather have Bettie accompany you? Alas, it is the will of God that she not be well at present." His eyes clouded over; the melancholy look grew more pronounced. Sweet-natured, vivacious, kindly Bettie was her father's favorite daughter, and Honor knew that her year-old son had died only a few weeks earlier. The summer of 1658 had thus far proved to be a cruel season for the Protector and his kin.

Honor shifted uncomfortably in the straight-backed chair. "I'm afraid that under the circumstances, the only suitable person I could think of to accompany me on a shopping trip would be King Midas." She gave Cromwell a rueful look. "Alas, good Uncle, our coach was set upon by thieves. The jewels that made up my marriage portion are gone. All I have left are a few coins and my engagement ring." The dark eyes glanced at her left hand to make sure that she hadn't somehow managed to lose the cherished pearl in the last half hour. "I know Tyler is well-off, but I despise coming to him dowerless. Nor do I have money for my trousseau. Damn and blast."

Cromwell's heavy brows lifted slightly at his niece's strong language, but his priorities were in order. "My dear! That's shocking! Were you harmed …

otherwise?" The question was phrased as delicately as the Lord Protector's bluff voice would permit.

Having announced the calamity, Honor dispensed with decorum and leaned forward, placing her elbows on the desk and her chin on her hands. "No. No, I wasn't." The denial was true, of course. Her rough retrieval from the copse had been brought on by herself, after all. As for the highwayman's adroit caresses, she'd suffered no real damage. Honor would forget them in a day or two, and no one ever need be the wiser. No doubt the bold brigand had already forgotten her. Honor must think of him for what he was—the enemy. Having thus fired up her sense of outrage, she was surprised to discover that she was unwontedly depressed. It was bad enough that she had been orphaned twice over, that her profligate brother, Palmer, had wasted their inheritance … but now she had proved almost as imprudent as he, having managed to lose her only property. She felt that it was *her* fault that she had been robbed. After all, she had failed to shoot the highwayman.

Honor couldn't guess how eloquent her face was as she stared unblinkingly at the mass of papers on the desk. As if reading her thoughts, Cromwell reached out to place a none-too-steady hand over hers. "Now, now, don't fret so. These things happen. All the time, I'm afraid. England's highways are a scandal. We could hang a thief a day, yet there'd still be no end to it. Many of these poor wretches, God help us, are former soldiers, and," he went on grimly, "not necessarily the opposition's. If only I had sent an escort!"

Honor shrugged. Short of deploying a small army, she failed to see how her uncle could have deterred the highwaymen. In any event, she had carried a gun, a precaution that even Master Ormsby had felt was adequate. She said as much to her uncle.

Cromwell's grizzled jaw dropped. "You carried firearms? God spare us!"

"God spared the highwayman," Honor replied tartly. "I couldn't fire the blasted thing." She leaned toward the desk, her piquant face earnest and intent. "Think of it, Uncle! I'd sworn on my parents' souls I'd make the Royalists pay for their deaths. But there I was, with that loathsome thief well within range, his back to me, no one else paying the slightest heed—and I just stood there, like a brick! Why, Uncle? Why?" The memory of her impotence goaded her into fury. "I feel as if I betrayed Father and Mother. How they must scorn me in Paradise!"

Cromwell frowned deeply. " 'Vengeance is mine, I shall repay, saith the Lord.' Take Holy Writ to heart, my child, and put aside your quest for revenge."

Honor sat up very straight, chin jutting aggressively. "How so, Uncle? Is that what you did at Drogheda?"

Her uncle blanched. The blood lust that he had unleashed in Ireland would forever taint the memory of him as a just and merciful man. She saw his jowls quiver as he bowed his head. "I was crazed. I was wrong. I have asked God to forgive me a thousand times."

"I'd do the same, had I but shot the highwayman dead in his tracks." Honor's temper was sputtering out. "Now I must ask instead that my parents forgive my cowardice." But Cromwell's train of thought had been diverted and the body under the dressing gown sagged. "I have often wondered if the illnesses I suffered soon afterward in Scotland were not a judgment from the Lord."

Though Honor knew that Puritanism embraced the concept of earthly punishment and reward, Aunt Lucy's philosophy had been more practical. A milkmaid who sprained her ankle wasn't paying attention; the smithy who broke his thumb with his hammer had his mind on something other than his work. While Aunt Lucy might not be able to make up her mind as to the precise cause, disasters were rarely considered divine retribution. Yet Honor knew that was not the prevailing Puritan view.

"Do you mean I've been wicked?" She felt not only chagrined but almost panicky. "Is that why I lost my dowry?"

Cromwell gave her a sharp glance, then fiddled with his stubborn pipe, which had already gone out twice. "Nay, not precisely that. Perhaps 'tis only a reminder to discourage pride and vanity. I do not suppose," he went on, changing both tone and subject, "that anyone in your party knew the thief's identity?"

"There were four of them," Honor responded, looking depressed. "The leader was called 'captain.' Mayhap he was once a soldier."

Cromwell considered. "Captain," he repeated, grimacing at the pipe. "Between Oxford and London?"

Honor nodded. "In the Chiltern Hills. He was polite and well-spoken, I'll give him that."

Lifting his eyes to the frescoed ceiling, Cromwell was silent for a few moments. "Ah!" The veins along his nose seemed to throb. "Youngish, tall, with a mask and cloak?" When Honor nodded again, this time with more vigor, his mouth turned down at the corners. "Captain Hood, I suspect. Have you heard of that particular rogue?"

Honor searched her brain. There had been stories of highwaymen near Whitehorse Hill but no closer than the Savernake Forest. As for names, Captain Hood's meant nothing to her. The blank expression told her uncle as much.

Oliver Cromwell rose from his chair, moving about the small, cluttered chamber on stiff legs. "Captain Hood is so called because he styles himself after the more noble Robin Hood, who robbed from the rich to give to the poor in the name of King Richard." A wry smile did little to erase the persistent melancholy of Cromwell's gaze. "This contemporary Hood robs in the name of his master, the man who would be king, Charles Stuart. At least that is the tale I've been told."

Honor nodded. This corresponded with what the highwayman had said to her. "How bold he is to ride so close to London," she remarked. "How can he escape capture?"

Cromwell looked quite grim. "He flouts our authority, throwing the gauntlet down in the very bastions of Puritan respectability. He was preying farther north, in the area of Derbyshire, but of late we have heard accounts of his depredations in the Oxford area."

"I'd give my teeth to meet him again," Honor declared, though a small inner voice asked why, when she had failed to exact vengeance at their first encounter. Wearily, she slumped back onto the chair and allowed her uncle to ply her with port. It was new to her palate, and, he assured her, not nearly as insidious as the stronger spirits, which had fallen into disrepute under the Protectorate.

It was also rather tasty, with a fruitlike tang. Honor sipped slowly, savoring the wine and willing it to calm her. Certainly she was growing sleepy. Indeed, she was exhausted. Uncle Oliver read the weariness in her dark eyes and suggested she retire. Honor agreed and finally was able to smile in a wan display of gratitude.

"First, our prayers," Cromwell said, kneeling down with some effort and beckoning Honor to join him. He spoke to God in fervent tones, offering thanksgiving for his niece's arrival, supplications for the family's health, especially Bettie's, and calling on the Almighty to mete out divine justice to Captain Hood and all his evil ilk. Honor began to nod off after the first ten minutes.

But when at last she lay huddled under a feather quilt, sleep would not come. Visions of masked men and bloodthirsty soldiers filled her exhausted mind while the child she had been shuddered behind a faded tapestry. She saw the blood again as booted feet thundered down stone hallways, and agonized screams echoed in her ears. She, who had never known any more frightening occurrence than the loss of an adventuresome terrier, was witness to such brutal butchery that only the fear for her own life could keep her silent and inert. Yet she was grappling with the tapestry, trying to push it aside. "I'll save you! I'll save you!" she cried, and was suddenly jarred into reality.

This was not Dale Manor in Yorkshire but Whitehall Palace in London. There was no tapestry, only the rumpled quilt. Honor pulled it closer, licked her dry lips and tried to empty her troubled mind. She might be destitute, but she was safe.

Sometime later, when she slept again, the nightmares had left her.

Chapter Three

THE FOLLOWING DAY DAWNED IN a hazy pall of smoke and soot, making Honor wonder what had become of summer.

"Never fear," clucked Aunt Elizabeth, sorting through the small trunk that Honor had sent ahead. " 'Twill burn off by noon. Yet I'll praise the Lord for the fresh air of Hampton Court." She paused, looking up from yet another drab black mourning gown. "Naturally your uncle and I will be in London for the wedding."

"I'm most appreciative," Honor said vaguely, looking up from an elegantly scripted note.

> Dearest Honor,
> I am delighted to learn that you have arrived safely in London. Fire-breathing dragons could not keep me from your company, but I must confront something far worse—a contingent of French Papists demand my attention about certain business investments that have been drastically altered by the recent allied success on the Continent. Be assured that as soon as I am able, I shall fly to your side.
> Your most devoted servant,
> T.

The missive had appeared that morning on Honor's breakfast tray. Obviously, Uncle Oliver had wasted no time in letting Sir Tyler know that his betrothed was in the city.

Judging from her fiancé's allusion to her safe arrival, Cromwell had not mentioned the robbery. Honor was distressed at the thought of having to somehow explain it all over again, but took courage from the fact that while Tyler might be upset about the incident itself, he wouldn't be nearly as undone by the theft of her dower jewels as she was. Gazing at the huge pearl on her left hand, she reminded herself that at least Tyler's ring had been spared. The alleged Captain Hood's ignorance had helped Honor save a small portion of face. Yet she despised him all the same.

"Well," remarked Aunt Elizabeth, refolding the note and handing it back to Honor, "I am sorry Sir Tyler is detained. But no matter, 'twill give us time to shop. Mall and Frances want to join us. The Good Lord willing," she added with a sudden frown that threw her otherwise good-natured features into shadow. "Bettie is very ill, you know." She spoke conspiratorially, as if by keeping her voice down, the Angel of Death might fly over without taking notice.

Honor made appropriate sympathetic comments. Mall, whose given name was Mary, had wed Viscount Fauconberg the previous autumn in a surprising show of compromise between the Cromwell family and kin to one of King Charles's staunchest supporters. Aunt Lucy, of course, had favored the match, at least at first. After all, hadn't Sir Harry initially supported the Crown before the Civil War actually broke out? But later, she had expressed qualms, wondering if perhaps Mall and her viscount were setting an example, no matter how sincere, that would open the doors to rampant opportunism on both sides of the political coin.

As for Frances, she too had been an autumn bride. But during the harsh London winter that froze the Thames and chilled the very marrow of rich and poor alike, her charming groom had coughed up his lungs and died before the spring could save him. Just a year older than Honor, Frances was still in widow's weeds and only recently had allowed herself to be enticed into going abroad. Honor remembered Mall as bossy and rambunctious, though possessing a great capacity for laughter. Frances was much quieter but owned a stubborn steak and trenchant wit. It would be interesting, Honor thought, to see how much both girls had changed since she had last seen them.

It was neither of the Cromwell daughters who timidly knocked upon the bedchamber door but the eldest surviving son, Richard. He had been a gawky adolescent when Honor had first laid eyes on him; later he had become an awkward young man. Now, as he fretted at the rumpled collar of his linen shirt, he appeared to have grown older rather than to have grown up.

"Coz," he said with anxious enthusiasm, "my good father told me you were here." With an uncertain glance in his mother's direction, he moved toward Honor and bent to kiss her cheek, at the same time managing to step on her left foot. Though she winced, she made no effort to pull away but patiently waited for Dick to draw back. "How pretty you are!" He grinned, a winning expression that gave his weak face sudden charm. “Pity Aunt Lucy died. She couldn’t have been that old.” Dick was ambling about the room, touching a tapestry here, fingering a plump pillow there, almost knocking over a figurine from the marble mantelpiece. “But we shall have a wedding soon, isn’t that so? Sir Tyler Vail, eh? A fine fellow. I think I owe him money. Or,” he mused, “is it the other way round?”

Elizabeth Cromwell eyed her son with maternal indulgence. His older brothers, Robert and Oliver, had long ago gone to their graves, leaving Dick and Harry, the youngest boy. Harry was a handsome, genial fellow whose excessive energies often propelled him into trouble. Conversely, trouble had a way of finding Dick. Tripping over a faint furrow in the Persian carpet, he continued extolling Tyler Vail’s virtues. It was only when Elizabeth Cromwell gently interrupted that he finally fell silent.

“We intend to show Honor the sights of London as well as peruse some of the shops,” said Aunt Elizabeth, putting a kindly arm around Honor’s shoulders. “She needs a trousseau.”

Dick gave Honor that winning smile as he shoved a clump of brown hair off his forehead. “Knowing my good lady mother, she’ll find you some bargains in the process.”

“I’m most grateful to her. To all of you,” Honor said, and suddenly realized how tiresome it was to depend on other people. It would be different, of course, with Tyler—a wife was supposed to lean on her husband.

Dick had bent down to kiss his mother’s cheek, missed the first time, then gave her a sound smack on the forehead instead. “My best to you all for a successful tour, but mind your purses. London grows more mischievous by the day.”

It was a caution Honor scarcely needed. So does the countryside, she thought to herself, but held her tongue and gave Dick a warm smile. It was hard to believe that a man as forceful and tenacious as Oliver Cromwell had sired such an unlikely son. She remembered Mall Cromwell as being made of much sterner stuff. It was a shame that Dick hadn’t gotten more of her backbone.

Indeed, it was Mall who proved the most valuable asset on their tour of London. While Elizabeth Cromwell’s reputation for driving a hard bargain emerged untarnished, Mall dealt smartly with the occasional Royalist rowdy or cheeky beggar. Honor kept close to Frances, who spoke touchingly of her late husband. Hoping that a few sympathetic words would convey her sorrow, Honor tried to pay close attention but was constantly diverted by the sights, smells and sensations of the city.

As Aunt Elizabeth had predicted, the heavy haze burned off shortly after noon, revealing a cloudless sky and a warming sun. Though she needed no more than the fringed Spanish shawl loaned to her by Mall, Honor insisted on purchasing a new cloak before even looking at any other items. It was a matter of pride that she would not go cloakless. At Aunt Elizabeth's suggestion, she charged the cloak, as well as the items in her trousseau, to Sir Tyler's accounts.

"He wouldn't demur," asserted her aunt, leading the way up Shoe Lane, "since, the Good Lord willing, you'll be man and wife come autumn."

The remark buoyed Honor's spirits. As they turned into Fleet Street, she wondered if Tyler would be holding her in his tender embrace in just another day. Feeling the soft, caressing fabric of her new green cloak, she allowed herself the luxury of pretending it was Tyler's arms that enveloped her. But another, far different image intruded: the elegant cloak reminded Honor not of Sir Tyler's chivalrous esteem but of the so-called Captain Hood, with his mesmerizing eyes and compelling voice. Ridiculous, she chided herself, to let the loathsome likes of a Royalist highwayman saunter across her mind's eye. He was a thief, mayhap a murderer as well, and if she'd had any nerve, he'd be cold as a carp by now.

It was much better to dwell upon her newly acquired trousseau. To her surprise, the Cromwell women hadn't insisted on somber Puritan garb. Even Frances's mourning gown was edged with several inches of fine lace, and Mall wore bold plum cut away at the waist to reveal a saffron petticoat. Honor was making mental inventory of the richly pleated skirts in deep blue, apple green, lilac, honey and rose pink that she had just acquired when a cart piled high with barrels of fish toppled over at the foot of Chancery Lane. Mackerel, cod and plaice slid about on the cobbles while the fishmongers cursed at a half dozen Londoners who were attempting to make some illegal catches of their own.

Honor, along with her companions, was laughing helplessly at the sight of flopping fish, careening barrels and embattled citizenry. A handful of young law students had now joined the fray, long robes flapping about their legs. Despite her mirth, Aunt Elizabeth recovered her sense of duty and scanned the street for some sign of law enforcement. Honor, however, was so caught up in the general chaos that she almost missed a familiar figure strolling arm in arm with a pretty brunette across the way in the Temple precincts. Seemingly oblivious to the raucous scene close by, Sir Tyler Vail was bestowing his most charming smile on the entrancing young lady at his side.

For a fleeting moment, Honor considered calling out her fiancé's name. But she suppressed the urge while her cheeks turned warm and her temper hot.

"What is it, child?" Elizabeth Cromwell inquired. "You look flushed. Are you ill?"

It would do no good to explain now, Honor reasoned. The cart had been righted, blocking their view of the Thames. "It's the excitement," she replied feebly. "I haven't been in London since I was seven." The pretty brunette certainly bore no resemblance to the "fire-breathing dragons" that Tyler had vowed could not keep him from Honor's side, yet there might be a logical explanation. Perhaps the young woman was kin to the French Papists Tyler was meeting with and he was showing her the sights of London. The more Honor turned this idea over in her mind, the better she liked it; by the time they returned to Whitehall, she almost believed it.

THE STOOP-SHOULDERED OLD MAN DRIVING the ox cart laden with hay didn't appear to give any notice to the raucous young Oxford scholars. With black academic gowns flapping around their legs, they raced under the arches of Christ Church, down toward the lane that hugged the lazy Cher-well. But if their interest had extended beyond their own high spirits, they would have observed that under the floppy, battered hat, a pair of eyes that were neither old nor dull had assessed—and dismissed—them with the speed of a wink.

The youths were now good-naturedly arguing over a punt that was tied up at the river's edge. The man on the cart's platform prodded the oxen forward, past the spires of Saint Mary's and Saint Martin's and All Saints. Swans, one of them coal black, glided by, giving the oxen haughty glances. The late-afternoon sun cast shadows of the leafy trees over the path and burnished the meadows beyond the river.

At Brewer's Lane, the man stopped and cautiously dismounted. With a grumbled command to the ox team, he lumbered toward one of Oxford's newer inns, the Brass Hand. But instead of going in through the front door, he sidled past a stone wall overgrown with crimson climbing roses and entered by the back way. A flock of chickens greeted him with rude, startled squawks.

The inn's kitchen smelled of roasting meat, boiled vegetables and a dozen mingled herbs. Next to the open hearth, a heavy-faced woman with lank red hair kept a beady eye on a huge haunch of beef that turned slowly on the spit. She expended the least possible energy in regarding the newcomer with only slightly less suspicion than she had fixed on the meat.

"Ooooh now," she wheezed, "it's yerself. I never know, now do I?"

"Nor should you," the man replied lightly, perching on a three-legged stool. "That's the beauty of it, Meg. I'm a man of many parts."

"Only one of 'em counts with a man anyways." Meg gave what passed for a chuckle but sounded more like the creak of a rusty hinge. "I suppose ye'll be wantin' himself?"

The man had taken off his battered hat, revealing a thatch of white hair that hung to his shoulders like faded straw. Yet his grin was young, in startling contrast to his aged demeanor. "Now, Meg, if I said I wanted *you,* I'd get my ears boxed for impudence. I owe him money and I need some information."

Meg gave the beef haunch a poke with a long, lethal fork. Juices spurted and sizzled onto the logs. "The usual?"

"That, too, but something more. Love makes beggars of us all." He struck a poignant pose for Meg.

"Ooooooh now," said Meg, the small eyes showing a bit more interest, "don't tell me you're in love. Again."

His answer was to lift one shoulder, which was no longer stooped. But before he could explain or Meg could pry, the sounds of a scuffle came from the common room. Wielding her sharp fork, Meg signaled for her guest to stay where he was while she investigated. As soon as she had left the kitchen, he alighted from the stool and went to the wall where a big skillet hung from a stout nail. Shifting the skillet to one side, the man peered through the peephole. It was not, as he had assumed, brawling students from rival colleges but Cromwell's soldiers. They were roughing up a tall young man over the protests of Master Sparks, the innkeeper.

"Fools and damned fools!" bellowed the innkeeper, swinging a chair in self-defense. "This here's a teacher, Master Bagley from Magdalen College!"

One of the soldiers ceased beating on the unfortunate victim long enough to growl at Master Sparks, "Begone with ye! And wasn't Oxford always a hotbed of Royalist sympathizers?"

The innkeeper spat. "Ptah! That was sixteen years ago they fortified Magdalen Tower! Bury the past with the past, afore I make ye pay damages! Enough, enough!" he roared, threatening to bring the chair down on the soldier's head. A barrel-chested man of fifty, Master Sparks had forearms like hams and a bulldog's face. The soldiers hesitated while the young teacher scrambled to his feet and made a haphazard attempt to shove the dark hair out of his eyes. There was a gash on one cheek and a long tear in his don's robes.

"Nevertheless, he's coming with us," the soldier asserted, backing off only slightly under the menace of Master Sparks and his chair. "He fits the description, after all. Black hair, youngish, over six feet and talks like he's learned." The soldier's flinty eyes regarded Bagley with malice. "We have the Lord Protector's word direct on it." Making a jerky motion, he called to his men to bring the prisoner along and make it quick. They had dragged Bagley to the door when the stooped old man shuffled in from the kitchen.

"No, no, no," he mumbled, shaking a finger that barely showed from under his long, frayed shirtsleeve. "Not young Bagley! I know him, I know them all." The battered hat was back on his head, which he tipped to one side and regarded soldiers, teacher and innkeeper alike with reproach. "Now who is it you might really be wanting?" The voice was a feeble squawk, not unlike the chickens at the back of the inn.

The soldier raked the old man with his flintlike eyes. "And who might you be, Father Time? Go back to the kitchen and stay with the womenfolk, eh?"

At least two of the other soldiers laughed even as they continued prodding the young teacher through the doorway. But the old man laughed even louder, a harsh, grinding rasp wrenched from his throat. "Father Time, Mother Rhyme, as it please you." He made an arthritic bow, then offered them a gap-toothed smile. "But Nobody's Fool, for all that. Why, I'd guess it's a highwayman you seek, and if yonder scholar is your man, then so am I!" He paused to scratch vigorously under one arm. "Have you tried Goring Gap?"

The soldier stiffened, apparently taking the old man seriously at last. "Goring Gap? Why there?"

The stooped shoulders shrugged. "Why not? Beyond lies Goring Heath, where the beech woods begin. One beech looks much like another, do they not? Few venture there, except the fairies. And old men." He shrugged again, then turned away, as if the matter were closed.

The soldier, however, hesitated. Goring Gap was some six or seven miles away but certainly close enough to the Oxford-London road. There was no point in hauling an innocent man before the magistrate, especially in Oxford, a city infamous for its clashes between Town and Gown. Despite a show of truculence, the soldier ordered his men to release their prisoner. "If we ever have cause to question you again, you'll rue the day," the soldier asserted in ominous warning.

Garbing himself in as much dignity as possible, Master Bagley marched back to his place by the fire and picked up his book, which had been sent flying dangerously close to the hearth. Meg Sparks appeared just as the soldiers straggled out.

"A fine mess," she muttered, but her first concern was for Bagley. "You'll live," she pronounced abruptly after a cursory examination of the teacher's cuts and bruises. "A fresh tankard of ale will help."

Master Sparks had gone back into the kitchen with the old man, who was wiping the charcoal from his teeth and shedding some forty years in the process. "Well? Did they seek Hood?" he asked, squaring his shoulders and rolling back his sleeves.

Sparks poured them both a cup of smuggled Scots whiskey from a vat marked by a skull and crossbones. "That they did." He took a stiff drink and wiped his mouth on his hefty forearm. "It seems," he went on, his black eyes glistening at the other man, "that Captain Hood, the dastardly knave, made off with Cromwell's niece's dowry."

The innkeeper had expected an eruption of mirth. Instead, he found himself staring at the face of a stricken man. "God's wounds!" his companion murmured, one hand gripping the whiskey cup so tightly that it threatened to shoot out of his grasp. "Cromwell's niece!" He slapped his other hand against his head, setting the white wig askew. "That's the maid I was going to inquire after! I took her cloak, as well."

"And no more?" Despite the younger man's startled reaction, Sparks couldn't resist having his little jest. He elbowed Hood in the ribs and poured himself another drink. "I wish I'd known who she was, when I sent word to ye, but I hadn't a clue, save that she was Mistress Honor Dale from Whitehorse Hill." He tried to look apologetic but failed. It was, after all, quite a grand joke all way round.

Except that Captain Hood wasn't laughing. Rather, he was taking a long, slow pull at his whiskey and looking grim. Sparks assumed a less frivolous manner and thumped Hood on the knee. "Well, man? What is it? Did the wench steal your heart even as you stole her jewels?"

Hood pulled off the wig and set it on a broomstick that was standing in the corner. "No. Of course not." He shrugged faintly and made a wry face. "She was uncommonly fair, that's all. The jewels were in the lining of her cloak and I promised I'd return it to her. I suppose I shall have to smuggle it into Whitehall right under Cromwell's bulbous beak." Though he spoke in his usual careless manner, Sparks noted there was no humor in his eyes.

"Well, now," sighed the innkeeper, "I suppose instead of just bare-bones facts of the passengers, you'll be wanting their pedigree, too. I must admit that lot wasn't particularly prosperous." Sparks was speaking good-naturedly, but he felt a genuine twinge of regret. If he was to get a share of the takings in return for information about the travelers on the Oxford-London route, he owed it to all concerned to make sure the profits were worth the risks. It was well and good to help Charles Stuart and make a few shillings in the process, but it was even better to stay alive. "The Cosgroves were said to be carrying a fair lot of gold. Mayhap I misheard."

"Mayhap." Hood was back on the stool, leaning against the wall, his hands shoved into deep pockets. "They're the sort to brag." He was staring at the beef haunch, which was acquiring a rich, crisp exterior. Except for the crackle of the fire and the sizzle of the meat, the kitchen had gone quiet. Sparks considered pouring another cup of whiskey, thought better of it and was about to give the spit a turn when Hood spoke again. "Dale, you say?" He saw the innkeeper nod. "But from Whitehorse Hill, not … Yorkshire?"

"That's right, had an aunt there. She died. The girl's to marry some London nob." Sparks moved the spit, allowing a fresh shower of juices to spatter into a pan Meg had put down for gravy making.

"What of her parents?" Hood asked, his forehead creased with what appeared to be puzzlement.

"Parents?" The innkeeper wrinkled his nose, a gesture that made his likeness to a bulldog even more remarkable. "Bless me, how should I know? Dead, I suppose. All I know is she's some kin to Cromwell and therefore no friend to the likes of us."

"Damn!" Hood's fist crashed down onto the cutting board next to the stool, startling Master Sparks. "It must be! If only I could be sure ...." He was frowning ferociously in an effort of concentration. "It's been ten years, the name was Dale, but it was Yorkshire, not Oxfordshire!"

"People move about," Sparks said reasonably, "especially in wartime."

Hood made no reply at first; he was staring at the fire. The play of shadow from the flames only emphasized the tortured expression on his face. "I was told they were all killed, right down to the last stable boy. It seemed right at the time, at least to me." His voice died away, like the echo of the wind on the moors. He finished off his whiskey and put the cup down on the cutting board. To his host, he offered an unconvincing smile. "It's possible that several Dales are related to Cromwell, I suppose. It's not an uncommon name."

Though Master Sparks had no idea what Captain Hood was talking about, he also knew it was better not to ask. "Any shirttail relation who can claim kinship to Old Noll will do just that if it helps them get a leg up."

"True." Hood set the wig back on his head, arranging the white hairs to cover as much of his face as possible. "Never mind," he said with forced cheer, pulling out a purse from his baggy pants. "Here's your share. You've done right well by us, though it's probably best to move on if Cromwell's men are on our trail."

Sparks didn't try to hide his disappointment. Life as an innkeeper was seldom dull, but Captain Hood's phantomlike presence these past few weeks had definitely added excitement. There'd been the money, of course, but if Sparks had to confess it, he took genuine pride in helping the exiled King. It wasn't right to murder monarchs, not in a civilized country like England. Thinking about Cromwell sitting in Whitehall and all but acting like a king himself was galling indeed. After all, the man was an upstart, of not much better breeding than Sparks himself. As he'd often told Meg, it just wasn't right—the next thing you knew they would be asking the people to vote on who they'd like to have running the country.

Hood was already at the door. He grinned widely and saluted. "Give my love to Meg. I may be back one day, but I'll not promise. I don't make promises I can't keep." Sparks moved as if to detain him but stopped halfway, still holding the empty whiskey cup. The door closed behind Hood, but not before the squawking of the chickens could be heard from outside. The innkeeper looked up to see Meg, carrying Bagley's tankard.

"Is he gone?" she asked, her beady eyes glittering at her husband.

Sparks nodded slowly. "He's gone for good. God help him."

Meg looked at Sparks with suspicion but said nothing. It wasn't like her husband to be religious. Still, there was something about the highwayman that inspired an admiration greater than mere respect. Maybe it was that quick grin or those farseeing eyes or the fact that he could assume a dozen guises without anyone being the wiser. Clever, he was, but kind, at least to those who shared his sympathies for King Charles. Meg gave the meat another turn and then got out a huge wooden tub for washing up.

A pity Hood would end up on the gallows, Meg reflected as she felt inside the rain barrel that stood just beyond the kitchen door. But that was the way it was with highwaymen. With Royalists, too, at least in the past. Shaking the water from her fingers, she peered up at the sky. It was clouding over, with the smell of rain in the air. The weather was changing.

Though Meg couldn't guess it, England was changing, too.

Amid the bustle of packing for the favorable air of Hampton Court, Sir Tyler Vail came to call on his betrothed. Despite her brief glimpse of him in Chancery Lane, Honor's recollection of his smooth, refined features hadn't really done the man justice. Surely, she thought, as he pressed his lips into her palm and gazed at her with clear blue eyes, Tyler must be the most handsome man she had ever met. The ash-blond lovelocks that trailed over his lace-edged collar were curled to perfection; the wide cuffs of his soft suede boots displayed well-turned calves. The chin might be just a shade short and the nostrils a trifle wide, but otherwise—if such a thing were politically possible—he was the perfect example of a Puritan Cavalier.

"My dear," he greeted her with enthusiasm, "how splendid you look! I've been counting the hours until we could be together."

Honor broke into a wide smile and let Tyler lead her to a seat by the window in the antechamber outside her temporary quarters. Shyly, she brushed the back of his hand with hers. The sun was streaming in behind her through the ancient wavery mullioned windows, turning her hair to molten gold and her eyes to dusky pools. Tyler bent to kiss her cheek, a tender gesture that did much to dispel any doubts Honor might have about the pretty brunette.

"My sweet dream," he said in a light voice, studying the clear, smooth skin, the wide, full mouth, the pert, turned-up nose, the intriguing hint of rounded bosom above the stiff white linen of her bodice. "If your uncle—and you—are willing, I should very much like for us to wed within the month."

Honor drew back, one hand to her breast. There would hardly be time for the completion of her trousseau … it was possible that Bettie Cromwell might not recover that soon … she wasn't really sure if Uncle Oliver would grant such hasty permission …. But of course if Tyler wished it, that was the way it would be. It was a man's prerogative to make such decisions, Aunt Lucy had always said. Though, of course, there were times when a man could make a mistake, in which case it was the woman's duty to tactfully step in and gently redirect his thinking.

"It's just that August isn't the happiest time for me," she said slowly, trying to push away the hideous memories of sunshine on steel, of charred ruins among the once bright flower beds, of bloodcurdling screams despoiling the summer calm. "Autumn is my favorite season."

Tyler reached out to wind one of Honor's golden curls around his manicured index finger. "My dear, isn't it best to replace sad old memories with happy new ones? Since your poor Aunt Lucy's unfortunate and lamentable demise, I presumed you would wish to put the past behind you and start our new life as quickly as possible."

The faint note of reproach wasn't lost on Honor. Of course he was right, she was being quite silly. "Let me think on it," she temporized. "I shall give you a firm answer when we return from Hampton Court."

Seemingly appeased, Tyler let go of the curl. He smoothed his pencil-thin mustache and the small pointed beard that added strength to his chin. "I suppose," he mused, "the time could be well spent making the necessary changes for you in my house on the Strand."

"Oh, yes," Honor agreed with enthusiasm. She was most anxious to see the house, which had been built soon after he had completed his distinguished service at the siege of Wexford. "I can't imagine living in London after spending my whole life in the country." Excitement bubbled within her. She had suffered greatly in her youth, but it appeared that Fate was at last smiling favorably on her: a handsome husband, a fine house, an entree into the highest echelon of English society. Her nightmares would be dispelled by dreams that were finally coming true.

"Then we must set about devising your suite." Tyler gave her his most brilliant smile, which always reminded Honor of May Day. Or at least the way it had been when she was very small, before Uncle Oliver decided that morris dancers and Maypoles and garlands with silk streamers were ungodly. He was quite right, she supposed, but at the age of three, Honor had been able to see only the innocent merrymaking rather than the darker, more sinful side that was always brought on by any sort of overindulgence.

Tyler, however, was speaking not of May but of mayhem. "War is such a bother. Victory or not, anytime we get involved with those Frenchies, it's trouble. Can't trust 'em, they're almost as sly as the Spanish." He sighed, anxiously tugging at the full open sleeves of his coat, and assumed an air of resignation. " 'Pon my word, foreign politics have a way of reaching out to intrude upon the least likely of Englishmen."

Honor gave him a puzzled look. Sir Tyler was ordinarily so glib. She'd much prefer to have him kiss her again instead of blathering endlessly about foreign affairs. Her tongue flicked unconsciously over her lips. Now that their wedding day was so near—perhaps even nearer than she thought—Honor wondered if he might attempt to stir her senses by kissing her full on the mouth.

But her betrothed was still rambling on about the French and the Spanish and the Catholics and war and peace and a changing foreign market. "Damme, the gist of it is that I'm temporarily without funds. Embarrassing, but there it is." He gave Honor's fingers a little squeeze. "The situation can be set right, of course, if you give me your dowry now instead of in October."

The reunion with her beloved had all but dashed the robbery from her mind. The very sight of Tyler Vail, so obviously affluent and self-assured, had managed to calm her. But here he was, suddenly sounding as if her dowry, surely of pitiful value compared to his great wealth, were actually of great importance. Honor stared at him with big, incredulous dark eyes.

Mistaking her stunned expression for distaste at his request, Tyler grew abject. "I know," he went on quickly, "it's sheer presumption on my part. You can't guess how miserable it makes me to even think of it. But I do so want to make everything fresh and bright and pretty for you. Blues and silver and white, don't you think? Or would you prefer greens and gold and cream?"

Still not quite able to take in the implications of Tyler's words, Honor shook her head. "I prefer nothing except your affection," she asserted in a weak voice. "It seems that I have …." She stopped, unable to meet his curious gaze. "During the journey from …." Again she halted, chewing the lips that had been awaiting Tyler's kiss just moments ago. "See here," she declared, finally squaring off on the seat to face him, "my jewels were stolen by a highwayman on the journey to London."

Her fiancé's face paled and his usual insouciant manner fled. "Impossible!" He barely breathed the word. "How could …?" He clamped his mouth shut and turned away, frowning at the frayed edges of the ancient Persian carpet. As Honor sat in motionless suspense, Tyler took several deep breaths, obviously trying to compose himself. At last he looked around to confront her but made no effort to regain her hand. "I simply cannot see how such a thing could have happened. I thought it was understood that you would take the utmost care to protect your jewels. What," he demanded, his voice rising with the anger he could no longer contain, "did you do, wear them all in full sight like the bloody Queen of Sheba?"

Honor drew back from his verbal onslaught, her shoulders pressed against the window embrasure. Certainly she had expected Tyler to be upset about the theft, but more so for her own sake than that of her dowry. Hadn't he made it quite plain that her dowry was of little consequence to him, that between his family inheritance, the rewards he'd earned for his military service and his genius for investment, he was a very wealthy man? Why was he being so callous?

"I stitched the jewels into my cape," she said through lips that scarcely moved. "I had my pistol in my boot. I traveled by daylight on a well-used route. What else should I have done, boarded them up in the coach seat?" The last few words were bitten off sharply, and Honor realized she was angry. It was, however, an emotion lost on Sir Tyler.

"There's no need to rail at me!" he retorted, getting to his feet and squaring shoulders made less broad by the fashionable sloping cut of his coat. "Turn your wrath on yourself for surrendering your worldly goods to some moronic marauder! Why, half those plundering sons haven't the sense to dodge dove droppings!"

The portrait Tyler sketched was so far removed from the cool, casual, yet courtly manner of the alleged Captain Hood that Honor hooted with derision. "And how many highwaymen have *you* met? This one might have graced Saint James's! He had style, charm, the speech of a poet!" Honor had risen from the window seat and was wagging a finger in Tyler's startled face. "Dove droppings indeed! A lot you know about it!"

Tyler started to back off, recalled his manhood and set his high heels squarely onto the worn carpet. "They should all be hanged, drawn and quartered! Royalist scum, I'll wager, a coward in the field, a hero on the highway!" He shook his head. "Odd's fish, you'd think you were defending the traitorous dog!"

To her amazement, Honor realized that Tyler was right. She *was* defending Captain Hood, putting into words perceptions about him that had never occurred to her before. Until now, she had considered the highwayman only as the enemy she had failed to foil. Certainly it would be imprudent to tell Tyler how she had tried to shoot the man—and had stood helpless, immobilized, turned to stone.

Honor redirected her anger. She stamped her foot and gave full vent to her frustration. "Damn and blast, I might have been kidnapped, tortured, murdered on the spot! All you're thinking about are my jewels! Most of them weren't even mine, but my poor mother's and grandmother's before her, a handful of cold stones only warmed by memories! Would you rather have my corpse than my dowry?"

Tyler emitted a great sigh, as if the worries of the world had been placed unasked on his own sloping shoulders. "Really, Honor, cease hopping about, you're giving me a bloody headache." To prove his point, he pressed angular fingers against his temples. "Now pray hush and let me think—I must find some way to surmount my straitened circumstances."

Finally absorbing her fiancé's distress, Honor forced herself to grow calm. The truth was, there were probably other precautions she could have taken, such as a false bottom in her portmanteau or making a formal request of her uncle to send an escort. Certainly Cromwell would have sent one, having already expressed his regrets over not having voluntarily done so. But that was hindsight—as was the unbidden thought that if Tyler had been concerned about her, he might have come to Whitehorse Hill to collect her in person. But Honor decided not to perpetuate the quarrel by saying so.

Indeed, the reality was that she and Tyler were engaged to be married. Whether they were rich or poor made little difference to Honor, though of course it was always easier to be rich. Hadn't Aunt Lucy once said that she saw no wrong in praying for wealth, since if one was financially secure the sins of greed and envy could be safely avoided, thus freeing one to pursue other virtues? Fretfully, Honor clasped and unclasped her hands, then suddenly paused, gazing down at her magnificent pearl ring.

"Tyler!" she exclaimed, twisting the gold from her finger. "I almost forgot!" Taking the ring off her hand, she proffered it to her betrothed.

Taken aback, Tyler vigorously shook his head. "Odd's fish, my little chicken, I'd not intended to bully you into breaking off our engagement!" He had the grace to look sheepish as he refused the ring and firmly closed Honor's hand around the huge gleaming pearl. "M'dear, I'd no idea you'd take such offense! I was merely blustering away there!"

Honor stared at the ring, then thrust it back at Tyler. "Don't be an idiot, Tyler. More than anything, I want to be your wife." She paused, oddly disconcerted by her declaration, then shook off the sudden mood and continued. "But the highwayman didn't take the ring. Surely it's worth a considerable sum. I don't need sentiment as much as contentment. Take it and replace it later, when your situation has improved."

Tyler stared at the pearl as if it were a crystal in which he could foresee their future. "Well! That's ridiculously generous of you, Honor sweet, but I really couldn't .... 'Twould make me look a bit silly, turning in that gorgeous symbol of our troth." He bent to kiss her forehead with dry lips. "Put that back on your pretty finger and meanwhile I shall think of something else. Mayhap your uncle can help," he added ingenuously.

"Mayhap," agreed Honor, "but all the same, I feel guilty. It wouldn't be right for me to wear such a costly piece while you agonized over your unfortunate circumstances." Determinedly, she took his hand and tried to slip the ring on his little finger. But Tyler only balked, turned very red and backed away.

"It's no good, Honor," he said in a thin voice, the usual affectation gone. "That ring isn't worth more than a poor parson's daily stipend. I bought it in Cheapside."

The bald revelation shocked Honor far more than if Tyler had confessed to stealing from the church poor box. Her wide-eyed gaze traveled slowly from his flushed, stricken face to the oversized pearl, which once again lay in the palm of her hand. The luster seemed to have faded, the color had taken on a sickly cast. Honor didn't know whether to laugh or cry.

Dazed, she wandered back to the window embrasure, where she stared vacantly out onto a little flower garden boxed in by tall yew hedges. Surely Tyler couldn't have been as profligate with his money as her brother, Palmer, had been with the Dale inheritance.

"Speculation in wartime can be most profitable," Tyler was saying in a strained voice. "It can also be ruinous. Alas," he went on wearily, moving to her side, "I was unlucky." For several moments he stood next to Honor, not touching her but waiting tensely for her reaction.

At last, after mulling over his explanations, Honor recognized that she had two choices: she could either believe Tyler—or not. And whichever she chose didn't matter, because she was going to marry him anyway. With a little shake of her head, she looked up at his patrician profile. Money aside, Tyler Vail was a splendid match. With a little shiver of pleasure, Honor envisioned attending social events on Tyler's arm while other women murmured enviously behind their fans about how a country chit had captured such an exemplary specimen of English manhood. Despite the harsh words that had passed between them, Honor couldn't help but smile at Sir Tyler.

Gratefully acknowledging what seemed to be her forgiveness, Tyler took her hand and pressed it against his smooth cheek. "It's not entirely hopeless, my angel. These reversals are only temporary." He inclined his head to kiss her fingertips. "Meanwhile, I shall merely ask your good uncle for some sort of advance to tide me—*us*—over."

Honor let out a sigh, though whether of relief or resignation, she wasn't sure. At least they had both made their confessions, surely a sign of trust between them. Like a pair of shipwrecked passengers, they had floundered about in rough seas but had finally reached the safety of solid ground. Honor dared to ask about the pretty brunette she had seen with him by the Temple.

Initially, his face clouded, then cleared like a mountaintop after a summer squall. "Philene Godard!" He uttered the name as if its owner were of no consequence. "A right deuced coincidence you should have seen us! I was merely perambulating with the little thing about the City, showing it off, as it were. She's niece to one of those pestiferous French Papists, going to marry some rich old geezer in Staffordshire. He's not a Papist, of course, heaven preserve us, but one of his sons was a soldier during the recent melee over there and married her sister. Quite a tangle, don't you know, my little pippin?"

It was more than a tangle to Honor, it was incomprehensible. Which, she told herself, didn't mean it wasn't plausible. As Tyler was toying with one of her thick, glistening curls and allowing his fingers to brush against her neck, Honor was more than willing to accept his explanation at face value. Offering no resistance, she gazed up at him expectantly, wondering if now he would dare to steal a kiss. As she recalled, her cousins at Whitehorse Hill had advised her to assume a demure, yet inviting, expression at such a moment. A sweep of eyelashes, a tantalizing upward glance, the lips just parted ever so slightly ... Honor ran through the gamut of instructions and was stupefied when Tyler squeezed her hand and released her.

"I shall call on your uncle tomorrow," he said, picking up his hat with its round, broad brim and the single feather. "It's always pleasant to journey down to Hampton Court this time of year. Lovely flowers and all that."

If Tyler noticed the sudden snap in Honor's eyes, he gave no indication. Indeed, he was already at the door when it opened behind him, revealing a servant carrying a large woolen sack. Seeing Sir Tyler, the servant bowed hastily, apologized for the intrusion, then presented the sack to Honor.

"This 'ere came for ye within the past 'alf hour, mistress. Mayhap you'd be wantin' to pack it with yer other baggage," he said, scrunching up his grizzled face. "Some wee lad no bigger 'n a minute brung it by." Having discharged his duty, the serving man bowed again and departed.

Frowning, Honor undid the cord that held the sack in place. Upon first glance, it appeared that another sack lay inside. But as she hauled the bundled cloth out into the light, she recognized her fine lamb's-wool cloak. A sharp intake of breath stirred Tyler's curiosity. He moved closer but was still baffled by his fiancée's apparent loss of composure at having found a cloak in a sack.

Heedless of Tyler's inquiring eyes, Honor examined the cloak, noting that the seams that had been undone to remove the jewels had been carefully restitched. Indeed, something had been added. Tacked to the silk lining was a piece of white linen some two inches square, with four lines of verse etched in a firm, blunt hand:

> What is the worth of hair so gold?
> Can joy be stolen from lips so cold?
> Should a man waste words on a maid of ice?
> Or is surrender bought at too dear a price?

Honor gaped at the bold words, abruptly turning away from Tyler so that he couldn't read her expression. How dare such a brazen thief send a message that was better suited to a lover than a traitor? He'd be a dead man, had her fingers been as resolute as her will. Or, a small voice asked, was it the other way round? Damn and blast, she thought savagely, why hadn't he ridden out of her life forever? Honor had vowed to wreak vengeance if they ever met again, but realized it was a hollow oath. She could encounter—and dispatch—fifty different Royalists before she ever saw the likes of Captain Hood a second time. Haphazardly, she wadded up the cloak and cast about for a place to put it.

"Really, m'dear, what's perturbing you so?" Tyler inquired. He was obviously irked at being left out on knowing the reason for Honor's sudden shift of mood. "Is that piece of apparel yours?" He jabbed at the rumpled cloak with his ivory walking stick. "I say, my little partridge—oh, zounds!" He had obviously just realized the garment's significance. "Don't tell me that was the cape in which you had—"

"Yes, yes, so I had," Honor retorted, marching to the portmanteau, which was stacked with her other modest baggage by the door, awaiting conveyance to Hampton Court. "We'll speak no more of it this day. I'm nigh onto ill with the subject." She yanked open the portmanteau and stuffed the cloak inside, then banged down the lid and dusted off her hands for emphasis. "Damn and blast," she muttered, ignoring Tyler's curious gaze.

"Well," said her betrothed in a conciliatory manner, "I can understand your upset. Most rattling, and I'd be the first to hang the highwayman high as Haman, but I confess I'm in a stew as to why the villain sent back your cloak. Usually those kind of fellows give such trophies to their doxies or whatever, excuse my language and all that."

Her longing for Tyler's embrace had been quashed. Honor's only wish was for his swift departure. "I must lie down," she announced, assuming an air of fragility that was quite foreign to her usual honest vigor. "It must be the reminder of the robbery. And," she added faintly, "the ensuing brutalities."

Tyler gaped. " 'Brutalities'? My little pigeon, whatever do you mean?" He reached for her, but she spun away, hand to head.

"I'd rather not speak of it. Ever." Her back was to him, her shoulders bowed. Tyler tapped the handle of his walking stick against his thigh and frowned. At last he shrugged helplessly and was gone. Honor gave the door a mighty kick behind him and then, for good measure, swung her foot at the portmanteau, as well. Innocent baggage, innocuous cargo, she told herself fiercely. It's Hood you want, not the stupid cloak. The verse was self-indulgent, the return of her cape self-serving. The myth of the latter-day Robin Hood was a farce. Of course she'd like nothing more than to have another chance to shoot the wretched man with his indolent air and Royalist sympathies. But that was hardly possible for the future wife of Sir Tyler Vail. Instead, she'd simply forget about Captain Hood. And his cheap verse. And those strange, hypnotic eyes. And his disturbing touch.

Honor put on her new green cloak and set her mind on the short journey to Hampton Court.

Chapter Four

Hampton Court Palace originally had been built in the 1520s by Cardinal Wolsey, Henry VIII's wily and worldly chancellor. But when Wolsey fell from power, Henry had confiscated the palace for his own pleasure and comfort. Situated on the banks of the Thames a short barge journey from London, the palatial dwelling had served Tudor and Stuart monarchs as a welcome retreat from the foul humors of the city. But during this hot and dry summer of 1658, even Hampton Court's gracious aura proved less than salubrious to the Cromwell usurpers. The Protector's favorite daughter, Bettie, had been brought from London to recover her health, but as the blue skies and blistering sun stood high above the mellow red brick palace, it became clear that Bettie had come not to prosper but to die.

Honor remembered her cousin as a pert, warm girl of immense personal charm. She had been pretty, with her chestnut curls and engaging smile, a natural pretender to the unofficial title of princess. But with her body eroded by pain and her spirit tested to its limits, Bettie reminded Honor of a withered flower vainly attempting to survive an endless drought.

The apartments Bettie shared with her husband, John Claypole, and their three surviving children overlooked the tennis courts. But despite the most heroic efforts at putting on a brave front, it was clear to Honor that no pleasant vista or comforting presence could long divert Bettie from her agony.

Yet she tried valiantly to rally when Honor came to visit. "You've grown to be very beautiful," Bettie said in a voice strained with suffering. "I was pleased to learn of your betrothal. I hope—in truth, I pray—that this is a love match."

"Oh, yes," Honor agreed almost too quickly. "We are quite smitten." Even as she gave Bettie a bright smile, Honor noted the ashen skin stretched tight across the bones, the thin, fretful hands that plucked at the goose-down comforter, the constant, disquieting shifting of the frail body as it sought some small, heretofore undiscovered place of ease.

But even in her misery, Bettie had the gift of attending to others' problems. "I am so sorry to hear about your jewels," she said, marshaling her waning strength. "But love will conquer all. I was younger than you when I married my dear John, yet we were so sure of our feelings. Never mind what people say about the convenience of arranged matches. Love is what matters. It's the *only* thing that matters." She closed her eyes briefly, and for a moment her entire being seemed to relax, as if the mere mention of the love she had shared with her husband could dull the pain. Honor, however, moved uneasily in the chair next to the big canopied bed. Of course she loved Tyler—wasn't he the most handsome and charming of men? Surely he must love her in return. A man in his present financial straits would hardly wed a dowerless maid unless he was genuinely devoted.

Honor turned as Oliver Cromwell came quietly into the room. These days he spent more time with his favorite daughter than he did with his ministers. Opening her eyes, Bettie gave her father a brave, if pitiful, smile. "Good father, I was telling Honor about the joys of holy matrimony. If she could be only half as content as I have been, she will lead a blessed life indeed."

Cromwell sank down into a chair on the opposite side of the bed as Honor noted his haggard face and unsteady hands. His manner, however, was one of forced cheer. "Ah, praise be to Almighty God, you will have many more years of wedded bliss. Why, Bettie," he went on in a voice that was pathetic in its self-delusion, "I do believe you're looking better today. Honor's visit has done you good. There's tonic in a change of faces, eh?"

Cromwell gave Honor a hopeful smile, which she tried to return, but it was Bettie who hastened to reassure her father. "Our cousin is a breath of spring, is she not?" Lifting a feeble hand in Honor's direction, Bettie winced with pain and bit her lips. "In truth, I hope to witness your wedding, Coz. Where will it be? London?"

"Yes," Honor replied after a moment's hesitation. "But I'm not sure yet which church." She glanced at her uncle for guidance.

"We haven't made that decision," Cromwell said, looking pinched about the lips, as if he could feel his daughter's pain. "The Abbey, perhaps. In the chapel."

Bettie nodded. "It's a lovely place," she said, barely above a whisper. "So peaceful, so full of God's presence …." Struggling against the latest onslaught of agony, she looked again at Honor. "I was married at Ely. But you must wed in the chapel at the Abbey … for me."

"The Abbey?" Honor spoke with wonder, knowing the great church only from accounts by visitors to Whitehorse Manor. "It sounds too grand for a wedding."

"Not if Bettie thinks otherwise," said Cromwell in that gruff voice.

"See how he indulges me?" Bettie remarked with a ghostly hint of what had once been an insouciant smile. "Praise God, no daughter ever had a fonder father!" Touched, Honor watched Cromwell and Bettie exchange loving glances, as if each were trying to give the other strength. Then Bettie faltered, another spasm of pain contorting her body. Honor looked away, unable to bear the visible suffering of both father and daughter.

THREE WEEKS LATER HONOR AND Bettie made the journey together down the Thames to the Abbey. For Honor, it was her first trip; for Bettie, it was her last. There was no bride or groom, no merry jests about the wedded state, no fulsome homily on holy wedlock. Instead, there was Bettie, cold and quiet on her bier, gliding through the August twilight. A silent flotilla of black-clad courtiers followed in the solemn summer stillness. Honor rode with Dick Cromwell and Mall's husband, Viscount Fauconberg. Neither Oliver nor Elizabeth Cromwell was present; so prostrate with grief was the father that the mother had stayed at his side to offer what small comfort might be given.

Standing at the barge rail, Honor stared down into the black, eddying waters of the Thames as they approached Westminster Stairs. The governing of England had all but come to a halt the past fortnight. Yet even the staunchest Royalist refused to criticize the Lord Protector, for Bettie's sweet nature had won over even her father's bitterest enemies. On more than one occasion, she had interceded with Cromwell, begging him to show mercy to a condemned Royalist. Her father had found it all but impossible to refuse her.

The love and respect Bettie had evoked showed clearly on the mourners' faces as they filed from the barge on leaden feet to make their way by torchlight up the moss-covered steps. Honor discovered that her own eyes were wet with tears and she wished that Tyler was with her to offer his assured masculine presence. But Tyler was shackled to his business interests in the city, apparently trying to convince his creditors that they must wait until Oliver Cromwell had emerged from his grief so that he could advance his future kinsman the necessary funds. Honor had been heartened by her uncle's generosity in granting Tyler's request for a sizable sum, but Bettie's last days had prevented the Lord Protector from actually signing the appropriate papers.

Perhaps now that Bettie would be put to rest in the Henry VII chapel at Westminster, the world could start turning again for all the Cromwells. Carefully watching her footing, Honor followed the others to the Painted Chamber at Westminster Hall, where Bettie would lie in state until midnight. Among the somber clergy and grieving mourners, Honor bowed her head before the ornate draperies of the hearse and prayed for Bettie's soul.

It was the second funeral she had attended for her kinfolk in two months. She could scarcely have envisioned that only four weeks later she would be kneeling at the bier of Oliver Cromwell.

EVEN AS STRONG A WOMAN as Elizabeth Cromwell might have broken rather than bent under the weight of the summer tragedies that had befallen her family. First a grandchild, then a daughter, and finally her much-loved husband of nearly forty years. Yet with superhuman effort, she stifled her own sorrow sufficiently to attempt comforting her remaining children.

Nor was Honor neglected during this rite of passage. Both her aunt and her cousin Dick made it clear that they were concerned for her future. They also made it clear that the wedding with Sir Tyler would have to be postponed.

"'Twouldn't be seemly, Coz," Dick asserted, looking extremely uncomfortable in his father's chair of state. Though Cromwell had never officially named a successor, it was generally agreed that the continuity of England's governance could best be achieved by passing the Protectorate to the eldest son. To hesitate or demonstrate a lack of confidence would only permit the Royalists time to rally their own forces and attempt to bring back King Charles.

"After all," Dick continued, shuffling a stack of official papers from one pile to another, "the first of October would be less than a month since poor Father's death." He paused, assuming a puzzled expression, as if he still couldn't believe that the senior Cromwell was gone. "You and Tyler had planned for a Christmas wedding—why not just revert to your original date?"

All things considered, Dick's request was hardly unreasonable. The only problem was Tyler, who was growing more and more impatient to wed. He was also very distressed over the late Protector's failure to take care of the promised advance; Cromwell had died before he could sign the papers.

"If my presence wouldn't inconvenience you and the rest of the family, I shouldn't mind," Honor replied carefully, "but Tyler has his heart set on an earlier date. He is, I fear, in great need of the money your good father planned to advance him."

"I don't know ..." Dick began, almost toppling an inkwell with a stray elbow. "It's not as if this pertained to official monies. We'd have to lend him some of our own, and to be frank, Coz, we aren't particularly flush at the moment."

To Honor, it seemed that every man she knew suffered from severe financial reversal. Certainly Dick Cromwell had an unenviable reputation for landing himself in debt. For England's sake, Honor hoped that the Lord Treasurer was a competent man. Yet if Dick was careless when it came to spending money, he had a stubborn streak when it came to lending it. Honor could elicit no more from her cousin than a vague promise to look further into the matter at a later date.

Tyler wasn't so easily placated. Upon visiting Honor at Whitehall one misty afternoon in late September, he expressed not just dismay but desperation. "See here, Honor," he lectured her with a wag of his forefinger, "my creditors are growing more than testy. It was one thing to be marrying Oliver Cromwell's niece. It's quite another to be marrying Dick Cromwell's cousin. Face it, m'dear, the man's an ass."

"He's also the new Lord Protector," Honor retorted, and received a baleful look from Tyler for rushing to her cousin's defense. Nevertheless, she continued doggedly. "With proper advisers, no doubt Dick will grow into the job." It was a shame, she had to admit to herself, that the more capable Henry hadn't been born the elder son, but surely his presence, along with Oliver Cromwell's loyal lieutenants, would keep England on an even keel. As soon as its citizens realized that, all would be well. "If you might be so good as to wait a few weeks …."

But judging from the stormy expression on his face, she could see that Tyler's patience was spent. He was flinging his walking stick from one hand to the other, while his buckled shoe tapped impatiently on the floor. "More's the pity I ever let Dick Cromwell pay back the money he borrowed from me last spring. To have him in my debt would be a tremendous boon." He paused, gazing thoughtfully at the carved boar's head on his walking stick. "It's all quite impossible. Much as I hate to say it, m'dear, we shall have to break off our engagement."

So unexpected were the words that Honor actually reeled, falling against a small gateleg table. Tyler started toward her but halted in midstep, his face a bit sheepish. "There, there, m'dear, it can't be helped. I'm aggrieved, too. We should have made a most delightful couple."

Still dazed by Tyler's shattering announcement, Honor steadied herself and gaped at him incredulously. What had happened to their tender feelings for each other, to the gentle wooing that had boded so auspiciously for marriage, to the love that they surely shared between them? But as had become his wont, Tyler was speaking not of love but of money.

"I don't suppose," he mused, almost more to himself than to Honor, "that there's any chance you'd profit from your aunt's estate?" The blue eyes darted in her direction. Honor continued to stare at him blankly. "No, I thought not. Still, it was worth inquiring into." Making a formal little bow, he saluted Honor with his walking stick and moved toward the door.

Honor started after him. "I don't believe this! You're panicking! I thought you loved me!" She kept her hands at her sides lest she shake him until his impeccably groomed mustache fell off.

Tyler had paused with his hand on the doorknob. He had the grace to look embarrassed but was devoid of consolation. "It's pointless to agitate yourself, my little duckling. Least said, soonest mended and all that. I'm not a heartless sort really, but whoever said it was possible to live on love must have had a yen for lean pickings. I don't."

Honor clenched her fists. "You're a callous cad, Tyler Vail! You never cared for me, only for my dowry and my uncle's position!"

"Well," said Tyler in a tone of reasonable reproach, "you must admit, the latter in particular was extremely impressive. Be reasonable, sweets, I'm not worthy. If I were you, I'd not think of marrying such a bounder as m'self." Abruptly, Honor backed away. The words had the unsettling ring of truth. Tyler Vail *was* a fraud, a liar, a cheat. Surely she deserved better. Except that penniless maids usually ended up as impecunious spinsters.

Even as her dark eyes sparked with contempt, Tyler was preparing to leave. Despite Honor's distress over his one-sided decision, he seemed as concerned as ever with style rather than substance. Again sketching an elegant bow, he offered her a rueful little smile, and was gone.

"MY BELOVED LATE HUSBAND, YOUR dear uncle of such solemn memory, taught me an invaluable lesson," Aunt Elizabeth said in calm, even tones. "All things are to be endured in Christ and for Christ. In the last weeks of his life, after darling Bettie's blessed release, he would repeat over and over the words of Saint Paul—'Not that I speak in respect of want: for I have learned in whatsoever state I am, therewith to be content. I know both how to be abased … and how to abound … I can do all things through Christ which strengtheneth me.' Heed those words, dear niece, for they sustained your uncle in many a tribulation."

They had not, however, prevented Cromwell from giving up his ghost so soon after the death of his favorite daughter, Honor thought with a cynicism that would have shocked her aunt. That other aunt, Lucy, would have seen things differently. Though she was a nodding acquaintance of Puritanism, she had always managed to see every side of any theological dispute. While allowing for Cromwell's submission to Christ, she would also have remarked that "the Lord helps those who help themselves," and then pointed out that it was very likely the Lord Protector would have died whether Bettie had preceded him or not, such being God's will in the first place or, perhaps, the inevitable weakness of mortal flesh, over which the Almighty had no direct control.

But it was Elizabeth, not Lucy, with whom Honor must deal at present, and the recent widow had given Sir Tyler Vail scant shrift. "He is clearly an unstable sort, unsuitable as a husband," she asserted, looking up from her needlework to make sure the point was not lost on her silent niece. "Your dear departed uncle and I once thought otherwise, but it appears he duped us. I understand he's gone abroad."

"I marvel at Tyler's talent in pulling the wool over the eyes of a man as astute as my good uncle," Honor remarked with bite. Noting the hurt expression on her aunt's face, Honor softened her tone. "He fooled me, too, but I'm a naive country lass. I wonder if perhaps Tyler didn't trade shamelessly off his Roundhead soldiering experiences." Though she didn't say so out loud, Honor also wondered if Tyler had ever worn a uniform, let alone distinguished himself in the heat of battle. He seemed capable of all manner of duplicity, from deluding young maids to deceiving Oliver Cromwell. At least she was beginning to realize that if Tyler had never really loved her, she had probably not loved him, either. Infatuation, Honor decided. That was what had overcome her. But love—as Bettie had said—could conquer all. If Bettie had been right, then neither Honor nor Tyler knew much about such exalted emotions.

Practical as ever, Elizabeth Cromwell chose to gloss over the past and look to the future. Unfortunately, Honor had been so wrapped up in her own ruminations that she had quite lost her aunt's train of thought. It was only when Elizabeth Cromwell raised her voice a notch that Honor felt obliged to pay closer attention.

"I can't think how you'd disagree," Elizabeth said pointedly, one hand poised with a long ivory needle above her embroidery frame, "that living in the countryside not so far from your childhood home would be advantageous to you. The Goudges are fine people, a bit strict perhaps, but most respected and prosperous. Their home at Creepers is the envy of the neighborhood."

Honor sat up straight in the chair, adjusting the brass fire screen so that the heat was diverted from her face. She hadn't the faintest idea what her aunt was talking about, except that it applied to herself. She knew no one named Goudge, nor a house called Creepers.

"Of course, she was Parthenia Bourchier before her marriage to Delbert," Aunt Elizabeth went on, serenely inserting her needle now that she was assured of Honor's attention. "My father was a city man of affairs, hers a country squire, yet the brothers remained close so we cousins saw each other often. Delbert was another matter," she went on with a wry little grimace. "He came from nowhere, to be honest, but his loyalty to your uncle's cause was indisputable. There has been some criticism that he was excessively cruel in exercising his duties in Ireland, but he certainly contributed to the submission of those terrible Papists. As a reward, he was given Creepers."

As much as Honor hated the Royalists, gruesome accounts of Drogheda and Wexford had always disturbed her. She had blurted her reaction to Cromwell on her first night at Whitehall. His subjugation of the Irish rebels had been necessary, of course, yet his lack of mercy had been criticized by even some of his supporters. As for Delbert Goudge, no doubt he had merely followed orders.

"Cousin Parthenia's letter was most encouraging," Elizabeth continued, pausing to bite off a piece of deep green thread. "With your consent, I shall write back tomorrow to tell her you're coming." Elizabeth Cromwell gave her niece a fond, frank look. "You know I would prefer keeping you with us. But I am so beset by troubles and the future is so unsettled that I see no other—" Abruptly, she closed her mouth, frowning at the half-finished tapestry. "Dick is a lovable, dear boy. But," she added on a deep sigh, "he's not your uncle."

"I know." Honor's voice was wistful. Her happily plotted life was being turned upside down. Instead of looking forward to being the wife of Sir Tyler Vail, she was headed for Creepers and a family named Goudge, back to the country to live upon the bounty of strangers.

Chapter Five

Creepers had originally been a small Staffordshire manor house, dating from the thirteenth century, but numerous renovations and additions had rendered the original structure almost unrecognizable. What remained was primarily a late-Tudor house of gray stone, covered in part by the trailing ivy that gave the residence its name. Long before the Normans, a family named Blaich or Blaike had lived at the edge of the River Dove near Rutbury. After the Conquest, one of King William's favorites was given charge of Rutbury Castle, but the Domesday Survey of 1086 showed one Harold Blaek as owning twenty acres, three roods and twenty-six poles of land between Burton Old Forest and the town. The family's name eventually became Blake, as descendants witnessed the passing panoply of English history on their doorstep. From King John to King James, monarchs passed through Rutbury. The castle had stood as a last bastion in the defense of King Charles. Thomas Blake had cast his lot with his sovereign, only to fall mortally wounded at Naseby. His wife and younger son had been driven from their home and had gone to live in exile abroad. Rutbury Castle was ordered demolished, and Creepers was confiscated. Thus, Blake's properties had been handed over to Delbert Goudge for services rendered to the Puritan cause.

The final chapter of the story was disturbingly similar to how Tyler Vail had acquired his house in the Strand. But many a Puritan supporter had earned his worldly goods in such a manner. The difference, Honor reminded herself, was that the Goudges seemed inclined to hold fast to their spoils whereas Sir Tyler seemed disposed to let his run through careless fingers.

In truth, Creepers was a house worth holding. It was not particularly large but the rooms were commodious and well furnished. The alterations over the years had resulted in an unevenness of floors between rooms, but the overall aspect was one of quiet, dignified charm. The same, unfortunately, could not be said of its occupants.

Delbert Goudge was a tall, rangy man of unrefined habits and a peculiar squint, which made him look ever dubious. His wife, Parthenia, was also tall and given to a stoutness that belied her constant admonitions to be temperate in all things. While Delbert ran the adjacent tenant farms with an unyielding hand, Parthenia oversaw the household in much the same fashion. Although she insisted upon practicing the virtue of Christian optimism and smiled a good deal, she rarely laughed and failed to see any humor at all in a world where she asserted the Devil worked relentlessly to snatch men's souls.

Of their three children, Faith was the nearest in age to Honor, and very unlike either of her parents. She had inherited her parents' height, but her figure bore more resemblance to her father's than her mother's. Still, had it not been for a long, sharply pointed nose, Faith might have been pretty. At fifteen, her younger sister, Clarity, was definitely destined for beauty, a fact that made her as unbearably vain as she was flighty. Indeed, Honor couldn't see how such a stern father and rigid mother could put up with such a smug child. It was clear that as the youngest, Clarity was also the most spoiled.

The oldest was the family's son and heir, Uriah, almost a duplicate of his sire in appearance if not in manner. Where Delbert Goudge was stubborn and narrow-minded, Uriah was spineless and of little mind at all. He dutifully followed his father about the Goudge holdings but openly admitted to a preference for fishing and hunting. A wife had been chosen for him, a squire's daughter named Prudence from a place nearby known as Buttermilk Hill, but Uriah seemed in no rush to claim his bride. In fact, he seemed in no rush to do much of anything, including getting out of bed in the morning. For the first week of her stay at Creepers, Honor heard Master Goudge attempt to rouse his son for the better part of an hour every day.

Not that she was permitted to loll about between the sheets at Creepers—it was expected that along with Faith and Clarity she would rise early to assist Mistress Goudge in the daily routine. Though there were several servants, Parthenia was a firm believer in busy hands.

"I've all but seen the Devil spring upon an idle maid and sear her heart with his hellish breath," said Mistress Goudge one crisp October morning as she vigorously churned fresh butter. "The next thing you know, she's sold her virtue for a farthing and masked demons with wings like bats have come to carry her away to perdition!"

Honor didn't know which was the more fearsome—Mistress Goudge's ghoulish account or the wide, toothy smile she offered her listeners upon the conclusion of her tale. Clarity seemed unmoved by either one, making a halfhearted effort to pull pinfeathers from a plump fowl. At the huge fireplace, Faith stirred the contents of a cast-iron pot with a long-handled wooden spoon. Judging from her expression, she was all too familiar with such anecdotes but had the good sense to suppress her boredom.

"Sin is a terrible thing," Mistress Goudge intoned, still with the fixed smile on her long face. "Constant vigilance must be exercised. I daresay your uncle often spoke to you of these matters."

Honor inclined her head in an ambiguous response. Oliver Cromwell had been the leader of the Puritan faction and a very devout man, yet his personal religion was of a less fervent—and more private—nature than that of Mistress Goudge. Indeed, Honor couldn't remember her uncle ever sermonizing. She had heard more religious diatribes in the week that she had been at Creepers than she had elsewhere in an entire year.

Before Mistress Goudge could launch herself again, the kitchen door banged open, revealing Delbert and Uriah. "That villain of a poacher, Will Tipper, has been sneaking around the mill, grinding his grain without paying his multure. Thieving knave that he is, I ought to have him put in the Rutbury stocks!" Master Goudge stalked angrily to the fireplace, where he inspected the kettle Faith was dutifully stirring. "Pea soup, eh? Make it thick, girl. Last time it was thin as rainwater."

Clarity, still pinching pinfeathers, giggled. "Faith's soup tastes like rainwater and her broth tastes like mud. Wouldn't you think she could get one of them right?"

"Nasty!" exclaimed Faith, dropping the spoon with a clatter. "You can't boil an egg! You won't even learn! How do you expect to ever get a husband?"

Clarity extracted a pinfeather and scrutinized it closely, wrinkling her small, well-defined nose. "Unlike some I could name, I shan't need a list of accomplishments ten feet long to find a man. And unlike those same ones I could name," she added with a smug little smile, "I doubt that I shall still be a spinster at nineteen."

Honor, who was facing her own twentieth birthday, found her sympathies with Faith, who had started toward her sister with retribution in her eye.

"Clarity, Faith," snapped Parthenia. "Cease this discord. Vanity, all is vanity. You think too much of the flesh, Clarity Goudge." She turned from her youngest to her eldest daughter with a rustle of black muslin skirts. "And you *think* too much for any female. The only reason you were taught to read was so you could dwell upon the word of God. We'll have no other books in this house but those written by holy hands. Understand?"

Cowed by her mother's admonitions, Faith backed away, returning to her soup pot. Master Goudge had watched the bickering with a disinterested eye, his big hands cupped around a large mug of cider. Uriah hadn't watched at all, no doubt having tired long ago of his sisters' quarrels. Instead, he sat upon a high stool, his long legs entangled, the lethargic gaze fixed on Honor. Ever since she'd arrived at Creepers, Uriah had followed her with his brown, bovine eyes; yet he had never spoken to her other than his initial greeting upon being introduced. Honor assumed that he was put off by her exalted Cromwell kinship, though it was possible that Uriah might be shy with women in general. Whatever the reason, his constant surveillance was disconcerting.

"Beans," said Mistress Goudge in her sharp, trenchant voice. She passed the big basket to Honor, who had just finished paring several dozen apples. As usual, she wondered where the cook and the scullery maid had gone—to market in Rutbury, perhaps, or out culling the remnants of the vegetable garden. It seemed to Honor that the servants had the more pleasant tasks. Except for cooking breakfast and supper, most of their duties were conducted away from the house.

As if she could read Honor's mind, Parthenia Goudge addressed that issue next. "You'll find humility in paring apples and snipping beans, Honor Dale," she asserted, finally satisfied that the butter was sufficiently hard. "It's no wonder that sinful king and his like fell before your uncle's mighty sword. Did King Charles ever churn or Queen Henrietta ever hoe? Did their nobles scrub or polish or sweep? Or course not! And look where such idleness got them! Exile or worse, and surely eternal damnation! I would rather serve my servants than have my servants serve me. See how Pharaoh forced the Israelites into bondage—and what good did it do him? Plague and locusts and all the horrid rest came to visit Egypt. There now," she went on, thumping Honor on the back, "don't you feel closer to God already?"

Honor winced. Mistress Goudge was the sort of sanctimonious person who made virtue sound like a dread disease. Honor gave her hostess the most innocent of stares. "I thought God was always with us," she said meekly, "and that Christ Jesus is in each of us. Is that not so?"

Lips pursed, Mistress Goudge lifted one straight eyebrow. "It is—and it isn't. Sin puts distance between God and Man. Especially," she added with a meaningful look at Honor, "the sin of pride."

Honor lowered her lashes and tried to assume a chastened expression. Outside, the autumn sun shone on the stands of ash and alder, which were shedding their red-gold leaves in the gentle wind from the River Dove. If Honor had been at Whitehorse Hill, she would have spent the day in the saddle, admiring the bold outline of Liddington Castle or riding into Swindon to explore the town. As it was, she found herself penned up at Creepers, her mornings devoted to kitchen tasks, her afternoons to household chores and her evenings to prayer and scripture study. If this first week had seemed like a month, the prospect of staying on with the Goudges yawned before her like eternity. Honor was far less afraid of being snatched away by the Devil than being condemned to a lifetime at Creepers.

The beans now snapped, Honor girded for the next assignment. Sure enough, Mistress Goudge was handing out large chunks of candied fruit. "Slice these fine as can be. We'll be using them later for fruitcake."

Honor picked up an orange segment; it seemed a shame to waste such a sweet bit of fruit in a dry old cake, she thought. But again, it appeared as if Mistress Goudge could read her mind. "Yield not to temptation in small things," she admonished, "lest you perish from succumbing to greater ones." With a glance at her husband for approval, Parthenia was encouraged to elaborate on her latest theme. "Why, only last spring, in Rutbury, the glazier's daughter, Bess, coveted her sister's wedding shoes. Of course her sister—a most virtuous sort named Nan—refused to let Bess wear them. So the wicked wench stole them away in the night. And then," she continued, taking a deep breath to emphasize the dire words to come, "not a fortnight later, Bess stole Nan's groom! They ran off to Uttoxeter," she added darkly, as if the nearby town ranked somewhere between Sodom and Gomorrah.

"It's true," said Master Goudge, "they went straight to Uttoxeter." He nodded solemnly three times before refilling his cider mug.

"My," breathed Honor. The single syllable was all she could manage for the glazier's daughter. Unfortunately, it was not enough for Mistress Goudge.

"See here," she railed, "I don't believe you're taking Christian principles seriously! Why, if I didn't know you were kin to the great Protector himself, I'd wonder if you didn't have some backsliding tendencies!" Mistress Goudge was holding her hands up in front of her, as if to ward off an assault from Satan. Honor wondered if open rebellion might earn her exile from Creepers. Surely it was worth a try. Aunt Elizabeth might be overwhelmed by family tragedy, but she'd never turn Honor away. Parthenia Goudge prattled endlessly about Christian virtue; Elizabeth Cromwell was more likely to practice it.

"You're right," Honor agreed, emptying the dried fruit from her apron onto the floor and briskly brushing off her hands. "I'm filled with sin and have no moral sense at all. I was actually raised by Druids. I must go now to commune with their ancient spirits and paint my body blue."

Ignoring the horrified expressions of the household members, Honor stomped out of the kitchen before anyone, even Mistress Goudge, could say a word. When she reached the stable, where a young boy with straw-colored hair eyed her warily, Honor stopped to consider her next move. Her natural instinct had sent her to the place most likely to provide escape. But as she studied the horses, who munched on feed and stamped restlessly in their boxes, she wasn't so sure of her feelings. London was a long way off, and though the journey to Rutbury had been uneventful, the previous trip had not. Perhaps she should merely go off for a good gallop, clear her head and think of some logical explanation for her impudent behavior. That it would satisfy Mistress Goudge was unlikely, but if she was to grovel and do penance, she might be restored to grace.

A sprightly black mare whinnied to Honor. She smiled at the animal, the first real smile since she'd come to Creepers. Finding a saddle and bridle, Honor led the mare outside. To her surprise, no Goudges were prowling in back of the manor house, looking for their wayward ward.

Taking the road that went toward Rutbury rather than the mill, Honor skirted the River Dove until she reached the turn into Burton Old Forest. Here the trees were mostly oak, some so tall they seemed to touch the sky. Over the centuries, the Blake family and their tenants had farmed only some of the land between the Dove and the Burton Road. The Goudges had kept to that tradition. The rest was forest, some of it growing since Saxon times.

The wind had picked up sharply, rustling the leaves in the oak trees and freeing Honor's golden hair from its confining white cap. As she spurred the mare to a canter, she actually laughed. Here, among the great stands of oak, with a sparkling little brook tumbling among the limestone rocks, Honor felt closer to God than she did in Creepers' kitchen.

The revelation prompted her to look down at her attire; she wore mourning, of course, black linen relieved only by the white cap, cuffs and collar. Incongruous enough out riding, but she had to laugh again when she saw that she still had on her apron. No matter, she was blissfully alone in Burton Old Forest with only the sound of the wind and the black mare's hooves. Honor urged the horse to a gallop and threw back her head, letting her long hair stream behind her in the wind.

She saw the goshawk before her mare did, glimpsing its sudden swoop on some unsuspecting prey. Yet she did not respond quickly enough to prepare her horse. The animal reared, whinnied and went down headfirst, throwing her rider onto the hard ground. Stunned by the fall, Honor didn't move for a long time; when at last she did, it was with great care, lest a bone might be broken. Both arms were bruised but otherwise intact. So was her right leg. The left, however, sported an ankle that was already painful and swelling at an alarming rate. She gingerly attempted to stand up but found that the left leg refused to support her weight. Hurriedly, she sat back down on the ground and tried to collect her wits.

The black mare was nowhere to be seen. Perhaps she would return to the stable, alerting the Goudges that something was amiss. But would the family care? Honor couldn't help but be dubious. Mistress Goudge would probably be only too glad that her charge had met with misfortune. A judgment, she'd insist, and would invoke God's name in all manner of just deserts. On the other hand, the Goudges couldn't let a niece of Oliver Cromwell starve to death in Burton Old Forest. Surely in time they'd come looking for her. But how long it would take for them to find her was a question Honor preferred not to dwell upon. She was less than two miles from Creepers, but there was a great deal of woodland to search between the Dove and the Belmot Road.

Glumly, Honor sat under a sturdy maple, which seemed small by comparison with some of the oaks she'd observed thus far. To her right, she saw the sudden plunge of an animal in a thicket; Honor leaned forward to see if the mare had returned. It was not a horse but a deer, from all appearances fleeing from some danger. The long-legged creature flew through the trees and disappeared. Honor was musing upon what had frightened the animal when her human ears picked up the sound that the animal had heard first: horses' hooves clip-clopping down the Belmot Road. It was too soon to be the Goudges, and in any event, the hoofbeats were coming from the wrong direction. Whoever it might be, they could rescue her. Honor struggled through the bracken toward the road.

At the halfway point, she realized that the horsemen would be well past her by the time she reached her goal, but she continued to scramble along on hands and knees until she saw that the men were almost directly opposite her. Peering more closely at the riders, her heart gave a sudden flutter. Three of the men looked quite ordinary—but the fourth wore an all-enveloping black cape, a broad-brimmed black hat … and a mask.

Honor all but choked on a gasp of startled recognition and fervently wished that she could burrow underground to hide from Captain Hood.

During the journey from London to Rutbury, there had been no mention of highwaymen prowling the roads of Staffordshire. Yet these thieving villains menaced all England, from Land's End to the Tweed. Hadn't Uncle Oliver mentioned that the purported Captain Hood usually roamed farther north than the Chiltern Hills? Rutbury was certainly north, in a logical line between London and the nearby cities of Derby and Nottingham.

Nottingham … Honor let the name roll about in her head. Robin Hood … Captain Hood …. Straining to look between two holly bushes, she could just barely see the outline of her nemesis's back. He was facing the others, who apparently were listening to his commands. Honor couldn't hear the words, but Hood's voice was just as she remembered it—cool, indolent, cultured. Not at all the sort of man to terrorize hapless travelers or rob a maiden of her dowry.

But there he was, bold as brass bells and doubtless lying in wait for his next brace of victims. If only Honor could warn them—or somehow frighten off the highwaymen. "Damn and blast," she muttered. Of course she hadn't brought her pistol. It reposed back at Creepers in a drawer under her linen.

Yet it occurred to Honor that revenge wasn't as important as rescue. Attempting to move her leg to relieve the pain, she began to see Captain Hood in a different light. It was possible, even probable, that he was of more value to her alive than dead. If there was any way she could ever get her dowry back, it was the notorious highwayman who held the key. As she watched him blend into the forest with his cohorts, Honor's lips twitched in a tight little smile. He had no idea that she had tried to shoot him. Surely a man—even a highwayman and a Royalist—who had seen to the mending of her cloak would hardly pose any serious danger. Then there was his verse, brazen as his kiss, yet civilized. Out of her pain and frustration, a plan began to form in Honor's mind. All she had to do was wait for the right moment.

Slowly, painfully, she inched over the rough ground. She had covered another ten yards by the time she heard the unmistakable clatter of a coach. Captain Hood and his men swiftly mounted their horses but held back until their objective was almost upon them. Then, with a signal from their leader, they thundered out onto the road. The driver swore out loud, the footman cursed, and from within the conveyance a woman screamed.

Hood kept to the side of the road as his men ushered the passengers from the coach. An obese older woman, a young girl with red hair, a gaunt man of middle age in preacher's garb and a gangly youth of about sixteen made up the party along with the two coachmen. Honor, peering through a tall stand of sword ferns, thought she recognized the lad as being from the village—one of Will Tipper's towheaded sons, perhaps. Amid much outraged grumbling and protest, valuables were handed over to the thieves. Honor studied the scene with something akin to amusement. The obese woman was threatening to faint, the preacher was promising eternal damnation in a solemn yet mild tone, which Mistress Goudge would have extinguished with one of her fearsome toothy smiles, and the redheaded girl was twittering mightily even as she darted inquisitive glances in Captain Hood's direction. It was, however, the gangly youth who had captured Honor's attention. He was deceptively quiet, gazing out blandly from under a shock of flaxen hair. Though he had already surrendered a small pouch, which presumably contained his money, he seemed poised for further action.

Sure enough, just as the older woman was handing her silver eardrops to the youngest of the robbers, the lad lunged at the largest of the highwayman, attempting to knock away his pistol. The firearm went off into the air with a loud bang as thief and victim wrestled against the side of the coach. Though the youth had height and bravado on his side he was no match for the burly strength of the robber. A single blow of the pistol butt to the temple brought the lad down. Angered by such temerity, the man raised his gun for a second time when a calm, authoritative voice commanded him to desist.

"Enough, Padge. Leave the lad be," said Captain Hood, dismounting from his horse and moving with that languid grace toward the others. "He merely wanted to be a hero. For that, I salute him." Bending down, Hood plucked at the boy's sleeve. "It's all right, my lad. You may tell your friends that you came within a whisker of thwarting Captain Hood."

The youth's glazed eyes tried to focus on the highwayman, but Hood was already moving away. Over his shoulder, he spoke to the redheaded girl, who was hugging herself in a manner that suggested something between abject terror and eager anticipation. "Your gentle ministrations will doubtless heal yon fearless fellow." Despite the mask that hid his upper features, Honor could have sworn that he winked at the girl.

Captain Hood and his men had withdrawn and were mounting their horses. It suddenly dawned on Honor that she would soon be left alone once more, for Hood was ordering his victims back into the coach. "Rutbury lies but two miles away," he called out in that easy, yet compelling, voice. "You'll find a good doctor there, off River Lane."

It seemed to take forever for the quartet of passengers to reload and for the coachmen to resume their places. At last, as the band of highwaymen looked on, the conveyance rumbled off down the road. "My master thanks you," Hood called after them with a tip of his big hat.

He had just turned in the saddle to face his men when Honor took a deep breath and boldly called his name. "Captain Hood! Help!"

The highwayman's horse shied as Hood swerved around. "What …?" Frowning, he scanned the tall ferns, the holly bushes, the piles of leaves that covered the ground. "God's ghost, what have we here?" Guiding his nervous mount in a semicircle, he stared at Honor with wry surprise. " 'Tis a wood sprite, creeping through the copse! What say you, vixen nymph? Do you hunt or are you hunted?"

The highwayman's jocular attitude riled Honor, for her ankle was throbbing harder with each passing moment. "I'm hurt," she called back, aware that it took a good deal out of her to speak at all, let alone shout. "I fell from my horse."

Hood tipped his head to one side, the big hat shielding half of his face. "Certainly that would explain your awkward position. It seems to me …." His words were cut short by Padge, who had come up behind his master and was speaking in a low, deep voice that Honor couldn't hear. Judging from the burly, square-set man's face, he had expressed some concern, but Hood only waved a careless hand. "Nonsense, Padge, if she'd meant to trap us, she would have been off as soon as we stopped the coach." Dismounting nimbly and tethering his gelding, Hood held his cape close to his body as he came through the bracken to the place where Honor lay. He started to speak again, but his mouth clamped shut as he looked down on her with those strange, clever eyes. "Jesu," he murmured, " 'tis the maid too good to dally with Hood!"

Honor couldn't blame him for not having recognized her sooner; she was so dirty and disheveled that even Aunt Lucy wouldn't have known her straightaway. She was not, however, prepared for the distinct, if fleeting, look of shock that crossed what she could see of his face. Anxiously, she wondered if he knew she had attempted to kill him. Perhaps her plan was more dangerous than she had guessed.

"Where do you hurt?" he inquired in a normal voice, then turned his head so that his men couldn't hear. "And where in God's name did you come from?"

"My ankle," she replied crossly, then lowered her own voice. "More to the point, where did *you* come from?"

His cloak hung about him in such a way that his comrades could see only his back, and Honor was jarringly reminded of his daring kiss on their previous encounter. Still, Hood did not touch her, nor did he answer her question but instead put another of his own. "Which ankle?"

Reluctantly, Honor plucked at her skirt. "The left," she responded, raising her hem just enough so that he could see the white of her stocking above the plain black shoe.

"What? No boots?" His eyes seemed to twinkle, and Honor grew more uneasy.

"I left in rather a hurry," she said petulantly.

"Indeed, you're still wearing your apron." He turned to his men, who were patiently waiting at the roadside. "Head back. I'll join you shortly." Padge started to lodge a protest, but again Hood cut him off. "There's no risk. I know my way."

The other bandits hesitated, looked at one another, then at Hood, and finally guided their horses back onto the Belmot Road. As soon as they were out of sight, Hood reached down to touch Honor's ankle. Though his fingers were briskly businesslike, she shivered.

"It's swollen but not broken," he announced after a brief probe that made Honor wince. He was still kneeling next to her but now had placed both hands on his thighs. "Do you have any idea what happened to your horse?"

Honor couldn't meet his gaze. "No." She was about to explain when more hoofbeats sounded on the road. Were the highwaymen returning? She looked beyond Hood to see Delbert and Uriah Goudge. "Damn and blast," she swore softly as the highwayman swung about to take in the newcomers. Honor's mind raced. Was it in her best interests to alert the Goudges and hope that they could overcome Captain Hood? She caught the glint of steel on the weapons slung across their saddles and darted a glance at her adversary. But

Hood had already pulled his pistol from his belt and was training it on the Goudges.

If, Honor thought desperately, she could knock the gun away while attracting the Goudges' attention at the same time .... But Hood's free hand came down firmly on her back, forcing her to lie prone on the ground.

"Stay, don't move," he commanded in a low, taut voice. Common sense told her to rebel; a wilder streak dictated otherwise. Should the Goudges be so lucky as to capture Hood and torture him into telling where Honor's jewels had gone, it was possible they might keep that knowledge to themselves. She didn't trust them, even though she knew she ought to side with her hosts rather than with a Royalist outlaw. She instinctively had more respect for the highwayman's integrity than that of the Goudges.

Hood was still watching the two men, who had drawn up alongside the road where his horse stood tethered to a young sapling. " 'Tis ours," announced Delbert Goudge, his harsh voice cutting across the thicket. " 'Twas stolen last year, remember?"

Uriah gaped at the animal as if he'd never seen a horse before, let alone the black gelding who was regarding both Goudges with suspicion. It occurred to Honor that in a battle of wits, the horse would trounce Uriah handily.

Delbert was still ranting about the horse, how it had been taken at about the same time as three other animals in the neighborhood, how he wouldn't be surprised if Will Tipper had been the thief. The man's reputation as a poacher was well-known, as were his Royalist sympathies. Surely, Delbert insisted, Tipper was flawed with unlawful tendencies.

"He's got to be nearby, setting his poxy snares," Master Goudge grumbled, reaching over to undo the horse's reins. The gelding, however, proved uncooperative, pulling away from Goudge, whinnying its disapproval. Shouting at the shying horse, Goudge swung his riding crop viciously. The big animal reared back and pawed at the air, startling the other two horses, who threatened to spill their riders. It was all either Delbert or Uriah could do to stay in the saddle. Freed from its tether, Hood's mount gave one last whinny before galloping off in the opposite direction, through the woods that led to the Rutbury Road.

Delbert Goudge was now cursing fiercely as he regrouped his rangy frame while trying to calm his agitated bay. Uriah's dappled mare was already under control, with its master reverting to his usual apathy.

Honor and Hood hadn't moved a muscle while watching the commotion at the roadside. As Honor's aching body still lay under the prison of Hood's arm, it occurred to her that the Goudges didn't seem to know about the robbery. They must have ridden partway through the forest rather than along the Belmot Road from Rutbury. It was possible that they weren't searching for her, either, though if they'd gone to the stable, one of them should have noticed that the little mare was missing.

"Should we follow?" Uriah's question was doubtfully phrased, as if he were accustomed to having his suggestions rejected.

Delbert was blowing his nose on the sleeve of his coat. "Might lead us to Tipper," he mused. The autumn wind rustled among the trees, shaking loose a fresh shower of leaves. Honor, now painfully stiff, swore to herself that she could actually hear the machinations of Delbert's brain. "Aye," he agreed, "Tipper might be at Granston Grind, filching stones. Then again," he added, as if any idea propounded by his son must lack merit by definition, "why would he leave his horse here?" Goudge scanned the copse; Honor couldn't imagine how he missed spotting them. "Someone's gone this way … recent, too. See there," he directed Uriah, pointing with a blunt forefinger, "boot tracks, fresh as the morning's milk."

Whether it was the gleaming metal in Hood's hand or the golden sheen of Honor's hair that gave them away, she never knew, but Delbert had seen something. He had started to reach for his weapon and cry out to Uriah when Hood's voice cut across the bracken like the slash of a saber.

"Don't move! If you touch your guns, you'll taste my own!"

Stunned, the Goudges froze in place, mouths agape. Honor felt the draft from Hood's billowing cloak as he leaped to his feet in one lightning move. Cautiously, she lifted her head and tried to shake her stiff arms. So intent were Delbert and Uriah on the highwayman's threatening figure that they hadn't seemed to notice her still lying among the ferns.

"Dismount." Hood had the pistol cocked. The Goudges exchanged uncertain glances, then reluctantly obeyed.

Delbert was the first to regain his voice and at least a portion of his courage. "Hood, isn't it? God's eyes, we thought you'd gone to the gallows by now!"

Honor had to admit that Delbert Goudge wasn't lacking in nerve. Uriah, however, was looking appropriately cowed. As Honor pulled herself up onto her elbows, it was the younger Goudge who first noted her presence.

" 'Tis her!" Uriah exclaimed, momentarily forgetting the pistol that Hood deliberately kept moving from one man to the other. " 'Tis our ward!"

The impersonal, yet possessive, description rankled Honor. It also seemed to startle Captain Hood. His head swerved just enough to catch Honor out of the corner of his eye while he kept the pistol trained on the Goudges. "That being the case," Hood remarked, reverting to his casual, effortless manner, "shall we barter over the fair maid's fair value?"

Delbert gave a little shrug. "What makes you think we want her back?" His narrow eyes raked over Honor, whose cheeks had turned warm at the deprecating exchange.

"In that case," Hood said smoothly, "I'll keep her. Take your horses and walk away. The next time we meet, I'll exact my price."

"Hypocrites!" screamed Honor, trembling with outrage. "You call yourselves Christians! How God must gag!"

Delbert drew himself up to his full, shambling height and darted a sly look in Uriah's direction before addressing Honor. "You call yourself a Druid, as I recall. Why not cut some mistletoe and say your prayers for deliverance, eh?" Chuckling mightily at his own humor, he jabbed an elbow at his son as if to poke him in the ribs. Uriah grinned vacantly.

Hood wasn't smiling. "Move out!" His voice again crackled with command. "And remember not to let your hands stray to your weapons. My sight is very keen."

"Uunh," Delbert grunted, taking up his horse's reins. "You'll find she's more trouble than she's worth. Ward or not, has Dick Cromwell sent us so much as a dandiprat for her keep? I don't care what *she* says, if we weren't good Christian folk we'd have refused outright—"

"Move!" Hood brandished the pistol.

Delbert stalled just long enough to make a brave show before starting down the road—but not without a parting sally. "Whatever use you make of her is your business," he said over his shoulder with a nasty smirk. "She claims to be virgin goods, but I'd be skeptical, if I were you."

Honor saw Hood's back go rigid, though his eyes never left the Goudges. Angrily, she watched the two men lead their horses away at a pace that was just short of leisurely.

"He'll hang, of course," she heard Delbert say to his son.

Uriah's mind was on more mundane matters. "Was it he who took our horse?"

With a jerky motion, Delbert swerved around. "Damn his eyes! I want the pleasure of hanging him myself!" He waved an angry fist at Hood before crossing the little stone bridge.

It was obvious, Honor thought dismally, that the Goudges valued their livestock far more than they did her.

She fervently wished that the damp ground on which she sat would open and swallow her up. Nobody wanted her—not Sir Tyler Vail, nor the Cromwells, and most certainly not the Goudges. The only person in the world who seemed willing to lay any sort of claim to her person was this brazen highwayman. As Delbert and Uriah disappeared around the curve in the road, Honor tried to steel herself for Captain Hood's next act of aggression.

But the first thing he did was to put the pistol back in his belt and emit a sharp whistle not unlike the lapwing's cry. To Honor's amazement, the big black gelding suddenly emerged from the trees across the road and docilely trotted over to Hood.

"Shandy," he greeted the animal, patting its neck in welcome. "I knew you wouldn't go far. You obviously remember your previous owners. They're not the sort to treat animals kindly."

"Or people," Honor snapped. *"Pigs.* I wish you *had* shot them!" She remembered her own murderous intentions toward Hood and covered her face with her hands. "Damn and blast, why is the world so awry?"

"It's been that way for years," Hood said shortly, then fingered his long chin and frowned. "Why hadn't I heard the Goudges had a ward?" He was speaking to himself rather than to her, and Honor didn't much care. She felt like flotsam tossed up by the waves, a worthless scrap to be buffeted about and left to wash ashore in some lonely, nameless cove.

Taking in her forlorn appearance, Hood turned uncharacteristically grim. Honor wondered what he was thinking—probably reproaching himself for the worthless threat to hold her for ransom. Or calculating that Delbert would change his mind once he was back under the thumb of Mistress Goudge. Whatever his reflections, Honor knew that he was pressed for time; it was more than likely that the Goudges would round up a search party and come looking not for Honor but for Hood.

The highwayman was still on one knee, his partially hidden face resolute. To Honor's surprise, he let out a heavy sigh. "I'm sorry. There's no remedy for it. I must take you back to Creepers."

For one wildly ridiculous moment, what remained of Honor's tattered spirits plummeted like a partridge shot out of a tree. Even if the Goudges weren't much interested in her welfare, surely she couldn't have the least desire to go off with Captain Hood, a man she had tried to shoot. He was a hated Royalist, he had taken liberties with her on their first meeting, he'd stolen her dowry. True, he had played the gentleman's part well today, showing concern for her pain and dismay at the Goudges' rude attitude. Yet the man was a villain, a criminal, the very root of her present dilemma.

"I'd rather go to the Tower," Honor blurted.

Captain Hood stared at her in surprise, then made an impatient gesture with his hand. "It was folly for me to suggest ransom. I doubt that Delbert Goudge would pay tuppence to retrieve his entire family."

"Could you blame him?" Honor snapped back. "Have so many wretched people ever been joined by blood before this?"

Hood's answer was to lift her up in his arms as if she were a sack of feathers. "We must ride to Creepers," he said, and she did not mistake the note of apology in his voice. Moments later, they were cantering through the forest, keeping clear of the more traveled byways. "We'll approach by the back, around the tenants' woodhouses," he said after a long silence. "Has the south field been plowed yet?"

Honor was amazed by his close knowledge of the manor house and its environs. She nodded in reply to his query, then continued to cope with the problem of settling herself in such a way that her body touched as little of his as possible. Hood seemed unaware of her difficulty as the footing grew more tricky and he had to slow the big gelding to a walk. Indeed, they might have been any carefree young couple enjoying an outing, rather than criminal and victim. Only the recurring tension in Hood's muscles every time a twig cracked or a leaf fell betrayed his need for constant vigilance.

They reached the south field just as the sun began to dip behind Buttermilk Hill. It was on this part of the Goudge land that their four tenant families worked. They lived beyond the stone wall edging the field in identical cottages known forever as the woodhouses, though they were presently made of limestone. The dwellings stood now in cozy symmetry, with smoke curling from each squat chimney. It was near the supper hour, and as far as Honor could tell, no one was outside.

"We can get a bit closer," Hood said, his voice low. "A good thing we still have some light."

He reined Shandy in at the stile by the paddock. Honor waited expectantly for him to put her down, though what would happen after that, she had no idea. To her surprise, he put a gloved hand on her dirty face and tipped her chin so that she was forced to look up at him. "You shy from my touch, as Shandy did with Master Goudge. Do you fancy I'd take a crop to your flesh?"

"I don't know," Honor answered sulkily. "You're an outlaw. Why should I expect anything but cruelty from you?" To her chagrin, she was all but mumbling, hardly able to glance up at his masked face.

Hood seemed faintly amused. "I force myself on neither woman nor horse, treating both with tenderness and respect. I stole a kiss the first time we met. It was, I hope, but a taste of the bounty to come." Idly, he trailed his finger down her neck, the smooth leather of his glove coming to rest just under the white linen collar. Honor's initial reaction was rage … until she realized that perhaps she'd discovered the highwayman's vulnerable spot. If indeed he was half so gallant to women as he had shown himself toward horses, this might be the weakness upon which she could play.

Trying to remember the demure yet enticing approach she had used on Tyler Vail, Honor started to flutter her lashes and then recalled that such wiles hadn't moved her erstwhile fiancé a jot. Would Hood prove any different? She settled for a weak little smile instead. "Alas, I know nothing of men's bold advances, sir. I'm but a simple country maid."

"Simple country maids do not stitch a thousand pounds' worth of jewels into their cloaks, nor do they try to shoot the men who rob them."

Hood's long mouth turned down at the corners as Honor gaped at him in astonishment. Did those all-seeing eyes have the ability to look out from the back of his head? Honor was overcome with frustration.

"We'll talk about these matters another time," he remarked as casually as if their tête-à-tête had been postponed by the guest of honor's arrival at an elegant soiree. "Indeed, we have much to discuss, you and I." With a gesture that just bordered on insolence, he flicked at her nose with his finger, then lifted her from the gelding to set her carefully upon the ground.

Puzzled as well as infuriated, Honor had to suppress an urge to ask the highwayman what he intended to do. Surely he didn't mean to leave her here alone by the paddock? It was a good hundred yards to the nearest woodhouse, and Honor was certain she couldn't crawl that far. He might give himself the airs of a gentleman, but he was a sham, overbold and underhanded. Just as she realized that tears were slipping through her heavy lashes, Hood pulled his pistol from his belt and fired into the air.

Wheeling the big gelding about, he grinned broadly at Honor. "We'll ride together one day, Mistress Dale! I promise you that!"

Honor stared after him as the fog began to curl up between the trees and the wood smoke hung heavy on the evening air. It had always been her favorite season—until this year. Now everything in her life had gone wrong. Even as she heard the voices calling from the doorways of the candlelit, timbered cottages, she wanted to call out after Captain Hood, to tell him that he might steal her dowry but he'd never have her heart.

Yet Honor kept silent. He had not, she remembered, mentioned her heart.

Chapter Six

THE BIG BLOND YOKEL WITH the eye patch hitched up his threadbare breeches and made a pass at tucking in his coarse shirt. "Where's drink? Where's meat?" he barked, pounding his grimy fist on the table. "Canna a man get fed hereabouts?"

The publican of the Three Gold Crows at Ingleton in Yorkshire was also the owner. He was a wiry sort, with crisp black hair and a small scar above one eye. He had bought the inn some twenty years earlier with his hard-earned savings, back when it was the Three Gold Crowns. While Ben Beard had supported King Charles, he had held no illusions about being a hero. When Cromwell's men had ordered him to take down his sign and replace it with something that had no Royalist connotations, Beard had protested the expense rather than the politics. But after being threatened with a beating, he had acquiesced, if on his own terms. The *N* had been struck out, a picture of a golden crow inserted, and the entire transformation had taken less than an hour and cost no more than a shilling.

For Beard, a practical, careful man, the ill-mannered country bumpkin before him posed no problem. "Hold yer horses," the publican replied without rancor. His manner gave the illusion that he was hurrying, but in fact he was purposely taking his time. "Now there, what'll it be? We got old beef and new lamb. Plenty of fine Todcaster ale, too."

The yokel glanced around the common room, taking in the only other customers, a pair of middle-aged lovebirds who were far more absorbed in themselves than in their surroundings. "I want memories," the yokel said, his rustic accent gone. "Memories of Preston. Of hunted soldiers. Of swift, rough justice—and no justice at all." The one eye, which had heretofore looked so vague, now fixed shrewdly on Ben Beard's startled face. "There was a young soldier who hid out behind your alehouse. The Roundheads hanged him. Do you remember?"

Beard sank down into an empty chair. "O' course. But it weren't my fault. Old Noll's minions took him. There was a dozen or more, armed to the eyeballs." He gave his guest a wary look. "Who be ye?"

"Never mind. The soldier was given away by a family who lived at a manor house nearby." The professed yokel spoke with an innate sense of command. "What was their name?"

Beard scratched the back of his head. "I dinna recall … it's been a proper long time "

Three gold sovereigns were produced from inside a ragged leathern doublet. "Not that long," replied the other man laconically.

Beard stared at the money, which winked in the flickering light like pools of fire. "The house is gone, put to the torch by Royalists seeking revenge. Or so 'tis said. The family's gone, too, all dead at the hands of King Charles's men. Except maybe the son. He fought with Old Noll but never returned hereabouts."

"Their name." The mouth, which had seemed so slack at first, tightened into a long, grim line.

" 'Struth, I dinna recall that, either …." He saw one eye flash with impatience and stirred about in the chair, as if making the effort of recollection. " 'Twas an apt sort of name, like Hill or Moore or Dale … aye, 'twas Dale, Dale of Dale Manor, in the Dales." He gave a small laugh. "Funny it slipped off my mind at first."

"And the family? Are you sure they all died?" The man's mouth clamped shut as he waited for the answer.

Again, Ben Beard reflected, though this time his concentration seemed genuine. "The lad who was hanged," he began, a hand to his brow, "was a great favorite of his fellows. He'd been seen hiding near the manor house, came all the way from Preston with a bad leg and a lame horse after the battle. Routed, the Royalists were, a pitiful defeat—if you sympathized with them, that is." He gazed out from under the shield of his hand to make sure he wasn't provoking the other man. "Anyways, Sir Langston Dale was a fierce Roundhead, kin to the Protector, and much hated, being as how the North always held to tradition. But what else could Sir Langston do, I ask ye?" The publican spread his hands palms up on the table. "I'm not saying he was right or wrong, all I mean is he done his duty. But it made the lad's comrades hotter'n the fires of Hades. They went flying off to the manor house and killed every living soul, down to the stable hands. Awful, it were, but that's war."

"That it is." The man looked away, off toward the shadowy corners of the common room. He had become more sorrowful than grim, and a weary hand passed over the thatch of blond hair. When he finally spoke again, his voice was heavier. "You're sure there was no one left? Not even … a child?"

Ben Beard shook his head. "There was some wild tale of a little girl who ran out of the fire and across the moors in naught but her shift. But even if 'twere true, what'd become of her out there?"

What indeed, thought Captain Hood. Wild animals, marauding soldiers, farmers with little sympathy for Roundheads of any age. It was a wonder the Dales hadn't been run off their land long before the fateful battles in the north that had turned the tide even there in Cromwell's favor. Then again, it had been summer, the most benign of seasons for a little girl lost on the moors. It was possible, he supposed, that her guileless innocence might have aroused someone's compassion. At ten years of age, she would have known enough to be cautious about mentioning her connections to Cromwell. But Sir Harry and Lady Lucy Ashford would have been safe references. A letter dispatched to Whitehorse Hill; grateful relatives sending for the child and rewarding her protectors; a home provided for the young orphan who had seen and suffered too much for anyone, let alone a girl of ten.

Hood put three more sovereigns on the table and stood up. "Thank you. I'll try the spring lamb next time. It's a great favorite of mine." Before his host could detain him, he was gone, an awkward, ill-dressed scarecrow of a man, half-stumbling out of the inn and up the steep footpath that led to the ancient drovers' lane. There, at the scarred edge of Scales Moor, he stood for a long time, looking out over the austere, relentless hills where the wind sighed in the valleys and the cry of the curlew mourned the passing of the old moon. Somewhere, out beyond the rushing waters of Thornton Force, was the charred cornerstone of Dale Manor. Though it was no doubt overgrown by gorse and heather, Hood sensed that the once fine house lived on in someone's memory. Perhaps it was Honor Dale who remembered it—and more.

Had she lost everything but her life in these bleak, wild hills? Yet Hood had suffered, too. Sadly, wearily, he shook his head. There was nowhere to search for his own memories, really—not even a potter's field. He imagined instead a hastily dug pit, mumbled prayers and a pitiful farewell to the broken body of his brother.

THE BLACK MARE HAD BEEN returned to Creepers by a lad from Anslow who had found the animal cropping among the cows in the family's little pasture. Honor's arrival had provoked considerably less enthusiasm, though not as much acrimony as she might have expected. Since Delbert and Uriah hadn't yet come back by the time the tenants from the woodhouses had carried her into Creepers, the female Goudges were ignorant of what had transpired with their ward. Mistress Goudge initially had managed to all but gloss over Honor's sprained ankle, concentrating instead on her rank impudence and wicked tongue.

Parthenia's harangue trudged through the morass of disobedience, sloth, impertinence, evil thoughts and, for good measure, heresy. Naturally, the theme of her sermon was "Pride goeth before a fall." Her refusal to hear any sort of defense prompted a perverse silence from Honor, who by this time had reached the point of exhaustion and wouldn't have recounted her adventures had the Goudges begged her to do so on bended knee.

Delbert and Uriah returned well after dark in an ugly mood, having met with failure in their attempts at capturing either Will Tipper or Captain Hood. Delbert grew even more irascible when he discovered that Honor had been restored to Creepers. In a heated exchange that awakened Honor three doors away, Master and Mistress Goudge battled their way to mutual comprehension. As far as Honor could make out, Delbert didn't confess to his blatant abandonment of their ward but implied that Captain Hood had kidnapped her despite his most valiant rescue attempts.

Eventually, their clamorous voices hushed and Honor went back to sleep. The next morning, she was surprised when Parthenia failed to take up where she had left off. Her toothy grin much in evidence, Mistress Goudge seemed almost congenial, like a gleeful ghoul. The closest she came to rebuke was a question regarding Captain Hood.

"Did the villain tamper with you?" she inquired while Faith rearranged the bolster on which Honor's foot was propped.

Still smarting from Parthenia's verbal barrage of the previous day, Honor didn't immediately reply. She noticed that Mistress Goudge's beady eyes seemed to spark with anticipation and that Faith had sucked in her breath. Clarity, who had just entered the bedchamber carrying a pitcher of water, wore an unabashedly eager expression. Honor couldn't resist tantalizing the trio just a bit.

" 'Tamper'?" She moved slightly in the narrow trundle bed and frowned. "La, mistress, I'm not sure what you mean."

The toothy grin widened. "I would think you could guess. Did he make … advances?"

It occurred to Honor that if she was to be completely honest, she would have to say that he had—at least on their first meeting in the Chiltern Hills. But she suddenly realized that the Goudges didn't know that this wasn't her first encounter with the highwayman. As she recalled, Aunt Elizabeth had informed them only that she had suffered a broken engagement, was impoverished, and had no place to live. It didn't strike Honor as prudent to tell them any more than they needed to know. She also had to recognize the fact that Captain Hood's words and deeds were not "advances" in the sense that civilized folk would define them. To the highwayman, such casual overtures were probably a mere fillip to his profession.

"He was quite gallant," Honor said, uttering a little sigh for the sake of Faith and Clarity, who were both motionless with suspense. "His only concern was for my wellbeing." It wasn't a lie, though it certainly wasn't entirely the truth, either. And he had certainly exhibited more solicitude for her than had the Goudges.

In fact, the family hadn't troubled to send for the local doctor. They did, however, summon Quentin Radcliffe, the curate from Saint Barnabas in Rutbury. He arrived two days after the accident in an aura of officious piety and implacable goodwill.

"I would have come sooner, my child, but our vicar was robbed by the same wicked thief who abducted you. Poor Master Busby is still recovering from the shock. I must say that the reward of a thousand crowns offered by our new Lord Protector should aid in the capture of this vile bandit and his ilk."

Honor looked up from the pillows to the tall, trim man who stood by the bed. While he wore the austere garb of a cleric, his roving gray eyes and sharp features gave him a more worldly appearance. But Honor was less interested in the curate's looks than in his words. "A thousand crowns! That's a lordly sum, sir!"

Radcliffe's shrug was a studied gesture of indifference, belied by the gleam in his eyes. "Dick Cromwell is determined to capture the knave. It seems that some relation of his was robbed, beaten and, ah, violated in a most bestial manner. Shocking."

More than shocking, thought Honor, for if the incident referred to her own encounter with Hood, as indeed it must, Radcliffe's account was also wildly exaggerated. But the curate was moving on to more spiritual matters, suggesting that thc three young women join him in prayer.

"Come," he urged Faith and Clarity, "kneel by me, so that our souls may commune more easily." Noting that Faith did so with a hint of shyness while Clarity sidled up next to him thigh to thigh, Honor was grateful to be bedridden.

"We must pray first for your recovery," Radcliffe said, folding his hands in front of him. "For what sin did the Lord send this punishment?"

Aunt Lucy would have said that either the mare was clumsy or Honor hadn't been watching the animal's footing. But such a response would not satisfy Radcliffe's Puritanical philosophy, which Honor realized she ought to share. Inasmuch as the curate was now rolling his gray eyes heavenward as if momentarily expecting a direct communiqué from his Maker, Honor decided to placate him and get on with the prayers.

"Insubordination," she replied, "leavened with pride."

"Ah!" exclaimed Master Radcliffe, waggling a triumphant forefinger. "Common vices in the young. Surely," he added, lowering his voice and all but leaning on the bed, "you are making up for it now."

Living at Creepers seemed to be making up for any number of sins, real or imagined, as far as Honor was concerned. Fleetingly, it crossed her mind that she could commit mayhem for the next forty years and have already paid the price.

"Praise be to Almighty God," Radcliffe intoned, "let us lift our voices to the Lord." Religious zeal oozed from every pore as he recited psalms, quoted from the Gospels and contemplated the Epistles. At last, Honor was vaguely aware that he was praying for her. Indeed, he was resting a too-familiar hand on the curve of her upper leg beneath the bed sheet. Pulling away proved useless; his touch followed her even as he kept his eyes turned up to heaven. "That Mistress Dale may bear her sufferings with a submissive spirit, that she may learn humility and be grateful for the mysterious workings of Your divine will, that she may profit from all her adversities in becoming a meek and dutiful daughter of You and this blessed house wherein she dwells. We ask this most fervently in the name of …."

Honor mused briefly on how many strange things were asked in God's name. For her own part, she was asking for only one thing: to find a way out of this oppressive place without having to throw herself back on the mercy of the Cromwells. That seemed like a sufficient challenge in itself, even for the Almighty.

Radcliffe had finally wound down, though his hand remained on Honor's thigh. "I trust you may feel the Spirit's healing presence," he said, gazing at her with all due solemnity. "Let us offer one final prayer."

Clarity's glazed expression remained fixed, though Faith was growing fidgety. Radcliffe was undaunted. "That Captain Hood may be brought to justice," he prayed fervently, "to be hanged by the neck until he is almost dead, then taken down and have his bowels cut out and his arms and legs severed while he is still alive to suffer the right punishment he has so richly earned. Amen."

The Goudge daughters weakly echoed Radcliffe, but the grisly picture he had conjured up made Honor actually feel ill. Not only couldn't she join in the awful prayer, but she was unable to keep the revulsion from showing on her face.

"Well?" Radcliffe pressed her leg. "Where is your amen?"

Honor swallowed hard and tasted bile. Her reticence was ridiculous, of course; hadn't she tried to kill Captain Hood herself? But shooting would have been a neat, relatively painless death; the curate's execution was too gruesome. "I feel faint," she finally said, and wasn't being entirely deceitful.

" 'Twill pass," snapped Radcliffe, who was looking displeased. "Let us hear you finish our prayer."

Honor opened her mouth, but no sound came out. She couldn't pray for Hood's death, even though she had willed it just three short months ago. Aware that Quentin Radcliffe was growing impatient and that Faith and Clarity were staring at her with a mixture of curiosity and fascination, Honor closed her eyes and shook her head.

"What's this? What's this?" Radcliffe demanded, shaking Honor by the leg without the slightest regard for her sprained ankle or her maidenly sensibilities. "Pray with me, mistress, or it will be said that you are bewitched by Captain Hood!"

Honor's eyes flew open. "That's a lie!" she breathed, somehow nettled by the accusation. "Please leave me! My ankle hurts and I'm tired!"

Radcliffe took his dismissal with ill grace, getting to his feet so abruptly that he all but knocked over Faith and stepped on Clarity's skirts. "No wonder God has seen fit to send you trials! You are contumacious, impious, mayhap even wanton! Poor Goudges—I must speak with them at once."

Dutifully, Faith filed out after the curate but Clarity held back, ostensibly to straighten the bolster.

"Don't mind him," she whispered, surprising Honor by giving a thought to someone besides herself. "He's a bit silly." Turning quickly at the shrill summons of her mother, Clarity wiggled her fingers in a frivolous wave, then danced from the room.

Honor let out a huge sigh of relief and wished that the Goudges, as well as Quentin Radcliffe, would all go straight to Uttoxeter.

Chapter Seven

QUENTIN RADCLIFFE DID NOT RETURN the next day, but another visitor came to call at Creepers. Matthew Thorn, who had been the village schoolmaster for the past year or two, presented an unusual sight. Blinded in his youth at Marston Moor, he also had a game leg. He kept his bearded face half-hidden by the folds of his hooded brown cloak, and this, along with his considerable height and the gnarled oak staff he carried, made Honor think of a medieval pilgrim. She could well imagine that his strange appearance might inspire at least a measure of awe in the breasts of his young pupils.

Yet under that eccentric facade was a superior scholar, well versed in the classics, history and mathematics. While another man so handicapped might have been reduced to begging for crusts at the edge of the gutter, Matthew Thorn had determined to make his own way in the world. He retained a companion, usually a former student, to read to him and correct written exercises. Unfortunately, the present term's aide was Jamie Tipper, whose attempted heroics Honor had noticed during the robbery. He still suffered from headaches due to the blow on the temple delivered by Captain Hood's henchman. Until Jamie returned to health, Mistress Goudge—ever vigilant in her war against idleness—had suggested that Honor come to Master Thorn's rescue.

"At least you've been educated," she allowed grudgingly, "though why, I cannot guess, since you're quite unable to quote Scripture." Parthenia's attitude toward Honor had once again hardened.

Honor let the remark pass. She did vaguely recall her parents' effort to teach her Holy Writ. But like so much of her life during the first ten years, the lessons were a blur.

Master Thorn had arrived on a chilly October day, when the east wind was stripping the trees of all but the most stubborn leaves. Honor watched him limp to the bed and feel for a chair as he grasped his bulky brown robes around his body. "We'll begin with composition," he announced without preamble in a husky voice as he delved inside the fusty material for a sheaf of papers. "There are fourteen pupils, ranging in age from eight through thirteen. Judge them accordingly. Their ages are on their papers."

At least she didn't have to deal with slates, Honor thought, as she skimmed through the formidable stack. Matthew Thorn must be an exacting teacher. Each lad had no fewer than six lessons to correct. "I shall do my best," Honor promised with a smile, then realized that it was a gesture lost on a blind man.

His hearing, however, was remarkably keen; Honor noted that he picked up Faith's footstep in the passageway several beats before she did. Faith came into the room carrying mugs of steaming hot chocolate and wearing her most diffident air.

"It's cold today," she said in a more nervous voice than usual. "I think it may frost tonight."

Taking the mug with careful hands, Thorn replied shortly, "It's too soon."

"But tomorrow is All Hallows' Eve," Faith responded, as if the date could exonerate her. "We had frost last year the third week of October."

The mug disappeared inside the drapery of his hood. "That was *two* years ago," he said in a voice that brooked no argument.

Flustered, Faith spilled a bit of chocolate on the bedclothes as she handed Honor her mug. "Oh, my—was it? I get so muddled!" Her cheeks turned faintly pink, the color giving evidence of how comely she might be except for that long, pointed nose. Honor offered her a look of sympathy but the other girl was distracted by the arrival of her sister, carrying a scruffy little puppy and wearing her auburn hair loose around her shoulders.

"Lyndon Styles has come a-calling," she trilled, tightening her grip on the dog, who seemed to be seeking escape. "I wonder who he wants to see—you … or me?"

Faith whirled around, accidentally bumping Honor's sprained ankle and provoking a sharp wince. "Master Styles is a widower, twice your age! You have too good an opinion of yourself, Clarity Goudge! Remember what Mother says about vanity."

Clarity yawned. "If I lived to a hundred, I could never remember everything Mother says about vanity—or anything else. I believe I'll go down and play the virginals for Master Styles. He's very fond of music. A pity you have no aptitude for anything but the drum."

Faith all but fell over Matthew Thorn in her effort to reach Clarity, but her sister, with the dog yapping for release, had already flounced off. Faith followed, her narrow face giving every evidence of extreme annoyance.

"I think," Thorn said, "I should have preferred to lose my hearing."

It was a sentiment Honor could appreciate. It also made her smile. She had not suspected the grim schoolmaster to possess even a dollop of humor, however dry. Yet his manner reverted at once, a long finger pointing to the compositions now lying by Honor's side. "Be fair, but firm. That's the mark of a good teacher. I shall come back in two days—no," he corrected himself quickly, "that's the Sabbath. On Monday, All Souls' Day."

Again, Honor started to nod, then remembered it was a wasted gesture. Matthew Thorn finished his hot chocolate, felt for an even place to set the empty mug on the floor and gripped his staff. She watched him with curiosity. As strange as his brown-robed figure might be, the man who dwelled within seemed the most ordinary person she had met thus far at Creepers. Honor was actually sorry to see him go.

She was glad, however, to have something to while away the hours abed. The swelling was beginning to subside in her ankle, but it would be at least another week before she could be up and about. She started the task with interest and found the work absorbing. As the faint sound of the church bells chimed midnight at Rutbury, she finally finished. In all, they were a satisfactory lot; the children obviously tried to do their best for the unfortunate master. Honor set the papers down beside the bed in a neat pile and blew out her candle. The old house was very quiet, though somewhere an owl hooted and a dog barked. Clarity's puppy, perhaps, or one of the hunters Master Goudge kept in a small kennel near the stables.

Happily, the pain in Honor's ankle no longer disrupted her sleep at night. She moved about, finding the most comfortable position, and closed her eyes. But the dog was still barking, now joined by at least two others. The kennel, Honor thought drowsily, and was gratified when the animals suddenly quieted down.

She was almost asleep when she heard the rapping noise outside her window. Puzzled, she propped herself up in bed and peered into the darkness. Her corner room was on the third floor, under the eaves, with a single dormer window looking over the outbuildings and home farm. The rapping sounded again. Could it be hail instead of the frost Faith had predicted? Honor lighted her candle and crawled to the end of the bed, the better to see outside.

The big hat all but concealed the mask, but the long, wry mouth was unmistakable. Captain Hood gestured for her to open the casement.

Somewhere, deep inside, Honor knew that she was about to make a momentous decision. Only a stupid, reckless fool would permit the notorious highwayman to enter her bedroom. Captain Hood was a criminal, a representative of everything Honor had learned to despise. He was a thief, an outlaw, a traitor, a charlatan. Knowing all this, it would take a completely brainless idiot to unlatch the casement and usher him inside.

Honor stretched as far as she could on the bed and clicked open the window. Hood put a booted leg over the sill, leaned on both hands and vaulted lightly into the room. He grinned at her in a vaguely sheepish way, then gazed inquiringly at his surroundings. Honor's bedroom was sparsely furnished with the trundle bed, a small wardrobe, a table and two chairs, all of oak. The roof slanted, making it impossible for a man as tall as Hood to stand up straight in the vicinity of the window. The only claim to decoration was a rather gruesome woodcut of Abraham about to sacrifice Isaac. Judging from Hood's now dour expression, he wasn't any more taken with the surroundings than was Honor.

"How very strange that you should have been sent here," he mused, keeping his voice low. "Have you heard that Sir Tyler's house has been put up for sale to pay off his debts?"

Honor had managed to sit up on the bed, decorously arranging the folds of her prim cotton nightgown. But her hand paused at the little ruffled collar. "I knew he'd gone abroad," she said in a girlish voice that made her flinch.

Hood had turned back to the window, standing to one side so as not to be seen. The long cape billowed slightly in the breeze, while the candle flickered on the nightstand next to the bed. Satisfied that no one lurked outside, Hood eased the casement shut and moved effortlessly toward Honor.

"I feared the dogs might give me away," he said, sitting beside her, "but I coaxed them into silence." Hood paused, looking down at the bare feet that poked out from under the hem of Honor's nightgown. "How fares your ankle? Better, I trust?"

"Oh … yes." She nodded vaguely, aware of the anxiety that was building inside her like a palpable thing. Why had he come? More to the point, why had she let him in? Should she call for help and rouse the household? If they captured Hood they could make him tell what had happened to her dowry. But the highwayman would be out the window and down the ivy before anyone came to her aid. Hood must know that—otherwise, he would never have taken such a risk. As for the gun, it would take too long to rummage for it in the bureau. Having raised the curtain, Honor deemed it best to play out the rest of the scene. Deliberately, she edged away from him on the bed.

"Are you afraid?" The question was casually put by Hood, though the shrewd eyes behind the mask seemed to twinkle.

"I don't know," Honor replied honestly. "Is there cause?"

Hood shrugged, a careless, artless gesture, so unlike the studied mannerisms of Quentin Radcliffe or even Tyler Vail. "I bring no danger to you, though you could bring it to me." He sounded quite serious, yet there was nothing in his attitude to suggest alarm.

In silence, Honor watched him take off his hat and set it on the floor. It was the first time she had caught more than a glimpse of the man. She saw that his hair was dark, almost black, and worn shorter than fashion demanded, curling up just slightly above his collar. The forehead was high, the skin tanned and the jaw clean shaven. The sharp features and decidedly aquiline nose made it too rugged a face to be handsome, yet Honor sensed the masculine attraction even without clearly seeing his fascinating, lively eyes. She tried not to stare but couldn't help herself. Nor was it particularly comforting that he was staring back.

"Why," he demanded in an unexpectedly harsh tone, "did you have to be kin to Cromwell?"

Honor lifted her chin. "Why must you be a supporter of King Charles and a thief?"

Captain Hood's expression was still grim even as he put a hand in the tangle of golden hair. "Better ask why you are so beautiful," he murmured roughly. "All Puritans should be plain as pikestaffs."

Damn the man, thought Honor, he is far too glib. "Why did you come? What do you want of me?" She tried to pull back, but his grip was as firm as it was effortless. If only she had been prepared for this encounter, she would have devised a strategy to make him reveal what had happened to her dowry.

"I intend to ask many things of you," he said, the rugged face hovering over hers. "For now I beg but two. Were you Yorkshire born and bred?"

The question was so unexpected that Honor was caught off guard. "Yes," she answered simply. "Near Ingleton. But," she went on bitterly, "the house no longer stands."

Hood's grip tightened in her hair, causing her to wince. His features tensed and his skin darkened. "Irony," he whispered bitterly, "all is not vanity but irony."

She wanted to ask what he meant, but she held back. For some strange, elusive reason, she feared his answer. Or maybe it was that she knew he had some terrible tale to tell that would arouse her sympathy and blunt her determination to best him in the matter of her dowry. To her relief, he seemed to have regained his aplomb, though he still had his hand entwined in her hair. "The second favor should cause us both less pain," he said, his mouth twisted into the hint of a smile.

She had forgotten about the other request and started to inquire as to what it might be when his kiss stole words—and breath—away. This was not like Tyler Vail's bloodless, pristine kisses but a slow, measured assault on her senses that made Honor dizzy. She felt his other arm go round her, pressing her against his chest, while the hand that had stroked her hair now caressed the nape of her neck.

The proper thing to do, of course, was to struggle, to rain blows upon this importunate fraud, to kick and fight and surely to scream. But Captain Hood seemed to render her will useless. Instead of fending him off, she discovered that her arms had slipped around him, that her mouth was yielding to his probing tongue, that she was utterly helpless in his embrace. The revelation should have been humiliating, but was instead delicious.

He drew away, just far enough to see her face, the shimmering dark eyes under gold-tipped lashes, the flush across her cheekbones, the inviting mouth still slightly open.

"I want you," he said simply in that low voice, which wasn't quite as calm as usual. "But not now, not until you're well." His hand strayed to the opening of her collar, but at last Honor jerked back. Her brain was in chaos. She needed time to order her thoughts. The man was ten times as bold as he had any right to be.

Yet, she thought, as away from his touch the excitement in her blood cooled, his very conceit should play nicely into her hands. "You take advantage of my helplessness," she accused him, but there was no bite in the words. "You also play upon my generous nature. Any other maid would have raised an alarm."

"No, not really." He spoke seriously but then broke into an engaging smile. "Most maids are very kindhearted. I always marvel at their bountiful natures."

Honor's eyes sparked and she had to look away; Captain Hood was on the brink of going too far. "You mock me, sir. You would toy with my affections yet make light of my feelings." Having gotten her temper under control, she risked gazing at him head-on. "For shame, Captain! To think I dared defend you!"

"I'm quite accustomed to defending myself," he retorted with more asperity than she had expected. "Let the gossips wag their tongues until they drop. Their prattle enhances my reputation and thus provides me with protection."

Honor lowered her lashes as if meekly accepting his rebuke. Hood made sense, of course. The more fearsome he was pictured, the less likely it was that he would be pursued by anyone but the most courageous. Or greedy. "There's a reward of a thousand crowns on your head."

To her surprise—and disappointment—Hood merely shrugged. "I know. It seems a bit steep, frankly." He bent down to recover his hat and got to his feet. "I must go. It would be folly for me to risk coming here again. We shall have to meet elsewhere next time."

"Next time?" Honor tried to look aghast. Had her feminine wiles finally worked their promised magic? "In truth, Captain, you are overconfident to think I would ever deign to see you again."

He brushed her cheek with one deft hand. "Nay, only hopeful. After all, you did defend me, didn't you?"

This time, she was sure that the omniscient eyes twinkled behind the mask. "I was trying to be fair," she pouted. " 'Tis hardly a sign of encouragement for any man, let alone your lawless sort."

"Lips speak without words," he remarked carelessly, going to the window and quietly opening the casement. "How well named is this place," he said in his usual indolent manner. "These vines would support an army." Noiselessly, he gathered up his cloak and put one leg over the sill. "Good night, lovely Honor." He touched his fingertips to his lips. "You won't regret that fate has brought you here. I promise."

A hand at her breast, Honor watched him disappear from view. Only then did she realize she was shaking all over. Hood's audacity was utterly reprehensible. She had to remind herself that it suited her purposes admirably. She might retrieve her jewels yet. As she tried to quiet her trembling limbs, however, she found herself smiling. As brazen as the highwayman was, he had asserted that he would never force himself on any woman. Perhaps she was naive, but Honor believed him. For all that he was a plundering thief and a Royalist outlaw, she sensed that he was a man of his word. Lying back down among the pillows and easing her ankle into its most comfortable position, she let out a deep sigh of satisfaction. For some reason, she was happier tonight than she had been in months. Her virtue would be safe with Captain Hood. It hadn't yet occurred to Honor that she might not be safe from herself.

EXCEPT FOR A SLIGHT LIMP, Honor had recovered by the second week of November. So had Jamie Tipper, but Master Thorn was still bringing his pupils' exercises to Honor. He had, he admitted, observed that she was much more competent at making corrections and suggestions than her predecessor. Besides, Jamie's time seemed taken up lately with Sarah Appleby, whose admiration for him had increased considerably after his display of courage at the merciless hands of the highwayman.

It pleased Honor to help Matthew Thorn. Not only did she feel compassion for him, but her academic duties excused her from some household drudgery, and in consequence, she was less in the company of the others. Parthenia's attitude remained ambivalent; she still spouted homilies like a blowfish, but she also seemed faintly wary of her unwanted charge. Master Goudge spent his days at the mill, in the fields or visiting with his tenants. Uriah often accompanied him, but when the Goudge son and heir stayed home, his constant, if guilty, gaze strayed to Honor, who had made up her mind not to let him unsettle her. As for Faith and Clarity, their incessant wrangling was not unlike a pair of untuned instruments rehearsing an ugly song. The longer

Honor stayed on at Creepers, the more determined she was to leave.

There was no immediate help coming from the Cromwells. In mid-November Honor received a letter from Aunt Elizabeth detailing the state ceremonies that had commemorated the Lord Protector's death. While Cromwell's remains had been buried for some time, his effigy had been set up in Westminster Abbey so that his subjects might pay their last respects. "Some say it was a popish gesture," his widow wrote, "but whoever rules England, whether king or commoner, must needs take upon himself the pageantry expected by the people."

Having thus dismissed the criticism of too much ceremonial pomp for a man whose life's work had been dedicated in part to abolishing such excesses, Elizabeth continued in a more personal vein. "Even now, we are resettling ourselves, being much involved in the refurbishing of Saint James Palace. Dick and Dorothy are moving into Whitehall, as is their due. As you may know, your dear cousin, being much affected by the catastrophe that befell you this past summer, has placed an immoderate sum on Captain Hood's head. Surely when the odious villain is captured, we will all rest easier in our beds and give great thanksgiving to God Almighty."

Aunt Elizabeth's heartfelt words echoed in Honor's brain. Her kinsman, the new Lord Protector, cared about her sufficiently to actively seek vengeance for the wrong that had been done to her. When Hood was caught and executed, her promise to her parents would be fulfilled. It didn't matter that she herself wouldn't personally dispatch the despised Royalist. As his victim, she would become the instrument of his death. Of course he would confess what had happened to her dowry before he was led off to the gallows. Honor should be filled with a sense of optimism and reassurance.

She was, in fact, shaken to her shoes. If she'd never seen Hood again after their fateful encounter in the Chiltern Hills, she'd feel differently, of course. But having gotten to know the blasted man, however slightly, she couldn't wish him harm. As for his kisses … Honor winced inwardly as she recalled the excitement she'd never experienced in Tyler's tame embrace. Certainly she couldn't consider the feelings Hood had aroused as extraordinary. It was Tyler's deficiency rather than the highwayman's prowess that was important.

How, Honor wondered, agitatedly brushing her hair before supper, had men who had known each other as friends and neighbors before the Civil War taken to the field and mindlessly murdered one another? Honor couldn't imagine such a terrible thing. How could anyone kill a person that he or she had known as other than the Enemy?

At table, Honor's thoughts still dwelt on Captain Hood. She heartily wished Dick Cromwell had never offered such a reward, particularly not on her account. Her attention wandered from the conversation, until the

Goudges' supper guest, Lyndon Styles, aroused her interest by bringing up her cousin's name.

"Tumbledown Dick," expounded Master Styles, "has no head for governing. No, no, not a bit." An overbluff, overhearty and overbearing man, Styles was a childless widower who was considered the catch of the neighborhood. He had considerable wealth and a pleasant house near Burton upon Trent. Of the former, he bragged endlessly; of the latter, he compared Totten Hall unfavorably to Creepers. In fact, Honor noted that though he flirted quite openly with both Faith and Clarity, his hooded hazel eyes lighted up only when he was discussing some admirable aspect of the Goudges' manor house. While Lyndon Styles might not covet his neighbors' daughters, he most assuredly coveted his neighbors' goods.

"Oliver Cromwell was feared, respected, if never loved," he asserted, addressing the other diners as if he stood in the House of Commons while they sat humbly in the upper stalls. "But Dick's another matter, a will-o'-the-wisp, a weak reed. If a vote were to be taken this very day on his ability to rule England, I'd wager he'd be the first to cast a nay. No offense intended," he added, giving Honor a patronizing smile. "No, no, not a bit."

Honor noted his ruddy complexion, the lack of candor in the hazel eyes, the coarse, straight, rust-colored hair that hung to his shoulders. Eligible he might be, but attractive he was not. At least Honor didn't find him so, but perhaps Faith or Clarity did.

"My cousin," Honor replied, emphasizing the two words, lest anyone under Creepers' roof forget the family connection, "is a kind, good man. He does not, alas, possess his father's great gift for governance. But then, who does?"

Everyone at the table shifted uncomfortably. The truth of the matter was that no one had come up with a viable alternative to Dick Cromwell. At least not anyone of the Puritan persuasion. The obvious choice of restoring the monarchy under Charles II was unthinkable. Indeed, it had not even occurred to Honor. Until now.

The awkward silence was finally broken by Parthenia, who took up the baton dropped by Lyndon Styles and carried it off into her favorite subject. "The congregation at Saint Barnabas dwindles. Why should God-fearing folk get the notion to stay away from holy services merely because their great captain is dead?"

On somewhat safer ground, the conversation turned to sinners in general. Honor toyed with the remnants of her pork pie and listened to the November wind blow lustily outside the windows of Creepers.

But she refocused her attention when she realized Lyndon Styles had launched into a diatribe against Captain Hood. "Talk of sin! The man's infamous!" he declared in a booming voice any politician or clergyman might envy. "Most infamous. Hood's plundered no less than three coaching parties west of Burton. Imagine! His audacity is not to be tolerated by decent folk!"

"The man's an eel," Delbert Goudge remarked, using his finger to dislodge a piece of errant pork from his teeth. "A pity we couldn't have found him last month."

"A fine haul he made, too," their guest asserted over raspberry trifle. "Wealthy merchants and their wives in one coach, a year's supply of port in another. But," he continued, leaning in Honor's direction, "a certain earl and his lady were intercepted on their way to Nottingham. Do you think he took their valuables?" Styles paused, hissing the final syllable through his teeth in a manner that Honor realized was habitual, as well as annoying. Glancing round the table, Styles was gratified to note that his audience, with the possible exception of the bland Uriah, appeared duly impressed. "No, no, not a jot! 'Pon my word, he greeted them as old friends and waved their coach off along the Great North Road!"

"Fiendish," muttered Delbert. "Those wicked nobles must have acknowledged allegiance to King Charles."

"Of course," Styles replied, helping himself to more wine. "I've heard cases of their ilk actually offering money and valuables to Hood for the Exile. Shocking, but true."

As Mistress Goudge motioned for the scullery maid to take away the dirty dishes, Clarity spoke up for the first time. "Mistress Dale ... our ward," she tacked on, in case Honor's true identity might otherwise go unremarked, "was actually kidnapped by Captain Hood. 'Twas a most harrowing experience, though I fear she's still too distressed to recount it."

Honor glared at Clarity, then gave a little shrug. "A trivial incident, actually," she said in dismissal, then turned her dark, probing eyes on Delbert. "Master Goudge's manly threats sufficed to secure my release. I remain in his debt."

At least Delbert had the grace to flush a bit. Honor was tempted to push him even further and possibly aim a barb at Clarity, as well, but her more unworthy self was thwarted by the appearance of Durwood, the Goudges' elderly manservant. All but confined to his quarters in damp weather because of his rheumatism, he was expected to provide little more than a reminder of his place in the household on social occasions. But at the moment, he was also displaying a considerable amount of animation for a man who generally looked more like a wax effigy than a living human.

Hovering at Master Goudge's chair, Durwood spoke in a thin, nasal wail. "The lady is faint, the gentleman has chest pains," he howled into his employer's ear. "May they ...? Shall I ...?"

Grumbling, Delbert Goudge got up from the table, excused himself and left the room with Durwood limping behind him. Parthenia also rose, smoothing her second-best lace cap and her charcoal-gray skirts. "Pray forgive me, Master Styles, but a woman's delicate touch may be required. Uriah," she briskly commanded in passing by her son's chair, "entertain our guest in my absence."

The idea of Uriah Goudge providing sprightly conversation or a turn on the lute made Honor's eyes roll upward. But to her great surprise, Uriah actually initiated conversation. "Seems to me," he began in a rather thick, toneless voice, "that if Charles Stuart came back to England, some of us might face hard times. What think you, Master Styles?"

The ugly subject now having been broached, Styles assumed a ponderous air and sipped at the dregs of his wineglass. "It's probable that anyone connected with the late king's execution would face charges of regicide. It's also likely that the more outspoken anti-Royalists would suffer. But," he went on, pushing away a bit from the table, "I wouldn't worry about your own properties. Lady Blake died in France, I'm told. No one else has any legal claim to Creepers. No, no, not the least." Again, he made that hissing noise for emphasis.

"There were two sons," Faith put in, shyly anticipating Styles's reaction. "Surely they could cause trouble."

Styles dismissed the Blake heirs with a wave of his beefy hand. "I heard they were killed fighting for the Royalists. Put your mind at ease, my friends. Your parents were given this land by the Lord Protector himself."

Uriah's usual blank expression showed a trace of lingering doubt, but he had no chance to make a rejoinder. Mistress Goudge had reappeared, her tiny eyes glittering with excitement. "A terrible disaster! Sir Ralph Ferrers and his bride have been set upon by Captain Hood less than a mile from our doorstep! The poor lady has swooned and Sir Ralph fears for his weak heart! Excuse us, but we must tend them both." She sketched a curtsy in Master Styles's direction. "I shall have Durwood fetch a bottle of sack." With that promise, Mistress Goudge scurried from the dining room.

Styles brought his fist down on the trestle table. "Hood again! We must give chase! Oliver Cromwell's men couldn't catch him—surely Tumbledown Dick's minions are doomed to failure!" He squared his broad shoulders and skewered Uriah with a challenging stare. "Well? Do we organize? Do we scour the countryside with every man and boy until Hood is finally brought to justice? Or do we sit like timorous women, allowing Hood to plunder and ravage at will?"

Uriah's face was working in an effort to reply, but it was Clarity who spoke.

"Imagine!" she gasped, her cheeks quite pink. "Hood dares to ride by daylight, almost under our noses! Isn't it too awful?"

Judging from the eager expression on her face, Clarity seemed to be thinking quite otherwise. Honor suppressed a rueful smile, wondering what Clarity would say if she knew that the notorious highwayman had been under her very roof less than a month ago.

But Uriah was now speaking in cautious, measured tones. "You may be right, sir. I suppose we must bring the brigand down." He sounded faintly dubious.

"There's the reward, a lordly sum even the owners of Creepers can't take lightly." Lyndon Styles's ruddy face glowed dark rose. "A thousand crowns!" He actually rubbed his hands together.

To her dismay, Honor once again discovered that the mere mention of capturing Hood made her quail. Abruptly, she stood up, remembering to curtsy to Master Styles and acknowledge the others. "I shall see if help is needed," she said in an oddly breathless voice. Since no one expressed any objection to her departure, she hurried out, following the sound of Mistress Goudge's strident tones.

The hapless Ferrers had not been brought into the parlor but into the room Parthenia Goudge somewhat grandiosely had christened with the new architectural term, the "withdrawing room." Originally, the ground floor of Creepers had been divided into the kitchen and buttery, separated by what was then called the screens passage, and the housebody or hall, which connected onto a single large parlor. Not long before the calamitous Civil War, the Blakes had divided the parlor into separate rooms. Judging from the bookshelves in the smaller of the two chambers, that space had been set aside as the library. Since the Goudges read nothing but Holy Writ, the shelves now contained only a few books and manuscripts but a great deal of pewter plate and ugly bric-a-brac. The newly created withdrawing room, however, was handsomely furnished, probably with pieces from the Blakes' previous tenure. It was here that Sir Ralph Ferrers panted on a cut-velvet settee while his young bride sniffed smelling salts in an upholstered armchair.

Honor expressed her desire to help to Master Goudge, but he shook his head. "We're managing well enough," Delbert replied curtly, still smarting from his ward's remarks at supper. "Though these gentlefolk may want to spend the night. They live at Smallwood Hall."

Feeling awkward now that her aid had been rejected, Honor shifted from one foot to the other and tried to see around Master Goudge. Sir Ralph was accepting generous gulps of brandy from Durwood. He appeared to be about sixty, a round mound of a man with fishlike lips and lank gray hair. His bride, however, was not much older than Honor. Indeed, upon closer inspection, her sloe-eyed beauty was as obvious as it was disconcertingly familiar. Honor stifled a gasp as she recognized Lady Ferrers. Philene Godard, the Frenchwoman Tyler Vail had squired about London, reclined in graceful distress under the watchful eye of Mistress Goudge.

In truth, Tyler had remarked that Philene was marrying "some rich old duffer" from Staffordshire, but at the time, Honor had had no reason to consider the matter further.

"Mes diamants," Philene was saying in a faint voice. *"Mes saphirs!"* Limply, she fell against the chair, waving away Mistress Goudge and her sal volatile.

On the settee, Sir Ralph seemed to rally. "Outrageous," he muttered, "damnably outrageous! I shall have Hood's head on Smallwood's gates!"

With that dreadful, mirthless smile frozen in place, Mistress Goudge motioned for Honor to leave. She might as well. They didn't need her help and she couldn't stand listening to one more vow of vengeance called out on Captain Hood.

But Parthenia was on her heels, skirts swishing like battle pennons. "See here," she said, all but shoving Honor up against the carved balustrade, "what do you know of Captain Hood?" Her eyes snapped with zeal. "Don't hedge. You know more than you've told us. Speak!"

Honor gaped incredulously at Mistress Goudge. "Master Goudge and Uriah have as many facts as I do," she answered, trying to keep calm in spite of Parthenia's fierce gaze. "Why should I hold back?"

Mistress Goudge inched even closer, actually stepping on Honor's hem. "Because you fancy him, that's why! And he, you! Otherwise, why bother to bring you back?" She stood very straight, arms folded across her bulging bosom, her long nose atwitch with indignation. "Deny your mutual lusts! Scorn your body's hot longings and tell me all!"

As she felt the newel post pressing against her back, Honor's patience disintegrated. "You talk drivel! Don't ask me where he hides, ask your cringing spouse! Or rather, ask him where Hood is *not,* for Master Goudge couldn't find a barrel in his breeks!"

Parthenia had gone white around the lips and her whole body was trembling. She gripped Honor by the shoulders, fingers sinking into flesh. "Strumpet!" she hissed. "Now we know why the Cromwells turned you out, why your betrothed threw you over! You're nothing but a sly little slut, parting your pretty legs for any jackanapes or rakehell who comes along! You ought to be in the pillory! I can see it all now, a vision sent not by God but Satan, with your fervid naked flesh moist from …."

Parthenia Goudge was a strong woman, but Honor had the advantage of youth—and surprise. Her hand flew up to grasp Mistress Goudge's chin and clamp her mouth shut, evoking not just pain but astonishment.

"You're revolting," declared Honor, tightening her hold on the other woman. "Your mind reeks of the jakes. Keep your evil thoughts inside your silly head and share them not with decent folk." With a quick, twisting movement, Honor broke free from the clawing fingers and pushed Parthenia aside. A second later, she was taking the stairs two at a time, her skirts bunched in her hands.

But Parthenia wasn't one to give up so easily. Her face a peculiar shade of puce and her hands tightened into fists, she called shrilly after Honor, "It's true! You burn for that brigand! And you'll go to hell for it!"

Honor paused on the landing. She was about to retort that hell would be preferable to Creepers but decided not to prolong the conflict. Continuing up the stairs, she raced to her bedchamber and gratefully collapsed on the trundle bed. She was still infuriated and knew it would take some time to compose herself. Indeed, she couldn't recall ever being so angry. Mistress Goudge had to be the most vile, mean-minded person she had ever met. Aunt Lucy used to say that as often as not—there were exceptions, of course—the people who annoyed one the most usually did so because they possessed similar flaws to one's own. Honor was sure that Parthenia was one of those exceptions. Surely she and Honor had no traits in common.

But, Honor reflected, when at last she had stopped breathing so hard, she must consider why Parthenia had unsettled her so. Perhaps in this instance she was closer to the truth than Honor wished to admit.

Chapter Eight

At Whitehorse Hill, Aunt Lucy had refused to abide by the Puritan suppression of Christmas. "Yuletide isn't Good Friday," she'd asserted in one of her rare, clear-cut opinions. "The dear Lord must get as tired of glum faces as I do."

Consequently, Christmas had been celebrated at Whitehorse Manor with the traditional customs: roast goose and plum pudding, garlands of pine and yew, sprigs of holly, a wassail bowl, and joyful carols. The Yule log burned brightly on the great hearth and gifts were exchanged. Honor had loved every minute of the season, from the first Sunday of Advent until Twelfth Night.

It was quite different at Creepers. There were no songs, no mistletoe, no ceremony in which the Holy Babe was tenderly nestled into a straw-filled *crèche*. From the end of November until after the New Year, Mistress Goudge led the family in yet more scriptural readings, increasingly longer prayers and stultifying sermons extolling the virtues of her own peculiar brand of Christian charity. Somehow, Parthenia's observance of Christmas in this Yuletide season of 1658 was linked directly with the capture and punishment of Captain Hood. Comparing the highwayman to King Herod, Mistress Goudge charged Hood with every imaginable sin, including the slaughter of the innocents. By the feast of the Epiphany, Honor was ripe for rebellion.

Ironically, her mood seemed to be shared by the majority of Englishmen. Early on in the year of 1659 the House of Commons was called to sit at Westminster. Those Royalist voices, muted but never stilled, grew strident as Dick Cromwell fumbled and bungled his way as Lord Protector.

The country's changing mood had a far more immediate effect on the Goudges, however. Less than a week after Parliament convened, Squire Wills of

Buttermilk Hill conveyed his regrets over the betrothal between his daughter, Prudence, and Uriah Goudge. Though his reasons were nebulous at best, it was clear that Wills had tested the political winds and found his daughter's future in-laws in the eye of the storm. Delbert and Parthenia Goudge were as enraged as they were humiliated.

"Satan's at work, make no mistake," Mistress Goudge had averred on a cold, gray afternoon that promised snow before evening. "They'll all rot in hell, I swear it."

Honor, who was carding wool for Faith, glanced up at Mistress Goudge. Judging by the vast numbers Parthenia regularly consigned to the netherworld, it was going to be a very crowded place. Admittedly, there had been no repetition of the ugly scene between Honor and her hostess. During the two months that had passed since then, Parthenia had definitely been cool to Honor but had kept her malicious tongue in check. Though she told herself she shouldn't fret about Mistress Goudge's manner one way or the other, Honor couldn't help but speculate. Had Parthenia let up in her virulent attacks because she still hoped to learn more about Captain Hood's whereabouts? Or had she actually been embarrassed by her wicked rantings? Honor didn't know but was grateful for the respite.

She had just finished combing out a particular stubborn tangle when Master Thorn arrived. He had given his pupils a fortnight off for the Christmas season, but now, in mid-January, they had returned to the classroom and Master Thorn had reappeared at Creepers with the latest batch of exercises.

"Young boys are heedless of the season's solemnity," Thorn said, after Honor had guided him to the parlor. "They think only in terms of holiday. Judge them accordingly," he cautioned, placing his staff next to the armchair on which he was sitting.

"Of course," Honor assured him, leafing through the papers and noting far more ink blots than usual. Despite the many visits Master Thorn had made to Creepers, she still hadn't gotten used to the idea that he was totally sightless. Thus, in his presence, she would often find herself maintaining a decorous appearance, composing her features appropriately and generally behaving as if he could actually see what she was doing. But of course that was impossible. Honor knew that she could tear off her clothes and recline stark naked without arousing the slightest response from Matthew Thorn.

Thus it was that when her rather coarse winter undergarments made her backside itch, Honor opted to scratch. Lifting up her skirts and petticoats, she succeeded in her attempt to get to the seat of the problem. It struck her as wondrous strange when an odd, garbled noise seemed to escape from the folds of Matthew Thorn's hood. She must, of course, have imagined such a peculiar sound, but her innate modesty compelled her to quickly withdraw her hand and cover herself with her clothing. She was arranging her skirts over her legs when Master Thorn spoke.

"I believe I've an ague," he said with a strange quiver to his voice. "I should head for home."

In all her dealings with Master Thorn, Honor had never learned where "home" might be. How, she mused as she saw him struggle to his feet, did he manage alone? Lighting fires, preparing meals, keeping any abode clean, no matter how small, must be daunting duties for a blind man. Someday she would ask, but she didn't yet feel she knew him well enough to pry. Watching him reach for his staff, she felt a sharp stab of sympathy. Leaping to her feet, she took his long, yet strong, hand in hers and guided it to the staff, which had slipped to one side of the chair. To her surprise, his fingers tightened, and his shrouded figure loomed over her in the wintry shadows of the parlor's rushlights.

"You must be very beautiful," he said unexpectedly. "Your hand is soft, your touch gentle."

The caressing note in Thorn's voice startled Honor. She stared down at their clasped fingers, feeling a little tremor crawl up her spine. Revulsion? she asked herself, and was ashamed at the very idea. "My mother was quite pretty," she said rather feebly, and wondered if it was true. She could scarcely remember what either of her parents had looked like.

Thorn let go of her hand just as Faith entered the room. "There was a messenger for you, Honor," she said, looking puzzled. "It was one of our tenants' lads. Here," she added, thrusting a folded piece of paper at the other girl. "The lad must have been bribed well. He won't say where this came from."

Curiously, Honor opened the note, which was hardly more than a scrap. As before, the bold handwriting was formed into a verse.

Tomorrow noon at Belmot Gate,
A lover's arms will surely wait.

The single initial *H* was scrawled at the bottom. Distractedly, Honor crumpled the paper and turned away so that Faith couldn't see the color that had risen in her cheeks. At least there wasn't time to explain; from the passageway she could hear Master Goudge cursing in a most un-Puritan-like manner.

"I'll murder that Will Tipper. By Christ's cross, I'll blow him to kingdom come," ranted Delbert, as Uriah dutifully trailed after his father into the parlor. "Poaching, that's what he's doing, clear and simple!" Master Goudge toned down his tirade just long enough to growl a greeting to Matthew Thorn. "The stocks aren't good enough for him! Where's my gun?"

Honor noted that as usual, Master Goudge's guns were above the limestone fireplace. Two old-fashioned harquebuses and a rather new pistol formed the Goudge armory. Delbert hauled down all three, handing the pistol to Uriah. "Clean and load," he commanded. "We'll flush Will Tipper out before sunset!"

Mistress Goudge and Clarity had now joined the rest of the family, as Matthew Thorn sought a path between them on his way out the door. In the commotion that followed, Honor was forgotten. Seeing her chance to slip away while Mistress Goudge cautioned husband and son not to shoot each other and to go with God, Honor crept upstairs to her room. Once inside, she bolted the door and did her best to smooth out the rumpled paper sent by Captain Hood. Belmot Gate … tomorrow, at noon ….

This time she would not go unprepared. She stood at the window watching Delbert and Uriah Goudge troop off across the fallow fields toward Burton Old Forest with their firearms at the ready. As the pale sun dipped behind the stark branches of the trees beyond the woodhouses, the plan to foil Captain Hood was revealing itself in Honor's brain.

THE BLACK MARE WASN'T PARTICULARLY contrite about throwing her hapless rider on their previous trip into the forest, but at least she seemed sufficiently biddable. A light snowfall had dusted the countryside overnight but the late morning was clear, with wisps of white cloud against a blue sky. Honor had informed the Goudges that she was heading for the village cobbler's shop to have her shoes mended. No one paid her much heed, the family members being caught up in their outrage over Will Tipper's flight from justice with at least three deer and a number of rabbits.

With the pistol hidden under her dark green cloak and tucked into a belt filched from Uriah, Honor cantered along the peaceful white road, which only a handful of tracks had flawed so far that morning. At the edge of Rutbury, she turned onto the Belmot Road, following the same route she had taken previously. Here, within the forest, the great gnarled oak branches were rimed with snow, though the protected ground was covered only in patches. As Honor approached the stream, the rocks wore smooth caps of snow while neat cloven hoofprints revealed that the deer had already come for refreshment.

The Belmot Gate, which led to one of the forest's enclosed game parks, was situated just east of the road at the edge of the little stream. Peering up through a maze of branches, Honor noted that the winter sun stood directly overhead. It must be almost noon. Dismounting, she let the mare drink from the icy waters, then listened intently for the sound of approaching hoofbeats. Only the brook's busy ripple and the occasional sound of snow slipping from the trees met her ears. Yet she had the uncanny feeling that she was being watched: the deer, perhaps, guarding their home from strangers.

Or the Goudges. The thought flashed through Honor's mind with lightning force. Their indifference to her trip might have been a sham. Perhaps the only reason they had treated her with any sort of decency was that they expected eventually she would lead them to Captain Hood—and the reward. Anxiously, she scanned the forest for any sign of either the Goudges or the highwayman. Pray God he would not appear before they did.

If she had been followed, then it stood to reason that Delbert or Uriah, or more likely both, would still be on the other side of the stream. Hood was already late; she would have to act swiftly. She could go on the attack, turn around and flush them out—but there was no guarantee that they would leave. Apprehension mounting, she scoured the woods. A snow-laden branch cracked suddenly, and she spun around. For just an instant, Honor saw both Delbert and Uriah clearly before they ducked behind a tree. She waited, but they did not reappear. Obviously, they believed she had not seen them.

Taking a deep breath, Honor gazed around the little clearing, as if seeking inspiration. It was the mistletoe, clinging to a young oak, that gave her the idea. In truth, she remembered with some scant measure of relief that it was Delbert who had mentioned it earlier during the exchange with Captain Hood. Getting a leg up on the little mare, Honor reached for the mistletoe and disengaged it from the tree. She found a sturdy broken branch, planted it in the snow and perched her prize on top. Momentarily at a loss as to her next move, Honor wished that Latin hadn't been considered too popish by her tutors. She knew some French, but its elegant cadences weren't appropriate for her intentions. In spite of herself, she jumped when a twig snapped somewhere behind her. If only she dared turn around … but she didn't. She couldn't allow any worldly distraction to disrupt the spell she was supposedly under. She must convince the watching Goudges of her trancelike state.

When Honor was fifteen, Aunt Lucy had welcomed a German antiquities scholar to Whitehorse Hill. He had come as many others did to study the strange outline of the horse and take his findings back to Heidelberg University. Honor had learned no German from him, but at least she could emulate some of the language's harsh, guttural sounds. Waving her arms over her head and dancing first on one foot and then the other, she began to chant in a throaty, if nonsensical, manner.

She shrilled earsplitting high notes, ground out low rumbles and howled quavering imprecations over and over and over. After several minutes, she was growing hoarse as well as weary. The little mare, which had started when Honor first began the raucous ritual, now stood as if fascinated. Honor desperately hoped the Goudges would flee the vicinity.

Sure enough, she was just taking a deep breath for her next paean when the sound of crashing branches met her ears. Either the Goudges were coming toward her—or heading toward the Belmot Road. Adding one final series of shrieks and grunts, Honor staggered over to the mare and leaned against its warm flanks. She could now hear the sound of receding hoofbeats, with no effort made at concealing the retreat. Honor took in deep gulps of cold air, seeing her breath form little trails of white steam. She had just reached out to pat the mare's neck when she heard another sound, this time from the opposite direction. She turned nervously to see Captain Hood next to a big maple, hat, cloak and mask firmly in place.

"Good Eros lets his schemes unravel,
He sends a maid with a voice of gravel.
I'd seek the peace of Death's dark shroud,
Yet still my love would sound too loud."

Hood swept off his hat and made an elaborate bow. "Don't mistake me," he said with his usual amused indolence. "I'm most appreciative of your awful efforts on my behalf."

"Your behalf?" Honor squeaked, one hand at her tired throat. "I did it for myself, to make them stop pestering me."

Hood was now three feet away, smiling easily, though his strange, elusive eyes held a spark of some emotion Honor couldn't define. "Nay, you did it so they wouldn't find me. Or do you intend to collect the thousand crowns yourself?"

"As you well know, I could do with a thousand crowns," she replied ruefully, wishing her voice didn't rasp so. She also wished Hood hadn't seen her make such a fool of herself. "You must think me a duck-brained ninny." With a studied, casual gesture, she ran her hand over her cloak to make sure that the pistol was still in place.

The highwayman brushed her cold cheek with his hand. "I think you're most inventive. Not everyone could conjure up Druid spirits to preserve themselves from the Goudges." He reached out to take the mistletoe from the tree branch and twirled it around in his fingers. "This excellent plant has been put to better use by Christians, though. At least it used to be so before the Puritans." He held the mistletoe over Honor's head and bent down as if to steal a kiss. "Shall we keep it as a talisman?"

"It's a parasite," Honor blurted, and wished Captain Hood didn't have the power to disconcert her so. She tried to meet his gaze but found herself nervously glancing back at the little mare, who was now contentedly nosing about in the short, tough grasses at the edge of the stream.

"I can trust you, can't I?" Hood's words took her by surprise, as did the hand that reached out to lift her chin.

Inwardly, Honor wondered why Captain Hood should think he could trust a woman he had robbed of her dowry. Perhaps he didn't know that the jewels had been her only earthly possessions. On the other hand, he seemed to know everything else. Had their positions been reversed, she would never have allowed him to worm a half inch into her confidence.

His hand still held her chin; she took a deep breath and met his gaze. Surely those shrewd eyes couldn't contain much naïveté. If he'd asked if he could trust her, then he must already know he could. Her heart was racing in her breast. Did Hood know something of her she didn't know herself?

"Why shouldn't you trust me?" she asked ambiguously.

He made no rejoinder nor did his expression change. Taking his hand away, he whistled for his horse, who came trotting around the maple, the reins swinging free. "Come," he said, grasping the bridle, "we'll ride together. I promised, did I not?"

That, Honor told herself, was what he'd said. But was it what he meant? She got back onto the black mare, noting that the sun had disappeared, leaving only a scanty patch of blue. More snow by evening, she guessed, and for the first time wondered where Hood would lead her.

It came as no surprise that they crossed the Belmot Road, plunging deeper into the forest. In less than a mile, they had reached the springs that were the source of the little stream that tumbled all the way to the confluence of Dove and Trent. The trees grew so tall and thick in this part of the woods that no snow and only the weakest sunlight penetrated the roof of sheltering branches. In places the thorns and hollies grew dense, winter feeding grounds for the deer whose tracks crisscrossed their path at almost every step. The heavy gloom and absence of human habitation made Honor uneasy. She felt as if she had entered not only a secret, hidden place but a distant, older time, as well. There was no trace of man ever having stepped here.

At last the underbrush cleared and the ground became quite level. Yet the oaks grew even larger; at least two of them just ahead were some twenty feet in diameter. The trees' mighty size seemed to dwarf their surroundings. Honor almost expected giants to reach down and pluck them from the saddle.

"Beyond this stand," Hood said, speaking for the first time since they had left Belmot Gate, "you'll see the greatest tree of them all, Beggar's Oak." His voice sounded unnaturally loud in the quiet forest. Slowing his mount so that Honor could catch up, he gave her a look that was teasing, yet challenging. " 'Tis said to be haunted. Are you afraid?"

She shook her head slowly. "No." Ghosts didn't frighten her. Hood, however, was another matter. She wished she could be sure of his intentions. Glancing about, she noticed that some of the heavier limbs were propped up by stout timbers. Up ahead, the branches formed an archway. The silence, the play of light and shadow among the trees, the sense of being sheltered from the real world reminded Honor of Westminster Abbey and the procession for poor Bettie. Reverence, thought Honor, and then gasped as they passed between two huge trees that stood like mammoth sentries, guarding an oak so vast that it must have flourished for a thousand years. At least twenty feet at its base, it was so tall that for all Honor could see, it might have soared straight to heaven.

"There it is," Hood said in his calm way, though Honor thought she could detect a hint of pride in his voice. "Beggar's Oak, worshiped by pagans, respected by woodsmen, feared by ordinary folk. No doubt your Druids paid homage here. What think you, lovely Honor?"

Words failed her. She sat with her mare next to Hood and his gelding, quietly contemplating the great oak like a pilgrim at a shrine. After what seemed like a long time, Hood pursed his lips and uttered a strange, shrill cry, not unlike the sound he had made to summon Shandy. Honor's brow furrowed as she looked at him, then she jumped when an answering call emanated from the vicinity of the giant tree.

"All's well," said Hood, prodding his horse to move ahead. "Shall we explore?"

Honor's only response this time was to urge the little black mare into a trot. They rode wide of the tree, coming round to the far side, where Hood stopped and dismounted. From virtually nowhere, the fourth member of the highwayman's band appeared, making a courtly bow. Honor studied him more closely, noting that he was quite young, perhaps only a year or two older than she was. The suggestion of a blond mustache skirted his upper lip and the eyes behind the mask were a lively blue.

"I'll tend to the horses, Captain," he said in a cheerful, surprisingly refined voice. "Wat and Padge have gone a-hunting."

"Good, Nip. We're running low on meat. I should hate to have to waylay a butcher's van." Hood waved amiably at the young man, who already held the reins of both horses. Nip's eyes darted in Honor's direction, giving her a quick, discreet appraisal. Embarrassed at what he might be thinking, she looked away, but met Hood's frank gaze. "Despite his years, Nip's more cynical than I. He'd never say so out loud, but he's convinced I'm a fool to bring you here."

Nip cocked his head to one side and managed a sheepish grin. "Now, Captain … since when have I criticized your judgment?"

"Within the hour, I should imagine," Hood replied easily. "Never mind, Nip. Whatever befalls, the blame as always is mine."

Nip was doing his best to maintain a carefree attitude, yet Honor sensed that the young man was worried. She couldn't blame him; Hood appeared to be taking an enormous risk. As Nip led the horses away, Hood watched him with speculative eyes, as if any doubts the younger man had sown might still sprout.

Yet as Hood turned back to Honor and took her arm, he was smiling. "Pray join me in my arboreal bower, mistress. Mind the acorns on my doorstep."

They were standing directly in front of the massive oak's trunk with the lower branches of the vast, spreading crown almost brushing the tops of their heads. Honor wondered if Hood meant for them to grab a limb and start climbing. Though a highwayman might hide in a treetop, surely he wouldn't live in one. Resting his hand on the red-brown gnarled trunk, Captain Hood set his shoulders and gave a forceful push. To Honor's astonishment, a four-foot-high segment of the tree gave in, then pivoted outward.

He made a courtly bow. "Welcome to Beggar's Oak, sweet Honor. Keep your head down as you enter."

Utterly amazed, Honor hunched down to clear the opening. Hood followed close behind, pausing to swing the false piece of tree trunk back into place. Once inside, Honor straightened up and stared incredulously at a high, round room where a brazier burned merrily in the middle of the dirt floor, giving off the only light. It took her several moments to accustom herself to the dusky interior, but shapes and forms began to fall into place. The room itself was more than ten feet in diameter and almost as tall. It was sparsely but comfortably furnished—a narrow bed with a thick wool blanket; a table with a curved bench; a cupboard that reached from floor to ceiling. At one side of the room a staircase, which presumably led to a loft, had been cut out in a spiral.

Hood was lighting a lantern and watching Honor with keen, yet curious, eyes. "Well? Do you find Beggar's Oak a mere hovel compared to Creepers?"

Honor's initial response was that any abode that didn't house the Goudges had to be an improvement. But in truth, as the lantern spread its light around the room, Honor found herself smiling. She turned to Hood. "I like it. It's … charming." Ingenious, too, she was going to add, but a sudden rustling movement made her whirl about. On the dirt floor at Hood's booted feet sat a fat red squirrel making indignant chattering noises.

"Rupert!" exclaimed Captain Hood, stooping down to pick up the squirrel. "I've not forgotten you. Meet Mistress Dale, from Creepers Hall."

The squirrel eyed Honor with far more suspicion than Nip had allowed himself to show. Tentatively, Honor put out her hand, but the little animal leaped down, scurrying toward the table, where he bounded onto the bench and gibbered angrily.

"He's not used to strangers," Hood explained somewhat apologetically. "He and his family have lived in this tree for generations. Rupert is the only one sufficiently condescending to come inside. I named him for that great fierce prince who has served King Charles so well. Rupert is as proud as his namesake and, in his way, just as loyal." Having concluded his reproaches, Rupert now descended to the floor, skittering toward the outer door, where he burrowed down and disappeared. "He has his private entrance," Hood continued, opening up the cupboard and taking out two battered silver cups. "Wine? Or port? We have a surfeit of the latter, there being a glut on the market at present."

Honor indicated the port and recalled Lyndon Styles's report that Captain Hood had recently commandeered someone's monthly supply. Now that her initial shock had passed, she was trying to gauge how much maneuverability she had within the close, circular confines of the little room. Obviously, the loft must accommodate the other three beds, though where Hood and his men hid their spoils, she couldn't guess. Another hollowed-out tree, perhaps, or even underground.

Handing her the silver cup, Hood raised its mate in a toast. "To mutual trust—'tis worthless unless it's shared, you know."

Honor saw that those shrewd eyes were unwontedly serious behind the mask. She suppressed a small wince and touched her cup with his, then took a slow sip. If Hood still had her jewels they might be in the cupboard. Or under the cot, since it appeared there were drawers peeking out from beneath the blanket.

"This is all fiendishly clever," she remarked, waving her free hand to take in her surroundings. "In truth, you are far more inventive than I."

"Pray sit, Honor," said Hood, indicating the bench. "The idea for this hideaway has been with me since I was a youth," he went on, removing his cloak and hanging it on a peg next to the door. "Another oak, not quite so large, was struck by lightning. The tree was partially hollowed out, though it still lived. My friends and I would hide there when our parents were angry or our tutor was looking for us." A reminiscent smile hovered at Hood's long mouth. "Eventually, we were caught out, not by our elders but by one of the neighbor lads who also happened to be a bit of a bully. Not only was our secret exposed, but his father unlawfully had the tree cut down."

He stopped to take a drink, then sat next to Honor on the bench. "That was almost twenty years ago, yet the memory lingered. When I sought a hiding place in the vicinity last year, I came across this tree as well as several others almost as large. It's been ideal. Oh," he added with a little shrug, "it's cramped and it's damp, but it's safe. We have made slits in the loft part, too high for a man to see from ground level but sufficient to give us air and to keep watch. Our pursuers look for us in the limestone caves, deserted stables, abandoned lodges. But never the trees." He spread his hands on the table and Honor noted how long and strong those fingers were, how weak and fragile her own looked by comparison. She actually jumped when he put his hand on hers. "What is it, Honor?" he inquired softly. "You've nothing to fear from me. Or am I wrong to trust in you?"

She saw the troubled look in those enigmatic eyes and lowered her lashes. Slowly, she shook her head, though she wasn't sure exactly what she was denying. He had slipped an arm around her waist, drawing her closer to him on the bench. Honor shifted just enough so that he couldn't feel the pistol beneath her cloak. Their faces were almost touching as he leaned forward to fathom the expression in her eyes. Honor felt compelled to return his gaze, yet that hypnotic stare further unsettled her. Somehow, she must get back on her feet; there was no way she could reach for the pistol unless he released her.

But Captain Hood clearly had no intention of letting her go. His lips were in her hair, then at her ear and along her neck. When he pulled back, it was to unhook the fastenings of her cloak.

Honor tensed and moved away. "Please, sir," she pleaded, "I'm all undone!"

"Not yet," countered Hood, "though that is my intent. Am I too clumsy?" he inquired with self-deprecating humor. "I notice this is not the cloak I returned to you. Was aught wrong with the mending?"

Flushing in spite of herself, Honor gave him a tentative, hopefully winsome, smile, then rose somewhat awkwardly from the bench. "The cloak was admirably stitched, though I should have been more grateful if you had left its contents intact." She had now broached the subject; perhaps Hood would volunteer some scrap of valuable information.

"Had that been my plan, I wouldn't have taken it in the first place." He spoke as easily as ever and without the slightest hint of regret. "I have my responsibilities, mistress. Though self-imposed, I'm obliged to carry them out even in the face of such an enchanting creature as yourself." He was straddling the bench now, taking another drink from his cup. "You'll find me a most obstinate sort, once I've made up my mind," he added in that cool, lazy voice that made Honor shiver slightly.

"I can be stubborn, too," she asserted, though she tried to keep her tone as casual as his. She had moved back as far as she could without running into the narrow cot. Obviously, he wasn't going to offer to make amends for her stolen dowry, despite the fact that she had given him ample opportunity. With a hurried if not particularly deft move, Honor pulled the pistol from Uriah's belt and leveled it at Captain Hood.

For a fleeting moment, as much as she could see of his face looked stricken. Then he swiftly composed his features and took another leisurely sip of port. "If you fear for your virtue, why did you come? This isn't a monastery, it's a den of thieves."

His offhand acknowledgment of that bald fact rattled Honor. "You said ...

you led me to believe …." Her voice, still ragged around the edges, trailed off, though she forced her hands to keep steady.

"That I don't force myself on women?" He shrugged. "That's true. Nor will I force myself on you. But that being the case, why did you come?" This time he spoke the words more roughly; Honor sensed that his patience was wearing thin.

"I want my jewels, or at least recompense. You left me with nothing in this world except …." She was about to say "my honor" but feared it would sound either like a complaint or like one of those plays on words that Hood relished so much. "That's why Tyler Vail wouldn't marry me. I had no other dowry. You didn't just steal my jewels, you took my future!" She spoke more rapidly now, self-righteous indignation fueling her tongue. "If it hadn't been for you, I'd be married to Tyler instead of here in this ridiculous tree!"

"Personally, I'd much prefer the tree. It may be a ridiculous abode, but at least it's genuine—and solid. I can't say the same for Sir Tyler." The highwayman brought one long leg up onto the bench. "If you thought twice about it, you'd thank me, not shoot me. Your baubles are destined for King Charles, as is all my ill-got gain. Surely his cause is more noble than paying off Tyler Vail's debts."

Honor might hold her former fiancé in contempt, but she hated the Royalists. Her face set and she gestured menacingly with the pistol. Surely Hood understood that she was quite serious. Just because she had failed to pull the trigger on their first encounter didn't mean she lacked the nerve to do it now. After all, his life stood between Honor and her future.

"Where is my dowry? Do you still have it in your possession?"

The brazier burned merrily, the lantern cast sharp shadows in the rounded confines of the room. For the first time, Honor noticed the lingering odor of cooked food, a pervasive mustiness, a woodsy smell of the very earth itself. Yet for all that which was so ordinary, the inherent strangeness of her surroundings and the bold man in the mask who stood before her made Honor feel as if she were in a distorted, disturbing dream. She gripped the pistol even more tightly and anxiously awaited his answer.

Hood made no move to dissuade her, except to shake his head. "You wouldn't fire that at me," he said almost wearily, like a parent who has lost patience with an unruly child. "Even if you did, the report within such close quarters would harm you almost as much as it would me. And it's likely we'd be blinded from the flash in this semidarkness. And what would poor Nip think when he charged in here to see what had happened?"

It had never occurred to Honor what might transpire if she actually had to use the gun. Of course, she hadn't been prepared to confront Hood inside a hollow oak while one of his men stood guard outside. Why, she demanded angrily of herself, did her schemes always seem to collapse in the face of reality? Her grip faltered and her face must have revealed her sudden doubts. Hood lunged so swiftly that she didn't see his hand sweep down in a hacking motion to knock the pistol onto the ground.

"God's teeth, that was a silly stunt, Honor Dale." Hood kicked the weapon away, sending it between the bench and table, then snatched Honor by the wrist. "We'll speak of your jewels some other time," he said, not hiding his annoyance. "Or," he asked in a voice that was gruffly at odds with his usual calm, collected tones, "would you care to barter for them?"

His hold on her wrist was overtight and Honor winced. She attempted to pull away, but her effort was futile. Hood's other hand was entwined in her hair, wresting the golden masses free from the numerous pins and a pair of tortoiseshell combs. "Doubloons from Spain, English sovereigns, a ducal coronet—I've seen gold of all kinds, yet none of it shimmers like this." His temper under control, he lifted a heavy strand to his lips while those mesmerizing eyes held her own gaze captive.

Honor tried to pull back but bumped up against the solid oak that supported the cot. Experimentally, he brushed her mouth with his as he finally succeeded in undoing her cloak. It slid to the earthen floor as Hood searched her face. "Well? Shall we barter?"

"Barter?" Honor's voice sounded hollow, her brain was fuzzy. The jewels, of course. Did he mean he still had them in his possession? "I told you, I have nothing with which to barter."

"Except your honor." Hood's kiss was swift and hard. She shuddered in his arms.

"Stop!" she cried, somehow managing to pull away just enough to speak. His face was so close, her mind was such a muddle. "Do you mean that? Would you give me back my jewels if I … if I gave myself to you?"

Hood's hands followed the curve of her back to her waist and on down to her hips. He gazed at her with a most serious, intent expression. "No." He ran his fingers lightly over her buttocks and she shivered at his touch. "I want you only if you want me. I said as much. I never lie—except that I would lie with you."

Honor moaned and went slack in his arms. The man's self-confidence was the size of his damnable oak. But it didn't matter—nothing mattered except those probing hands and that searching mouth. The golden hair spilled over his arm as he lifted her carefully off the ground and lowered her onto the cot. Parthenia Goudge was right: Honor lusted after Hood as shamelessly as any Shoreditch whore. Yet it was different, it had to be. In that shattering, wondering moment as he paused, gazing down at her with a desire that was almost tangible, Honor knew that she loved this outlaw, this thief, this

Royalist brigand. Her emotions were raw, her soul was bared. She lay back on the narrow cot and held out her arms to Captain Hood.

His fingers worked adroitly at the jet buttons of her black gown. She wore no heavily boned corset as fashion required but only a thin silk chemise held in place with a drawstring. Hood tugged at the little loops which fell away like tiny satin snakes against the curve of her bosom. He made no move to pull away the fragile silk but instead cupped her breasts in his big hands, molding them sensuously until their tips peeped above the fabric.

"Enchanting!" he breathed, his lean, hungry gaze traveling up to her face and back again to those perfect white globes with their pert pink buds. Slowly, tantalizingly, he moved the flat of one hand over her nipples, again and again, each time with more pressure until Honor wanted to cry out with agonized delight. But all she could muster was a writhing motion until her hands moved with a will of their own to press his fingers against her flesh. Quickly, he bared her to the waist, then undid the fastenings that held both muslin skirts and petticoats in place. His tongue flicked urgently at her nipples, setting off a fire that raged throughout her entire being. Instinctively, Honor wound one white-stockinged leg around his thighs, her fingers clawing at his shirt.

He paused long enough to remove his own clothing, and in that sudden lull, Honor was forced to focus on his lean, sinewy body. Light and shadow played off his finely toned flesh as he slipped down her stockings and then, that last vestige of virtue, a long-legged undergarment that had staved off the winter weather far more effectively than it had Hood's ardent hands. For just an instant, Honor shut her eyes, unable to watch him look at her nakedness. But he was speaking to her again, in low, almost shaken tones. She scarcely recognized his voice, yet felt as if she had known it for a lifetime.

"Truly, I have found the Golden Fleece," he murmured, placing his hand between her thighs. "God help me that it isn't fool's gold!"

Honor shuddered violently. "Heaven help *me,*" she breathed, " 'tis the wealth of Midas I would give you!"

Cautiously, tenderly, he plied that secret flesh, making Honor seethe with anticipation of a miracle she couldn't possibly understand. Could Tyler Vail have made her ache so much with longing? Could any man, except this bold brigand with his house of oak and air of mystery? But even as her thoughts whirled inside her brain, Captain Hood had ripped off the black mask and tossed it onto the ground. She saw him fully for the first time, a ruggedly masculine face that was suffused with desire, inflamed with passion. As he entered her body with slow yet sure thrusts, one fragment of reality pierced her haze of yearning: *his eyes are green.*

And then there was a sudden, sharp burst of pain, so swift that Honor's entire body was tensed for revolt. Yet the moment passed so rapidly, the rapture that followed was so complete, that when she felt his shattering release within her, they both cried out with the joy of sweet deliverance.

A moment later, Hood had gone very still, allowing their bodies to commune and their brains to catch up with their senses. Honor lay beneath his weight, yet not conscious of any burden. Indeed, she could think of nothing but the wonder of his lovemaking, of the fulfillment, of the happiness he had given her. She locked her arms around Hood's neck and smiled up at him in a beguiled, dazed manner.

Indeed, as he reluctantly withdrew from her, his own face was a study in emotional chaos. Honor recognized pleasure and elation, but as she began to spiral down to reality, she also detected a hint of discomfiture. Or perhaps it was the absence of his customary self-possession. He was no longer a cool, casual stranger but a flesh and blood man with flaws and failings.

"Who are you?" she asked in a hushed voice. "Who are you really?"

Slowly, he rolled off her, though the cot was so narrow that he had to prop himself up on his side. "A fair question, I suppose." Heaving a great sigh, he stared up at the curiously hewn ceiling of the little chamber. "Are we beyond secrets?" He turned just enough to see her profile.

"I should think so," Honor replied, still awash with new, untried emotions.

Hood moved again, a hand on her hip. "My name is Justin Blake. I was born and raised at Creepers Hall."

Honor gaped at him, her dark eyes huge. But even as she stared, she realized she should have known all along. He had known so much of the neighborhood, of local inhabitants, of the house itself. "Justin Blake." She tested the name on her tongue. "It's very … strong. An open, honest name."

"Which has put me behind a mask." He made a wry face. "It has also made me hate the Goudges."

"That's easy to do," Honor remarked idly, then became aware of her nakedness and flushed. "Damn and blast, I shouldn't …."

He stopped her with a kiss. "You should. Always. At least with me." He kissed her again but pulled the heavy blanket over them both. "I used to dream of the day Creepers would be returned to me," he said, staring beyond Honor to the brazier, which was beginning to burn low. "Yet I feel that's not as important to me as ridding England of the Puritans and putting King Charles back on the throne."

Honor shivered. "Why must you be a Royalist?" she asked in a low voice.

He lifted one bare shoulder. "For the same reason you are a Puritan. We were born to it." He passed a hand over his dark hair, then caressed her cheek. "That's not quite true, perhaps. I believe in what I was born to. Do you?" Honor blinked. "Of course!" She paused, running her tongue across her upper lip. "That is, I must. My parents were Puritans, Uncle Oliver was the great

Puritan leader, even Aunt Lucy was a Puritan … of sorts." Honor fell silent, suddenly aware that she'd never really given her political convictions much consideration. All these years it had seemed enough to hate the Royalists. They must be wrong; they'd murdered her parents.

But Honor wasn't ready to talk about that awful memory yet. "The first King Charles was unjust, the country's leadership was corrupt and inept. As for morality, there was none. The Church of England smacked of the Church of Rome. All England had sunk into a morass of scandal and debauchery."

Justin regarded Honor's prim little speech with amusement. "Or so you've been taught. If you really believed in strict Puritan principles, what, my wild and wanton lady, are you doing here with me?"

Indignantly, Honor tried to sit up, but he put both hands on her breasts and pushed her back gently.

"You know I didn't come here to let you ravish me," she protested without much vigor. His fingers were again teasing her flesh, making lazy circles around each taut pink nipple. "Your family … I heard they were all dead. Was that merely a rumor started by the Goudges?" She looked into those green eyes and wondered if she dared plant little kisses on his brow.

She was both surprised and disappointed when he ceased trifling with her breasts. "I don't know the source," he answered, suddenly grim. "I heard the same about yours. It seems we are the sole survivors of an unfortunate few."

Honor frowned. "How did you know? About my parents, I mean." For one brief moment, the terrible vision returned. She closed her eyes and laid her head against his chest. "Please … must we speak of it … now?"

"It's best we don't. Mayhap not ever." The tense note in Justin's voice jarred Honor, but before she could say anything more, he smoothed the hair back from her forehead. He was kissing the hollow of her throat when a soft, yet persistent, knock sounded at the door. "Nip," he said to Honor in a low voice, and then spoke louder. "What is it? Are we treed at last by the sheriff?"

Nip's words were muffled by the thick bark. "It's snowing. The wind has come up, too."

Justin let out a deep sigh, then lightly brushed Honor's lips with his. "I shall escort you as far as the south field. We may be in for a blizzard. At least it will cover our tracks."

As Justin flipped away the blanket and got up from the cot, Honor suddenly felt chilled. As reluctant as she was to leave him, she still responded to some innate sense of modesty and kept her back turned as she dressed. Moments later, they were at the door, where Justin paused with his hand on the rough wood. "I must see you again. Soon."

Honor swallowed hard. "Soon," she echoed, not daring to think what the future might bring. She studied his face, committing the rugged features to memory, wishing that they had met in some other place, at some other time. "Your mask!" she exclaimed. "You forgot to put it back on!"

He shook his head. "You could be my undoing, you know." He spoke lightly, but Honor felt a shiver along her spine. The north wind, perhaps, howling its way through the cracks and crannies. She hugged herself under the cloak and suddenly remembered the pistol. It still lay on the floor, now guarded by Rupert, the little red squirrel. She collected the weapon and stared down at the cold steel in her hands. How could she ever have dreamed of using it on this man?

"You knew, didn't you?" she breathed, gazing up at Justin.

"Knew?" He feigned ignorance, then gave her a crooked grin. "I did. Though had I been wrong, I should have come back to haunt you the rest of your days."

The faintest of smiles touched Honor's lips. "I believe you will do that anyway," she said. As Justin held the door open for her, she gave one last look over her shoulder at the roughly crafted little room. Rupert still squatted on the floor, his paws clasped around an acorn. Honor noted that he was staring up boldly at her; she could have sworn that he winked.

Chapter Nine

THE SNOW WAS FALLING OVER Creepers like a thick veil, blurring its chimneys, blanketing the herb garden, piling up against the sturdy walls of the woodhouses. Except for the soft murmur of the wind, the silence that surrounded the manor house struck Honor as ghostly. So wrapped up in her world was she, so overtaken by her newly found emotions, so distanced from the harsh, warped life among the Goudges, that she could almost imagine what Creepers had been like when the Blake family had lived there.

After she had taken the little mare into the stable and tended to the animal's needs, she returned outside to stand and stare anew at the house. Had Justin played here as a boy? Had he learned to ride his first pony in the paddock? Had he climbed the stile and gone off to fish the Dove with a birch rod over his shoulder? Honor smiled to herself, the snowflakes dusting her lashes, the visions dancing before her. How she wished it was he and not the Goudges who still owned Creepers! But then he wished the same. She sobered, suddenly shivered with cold and started doggedly for the house.

Any notion of sneaking in without the Goudges knowing was dashed by the apparition of Parthenia, emerging from under the back stairs with a taper in her hand.

"Wicked!" she raged, bearing down on Honor only to retreat as if overcome by fear. "Pagan rites! Heathen rituals! I can't believe it!"

Honor made as if to brush past Mistress Goudge, but Delbert was coming down the stairs. "I tell you, we saw her, plain as the nose on your face! Dancing and prancing and carrying on!" He swung around at the bottom of the stairs to join forces with his wife. "It isn't right, I tell you! It goes against God!"

Honor eyed both Goudges and tried to gauge their wrath. Delbert's seemed genuine; Parthenia's, as usual, lacked sincerity. It occurred to Honor that the hypocritical woman couldn't even come to grips with blasphemy in a credible manner.

"Actually ..." she began, but was cut short by Mistress Goudge.

"Witchcraft! That's what it is!" Parthenia jerked up her aggressive chin as if defying Honor to refute the charge. "We've summoned Master Radcliffe to exorcise the demons!"

"This is ridiculous." Honor spoke calmly, though the brightness of Parthenia's beady eyes warned her that the situation was extremely serious. "I simply dislike being followed. My privacy was respected at Whitehorse Manor." Squaring her shoulders, she made an attempt to walk between the Goudges, but Delbert stopped her with a heavy hand.

"Stay, pagan priestess. You'll come with us into the withdrawing room." He jerked his head in that general direction but Honor balked.

"I'd rather not. I'm cold and wet." Hungry, too, she realized, and noted that her gloves were caked with snow. She also saw that Uriah had come into the hallway, followed by an agitated Quentin Radcliffe, who was shaking wet drops from his cloak like a puppy.

"Ah! Master Radcliffe!" Parthenia pivoted but didn't leave Honor's side. "Bless you for coming despite the weather. In here, in here." She grasped Honor by the other arm. Both husband and wife propelled her into the withdrawing room. To Honor's surprise, Clarity and Faith were already there, standing like firedogs by the lighted hearth. Clarity looked faintly excited; Faith tended more toward apprehension.

"This is all quite extraordinary," Radcliffe declared, shedding his cape and brushing anxiously at his sandy curls.

"Druid rites!" He glanced at Honor, who was having some difficulty removing her stiff gloves. "Holly and mistletoe?"

"I cut holly only at Christmastide, to honor the Christ Child. It is sacred to me only as a remembrance." Honor's gaze was unwavering; the curate was the first to look away.

"Well." Radcliffe cleared his throat and extracted a well-thumbed book of devotions from his pocket. "I must find the right passages. I don't often do this sort of thing "

Having finally peeled off the gloves, Honor turned to Radcliffe. "Do what? I demand to know what manner of farce transpires here. If you are taking a mere prank seriously, I must insist that you come to your senses immediately." She tossed back the damp golden hair and moved toward the fire. Faith and Clarity edged away but kept fascinated eyes fixed on Honor.

Parthenia's laugh was a jangle of spite and outrage. "Pranks! Sense!" She snapped her fingers. "Come here, girl. On the settee." A long finger pointed at the place where Philene Godard Ferrers had reclined in distress a few weeks earlier. "Lie down."

Honor, limbering her fingers by the fire, turned to gape at Mistress Goudge. "I'm not tired, only cold and hungry. Leave me be." Her voice was impatient; the cloak swung defiantly as she again faced the flames.

She cried out when Delbert and Uriah grabbed her, hauling her bodily across the room and dumping her unceremoniously on the settee. Suddenly afraid, Honor tried to resist, but the two men held her down.

"I find no reference to Druids," Radcliffe murmured, more to himself than the others, "but much of witchcraft. Let me see, here we are, 'Witches and Familiars.' This should suit the occasion, I trust. Take off her clothes."

"No!" Honor screamed in protest and vaguely heard Uriah's grunt and Faith's gasp. Struggling to escape from her tormentors, Honor kicked out with her feet and flailed with her hands. But Uriah and Delbert were strong men. They held her firmly but refrained from actually proceeding further.

"It's a question of identifying the familiar and where it's suckled," Radcliffe explained carefully. "The breasts are obvious." He paused, glanced at Honor's bosom straining beneath her cloak and licked his lips.

"Stop it!" Honor's voice cut across the room like shattered glass. With a mighty heave, she wrested one arm from Uriah's grip and plunged inside her cloak to pull out the pistol. "Enough!" Honor commanded, leveling the weapon straight at a stunned Delbert's forehead. "You are all perverted!" She shook off Delbert and sat up straight, keeping the weapon trained on Uriah. Still at the fireplace, Clarity and Faith clung to each other. Parthenia's thin lips worked noiselessly, as if she were summoning up a curse of her own. Honor motioned for Delbert and Uriah to move back.

"Now," she said in a much calmer tone, "let's end this absurdity. You know perfectly well I'm neither a Druid nor a witch. Druids were real, but I'm skeptical of witches. The only ones I've ever heard of were pathetic old women whose wits were addled by age. The rest is sheer superstitious nonsense."

Her audience was not to be easily won, though Uriah appeared to have had his curiosity piqued and Faith looked vaguely embarrassed by the whole situation. "I shouldn't have played a joke on you," Honor continued, suppressing a desire to remark that any sort of humor would be lost on the Goudges, "but I did, and I'm full sorry for it. Uncle Oliver must be turning over in his grave and Cousin Dick would be ashamed of me." She paused, making sure the others took in her reminder of exalted family connections. Parthenia's eyelids fluttered and Honor knew a point had been scored. In acknowledgment, she lowered the pistol. "I was rude and insubordinate. A few hours lost in the snow have restored my … manners." Her dark eyes flickered as she recalled that what she had lost that day could never be restored. Yet it was imperative that she appear penitent. The Goudges seemed to have a well-supplied arsenal with which to combat those who thwarted their collective will. Until she devised a means of permanent escape, she must at least attempt a truce.

"You are not at all what we expected," Parthenia asserted between taut lips. "I can't begin to articulate my disappointment. How can we help you save your immortal soul when you are determined to writhe forever in hell?"

"The wages of sin are death," murmured Radcliffe, apparently feeling an obligation to exercise his office in at least some small way. He had, after all, ventured out from his cozy hearth in a blizzard.

Warily, Honor got to her feet. Her greatest concern was to reach the relative sanctuary of her little bedroom. "I've apologized, I promise to behave in a more seemly fashion henceforth." She assumed a demure, tractable expression but kept the pistol at the ready. "What more do you want of me?"

Uriah started to open his mouth, but his father elbowed him sharply. "Obedience, humility, all the virtues. Same as Faith and Clarity." He nodded vaguely toward his daughters but lacked conviction.

"I still don't think this escapade is all it seems," Parthenia said sharply. "We're not fools, you know."

Honor kept silent just long enough to cast doubt on Mistress Goudge's claim. Yet the words were true enough. The Goudges were grasping, narrow-minded, spiteful hypocrites—but they were definitely not fools. Underestimating them—at least Parthenia—would be a grave mistake. "I shall pray for a more seemly attitude," Honor promised, gliding past Radcliffe and Mistress Goudge. Well aware of the incongruous picture she must make with the pistol in her hands and the docile expression on her face, she made her exit without further interruption.

Parthenia's rasping words followed her into the hallway. "Up to no good, I'll wager, Druid or not! Is she meeting someone?"

Honor put one hand firmly on the balustrade. It would almost be better for them to think she was a pagan witch than to find out she had lain in Captain Hood's arms. His secret was now hers, as well. Honor realized that she must guard it as zealously as he did. No one must ever, ever suspect that she knew the highwayman—or that she loved him. Slowly, but purposefully, Honor ascended the stairs. Her little room at the end of the hall should offer temporary haven.

Yet for all its homely comforts, she found no ease there. Purity was a virtue to be guarded as zealously as life itself. Only the most wanton—or ignorant—maid let herself be seduced. Even Aunt Lucy, inclined to sympathy toward a simple scullery wench or an errant chambermaid, had impressed upon her daughters and her niece the necessity of preserving one's chastity. But at the first temptation, Honor had recklessly surrendered herself to the highwayman. It was a grave sin, and for once, Honor expected to be punished—not by the superstition-ridden Goudges or the silly theology of Quentin Radcliffe but in some other, more devastating manner.

Ironically, the worst hardship she could imagine was never to lie again in Justin Blake's arms.

BY EARLY MARCH THE SNOW had all but melted, though the chill, damp air held no sign of spring. Despite the gloom of winter, there was excitement at Creepers. An order from Dick Cromwell had been handed out for a survey of Burton Wood. Deforestation would follow, and many of the local landowners, including the Goudges, anticipated sizable profits from the trees.

An evening fog chased itself among the chimneys at Creepers while several of Rutbury's more prominent residents gathered in the parlor. Apprehensive about her cousin's order, Honor wanted to listen in on the conversation but was briskly informed by Mistress Goudge that the issue was solely a male prerogative. Reluctantly, Honor drifted away but thought she noted a spark of resentment in Parthenia's beady eyes. Mistress Goudge might absent herself from the gathering, but Delbert would make no decisions without his wife's counsel. As for Honor, she could not dispute the arbitrary exclusion. During the weeks since her passionate encounter with Justin Blake, she had coexisted in relative peace with the Goudges. Parthenia's suspicious eye seemed constantly upon her, but Delbert had reverted to his previous disinterest even as Uriah's vapid stares took on a guilty cast. As for Faith and Clarity, they seemed vaguely in awe of Honor, as if her open rebellion were a source of admiration—and hope.

It was Clarity, in fact, who carried the news of the men's discussion to Honor the following day. Honor was churning butter, a task that seemed to take forever and would be better left to the servants, who had gone off in search of kindling instead.

"We are going to be rich," Clarity announced, perching prettily on a three-legged stool. "Even richer than we already are!" She hugged herself and dimpled at Honor. "All those trees! And so many of them on our land! I shall have a marriage portion fit for a marquis!"

Honor glanced down at her hands to see if she'd acquired blisters yet. "I thought you didn't believe in titles," she remarked dryly.

Clarity was unscathed by the comment. "I believe in being rich. Politics and religion are all quite silly." She stretched languidly, admiring the curve of her bosom under the somber black gown. "I shan't be satisfied with a country squire like Lyndon Styles or even some stuffy old knight like Sir Ralph. How he wheezes! I could scarcely hear the others over the noise last night."

Honor paused in her churning and looked up at Clarity. "You heard them? How?"

Clarity lifted one slim shoulder. "There's a panel between the parlor and the withdrawing room, in the back of the bookshelves. I found it years ago when Faith and I had to clear away all the Blakes' blasphemous books. It's proved convenient."

Grimacing, Honor wished that she had known of the secret panel earlier. She was not above eavesdropping when it came to critical matters. "In truth," she remarked with studied detachment, "it sounds like a shame to me. The forest is a beautiful place. What will become of the animals?"

Clarity gave another faint shrug. "They'll go elsewhere. What does it matter? There are trees aplenty in England." She didn't notice Honor's glance of dismay. "Of course my father and the others think they'll flush Captain Hood from his hiding place. The reward would be a fine thing, but I'd hate to see him hanged. He sounds most romantic."

Honor's grip tightened on the churn. She had worried all along that if the deforestation order was carried out, Justin's hideaway would be discovered. Reports of a half dozen robberies between Burton and Nottingham indicated Hood and his men were still in the vicinity. The news had both comforted and galled Honor. Why had he not tried to contact her? Had he merely trifled with her body as any scoundrel might do with a foolish maid? Was his defection the punishment she'd expected for her sin? Yet he had confided in her; he had put his safety in her hands. No matter that he was a Royalist thief, she could not rest until she delivered a warning to Beggar's Oak.

Keeping her voice deliberately casual, Honor ignored Clarity's moonstruck remarks. "When is all this to happen?"

Clarity frowned at a ragged fingernail. "The survey begins tomorrow. Lyndon Styles will supervise."

Again, Clarity's self-absorption prevented her from seeing the startled reaction on Honor's face. Tomorrow! Honor's brain swung into action, searching for a plausible excuse to leave Creepers by herself. "Where does Matthew Thorn live?" she asked, hoping Clarity wouldn't find the question a queer sort of diversion.

But the other girl's face was blank as she slipped off the stool and shook out her skirts. "Somewhere by the river. I'm not sure." She was as disinterested in the schoolmaster as she was in the forest creatures. "I hear Mother. I must look busy or suffer a lesson on idleness." Clarity reached for a sack of potatoes and a paring knife. But Mistress Goudge's quick step passed by and continued on outside. Taking advantage of Parthenia's departure, Honor thrust the churn at Clarity.

"I've all but finished," she said, offering the other girl her most winning smile. "But I must take some lessons to Master Thorn. He has difficulty walking in this foggy weather."

Apparently it never occurred to Clarity that a blind man would not be hampered by fog. Nor did she offer any suggestion as to who might know where Master Thorn lived. Honor was just as well pleased; she'd at least have an excuse for not actually calling on the schoolmaster.

The fog had lifted by the time she reached the great stand of trees. The earth's rich dampness mingled with the smell of winter's decay. Honor glanced about for the first brave sprouts of greenery. To her delight, the sweet violet had burst from the ground with its heart-shaped leaves and scented purple flower. "Wood violets," Aunt Lucy had called them, and to Honor, their bold arrival had always held the promise of spring.

Somehow it was easier for Honor to concentrate on Nature's wonders than on the realities of her self-appointed task. This time she was sure she hadn't been followed. Delbert and Uriah had gone out at dawn, presumably to the brick kiln in the village. Parthenia had been nowhere in sight when Honor left, Clarity had displayed her usual indifference to the activities of others, and Faith was stitching herself a new dress for the Sabbath. Yet Honor was uneasy, afraid that she wouldn't find Justin at Beggar's Oak—and anxious as to what might happen if she did.

Without the highwayman as her escort, the enormous tree appeared forbidding rather than awe inspiring. It also seemed deserted. No outlook stood on guard, no sign of horses was in evidence, not even the chatter of the saucy squirrel greeted Honor as she reined in a few yards from Beggar's Oak. Where was Captain Hood—Justin, as she now called him to herself. Had he moved out in the past few days to ply the London-Oxford Road? Or west to the coastal routes of Exmoor and Devon? Honor stared blankly at the oak's scaly bark, aware that her untrained eye couldn't detect the real trunk from the false.

"Damn and blast!" she cursed aloud, startling the little mare. As her hand soothed the animal's neck, she suddenly heard that strange birdlike call that had passed between Justin and Nip on her first visit to Beggar's Oak. Looking in every direction, she tried to find its source but saw nothing except for the huge trees and the glowering gray clouds. Honor shivered under her cloak and patted the mare again, this time not only giving but seeking comfort.

The high-pitched sound was repeated. Honor turned in what she gauged to be the direction from which it came but still saw nothing. Puzzled, she was about to dismount when a flurry of booted feet and flying cape descended to the ground some ten feet away. Honor failed to stifle a scream as Justin Blake steadied himself and grinned from behind the mask.

"My love! You braved winter's cruel weather to see me? I'm enormously flattered!" He pulled off his hat and made a deep bow as the little mare moved skittishly under Honor.

Despite her mingled astonishment and relief, Honor's temper was piqued by Justin's remark. There he stood, unruffled, as if the time apart had meant nothing to him. She knew the risks involved in any attempt to seek her out yet felt that her surrender had been ample evidence of her own willingness to take great chances. Did he not share her feelings, or, as she feared, did he regard the episode as a passing pleasure?

"I brought you news," she said stiffly.

"Ah." He had moved closer, one gloved hand on the mare's bridle. "Concerning what, sweet Honor?" His curiosity seemed mild indeed; he seemed more irritatingly self-possessed than ever.

Your neck, she wanted to snap back at him, but the very thought caused her to shiver. "Must we stand about like a pair of forest elves? I feel as if every sort of creature must be spying on us."

Justin hesitated, then made an elaborate bow. "Enter unto my rustic bower, mistress. Pray excuse the clutter, but the servants have gone to the Saint Valentine's Fair."

For Honor, brought up under Puritan rule, the allusion to celebrating a saint's feast day was as much of a myth as Justin's nonexistent servants. Inside the tree, the brazier burned as before, a kettle of steaming barley soup hung from an iron stanchion, and a bottle of red wine sat on the table. She couldn't help but wonder how the four men could live in such cramped quarters for any length of time. Surely it was a tribute to Justin's leadership that they managed without trying to kill one another. She remembered a particularly harsh winter some five years ago when the inhabitants of Whitehorse Manor had been marooned for almost a fortnight. Even amiable Aunt Lucy had grown testy, and the three young girls had all but physically assaulted one another before the thaw.

Honor sensed that Justin was more indulgent than expectant. Nonetheless, she would communicate the news she had brought. "There's to be a survey of the forest. The trees are to be cut down, by order of Dick Cromwell." Justin twirled his hat in his hand. "I know." Unperturbed, he looked musingly at Honor. "I'm blessed with extra ears, some of which are not my own."

It occurred to Honor that he might give her credit for possessing one of those pairs, which had hoped to be of aid. But he seemed oblivious to the risk she had taken on his behalf. "I wasted my time then," she said, and realized she sounded sulky.

"That depends," he remarked lightly, uncorking the wine bottle.

"On what, pray?" Honor asked stiffly as he poured out two tumblers of wine and handed one to her.

But the highwayman's facile mood deserted him. He put out a hand to tip back the hood of her cape. The golden hair was confined not by a snug linen cap but by a white bandeau. "On whether you came to warn me … or to love me," he said softly.

"I told you," she asserted doggedly, "I brought news." Her attempt at severity failed when Justin twined a thick lock of her hair around his fingers and brushed her cheek.

"You brought yourself." The eyes behind the mask were shimmering, like a mountain lake. Honor felt mesmerized as she watched him take the tumbler from her and set it down on the table next to its mate. "Be honest," he urged, "do you offer me stale news … or yourself?"

"No!" The refusal burst from Honor's lips. "You toy with me, like a child with a ball. If it rolls his way, he'll catch it. If it doesn't, he ignores it, he won't trouble himself to go find it." Her chin jutted and her eyes sparked. "I won't allow you to use me thus!"

His features hardened. "Then you should not have come." His free hand gripped the pugnacious chin. "When you are away from me, I can try to keep your image at bay. Often, I succeed, but then a glint of gold or a pair of dark eyes will remind me, and I'm immersed in memory." His mouth twisted with self-reproach. " 'Tis wrong. I cannot afford to dream."

"Why not?" Honor demanded, pulling free. She envisioned her own future as an unattainable desire in Justin's imagination. "Can't any man dream?"

Little clouds of steam rose from the iron kettle, a cozy mix of broth and beef. But there was nothing warm or homely about the face behind the mask. Justin had turned grim. "My dreams were dashed long ago. I put my trust in Fate. Now you tempt me to do otherwise."

"That's nonsense," Honor countered hotly. "We make our own way in life, and if we do God's will, we're rewarded. If we don't," she added, aware of the sudden doubt in her voice, "we're punished. Or so I was taught."

"How busy God must be!" Justin remarked, injecting only a hint of his usual glibness into the words. "We all suffer, we all rejoice. I see nothing providential in life's daily toil, only that its end is inevitable."

Honor had not come to Beggar's Oak to argue but to warn. Instead, she was discovering a disconcerting side of Justin Blake. With a futile gesture, Honor tried to convey her frustration. "You blame me for unsettling your fatalistic notions? What have I done except try to help you?"

A pained expression crossed Justin's face. "That's unfair, an offense to both of us. You ride up to Beggar's Oak like any mindless maid seeking her lover. You are heedless of the danger to yourself as well as to me, and to my men." He was speaking much more rapidly than usual, as if he were firing the words from a gun. He had moved closer to Honor, placing his hands on the rough-hewn cupboard behind her head. "I plead with you to go away, to end what can only be a torment to us both. But you are here and now I can't let you go. Not yet."

His hands remained braced against the cupboard, imprisoning Honor even as his mouth came down on hers. The words she would have uttered in protest were lost in the mingling of their lips as his kiss deepened, disturbed, demanded. Her body, which had been rigid with tension only moments ago, collapsed pliantly against him. Honor savored his mouth, drank in his kisses and dizzily surrendered herself to the sudden impatience of his touch.

As their garments fell away in a soft rustle of linen and wool, Honor submitted her nakedness to his delighted scrutiny.

"You are so beautiful," he said in a hushed, awed voice. His hand remained in her hair as he stood before her in primeval masculine splendor. To her astonishment, she was as eager to explore that taut, lean body as he was to possess every inch of her soft, rounded flesh. She took one step toward Justin and locked her fingers behind his head.

"If this is torment I relish it like rain on parched earth," she whispered, kissing his rugged face again and again.

"More like dew on the rose," he replied, caressing her buttocks with both hands. "There is no dry, arid quality in you—you are vital, flourishing life. If only," he went on, burying his face in the curve of her shoulder, "I could see into the future!"

She stroked his back from neck to hip. "Why can't we forge it together? Why must the world intrude?"

His answer was to lift her high in his arms, like captured booty wrested from grudging hands. Honor took a deep breath, then closed her eyes as he lowered her onto the narrow bed. His mouth devoured every inch of her, his fingers plied the most secret places, his body consumed hers in a rite of passion as ancient as time, as new as the dawn. She responded with an ardor that matched his own, like fire to flint, like waves to wind. There was no guilt, only need. And, as Honor's heart drowned out her conscience, there was love. When at last they lay replete in each other's arms, Honor was overcome with fatigue and began to doze against his chest.

"I should go," she murmured drowsily, but instead nestled even closer.

"Bide awhile," Justin urged, smoothing the tangle of golden tresses from her temple. "I'll watch over you."

Honor's reply was a smothered purr of consent. Yet even as she started to drift into sleep, she felt the rhythmic movement of his body next to hers. "Justin!" She called his name sharply and sat up, shaking herself vigorously. If they both slept, who would stand guard? Clearly, Justin had been at the sentry's post when she arrived. No doubt her mare was still outside, cropping contentedly but offering evidence that humans were nearby.

Justin blinked and stretched. "What is it? Is something wrong?" With some effort he focused on Honor, who had clambered out of bed and was gathering her clothes.

"You're right, Justin," she asserted grimly. "I'm a detriment to you. You grow careless in my presence. Where," she inquired, hurriedly slipping into her undergarments, "are the others?"

He pulled himself into a sitting position and ran his hands through his dark hair. "They forage. We spend but a fraction of our ill-got gain for ourselves. Ergo, we degenerate into chicken thieves." His lopsided grin was both comic and endearing.

"In truth, Justin, I can't picture you crawling about a henhouse with feathers in your cloak. Surely there must be Royalist supporters who would provide victuals."

He stood up, making no effort to cover his nakedness. Honor paused, a hand at her bodice, and suppressed a desire to reenter his arms. "There are some," he conceded, noting the parted lips and arrested fingers, "but not enough." With that leisurely male grace, he moved around the brazier to touch her cheek. "Would you ride with us, sweet Honor? Would you risk all to gain all?"

Honor stared into the green eyes, which suddenly glittered like emerald fire. Her initial reaction was that he jested, but the sharp cast of his features and the aggressive jaw gave frivolity the lie. She longed to be with him, to share his life, to be his comfort and his companion. But to join his band of Royalist thieves? Deep within, memory stirred, of agonized screams, of bloodstained walls, of laughing soldiers mocking death. Justin Blake was the man she loved, but Captain Hood espoused a cause she loathed. Honor recoiled from the idea of aiding the enemy who had murdered her parents.

"I..." Honor tried to speak, but her voice failed. She saw the sudden twist of Justin's mouth and was ashamed. "I could never ...." Turning abruptly, she hid her face from him and felt the tears sting her eyes.

"Of course." The words were stiff. "It was an absurd request. I must have been mad to ask such a thing of you."

Biting her lips, she fought the tears but still kept her back to him. She could tell that he, too, was getting dressed, very quickly, and keeping his distance as far as the circular confines of the room would allow. Matching her pace to his, she threw the cloak over her shoulders and tied the bandeau around her hair. A moment later they were facing each other, with Justin's hand at the door.

Honor knew she should not put the question to him but couldn't help herself. "Will I see you again?" She was annoyed at the plaintive note in her voice.

"I told you," he answered lightly, "I believe in Fate."

Honor's gaze was bleak. "I've failed you," she murmured as he peered out through a tiny hole in the door.

"We're victims of our upbringing," Justin replied, still in that casual tone. "We live by what we've been taught. Often it's proved wrong." His hand was at her back, guiding her through the opening in the tree.

Stepping over the threshold, Honor turned to look back at him. "We're strangers, aren't we?" she asked dully, and then was disturbed by the idea that she seemed to trust him with her body but could not let him share her soul.

"As I said, we come from different worlds. It's no one's fault, but it builds great barriers." His hand fell away as he put his fingers to his mouth and made the birdlike call that Honor had come to recognize as the highwaymen's signal. In return, a similar cry floated on the winter air and he nodded once. "My men are coming back. I trust they've been successful."

Acknowledging the futility of further disagreement, at least in front of Justin's comrades, Honor moved silently toward the little mare, who had patiently waited for its rider. With a sweep of her cloak, she climbed into the saddle, gave the mare a nudge and rode out through the grove of giant oaks.

Chapter Ten

SAINT BARNABAS CHURCH RESTED BY the Mill Fleam in the ragged shadow of Rutbury Castle. Originally both priory and parish, the church had suffered at the hands of Henry VIII's reformers. The castle's stone skeleton gave evidence to Cromwell's relentless assault on the Royalists who had vainly tried to save Rutbury from the Puritan usurpers.

It was the third week of April when Honor happened to glimpse Lady Ferrers in the graveyard outside Saint Barnabas. Honor had visited the church on a whim, to search out the Blake family's graves. Somewhat to her surprise, the large stone marker over the family plot had been left untouched by the Puritans. Time and weather had blurred many of the names, but she could make out some five generations, going back to the time of Henry VII. The last Blake to be buried at Saint Barnabas was a child named Philip, in 1631. He had been only six months old and Honor conjectured that he might have been Justin's brother. She was scraping off a growth of lichen from another Blake marker when Lady Ferrers came in from Church Street with a plump little maid in tow.

The former Philene Godard didn't appear to recognize Honor but nodded in a vague sort of way before approaching the church vestibule. Somewhat furtively, Honor watched her go inside, no doubt to the Ferrers family vault, which was located on the east side of the nave. Stalling for time, Honor continued her study of the tombstones, which provided a capsule history of Rutbury. The first Ferrers apparently had been in William the Conqueror's van and had built Rutbury Castle on a hillock above the river. He had also constructed the church and priory, apparently in thanksgiving for his wife's safe delivery of a Ferrers heir. The six centuries of continuity were not lost on

Honor, but she wondered if the present Lady Ferrers gave a fig for English tradition. Assuming a pensive air, Honor saw the Frenchwoman emerge from the church's west entrance. Her taffy-colored embroidered skirts swished above saucy layers of petticoats while the little maid trailed behind at a decorous distance.

This time, Philene paused on the limestone walk to greet Honor in a surprisingly direct manner. "You're from Creepers, is that not so?" she asked with a lilting French accent. "You are one Goudge?"

Honor kept from bridling at the mere suggestion. "No. I'm … their ward. My name is Honor Dale, from Whitehorse Manor in Oxfordshire." She watched the other young woman carefully to see if the name meant anything to her. Surely Tyler Vail would have at least mentioned his fiancée.

But Philene Ferrers's lovely oval face remained blank. "Oxfordshire? Where the great university is located?" She saw Honor nod. "Ah—I know of it. But I know little of English geography, alas."

Alas indeed, thought Honor. Either Philene had a faulty memory or Tyler had kept his betrothal a secret. It shouldn't matter at this late date—but somehow it did. Honor abruptly changed the subject. "Your husband's forebears rest inside the church, I believe. I've seen the tombs at Sunday service."

The blue eyes blinked once. "So tiresome, those services. The vicar drones on and on about nothing, and the curate bellows forever about everything. I shall become a Catholic again after …." Philene clamped her bow-shaped lips shut, then dimpled self-deprecatingly at Honor. "But I mustn't say such things in this country, eh? Catholics are hated even more than the High Church followers. You are, of course, a Puritan?"

"Of course." Honor lifted her shoulders in a gesture that dismissed all other possibilities. "Your husband is a Puritan, too, I gather."

Philene cast a swift look at her maid, who was patiently standing next to a border of primroses and looking suitably demure. "My husband, he is what you would call 'Reformed.' " She molded the word carefully on her bowshaped lips, as if it were an unpleasant sensation.

Ancient lineage notwithstanding, Sir Ralph seemed to have cast his lot against the monarchy and thrown his support behind the Commonwealth. "I suppose," Honor said with what she hoped was her most ingenuous expression, "that Oliver Cromwell rewarded his services by allowing him to keep his fine home at Smallwood."

"I suppose." Philene was losing interest in the conversation. "But it is a dull place, far from any amusements." The long dark lashes fluttered over iris-blue eyes. "He promised we'd go often to London, even to Paris. But it's been almost ten months since we wed and we have gone no farther than the Burton

Road, only to be waylaid by robbers. I lost many beautiful jewels and cried for three days. Now my dear husband is afraid to go anywhere until that nasty highwayman is arrested." Lady Ferrers was pouting mightily. It was possible that her manner might beguile her husband, but it had absolutely no effect on Honor. "*Mais*, he was very handsome," Philene remarked with a sly little smile, "even if he caused me much hurt."

"Hurt? Or loss?" Honor inquired a bit uncertainly. She had the feeling that Philene's failure to grasp the subtleties of the English language was hampering their conversation.

"Ah, *mais oui,* loss!" Lady Ferrers laid a delicate hand on her bosom while the little maid snickered. "He stole my diamonds, my sapphires, but not my heart! Handsome or not, I would refuse to be enticed by a thief!"

"I should think not," Honor murmured, feeling her cheeks grow warm. "Forgive me, I thought perhaps he'd made … advances."

Lady Ferrers's fine eyebrows lifted. "Well, *certainement,* it would be the insult if he failed to do so, eh? And," she went on, fixing Honor with that sparkling iris gaze, "then I would have been even more angry."

Honor forced a weak smile. "Yes, of course. But surely you were well chaperoned." The discourse had taken an unexpected turn. To her dismay, Honor was afraid to hear the reply.

Philene lowered her lashes and flicked her tongue over her lips. When she spoke, her voice was scarcely audible. "He stole a kiss." She looked coyly at Honor, whose face had turned to stone. "Imagine! There, in the coach, while my poor husband clutched his chest and moaned! Such audacity!"

Behind her mistress, the little maid giggled. Honor felt like throttling them both but kept the false smile pasted on her face. "I daresay," Philene amplified, "he would have stolen more had he been given the chance. As it was, I expressed my outrage most strongly." To prove her point, she assumed an uncharacteristically severe expression.

Honor lifted her chin in a more hostile gesture than she'd intended. "Perhaps he'll come back … and take what he missed."

Philene had the grace to blush. "La, Mistress … Dale?" She paused to eye Honor questioningly. "*Mafoi,* I should not encourage such a one, however handsome!"

The conviction of her words was undermined by the glint in her eyes. Honor tried to compose herself and was about to make a rejoinder when a lad with curly black hair careened to a stop by the lych-gate. "Ladyship!" he called, stopping to catch his breath, "Sir Ralph is ill! Can you come? I brought an extra horse."

Philene turned slowly, the blue eyes wide. "His heart?"

The lad nodded, looked as if he were about to cross himself, thought better of it and settled for placing a hand on the lapel of his green cloth coat. "Terrible bad pains, here. Worse than before."

"Mon Dieu," lamented Philene, glancing vaguely at Honor, "I've warned him not to drink so much of the red wines!" With a flick of the wrist directed toward the maid, Lady Ferrers hurried from the churchyard.

Honor watched the trio disappear before ambling restlessly back among the tombstones. She had never considered graveyards particularly morbid. It was the soul, not the body, that counted, and she rarely considered what happened to mortal remains after death. Indeed, she had no idea where her parents had been laid to rest, or even if they'd been given a proper Christian burial. Sometimes the thought bothered her so much that she couldn't bear to dwell on it.

But if pondering the fate of the dead could depress her, considering the feelings of the living was almost overwhelming. If Philene Ferrers could be believed, Captain Hood bestowed kisses on women the way bees stole pollen from flowers. He was, Philene insinuated, a bold seducer, a thief in every sense of the word. Yet he had confided in Honor. He had revealed a different side of himself, ostensibly a less confident, more vulnerable being than the facile highwayman who hid behind the mask.

Which, Honor wondered as she drifted aimlessly through the garden, was the real Justin Blake? Was he a rogue, a rebel, a rake? Or was he fired by integrity, idealism, illusion? It occurred to Honor that though she might love Captain Hood, she didn't know him. They were, as she had suggested to him earlier, strangers. Oblivious to the riot of golden daffodils and early irises, Honor moved out through the lych-gate. Spring, with its promise of hope and new life, was turning the countryside into a patchwork of bright color. Yet Honor's heart was cold, as if still in the grip of winter.

Most of the county came to Sir Ralph's funeral, which was held on Easter Monday. The grieving widow was supported by his three sons from a first marriage and Lyndon Styles, who had assumed the role of Rutbury's chief mourner. There was, of course, much speculation that Master Styles also aspired to Lady Ferrers's bed.

Honor attended with the Goudges, who seemed more disturbed at the loss of the most exalted personage in the vicinity than for any sentimental reasons. It was even possible that Faith and Clarity's show of tears was for the apparent defection of Lyndon Styles rather than for Sir Ralph.

Quentin Radcliffe gave the eulogy, using 1 Samuel, chapter 9, verse 3, "The Lost Asses." " 'Take now one of the servants with thee, and arise, go seek the asses,'" boomed Radcliffe from the pulpit. "And so Sir Ralph obeyed, enjoining his neighbors to search for the godless bandits who roam our roads and forest. Yea, though he might slay the hare and cut the tree, he would find these spawns of Satan. But the Devil stood between Sir Ralph and his holy crusade. Now, I charge you, in the name of God Almighty, to gird your loins, pluck up your courage and take ax in hand to drive the wickedness from Burton Old Forest!"

Appalled at Radcliffe's attempt to twist a sacred service into a means of achieving self-serving ends, Honor surreptitiously glanced about the church. Delbert Goudge was nodding solemnly, Lyndon Styles was presenting a stalwart appearance even as he patted the widow's shoulder, and most of the other men present wore determined expressions befitting Richard the Lionhearted's doughtiest knights.

Honor forced herself to concentrate not on the rapaciousness of the mourners but on the finely wrought stained glass window with its blue shield set between six small lions rampant. Across the aisle, near the alabaster tomb of the Ferrers, Matthew Thorn stood as stiff as any monument, his staff at his side. Honor wondered what he was thinking. She was almost sure that his reaction to Radcliffe's eulogy would be similar to her own.

Radcliffe had finally run out of steam and the congregation was singing a doleful hymn that grated on Honor's ear. Parthenia's shrill voice rose above the others, as if she were trying to shriek her way to heaven. When Vicar Busby offered the final prayers, Honor all but bolted from the pew. Several members of the congregation were milling about the vestibule, calling their neighbors to arms.

"Hood might as well have murdered poor old Ferrers," asserted a bristling Lyndon Styles. "We owe His Lordship Hood's life."

A pert face with lively blue eyes thrust itself between Styles and Honor. "You owe a lot of things to a lot of people, but not that highwayman's life." Despite having what Honor guessed was a normally benevolent nature, the woman now wore a pugnacious expression. Lyndon Styles was clearly caught off guard.

"Now, Mistress Tipper, you of all people ought not to speak of owing!" he reproached her. "If ever a man took rather than gave, it's Will …."

"Took *back*, you mean," Judith Tipper interrupted with a wave of her fist. "Will and I never did hold with Roundhead ways. Every Puritan from Uttoxeter to Burton took advantage of us! I hope Hood steals you all blind!"

Styles's ruddy face looked near to rupture. "Your son was savagely beaten by those scurrilous thieves! Have you no loyalty to your own flesh?"

Mistress Tipper was scornful. " 'Twas an adventure for the lad. Jamie yearned to be a hero for the Appleby maid and got a rap on the head for his daring. As for Hood, he's merely playing a ridiculous game forced upon him by the Roundheads. To think that Rutbury was once a Royalist stronghold!"

She put a hand to her Sabbath-best cap and emitted a groan.

Lyndon Styles was not to be silenced so easily, however. Encouraged by the little crowd that had gathered around them, he was about to launch a counterattack when Matthew Thorn's husky voice cut in. "Here, now," he rumbled, "is it necessary to remind good Christian people that we are in the House of God?"

"Necessary?" snapped Mistress Tipper. "It's imperative! Most of these hypocrites don't know God from cod!" With that parting sally, she sailed down the main aisle. Honor watched her departure with admiration, wondering if Parthenia had met her match.

It was Matthew Thorn who accompanied Honor from the church, his stout staff thumping along the length of the nave. "Alas, our neighbors seem ready to deforest their surroundings with or without Dick Cromwell's written consent. I trust you're not privy to your cousin's will in this matter?"

Honor wasn't privy to any of Dick Cromwell's erratic attempts at clinging to the Protectorate, but before she could tactfully avoid saying so, Faith came hurrying toward them.

"Honor!" she cried. "Come! We must leave. Father has tried to punch Squire Wills!"

Puzzled, Honor stared at Faith. "But why? Is he still angry over the broken betrothal?"

Nervously, Faith glanced beyond the graveyard to a cluster of people at the roadside. "Father is claiming some of Squire Wills's trees as his own. He thinks that because Prudence isn't marrying Uriah we should be given some of her dowry as an appeasement."

"And the good squire disagrees?" Honor inquired dryly as she watched the group pull apart, half apparently moving away with the Goudge faction, the other with Squire Wills.

Next to Honor, Matthew Thorn grunted. "So the wrangling has begun," he murmured.

"Indeed," Honor replied, telling herself that she should have foreseen the infighting. Greed was often a greater obstacle among allies than the opposition. Before she could say as much, Parthenia Goudge sprang through the lych-gate, gesturing vigorously at both Honor and Faith.

"Come along, come along, we've much to do. Half of Rutbury has gone mad!"

Repressing the desire to ask which half, Honor bade Master Thorn farewell and followed Faith up the limestone walk. The family's spotless open carriage, used only for church services, stood across the road. Durwood sat stiffly on the driver's platform, his rheumatic hands barely able to hold the horses' reins. As the three women hurried to join Delbert and Uriah, a rumble of criticism arose from the mourners who still flanked Squire Wills.

"Dog meat, all of them," muttered Parthenia, heaving her stout body into the carriage. "Where's Clarity?"

Faith moved over on the cushioned seat to make room for Honor. "Lady Ferrers asked her to help out at Smallwood. Visitors from London are coming, no doubt to pay their respects to Sir Ralph."

Parthenia smacked at her billowing skirts and snorted. "A lot of good that does him now! They'd better not be troublemakers! And why didn't Clarity ask permission?"

"She did." Delbert glowered, his temper still smoldering. "How else are we to keep an eye on Lyndon Styles or any of these other turncoats?" Pulling a wrinkled handkerchief from his pocket, he blew his nose with great energy. "Think of it," he continued, leaning forward on the seat as Durwood weakly flicked the reins. "That oaf of a Wills and his cronies will hardly take a piss before waiting to see which way the political winds blow!"

"Master Goudge!" reprimanded his wife sharply. "Cease that vulgar speech lest the Good Lord snatch away your tongue!" Parthenia sat very straight, bust out, shoulders back, oblivious to the carriage's swaying motion under Durwood's feeble guidance. "Let the Devil take Squire Wills and all his ilk. We'll find another bride for Uriah, a better match than that simpering little sow from Buttermilk Hill!"

"Who, may I ask?" Delbert demanded with fire in his eye. "Lady Ferrers?"

Parthenia ignored her husband's heavy-handed sarcasm and gazed at the object of their discussion. Uriah was calmly sitting next to his father, shredding a thick piece of straw and sneaking occasional looks at Honor. "That French hussy might do," Mistress Goudge said, clearly calculating advantages and disadvantages. "If Sir Ralph had an ounce of sense, which I doubt, he would have left everything to his sons. His widow may well find herself packing to go back to that Papist-riddled homeland of hers. Still, I wouldn't wish the likes of some foreign baggage on our boy. There must be a dozen suitable maidens close by."

It seemed to Honor that as Parthenia's words trailed off, both she and her spouse had turned in concert. Sitting next to Faith, Honor all but squirmed under the probing gazes of Master and Mistress Goudge. The fresh April air no longer smelled so sweet, the breeze stopped blowing through the tall cotton grass, and alongside the road, the River Dove seemed to stand still. Surely the Goudges couldn't mean to marry her to Uriah.

"Well?" rasped Parthenia. "If Dick Cromwell can hold on to the country, it would be a miraculous mating."

Honor's first reaction was to deny that Dick could hold on to his hat, let alone the government. But even for her own sake, she dared not be so disloyal.

Indeed, the utterance of such words could be construed as treason. Honor refused to put such a weapon in the Goudges' dishonorable hands.

Delbert was stuffing the wretched kerchief back in his pocket. He leaned his bulk into his son as Durwood allowed the horses to lead him onto the road that curved toward Creepers. "Well?" he inquired of his son. "What think you?"

"About what?" inquired Uriah blankly.

Parthenia bristled and Delbert sighed. "Never mind," he said. "For now." He sat back on the carriage seat and probed his nose with thumb and forefinger. Honor looked the other way. Ahead lay Creepers; to her left lay the road to Beggar's Oak. She felt more like a prisoner than ever.

Yet another heated debate was going on at Creepers, this time in the paddock. Lyndon Styles, holding a bay hunter by the reins, was arguing that a delegation should ride to London and obtain official permission to start cutting down Burton Old Forest. "We need an answer *now*," Styles asserted, underscoring his point with a wave of his crop. "God's eyes, man, the spring is almost gone!"

"So?" Master Goudge was trying to keep calm as well as avoid committing himself in the face of an unstable political situation. "Then we've still got the summer. Have you no faith in the Protector?"

Styles glared at Goudge from under hooded eyes. "Why should I? He'll be lucky to escape his creditors, let alone his opponents! The man's finished, dead as a decoy!"

Honor, who was just inside the stable currying the little mare, saw Styles give a tug to the bay's reins. Unfortunately, his assessment of the younger Cromwell was accurate. In the four months since Parliament's return, Cousin Dick's hand had slowly but surely slipped from the government's neck. While she felt sorry for her kinsman, Honor realized that his fall could save her from the proposed marriage to Uriah.

It was Clarity, however, who entered the stable from the rear door, a saddle thrown over one slim arm. "Trees, trees, trees," she complained, hanging the saddle in its place on the far wall. "I wish I were back at Smallwood, where conversation is far more amusing."

Making one last pass with the curry comb, Honor shot Clarity a look of rebuke. "Amusing? I thought Smallwood was plunged into mourning."

Clarity moved around Honor to close the door on the vociferous argument between Master Goudge and Lyndon Styles. "Lady Ferrers isn't narrow-minded and strict like ...." Her eyes darted toward the door, as if she expected Mistress Goudge to walk through wood. "Never mind, but I hated to come home."

Honor didn't blame Clarity. She even wondered if once out from under Mistress Goudge's stifling influence, both daughters might turn into decent human beings. Clarity had the warmth; Faith possessed compassion. For once, Clarity was not speaking of herself but of Philene Ferrers.

"Being more worldly, the French don't consider love a sin," Clarity was saying as she checked out a saddle girth. "Or mayhap it's because they're Papists. Imagine," she breathed, turning to Honor with sparkling eyes, "if such a recent English widow was to take a lover so soon!"

"A lover?" By reflex, Honor glanced in the direction of the paddock. "Squire Styles?"

Clarity wrinkled her nose. "Of course not! He's a pompous boor compared with the highwayman."

At first no words passed over lips that had suddenly gone dry as Honor tried to counter Clarity's statement. But as the other girl began to regard her with puzzlement, Honor fought for composure. "You mean Captain Hood … or …?"

"Of course." Clarity was quite matter-of-fact, clearly practicing the art of sophistication for her next visit to Smallwood. "I saw him climb through Lady Ferrers's *boudoir* window." She pronounced the French word carefully, if broadly, but Honor was much more interested in facts than linguistics. "Who else could it be?" Clarity asked with a shrug as she began to coax her favorite gray with an apple. "Any honorable suitor would come up to the front door, along with Squire and the rest."

Fighting to keep her disquiet to herself, Honor merely nodded. For all of Clarity's flightiness and vanity, she was no fool. Who indeed would come by stealth to Smallwood?

Who had come that way to Creepers?

Honor mumbled something about candling eggs and stumbled outside into the now empty paddock. As luck would have it, she met no one else between there and her chamber, where she burst into tears as the pain of betrayal pierced her laboring heart.

LATER, WHEN SHE HAD WASHED her face and tried to untangle her hair with a tortoiseshell comb, Honor made a desperate attempt to put Clarity's news in perspective. The May sunshine, which had briefly crept behind the lamb's-wool clouds, now came out to cast long shafts of light through the mullioned windows. Yet Honor's spirits were scarcely lifted by the fine weather. If Hood had betrayed her with the Frenchwoman, there was absolutely nothing she could do about it. Honor had no hold on him, they'd spoken no vows, there had been no mutual declarations of love or promises of fidelity. Nor was Philene Ferrers a Puritan. A liaison between her and Captain Hood not only wounded Honor but pointed up the differences between herself and the highwayman.

Unable to sit still, Honor moved restlessly about the little room. Glancing from her window, she saw Uriah talking to Jamie Tipper. The youth, who had been hurt during the robbery six months ago, had grown both taller and broader. Though fully recovered from his injury, he had never resumed his post as Master Thorn's assistant. Apparently, since both he and Sarah Appleby had discovered his manhood, Jamie's interests had become more adult. Certainly he seemed very grown-up next to the younger boy who had rushed up behind him waving a sheaf of papers. The lad possessed the same flaxen hair and long legs as Jamie, causing Honor to decide they must be brothers. Listening patiently to the boy's agitated explanation, Jamie turned to Uriah, who seemed to take some time to respond. At last, he pointed up to Honor's window and indicated the back door. Less than two minutes later, Honor was admitting him to her chamber.

"I'm Jeremy Tipper, Jamie's brother," he piped, standing stiff as a soldier. "Master Thorn asked me to deliver these lessons. He's taken ill again. Thank you." He spoke all in a rush, barely pausing for breath, and Honor judged from the relieved expression on his faintly sunburned face that he had discharged the sum of his duty without a flaw. Jeremy was no more than ten or eleven, a spindly child with nervous gray eyes. Only the stubborn chin reminded Honor of Judith Tipper.

"Master Thorn gave you these?" Honor asked, gesturing with the papers before setting them down on her dressing table. Impossible as it might seem, she was speaking in a normal voice, as if her world had not been shattered within the hour.

But Jeremy was shaking his head with vigor. "Nay, mistress, he left them by the henhouse."

"Oh. He lives nearby then?" The query was wooden, but Honor knew she had to force herself to act as if nothing extraordinary had happened.

"Not exactly," Jeremy replied, puffing up his thin chest. "He lives by the river, in a cave."

"A cave!" Honor couldn't help but gasp, a reaction that seemed to please young Jeremy, who obviously seldom had such important news to convey. "I should love to explore the caves," she went on, though the idea had never before occurred to her. "Perhaps you could take me someday."

His gray eyes sparkled. "There's spires and crags, too, great rocks huge as a house. This is a wondrous place, better than the rest of England," he asserted, the thin chest all but bursting like a rooster's at sunup.

"You've traveled much then?" Honor asked, surprised that she was able to offer Jeremy a feeble smile.

"My, yes," Jeremy answered. "I've been to Burton and Paget's Bromley and even Uttoxeter."

"I'm impressed," Honor declared. "You are indeed the ideal guide."

Jeremy cast a quick glance up at Honor, then looked away, though his grin was as wide as it was shy. "I can show you tree creepers and giant bellflowers and even Toad's Mouth Rock. That is," he amended as the grin disappeared, "if you can be gone for more than three hours."

"I'll see about that," Honor replied, assuming as serious an expression as his. From outside, they both heard his name called by Jamie. Jeremy started past Honor, trying to remember the rest of his manners. A jerky bow gave evidence to his upbringing. In a flash, he raced from the room and down the hallway before Honor could say goodbye.

Jeremy's youthful innocence had charmed her, momentarily dispelling the gloom under which she had fallen. But his leave-taking only served to remind her that she had lost her own innocence, not once but twice—first, to King Charles's murderous soldiers, and again, to a faithless Royalist highwayman.

Chapter Eleven

When Honor had told Justin Blake that she believed people could fashion their own fate, she had been sincere. Preachers claimed that a good man acquired wealth because God rewarded him. Honor, however, saw a different reason for the same result: a diligent person made money because he worked hard to earn it. In that vein, she set out to unravel the enigma of the highwayman's amorous conduct. She had to know the truth, and only a confrontation with him would serve her purpose.

As twilight settled in over Creepers two days later, Honor saddled up the little mare and slipped off toward Burton Old Forest. The past days, which she'd spent mulling over Hood's alleged infidelity, had robbed her of sleep, taken away her appetite and reduced her usual high energy to a low ebb. Something had to be done, and only Honor could do it.

Certainly Captain Hood had behaved as if he not only desired her body but yearned after her heart. At least he had alluded to a future, however tenuous, for the two of them. He had also given her the means to undo him—and his cause. Surely that was a sign of ultimate trust, especially in light of her Cromwell connections. His betrayal of her made no sense; he could only break her heart. But Honor could take his life.

With this conundrum whirling in her brain, she rode deeper into the forest. The light thinned, the bog oaks blotted out the sky. Honor reined up, unsure of the way in the gathering gloom. Belmot Gate, the little brook, the abandoned byre were all behind her. But in the darkness the trees looked alike, a great army of stalwart trunks and massive branches, as indistinguishable as the soldiers of a regiment poised for attack.

The owl that hooted overhead startled both Honor and the mare, but it was the sound that immediately followed that raised a real alarm. Hoofbeats at a canter caused Honor to sit her horse in motionless apprehension. The minutes dragged by as she waited for the lone rider to pass. At last, some twenty yards away, an old-fashioned steeple-crown hat, a flowing cloak and perhaps a beard presented only a sketchy impression. But there was something familiar about the way the man sat his horse, and even the animal itself was no stranger to Honor. With a gasp, she recognized Shandy first—and then Captain Hood. Her first impulse was to trot after them, but when Hood turned slightly in the saddle, she shrank back. Her bold plan was doomed. Hood had business elsewhere, that was clear, and any prolonged discussion would be untimely.

With a bitter taste in her mouth, Honor also realized that even if she had found Hood at Beggar's Oak, the chances were that they would have ended up making love, not peace. So it had been before; so it would be again. They would resolve nothing by pleasuring each other's bodies instead of pouring out their hearts.

But at least Hood's unexpected appearance served a purpose. If Honor kept her distance but didn't lose him from sight, she'd get back to the Belmot Road safely. They had gone only a few hundred yards when it dawned on her that he was heading not for the vicinity of Creepers but for Buttermilk Hill. Even as the slip of a moon rose over Stubby Lane, Honor knew she should turn back. Now that she had her bearings again, she could find the way. But up ahead, just barely within view, Captain Hood was turning off between a row of poplars that served to break the wind for a burgeoning field of corn. Her better nature—or was it fear?—told her to ride on, to head for the river and the village. But with a defiant swing of her golden hair, Honor plunged after Hood. She had gone only halfway along the edge of the field when she saw the outline of a big house and knew instinctively that it was Smallwood.

Giant rhododendron bushes, some of them still in full bloom, cut off Honor's view. Carefully dismounting, she crept between the glossy-leafed shrubs until she could see what must be the back of the house. Only a few candles still glowed at the windows, but Hood was silhouetted against one of them, a hand at the glass. Inside, Philene Ferrers sat at her dressing table, the plump little maid hovering at her mistress's elbow.

Honor turned away. She didn't need to see any more. She had found out what she had wanted to know.

THE ORIGINAL MANOR HOUSE AT Smallwood had been demolished in the early fifteenth century. Its successor had burned to the ground shortly before Queen Elizabeth's coronation, and the present house was a late-sixteenth gem of perpendicular architecture. Some visitors likened it to a miniature version of fabled Hardwick Hall in Derbyshire; others compared it to Burghley House in Buckinghamshire. All agreed that the house was a handsome, commodious dwelling with its tall mullioned windows, long second-floor gallery, great fireplaces and the towers with weather vanes that flanked the main entrance.

It was at the bay window in the rear of the house that the cloaked figure rapped softly in the moonlight. The woman seated in front of her mirror fixed her eyes on the reflection, then called to her maid.

"Mignon?" Philene Ferrers waited for the petite servant to emerge from the wardrobe; almost at the same moment the figure outside stepped back into the shrubbery. "Mignon, *je suis très fatiguée.* You may leave me now."

The little maid curtsied from the room as Philene plaited her long dark hair and secured it with a satin ribbon. Again she looked in the mirror; again she saw the cloaked figure. This time she rose on slippered feet to lock the door and blow out the candles before she opened the window.

"Quickly, *mon cher,*" she whispered, standing aside so that her nocturnal visitor could swing over the sill. *"Mon Dieu,"* she exclaimed, noting the heavy beard and bushy brows under the steeple-crowned hat, "who is this man that invades my *boudoir*?"

Captain Hood's grin flashed in the dark beard. "I am but half a man tonight, Philene." He bent to kiss her cheek, ignoring her shudder at the touch of his coarse beard. "There was little time to assemble a full-blown character after I received your message."

"Bien-tout." Philene shrugged, all traces of coyness gone. She moved briskly to a little cabinet and felt for glasses and decanter. "Brandy? I would offer port, but you stole our merchant's supply."

Hood sat down on the settee with its bold pattern of chrysanthemums. "If Shandy drinks brandy, then so should Hood." He made a face at his impromptu verse. "I grow weary of mind and body, Philene. How long must we wait?"

"You? Weary? La, *mon capitaine,*" she said, laughing low in her throat, "such is not your mode!" Handing him the brandy glass, she dropped down next to him on the settee and carefully arranged the folds of her suitably somber black robe. "My recent visitors tell me that all is astir in London now that Tumbledown Dick Cromwell has resigned as Lord Protector. The trees, I fear, will be cut down regardless. Monsieur Goudge commences tomorrow."

"Damn his eyes!" The curse was soft but sharp. "Why doesn't General Monck act? How," he demanded, gesturing sharply with his free hand, "could it come to this, that a single soldier should hold the fate of England in his hands?"

Philene was trying to keep calm for both their sakes. "He has the loyalty of the English Army behind him. That attests to his integrity as well as his ability to command. Yet he was Oliver Cromwell's man and those were his soldiers, is that not true?"

Hood nodded abruptly. "Cromwell's Army has become Monck's Army. And Monck has never had any faith in Dick Cromwell, nor does he care much for our new Puritan leaders—Lambert and his ilk. So Monck appears to consider King Charles the least of various evils. But instead of stating his position—which would resolve the matter for everyone, in my opinion—he sits in Scotland like a crow perched on a crofter's hedge. For a soldier, the man is overcautious."

"Perhaps he needs the push." Philene turned to look at Hood, her face no longer fresh in the gloom of the bedchamber. "We must pray that the Army and Parliament see—how do you say?—eye to eye. Alas, dear Justin, if they do not, we may be rid of the Cromwells, yet unable to put Charles back on the throne."

He drank down more than the prescribed sip of brandy, then frowned. "If Monck declared for the King, all of our troubles would be over. Give the Devil his due, Oliver Cromwell was a great leader. There is no one to fill the void—except for the rightful King. I'm confident that Charles will come back. He's fated to rule."

Philene cocked her head to one side. "Yes, perhaps that is so. But Adrian will not come back."

"No." He stared into the brandy glass. "I went to Ingleton, you know."

"Did you?" She swerved on the chaise, the iris eyes suddenly bright in the darkness, like a cat's. "So?"

Justin didn't look up. "Her family—Honor's—were killed by Royalist soldiers. For their role in betraying Adrian."

For a moment, Philene was very still. At last she spoke, the lilting voice husky. "Her family? Oh, there is irony!" With a fluttering gesture, she pushed the long plait over her shoulder. "Does she know?"

He shook his head. "It's better that she does not. For now."

Again, Philene did not comment immediately. Instead, she put a hand on Justin's arm. "She loves you very much, Justin. I made her jealous. It was, oh, so easy."

He turned halfway, a rueful grin showing in profile. "It's not fair, Philene. It's not fair to her, it isn't fair to you."

A very Gallic shrug dismissed his assertions. "Spare your pity, *mon cher.* It is up to her to decide what is fair when it comes to loving you. As for me, I had three miraculous weeks with your brother before he went back to die in England. My papa said I was too young to wed, but I defied him. I married Adrian by moonlight in the chapel at Sainte-Geneviève. I knew my bridegroom was a soldier—I knew he might be killed. But I risked everything—and won as well as lost. I have no regrets."

Justin put his hand over Philene's. "I know, I understand all that. But this marriage to Sir Ralph … it wasn't necessary for you to sacrifice yourself."

"Zut!" Philene tossed her head, the long plait swinging down her back. "Me, I sacrifice nothing! Sir Ralph wheezed and wallowed about in my bed, but nothing more. It was like sleeping with a big pig. Crowded, but harmless." She heard his stifled laugh and clapped him on the shoulder with her free hand. "*Alors*, how else would I learn all these things for you to know? Tyler Vail was a useless source, privy only to London gossip. If," she went on, giving him her most ingenuous look, iris eyes wide under dark lashes, "he'd married Cromwell's niece, that would have been more helpful."

Justin all but choked on his brandy. "But at what a price!"

Philene's smile was arch. "For whom? You? Me? Or the enchanting Honor Dale?"

Releasing her hand, Justin rose and set the brandy glass down on a tiny side table. "She followed me tonight. She was waiting near the bog oaks."

"Ah!" Philene also got to her feet, but the expression on her face clouded. "But why?"

"I don't know." Justin was genuinely baffled. "She must know that I came here. Ergo, she must despise me for it. I wonder if that isn't just as well." He fingered the bearded chin, then picked up his hat.

"Perverse man!" exclaimed Philene. "You English make life so complicated! Put love first, and all else will be easy." Justin jammed the tall hat onto his head in such a manner as to give himself a more raffish appearance. "As easy as it was for you and Adrian?" When he saw Philene flinch, his mouth set in a grim line. "You, of all people, know better, Philene. I can promise Honor no more than my brother could to you."

The iris eyes were steady, the stance of her slim body radiating conviction. "For me, for him, that was enough."

Justin's first reaction was to contradict her, but Philene's calm certitude had caught him off guard. His customarily agile tongue deserted him, as it often did when the mask was stripped away. Inwardly, he might scoff, but only a fool would argue with a woman whose love had transcended death.

Or did only fools love that much? Justin said nothing at all but brushed her cheek again with his lips and disappeared into the night.

WHEN THE REST OF RUTBURY heard that Delbert Goudge had chopped down six oaks in a single day, there was a frenzied scramble for ax and saw. Honor watched from the gate by the woodhouses as a steady stream of men armed with cutting tools poured down the Belmot Road toward Burton Old Forest. As they swarmed into the woods like so many greedy wasps, Honor realized that they were bound to discover Beggar's Oak sooner or later. Perhaps Hood had already fled. If so, he hadn't bothered to say goodbye, at least not to her. Philene Ferrers was another matter.

Unable to watch the parade of despoilers another minute, Honor headed for the village. But even there she saw further evidence of Rutbury's rapaciousness as women and children collected yet more tools and devices in the old market square. With contempt boiling up inside like bile, Honor marched off down the road to the river. A quarter of an hour later she was far from the raucous sounds of Rutbury, dipping her bare feet in the cooling waters of the Dove.

There, under the warming midday sun, Honor tried to push her troubles aside, if only for a short time. By an act of will, she let the rippling waters soothe her soul and the soft wind in the trees relax her body. High above, the curlew cried, evoking long-forgotten memories of her childhood in the Yorkshire Dales. She saw her mother on the terrace, but her back was turned; her father was down at the forge, but his head was bent. They were both so real, yet faceless. Why was it that she could never really see them or remember what they looked like? The very least that she should have been left with was memories. Honor shifted restlessly on the grass and opened her eyes.

Downriver, a fisherman stood virtually motionless below the weir. He was dressed like a farmer, in baggy breeches and a coarse shirt. Honor marveled at his presence on the Dove. Surely he must be the only man in the vicinity—except for Matthew Thorn—who wasn't off hacking up trees in Burton Old Forest.

Moving gingerly, Honor got to her feet and slipped back into her shoes. She'd put her stockings on later; it wouldn't be seemly to lift her skirts in the presence of even the most absorbed fisherman.

But the man was pulling in his line. "Have ye bait?" he called in a harsh country voice.

"Bait?" Honor shook her head as the fisherman moved toward her. He was a big man, with a shambling step and a thatch of straw-blond hair. Yet for all his rustic aura, she could have sworn there was something familiar about his manner. "Midday makes for poor fishing," she started to say, and then gasped. Now that he was within ten feet of her, she recognized Captain Hood underneath the farmer's disguise. "Damn and blast!" she breathed. "Where did you come from?"

He set down his birch rod. "They scour the limestone caves when I am in the woods. So when they search the woods, I go to the caves. It's very simple, lovely Honor. Do you like my wig?"

She ignored the question. "You followed me!" she accused, lashing out with no regard for having done the same to him. "How dare you!"

He was trying to maintain his laconic pose. "Let's say it was Fate that led me here."

"Fate! I loathe the word!" Inside, she wished he *had* followed her; at least it would have indicated he cared. "Why are you here, then? Is your paramour otherwise occupied?"

"My 'paramour' is having a sort of fit," he said dryly, inching closer. "I would not use such a pejorative word but rather call her 'my love.' "

Honor's dark eyes sparked defiance. "You talk drivel," she challenged. "You were at Smallwood. I know it for a fact."

"Smallwood, Burton Wood, kindling wood, what does it matter?" The green eyes danced under the fringe of straw.

"It matters to me!" She whirled away, turning back toward the river. "You're faithless, unkind, worse than a mere thief!" Her back was to him, as she dared not meet his eyes. "How many women do you have tucked away in Rutbury? I'd wager the coaching roads of England are peopled by your bedmates!"

Had she not been looking in the other direction, Honor would have seen him pass an impatient hand over his forehead and shake his head in frustration. He was tempted to tell her the truth, but it was still too soon. "You're making childish assumptions, Honor," he declared, well aware that reason would get him next to nowhere with a woman. With his hands jammed into the deep pockets of his baggy shirt, he paused in midstep, taking in the tumble of golden hair down her back, the soft fall of gathered skirts at her slim waist, the stubborn set of those creamy shoulders he'd covered with kisses "If you hate me so much," he finally said, again moving closer, "why not go for the sheriff or the church elders?"

Warily, she turned her head just enough to catch a glimpse of him from behind. "I should," she huffed. "I should have done that at the start."

He was now only a scant six inches away, though he made no attempt to touch her. "But you didn't then. Can you do it now?"

Honor fixed her gaze on the sparkling green waters of the Dove and wished that she weren't reminded of Justin's clever eyes. Biting her lip, she stalled for an apt reply. "If I did, I'd be a thousand crowns richer." Perversely, she forced herself to imagine a pile of gleaming coins, more than enough to escape from Creepers and provide a marriage portion. But even in her mind's eye, the horde turned dull. All that she could really think of was Justin at her back, his presence more compelling than gold. "Why," she finally asked, slowly turning to face him, "did you go to Smallwood, if not to lie with Philene?" Honor refused to capitulate too easily this time.

He put a hand out, lightly brushing her arm. "Don't pry further, Honor. You ask questions that have dangerous answers."

Irritated, Honor shook him off. "To whom? Mayhap only you, Justin, as you dally with the ladies of the neighborhood!" Deliberately, she let the hurt she had been nurturing these past weeks rise to the surface and unleash itself in a barrage of recrimination. "Even if I believed you were faithful, it would not make up for your neglect! Your code is as self-serving as any other man's, no matter what he calls himself! Royalist, Puritan, troll or tyrant, you're all hypocrites!"

Stung, Justin backed off a step or two and stood with fists on hips. "You're gullible, Honor, listening to rumors and comparing me with the likes of Tyler Vail and the Goudges. Never mind their pious speeches, they use politics and religion for their own ends. Self-serving they are, hypocrites too, but they care for neither God nor their cause half so much as they care for themselves."

Having run out of breath with her tirade, Honor had also dispersed some of her ire. "What makes you so different?" she demanded less heatedly, if still truculently.

For a moment, he didn't respond. When he did, his words were quiet and measured. "Justice. A need for order and balance. The belief that extremes, whether Papist and absolute at one end of the scale or repressive and Puritan at the other, are wrong. I don't merely react, I act. And I *believe*."

Honor rocked slightly on her heels, teetering close to the river's tumbling waters. She wanted to believe too, especially in him, but she had been brought up to think—and feel—quite differently. Yet her anger was all but dissipated, not only by his declaration but by Justin himself, attired in that ill-fitting shirt and baggy pants, with the straw-colored wig gone askew in the heat of their argument. She was torn between laughter and tears, doubt and faith. What anger she still possessed was directed as much at herself as at him. "Damn and blast, Justin Blake Hood or whoever," she exclaimed, stamping her feet on a flat rock, "I can't quite—"

The rock was not only flat but slippery. Honor lost her balance, feet going out from under her in a flurry of skirts and petticoats as she plunged backward into the River Dove. Luckily, the water was neither deep nor swift. Her painful landing left her half-immersed in a sitting position, sputtering and swearing like a sailor.

"God's great ghost," Justin burst out, trying to stifle his laughter, "I had no idea prim Puritans knew such vile language! Don't tell me you're a secret Papist?"

Struggling to right herself in the water, Honor slipped again, soaking herself up to chin level. "I wish I'd stayed at Whitehorse Hill!" she grumbled, even as Justin grabbed her by the arms. "I hate this horrid place! A pox on Rutbury! I hope Creepers falls down!"

Her wrathful tongue had gone too far. He gave her arm a sharp shake. "Whatever Creepers has become," he admonished, digging his heels into the riverbank, "it was once a blessed, happy home. I'll not have you degrade it with your errant tongue!"

Honor's dark eyes flashed even as she tried to right herself in the rambling waters. "Blessed, my foot! The Goudges have degraded it by their very presence! Creepers is a cesspool!"

Justin's response was to let go of Honor abruptly, sending her splashing back into the river. Wild with rage, she dived for his left leg, catching him by surprise. He fell forward, chest first into the river, almost landing on top of her. The straw-colored wig flew off, sailing downstream.

"Damn your soaking hide!" he cursed, trying to get a foothold on the slippery rocks. But even as he fought for balance, Honor grabbed his other leg and tumbled him into the river. The wig jauntily bobbed on the current, catching on a weir some yards away. Seeing the helpless expression on his face, Honor burst out laughing. Justin gave her a stormy look, started to rage at her and then subsided into a sheepish grin. They both laughed then, sitting in the rippling waters, the sun high above them, the birds providing a musical accompaniment from the nearby trees.

"You're a minx," Justin said at last, finding the sodden folds of her dress under the river's surface. "You'd make an enchanting Lorelei."

Her laughter died away but she was still smiling as he ran his fingers along her slender legs through the wet garments. "Can you swim?" he asked, his voice suddenly low.

"A bit," Honor replied, finding herself surprisingly breathless. "But it's too shallow to swim."

"True." He lifted one insinuating eyebrow. "But it's deep enough for some kind of sport." His gaze traveled to Honor's breasts, taking in the way the wet muslin fabric outlined every nuance of her flesh. He moved closer so that his knees locked around her thighs under the ripples. "I daresay we are the only two people in Rutbury who are not in the forests making mayhem. I suggest we not waste this blessed solitude."

Her first reaction was to glance anxiously at their surroundings. But he was right; the Dove held no lure this fine May day for Rutbury's inhabitants. Honor saw only the soft green grass, the stands of ash and alder, the gentle sloping hills that rose up from the gorge, the occasional outcropping of limestone rock. For all the private peace of the River Dove, the world might be asleep.

With parted lips, she stared at him. His wet, dark hair glistened like ebony in the sun, the green eyes reflected the green-blue waters, and his broad shoulders seemed to all but burst from the shapeless homespun shirt. She took in a quick little breath as he unfastened her bodice and slipped her clinging dress and shift down over her breasts. Her nipples already taut from desire,

Honor quickened at his deft touch. With one hand, he scooped water from the river and languorously let it trickle between the ripe, aching mounds, causing her to shiver with excitement. Tantalizingly, he tongued each breast in turn, drinking in the excess droplets as well as the wonder of her sleek, shining skin.

"Justin ..." she gasped, eager fingers entwined in his wet hair. The nagging questions that so distressed her were hurled aside, dashed away by her great need of him. He was kissing her neck, her throat, her ear, even as his hands slid the rest of her garments down into the riverbed.

For an instant, Honor panicked. "My clothes! They'll float off to Burton!"

"Nonsense," he murmured, trailing little tingling nips with his teeth along the curve of her shoulder. He paused just long enough to plunge one arm into the water and gather up the discarded clothing. With an accurate toss, they flopped onto the grassy bank. He leaned away from her to pull off the ill-fitting shirt and pants. The clogs he'd worn had already wedged between two large boulders a few feet away.

She watched the muscles of his upper torso tense as he stretched out in the water to reach for her again. Now that she was free of her clothes, she had let herself drift with the current, half-reclining so that only her head and shoulders were revealed above the sun-dappled Dove. Justin captured her by the ankle, grinning wickedly as he towed her closer. His hand flashed up along her calf and thigh to wrap one arm between her legs while the other encircled her shoulders. Carefully, yet adroitly, he found his balance among the rocks and stood up, holding her facedown a few scant inches above the water.

"Are you quite certain you can swim?" he asked teasingly.

Her golden tresses tumbled over her back and breasts, touching the river's surface. She was looking straight into the cheerful ripples and saw the swift darting of small fry among the pebbles. Suspended as she was between earth and sky, she could think of nothing but the passion this mysterious Royalist had aroused in her. Turning her head, she saw the heat of desire in Justin's face. He was cautiously moving backward, closer to the bank, yet a few inches at a time upriver. There, as the Dove curved around a meadow of daisies, the rocks and pebbles gave way to a sandy pool. He turned her in his arms and gently laid her down in the water.

The little pool was very still and very green, the verge dotted with deer prints. Later in the season, the quiet water might turn stagnant and no doubt disappear by summer's end, but now it was a perfect sylvan sanctuary, no more than a foot deep and almost ten times as wide. With her hair fanning out from her head, Honor looked like a painting of an angel with a radiant halo. Justin said as much and kissed her nose.

"You bring me close to heaven," he whispered, covering her body with his. "For me, hell is where you are not." Honor drank in his words and his touch, a heady brew that left her senses dazzled. Under the gently lapping waters, he explored her tender flesh even as her trembling fingers caressed his male strength. Their hands grew more urgent; the pool eddied with their fervor until at last they took possession of each other, shattering the noonday calm with their ecstatic cries.

Sunlight and shadow played upon their replete bodies as a faint breeze picked up off the meadow, making the daisies sway to a coquettish dance. Honor pushed herself back with her elbows until she was half out of the water, breasts gleaming, hair atangle, eyes still closed as if to keep the world at bay. Justin got to his knees and locked both hands behind his head, shaking himself vigorously.

"God help me," he ventured in a husky voice, "I dream of making love in our bed, in our own house, in our own lawful company."

"Dream, then," she urged, also sitting up and tucking her feet under her. "What are dreams but the touchstone for reality?"

He grimaced, the green eyes as deep and shadowy as the sylvan pool. "Dreams are elusive. I learned early on that nothing is certain, including life itself."

"Stuff and nonsense," Honor replied, summoning her energy to stand up. "I learned the same, yet I refuse to give up my hopes for happiness." She was moving away through the grass where their sodden garments lay in a heap. "You're melancholy sometimes, Justin," she said, unaware of the effect her nakedness had on her lecture.

"You're beautiful always," he averred, joining her to sort out their clothes. "The sun dances on your skin like a happy child."

"You divert me," she insisted, deliberately stepping away from him. "I'm serious, you veer from flippancy to despair. 'Tis most vexing."

He looked away from her, toward the weir. His wig was gone, apparently a victim of the wind. "It seems I shall have to concoct yet another disguise," he remarked, wringing the wet from his shirt.

"You avoid my charges," Honor declared, straining to put the damp dress back on. "Why must you fend off bliss with both hands?"

"I don't," he responded, looking vaguely truculent as he pulled the baggy pants back on. "Life bring us both joy and sorrow, but how and why and when, no man can gauge. To expect good fortune is to court disappointment. That's why I take nothing for granted."

Honor was struggling to refasten the bodice of her gown, which seemed to have shrunk. "Damn and blast!" she exclaimed. "My clothes are ruined! Dare I wear any of my London finery at Creepers? And don't look at me like that. You remind me of a spaniel I once had at …."

Her voice trailed away as her hands paused over the opening of her bodice. For one vivid moment she had seen an image of the taffy-colored dog, peeking out from behind her mother's skirts. Then the picture faded, leaving her pale and shaken.

Justin was looking at her with worry in his eyes. "What is it?" he asked.

Honor didn't answer right away. When she did, her voice was vague and thin. "The pup died … I forgot to latch the kennel gate … it was winter, and the wolves came down and killed it."

"Honor." He took her in his arms, his chin resting in her damp hair. "Don't think on it. It was a long time ago." But she had fought off the tears and now pulled back just enough so that she could look up at him unflinchingly. "That's what troubles me. I haven't thought of it for years. I try not to think about the past, ever."

In those dark eyes, he searched for the long-gone days of war and murder and revenge. They were all there, imbedded somewhere in her brain as surely as they were in his. It occurred to him that neither could look to the future until each had resolved the past.

"Perhaps we should both consider what we have now," he finally said, trying not to let his hands roam farther than her waist. "Past and future are not ours to fashion."

"Perhaps." Honor spoke without much conviction, but she offered him a feeble smile. "For now, I'm sure of only one thing, that nothing else matters when I'm in your arms."

"True," he admitted, savoring the softness of her body next to his, "but the world does not permit us to ignore its intrusions."

She placed her hands on his chest, oblivious to the damp, coarse feel of his shirt. "Puritans abjure passion between husband and wife, they condemn marrying for love. I don't think that's right. Does that make me not a Puritan?"

His expression was solemn as he turned just enough to kiss the palm of her hand. "Only you can make yourself a Puritan—or not, as you decide what you believe."

But even logic couldn't erase a lifetime of habit. Reluctantly, Honor moved away a few steps and ran her hands through her still damp hair. "The truth is," she admitted, "I've never thought about it, except for why I hate the Royalists. But that's obvious. I could do nothing else, considering."

"Consider both sides," Justin said, still unusually solemn. "Consider that in a civil war, blood is let too freely by everyone involved."

Honor thought she detected a grim note in his voice, but when she turned questioning eyes on him, he failed to elaborate. Certainly his mood had changed, for he was now sitting down, putting his clogs back on. Distractedly, Honor finished dressing, and wished that Justin would offer her some assurance that their future wasn't hopeless. Yet deep down, she knew he could not yet do that. He was a man who found hope hard to come by.

He stood again, the unbecoming clothes hanging limply on his tall frame. He tossed the fishing rod from one hand to the other and gave Honor a wry grin. "I must head upriver. Don't scowl," he admonished, caressing her lips with his kiss. Then he turned away, setting himself a leisurely pace along the Dove. Honor watched him until he disappeared around the bend in the river and was lost in the soft greenery of an English May.

Chapter Twelve

JEREMY TIPPER STOPPED BY THE entrance to yet another cave. For almost an hour, he and Honor had been prowling the riverside, but so far they had seen no sign of human habitation. "I was all but certain ..." Jeremy mumbled, standing first on one foot and then the other as he scratched his head. "Master Thorn said he lived by Cotter's Weir." He pointed downstream. "There it is, yet the caves are empty."

Having now gone over the ground where she and Justin had so passionately melded their bodies only a few days earlier, Honor was distracted by burning memories. "Don't fret," she cautioned the lad. "We've had a pleasant outing regardless." Taking a deep breath of the sweet meadow across the river, she paused to admire the daisies, red campion, yellow trefoil and golden vetch that flourished in the May sunshine. "I suggest we head home," she remarked, gathering up her skirts and hopping from one stepping-stone to the other along the path that led from the river to the Burton Road. "It may be that Master Thorn guards his privacy even from his pupils." Certainly the schoolmaster had never struck Honor as a sociable sort.

But Jeremy's elfin face wore a dogged expression as he climbed up the bank to the road and turned to look back at Honor. "You asked me to lead you to him," he said in a fretful voice. "Would you have me go back on my word?"

Honor circumvented a clump of wood sorrel as she reached the roadside. "Another time, perhaps," she suggested. Her smile froze as a coach hurtled around the bend. "Jeremy!" Honor screamed in warning.

The youth jumped away from the grinding wheel, lost his balance and tumbled back down the bank. Flinging a curse over her shoulder at the driver, Honor plunged toward Jeremy, who was lying very still. "Sweet heaven!"

she exclaimed, afraid to look. "Jeremy? Jeremy!" She called his name on a rising note as panic set in. There was a gash on his forehead and a cut on one hand. Kneeling beside him, she saw that his eyes were closed, though he was breathing. Even as she heard someone call from above her, the lad moved his arms and his eyelids fluttered. With relief, Honor noted that the gash was long but not deep, the cut merely superficial. She started for the river to cup cold water when the voice called again from the roadside.

"Mistress Dale!" The booming voice belonged to Lyndon Styles.

"Damn and blast!" Honor muttered, shielding her eyes from the sun as she looked up to the edge of the bank where the squire was perched. "The lad is hurt," she called, waving an arm in an urgent manner. "Give us your aid!"

Moments later she was bathing Jeremy's forehead while Lyndon Styles gingerly climbed down to the river. "Silly child," he remarked, dusting off the pleats at the knee of his yellow cloth breeches. "He ought to have looked where he was going."

"So should your reckless coachman," Honor snapped without taking her gaze from Jeremy's pale face. Though he was still dazed, the boy's eyes were focusing again.

"It's Lady Ferrers's coachman," Styles huffed, as if somehow that fact would set matters aright. "Milady is nigh on to fainting."

Honor wasn't about to waste any pity on the Frenchwoman's alleged delicacy. "Lady Ferrers had best be nigh on to making room for Jeremy. Help me carry him up the bank, if you please."

Judging from the indignant expression on Styles's ruddy face, he was not pleased at all, but he did bear the bulk of Jeremy's weight up to the road. To Honor's surprise, Philene was standing by the coach, looking more concerned than vaporous. It was she who ushered them all into the coach and then swiftly commenced examining the lad for serious injury.

"Praise *le bon Dieu,* he seems bruised only," she pronounced, signaling for the coachman to start up again. "This Cyril, he drives like a demon! I shall scold him once we are back at Smallwood."

"I should think so," Honor retorted, though she had to admit that Philene was exhibiting more consideration for Jeremy than might have been expected. "Jeremy, of course, must be taken home first."

Though Lyndon Styles appeared disgruntled, Philene merely nodded. Honor sat next to Jeremy, her arm holding him as steady as possible against the jolting of the coach. Though he hadn't yet spoken, his expression told Honor that he was more excited by his adventure than damaged.

Except for an occasional irrelevant comment from Philene, the brief ride to Stubby Lane was conducted in silence. The Tipper residence was a sprawling cottage, apparently added on to as needed by the birth of each of their four children. The arrival of the coach set two mongrel dogs to barking, frightened at least three dozen chickens and brought a startled Judith Tipper away from the well, where she'd been drawing water.

As Honor briefly recounted the accident and Jeremy demonstrated his wholeness by fending off the dogs, Mistress Tipper's bright blue eyes fixed upon the errant coachman. Philene, however, was leaning out the window, making Gallic gestures and offering profuse apologies.

"You must accept this," she insisted, holding out a handful of coins in her gloved palm. "I am most contrite, and this is my penance."

Honor could hear Lyndon Styles grumbling inside the coach, but Philene remained adamant. Yet Mistress Tipper seemed reluctant. Honor decided to intervene. " 'Tis unlikely, but you may need a doctor. Her Ladyship means well."

Judith Tipper was uncharacteristically inanimate for the better part of a full minute but finally went over to the coach and accepted Philene's offering. "I'd rather not, but at least Will won't have to risk his neck stealing it," she said, not without a flash of sardonic humor.

Taking her leave of Jeremy, Honor stepped over a broken wagon axle and shooed off a pair of plump geese who seemed oblivious to the barking dogs. Back inside the coach, she was surprised when Lady Ferrers invited her to join them at Smallwood for supper.

"We can send a message to the Goudges," Philene said, "so as to spare them worry."

"They wouldn't worry about me if I disappeared for a year," Honor retorted, wishing that she could tone down her responses to Philene. Despite Justin's denial, Honor still felt uneasy about Clarity's account of his reputed visit to Smallwood. But she was curious as to why Philene should invite her to sup in the first place and wondered if such an occasion might give an opportunity to learn more about any possible connection between Hood and the Frenchwoman. Besides, anything was better than going back to Creepers.

Skirting Buttermilk Hill, Squire Wills's rich pastures lay like green velvet under the late-afternoon sun. On the horizon to the west, a slow-moving wagon headed home from the forest. Honor couldn't see it clearly, but she knew it would be loaded with newly cut wood. She was frowning in disapproval when several horsemen galloped from the other direction. The wagon stopped; Honor leaned out the window, trying to get a better view, but Philene's carriage was already turning into Smallwood's back gate. Honor's attention was now captured by the towers and chimneys of the Ferrers's handsome house. While it lacked the cozy charm that Creepers must have once had, Smallwood's style and grace took Honor's breath away. Choosing between the two residences would be a matter of taste, Honor thought to herself, as the coach pulled up under the porte cochere. She would prefer the intimacy of Creepers, but either way, it seemed a shame that the Blake home had been surrendered as booty to the Goudges and the family seat of the Ferrers had gone to a flighty Frenchwoman who had been married to the owner for less than a year.

Liveried footmen dashed out to meet the coach. Lyndon Styles demanded that his cloak be taken away for a thorough pressing, then peremptorily took Philene's arm. "I had," he said in a whisper that carried almost as well as any other ordinary voice, "expected a, what do you Frenchies call it, a *tête-à-tête*."

Philene's laughter floated on the late-afternoon air like spun glass. "La, *mon cher* Squire, would you compromise a poor widow? You English are, how do you say, so blunt?"

As they entered the house and headed for the sitting room, Honor began to understand Philene's insistence on a third supper guest. But whether she was there as dupe or duenna, the occasion still might prove worthwhile. Noting Philene's black velvet riding habit with its silver loops and bowknots, Honor wished she were attired in something other than her plain gray linen with the obligatory white cuffs, falling band and apron. There was a rip in one sleeve and the hem had come undone in back, casualties of her efforts to rescue Jeremy Tipper. If nothing else, the difference in the two women's garb signified their contradictory philosophies, Honor reminded herself, and wondered why she would have felt happier in velvet than in linen.

The role of gracious hostess came naturally to Philene, though Lyndon Styles appeared only slightly appeased. "How good it is not to mourn alone," Philene exclaimed, taking off the black-plumed, steeple-crowned hat and setting it on a mirrored chest. "Shall we drink good wine?" Not waiting for a response, she tugged at a heavy bell cord. To Honor's amazement, a well-dressed servant appeared while Philene's hand was still at the pull.

"Milady." He bowed deeply, then arched his brows. "I regret to report that the stag is in the garden again."

"Ohhh," gasped Philene, running one graceful hand through a cluster of shining dark curls at her temple. "Such a nuisance! Has he trampled my roses?"

"I'm afraid so, milady," he responded solemnly. "And much more. He is quite out of control."

Lady Ferrers threw up her hands. "*Hélas!* I grow annoyed with this animal! How I hate the hunt, with all its barking and bang-bang and silly noise! Yet that stag bedevils me. Come, Steward Loxley," she said, "let us look together." Standing on the threshold, she inclined her head toward her guests. "The wine will come. Partake and enjoy until I return."

"Don't suppose," rumbled Lyndon Styles after the door had shut behind

Philene and the serving man, "that she'd let me gun the beastie down?"

Honor was gazing at a portrait of the late Sir Ralph. Noting the absence of girth and gray hairs, she judged the painting to be at least ten years old. "She might," Honor replied absently, "seeing that the animal's a pest."

The arrival of three French wines diverted Styles from his purpose. Honor accepted a glass of Burgundy while the squire drank Bordeaux. A heavy silence fell between them as Honor wandered about the handsomely furnished room, studying an embroidered satin pillow, an Italian clock, a chased silver urn filled with spring flowers. She was inspecting another portrait, a stern-faced woman with jet-black curls and matching eyes, when she realized that Lyndon Styles was standing directly behind her.

"An excellent study," he commented, his voice a trifle hoarser than usual. "The first Lady Ferrers, I believe."

"Oh." Honor's response was faint; she could feel the squire's breath on her ear. "It's warm today," she said in a hurried voice, "and this wine makes me flushed. I believe I'll step outside for a bit of air."

"But," Styles protested, placing a beefy hand on Honor's smudged cuff, "our lovely hostess should be back soon."

That was true, yet Honor thought that Philene had already been gone long enough to rout half the stags in Burton Old Forest. Pointedly staring at the squire's hand, which still rested tentatively on her arm, Honor made an attempt to brush past him.

But Styles blocked her path, seemingly oblivious to her effort to escape. "Charming creature, our Lady Ferrers," he remarked in his sententious manner, "if a trifle silly, as is the wont of foreign women. Imagine, compensating those thieving Tippers for that careless child's accident!"

Angrily, Honor succeeded in pulling away. "He wasn't careless, as you well know! As for Lady Ferrers, I found her generosity most admirable. Mistress Tipper's husband may be a poacher, but she strikes me as an honest soul."

Styles tried not to let either the physical rebuff or the verbal rejoinder disrupt his aplomb. "Seething with vengeance, though. The Tippers have never forgiven the Goudges for turning them out."

"The Goudges?" Anger fled in the wake of surprise. "I don't understand."

Having regained the upper hand, at least conversationally, Styles pursed his thick lips like a blowfish. " 'Struth, Will Tipper was steward to those wretched Royalists, the Blakes. The Tippers lived for years in the lodge at Creepers."

"I see." It was no wonder, reflected Honor, that she had found Judith Tipper so admirable. No doubt she had come to Creepers as a bride and watched Justin Blake grow from childhood to adolescence. But did the Tippers know that their young master lurked nearby in his guise as Captain Hood? Judging from Jamie's attempt at heroics, Honor thought not. Or at least the Tipper children didn't know the truth.

"Criminal, that's what I call Will Tipper, and Curate agrees, as do the Goudges and most of Rutbury." Styles was fulminating in his most pompous country squire manner, shiny boots planted at an angle to give him the stance of a man addressing a much larger audience. "The stocks, or worse, is where I'd have him. As for Captain Hood, the gallows is too merciful. Law and order, that's what's lacking in this country these days. We need a firm hand on the reins, a strong rider in the saddle, a resolute—"

"*I* need air," Honor interjected, with no regard for tact. "Pray excuse me, I'm suffocating in here."

Unused to such cheek, Styles gaped at Honor as she scurried from the room. Heading outside, she was genuinely grateful for the fresh spring air with its scent of narcissus and lilac.

The sun was just beginning to dip in the western sky. Honor remembered seeing a rose garden off the porte cochere. Pink, red, white and yellow buds were opening along the tall trellises that flanked a long oval pond. It was a formal setting, yet Honor realized it offered a perfect view of Lady Ferrers's boudoir, assuming that it adjoined the sitting room where she had received her guests. There was, however, no sign of Philene in the rose garden, nor any indication that her precious plants had been ruined by a ravenous stag.

Cautiously, Honor began to prowl about the rest of the grounds, observing that the gardens at Smallwood were not only more lavish than at Creepers but far more extensive. Stepping-stones led down to a grotto where a small fountain played. A grape arbor ran the length of an enclosed tennis court. Clipped yew hedges surrounded yet another pool, which was filled with water lilies. There was a dreamlike quality to the setting, as if the stodgy Sir Ralph and his grim-faced first wife had poured whatever reserves of whimsicality they possessed into their gardens.

It was the sharp cry of the lapwing that brought Honor back to reality. She pivoted at the edge of the lily pool and listened intently. Twilight was descending, lengthening the shadows of the birch grove beyond the stables. The bird cry had come from that direction. Honor kept close to the yew hedge, moving onto a limestone path, where she assumed the air of a casual stroller. When she reached the stable, however, she again stepped back into the shadows. The windows were high on this side of the structure, perhaps ten feet up. Honor looked around for something to stand on but nothing more promising than a sack of potting soil presented itself. Frustrated, she crept around to the end of the building and was rewarded with a rear door, which sported a tiny latched peek hole. Quietly unhooking the latch, she peered inside.

It took her a moment to focus. At first it seemed that the stable was empty. Her line of vision revealed only bales of hay, a pitchfork and a harness. Yet she could hear noises, somehow subtly different from the ordinary sounds of horses at rest in their stalls. Leaning from one side to the other, Honor tried to extend her narrow view of the stable's interior. At last she made out the black sweep of Philene's silk skirts and, just beyond, the booted leg of a man.

"There now!" Philene's words were barely audible through the stout door. "No more arguments. You will stay here tonight."

Honor saw the black silk retreat, indicating that Philene must have stood up. Pressing closer, she tried to see more of the man, but it was his voice that gave away his identity. "Padge will come. I'll whistle again," insisted Justin Blake. Honor was shocked by how weak he sounded.

"Padge and Nip and King Charles himself can come, but you will not go," Philene declared in firm, composed tones that were quite unlike her usual coquettish manner. "If I must, I will have Loxley tie you up." She still spoke with determination, but a note of humor had surfaced. "Shame on you, *mon cher,* you heed Philene. I should have been a surgeon!"

"It's but a scratch!" Justin spoke in protest but the break in his voice weakened his case. Someone else—Loxley the steward, Honor thought—had moved in front of Honor's peephole.

"Her Ladyship knows her business, sir. Your brother, rest his soul, swore she could bring a man back from the dead," said Loxley.

"It's my own fault," Justin asserted. "I should have left Burton Old Forest. My presence only incites the neighborhood to greater greed."

"Perhaps." Philene sounded tight-lipped. "In a few days, when you are well, you must head north."

"Yes." The single word was weary, without enthusiasm. Honor heard Philene's skirts rustle in testimony to their wearer's impatience. "You say it, you don't mean it. You stay because of *her.*" There was a pause but no reply from Justin. Philene emitted a deep sigh. "Light the lantern, Loxley. It grows dark."

Loxley moved away, following his mistress to the front door. Honor could now see Justin quite clearly. He was lying on a pile of straw, bare to the waist except for an ominous bandage stretched diagonally across his chest. She had just moved, as if to go to him, when a hand clamped over her mouth and an arm tightened around her shoulders.

"Roundhead spy!" a voice hissed low in her ear. "One word and your life is forfeit!"

Honor squirmed and kicked, but to no avail. She recognized the voice, low and angry though it was. It belonged to the steward, whose composed manners had given way to wary menace. Honor tried to shake her head, but he was hauling her away from the stable, back toward the hedge. Unceremoniously dumping her on the ground, he knelt beside her, pinning her wrists together above her head. "Speak out, what did you see?"

Honor's brain whirled as the man's pale blue eyes seemed to drill holes into her face. Who was Philene? Who was Loxley? Justin trusted both. But how much did they know? The fierce, frightening expression told her that this man held Justin's safety as close to his heart as she did.

"Nothing!" she insisted. "That is, nothing that would harm Captain Hood. I wish him as well as you do!"

The steward's face fell, then changed into a scowl. "Rot!" He gave her wrists a sharp tug. "You're Cromwell kin, and Goudges' ward to boot!"

"That hardly makes me a spy!" Honor shot back, her temper getting the best of her fear.

The man didn't look convinced. "You look like a Puritan to me. Are you?"

Wriggling in his strong grasp, Honor started to reply that she was indeed, but something made her pause. "I was raised a Puritan, yes," she finally answered, her voice sounding strangely detached. "But I'm a friend to Captain Hood. I swear it."

Honor's declaration seemed to sway her captor. "Are you lying?" He didn't wait for an answer but hauled Honor to her feet. "Let's ask Hood if he knows you."

Honor had to run to keep up with him as he dragged her back to the stable. Apparently the rear entrance was locked from the inside; they hurried all the way around the building to the front door. It was only when they entered that the steward slowed down. Cautiously, he approached Justin, who appeared to be asleep. "Sir?"

Justin stirred as Honor noted that the big bandage was now badly bloodstained. With obvious effort, the highwayman opened his eyes and blinked.

"God's ghost," he whispered. "Honor?"

She started to blurt his given name but caught herself in time. While some of Smallwood's inhabitants might know Captain Hood, it didn't mean they were acquainted with Justin Blake. "What happened?" she asked in a hushed voice, sinking down on the straw beside him.

Weakly, he waved a hand. "It was a ridiculous affair! Bad timing, impulsive." He stopped for breath and looked from Honor to the steward. "What goes here, Loxley? Is all undone?"

Loxley was looking bewildered as well as embarrassed. "I found the wench … *lady*," he corrected himself, "spying outside."

"I was looking for Lady Ferrers," Honor put in, giving Loxley an impatient glance. "Never mind that now, what matters is … Captain Hood. Were you shot?"

"Nay," he answered, reclining deeper into the hay, "I was stabbed. By one of Lyndon Styles's loathsome creatures. Damn all, it was my own fault. Padge and I waylaid a wagonload of oak cut down by Styles's scavengers and meant to set it afire. There were only two of them, or so it seemed, and the task should have been an easy one. What we didn't know was that two more were alongside the road, following Nature's call."

Honor remembered the wagon she'd seen on the horizon as they approached Smallwood. A shiver crept up her spine at the realization that even as she rode in comfort through Smallwood's gates, the man she loved was being stabbed by one of Lyndon Styles's henchmen. "But …" Honor stumbled over Philene's name. "Lady Ferrers has tended to your wound?"

Justin nodded, one hand brushing against the bloody bandage. "Philene is most competent. She has a gift, or so my brother told me."

Honor studied the bandage closely, trying not to wince at the sight of so much blood. "Dare I ask how your brother knew?"

Justin gave her a wry grin. "You dare. Now that you've been spying through stable doors." He gave Loxley a brief, reassuring glance. "Philene was wife to my brother, Adrian. She would have been Lady Blake of Creepers had the Roundheads not ruined all."

In the past, Honor would have bristled at such antipathy toward Puritans. But now she felt only sadness. "I had no idea. Why couldn't you tell me about Philene? Did you think I'd betray you?"

Justin shook his head slowly. "Nay, but you can't reveal what you don't know, even in all innocence. Nor was there any need."

"But there was!" Honor made fists of exasperation. "I thought she was your mistress! You knew I was wild with jealousy!"

"A passing affliction," Justin remarked, his eyelids drooping with pain and fatigue. "Had you known, no doubt you would have raced here to offer your aid to my sister-in-law and, in so doing, possibly aroused suspicion of you both. As it was, you arrived at Smallwood in ignorance, avoiding any taint of complicity. Shall I have Loxley beat you to enhance your camouflage?"

"Really, sir!" Loxley was once again the perfect servant. "Indeed," he added, looking flustered, "I owe Mistress Dale endless apologies as it is. I was rather rough with her, I fear."

"All in a good cause," said Justin with a wink for Honor. "Now go, leave me to my slumbers before Lyndon Styles wonders what's happened to you and Philene runs out of excuses."

Honor longed to kiss his cheek, which looked faintly bruised. It dawned on her that he wasn't wearing his mask. "But … how long have you known …." She halted, making a vague gesture at Loxley.

"Loxley served with my father as Naseby, and then was Adrian's aide-de-camp in France. And in the field." He gave the steward a full-fledged grin. "We go way back."

"Oh." Honor felt relief, but also a sense of being an outsider. Loxley, Philene, even the Tippers, had known Justin Blake for years. Yet she, who had known him but a few months, was certain that she loved him best. "Where is Padge?" she asked, finally getting to her feet.

"At Beggar's Oak, I trust," Hood answered. "I thought he might be lurking nearby but I called and he didn't come. He'd seen Loxley riding to the rescue."

"A lucky chance," murmured Loxley. "I'd gone for a gallop to clear my head before enduring the squire." He looked away, embarrassed at the indiscreet reference to his alleged betters.

For an awkward moment, Honor gazed about the stable. "I'll leave you now," she said uncertainly, then threw up her arms. "Oh, Justin, isn't there something I can do? Can't I stay with you tonight?"

Justin smiled at her fervor but shook his head. "Nay, it's too risky. Go back to Creepers. Loxley will give you escort."

Honor could do nothing other than agree. Staying on at Smallwood, even as Philene's guest, might pique too much curiosity. Yet Honor felt no compulsion to return to the Goudges, nor any aversion to settling in under what had turned out to be a Royalist roof. Had Aunt Lucy's ambivalent attitude undermined her Puritan zeal, or had her feelings for Justin transcended all else? Blinking away a sudden onslaught of tears, Honor gazed at Justin, and could have sworn she felt his pain. "I'll do as you say," she said, summoning up a wan smile. "Does Styles know what's happened?"

Justin glanced at Loxley, who shook his head. "Apparently the squire was otherwise occupied while his henchmen did their dirty work." Leaning back into the straw, he touched his fingers to his lips in salute. "Your eyes glisten, lovely Honor, with tears of gold. They serve as a testament to your goodness."

To my love, she wanted to say, but instead gave him a feeble smile of farewell. He was asleep before she had left the stable.

Chapter Thirteen

FAITH'S USUALLY EVEN DISPOSITION WAS upset the following day by Honor's restlessness. The two young women were in the buttery, shelling spring peas, but after every sixth pod, Honor jumped up from her stool and paced. "Whatever is troubling you?" Faith finally demanded, setting her kettle down on the tiled floor. "Are you expecting a visitor?"

"No," Honor answered abruptly, then fussed with the bandeau that held her hair in place. "Rather, someone may come by with news of Jeremy Tipper. Master Thorn, perhaps." It was only a small fib, since the schoolmaster would be the most likely source of information about Jeremy. But if she'd had to tell the truth, Honor wouldn't have known whom or what she really expected. A message from Philene, perhaps, about Justin's condition, or even someone sent by his companions at Beggar's Oak. As it was, she felt quite helpless at Creepers, cut off from any news of her lover.

Distraction came in the form of Delbert Goudge, accompanied by Quentin Radcliffe and Lyndon Styles. "Ale!" he bellowed, all but knocking Faith over. "Brown bread and cheese, too! We need our bellies full to help us make great plans." Yanking off his hogging jacket, he led the others toward the parlor.

"My!" exclaimed Faith, obediently setting out three tankards. "Men have such enormous responsibilities. Praise God I'm female. There's so much less to worry about."

"Mmm," replied Honor, hardly aware that Faith had spoken. "Here," she offered, suddenly animated, "let me carry in the bread and cheese."

If Faith found Honor's change of mood peculiar, she gave no sign. After the beer had been poured and the food passed around, Honor lingered behind, then slipped into the library after Faith had returned to the pantry.

The secret panel was easy enough to discover; it was located at eye level behind the works of Praisegod Barebones. Honor took the precaution of latching the door but worried only about an early return from the village by Mistress Goudge and Clarity. She could contend with Faith, and Uriah would believe almost anything. As for the others, they were clearly settling in for a lengthy discourse.

As Honor had expected, the main topic of their conversation was the forest. But as she had also feared, the subject of Captain Hood was much on their collective minds. Leaning with one arm on the bookshelf and the other braced against the wall, Honor listened with rapt attention.

"Fools indeed," snorted Styles, apparently in reply to a comment from the curate. "It seems to me that next to capturing Hood, wounding him was a victory. He's been slowed down and may not recover."

Giving her head a little shake of denial, Honor strained to hear Delbert Goudge, who was more inclined than the other two to mumble in polite conversation, "… have gone? Caves, mayhap, upriver. Or Derbyshire."

"Doubtful, doubtful," said Radcliffe, punctuating the response with a hiccup. "He's still close by, I'm sure of it. In that we can't seem to get to him, might I suggest that we devise a means of getting him to come to us?"

"Uuh," scoffed Delbert, "and how's that? By baiting a trap on the coach road?"

"Too obvious," Radcliffe replied, and Honor could hear the smirk in his voice. "You, Master Goudge, have the perfect bit of cheese." To emphasize his point, the curate delicately smacked his lips over the last bit of cheddar on his plate. "By cheese, by heaven, I mean Mistress Dale, your ward."

"Honor?" Delbert growled her name with contempt. "Bah! What's she to do with Hood?"

Radcliffe cleared his throat. "It seems," he said, lowering his voice so that Honor had to press her ear against the thin panel, "your blessed wife has told me that there is mischief between them of a most unholy sort that has nothing to do with witchcraft or pagan rites."

"Bah!" repeated Delbert. "That's worthless female prattle! Parthenia's given to odd fancies. Though," he added quickly, as if his wife, rather than Honor, might lurk in the library, "she's a fine woman in every other way. Didn't Hood bring the girl back safely last autumn?"

"To be frank," put in Lyndon Styles, "I found that suspicious in itself. She is Cromwell's niece. Hood could have raised a fortune for her."

"Not from us," grumbled Delbert, but something in the others' attitude must have disconcerted him. "That is, it would have been Dick Cromwell's responsibility, eh?"

"That's beside the point," a faintly testy Quentin Radcliffe asserted. "Let's return to the issue at hand. We must somehow trap Hood. For all his criminal acts, he likes to play the gallant. It enhances his reputation. Now tell me, Master Goudge, is it not true that you intend to wed the wench to Uriah?"

Honor froze in place as she heard Delbert's affirmative, if rambling, reply. There was a kink in her neck and perspiration beaded her forehead. She could hardly breathe as she waited for the conspirators' plan to unfold. So engrossed was she that at first the pounding on the library door might have come from another county. It was only when the latch was rattled that Honor whirled about. Clumsily, she slid the panel shut and stuffed Praisegod Barebones back into place. A moment later, she was opening the door to a befuddled Uriah.

"Where's Father?" he asked, glancing about the room.

"Father?" Honor swallowed hard, trying to regain her composure. "Oh, your *father*. He's visiting with Squire Styles and the curate in the parlor." She was already out in the corridor, discreetly mopping her brow with the white cuff at her wrist. "If you're joining them, I'll fetch more ale."

But Uriah was looking glum. "Faith said I ought to, but why for?" His vague gaze rested somewhere behind Honor. "He never listens to what I have to say. Nobody does."

Relieved by Uriah's lack of interest as to why she had locked herself in the library, Honor willingly offered sympathy. "That's not kind of them, Uriah," she declared, moving back down the hall slowly but surely. "I'm sure you have many excellent ideas."

"No." Uriah spoke without inflection. "Or at least not any useful ones."

"I doubt that very much," she insisted, now leading him out the back door to the herb garden. Somehow she must get rid of him and return to the library to hear the rest of the plot to ensnare Justin. "Why, I should think . . . ." Stopping abruptly, Honor realized that her efforts were misguided. It might be better to seize the moment and enlist Uriah's help. "I should think you would know your own mind about a lot of things," she continued more rapidly. "Such as marriage. Surely you're not going to let them foist me off on the likes of you! I have no dowry, no family connections of importance anymore, nothing! You, on the other hand, must be extremely eligible."

Uriah's lower lip protruded. "Not so. If I was, why didn't Squire Wills let me wed his daughter?"

"Did you want to?" Honor asked, aware that Uriah was actually meeting her gaze for the first time.

"Hmm." His spurt of boldness fled, and he lowered his eyes to ground level, intently studying his worn shoes. "Prudence was plain and talked only of her loom. Her weaving is handsome, I'll give her that, but not being a talker myself, I should have preferred her to say more interesting things." He compressed his lips and furrowed his brow, as if reviewing the rather lengthy speech he'd just uttered. "So maybe," he concluded, "it's for the best that she and I won't wed, seeing as how I prefer you anyway."

Honor sucked in her breath. It had never occurred to her that Uriah actually might *want* to marry her, but if his crimson ears and hopeful expression weren't evidence enough, the tentative hand on her arm convinced her that he was serious. "But why, Uriah? I don't love you," she blurted.

"Of course not." He seemed surprisingly complacent as he again looked directly at her. "That's not the way it's supposed to be with Puritans. Too much love breeds 'woeful imps.' Or so I read in a book my mother gave me."

"Really." Honor's voice was faint. She had always known that Puritans put little stock in love, but Aunt Lucy's more romantic nature had left its mark. Honor had been infatuated with Tyler Vail; otherwise, she could not have imagined marrying him. But now she was in love with Justin Blake and could not imagine marrying anyone else.

"So it's I who am in the wrong," Uriah continued, as serious as Honor had ever seen him, "for I do love you very much. But since you don't love me, our wedded life may turn out well enough in spite of my weakness."

Gently but firmly, Honor pulled her arm away. "I think you do neither of us any favors. You would not want an unwilling bride, Uriah. It would make you unhappy, too."

Uriah held out his hand as if Honor's arm still rested within his grasp. "Oh, no," he replied with unwonted haste, "for I would make you happy. I would do all that I could to please *you*, and thus, your joy would be as great as mine. I have," he added gravely, "made up my mind about our life together."

Honor blinked at his solemn fervor and tried to summon up the words that would refute his statement without hurting him. But her appraisal of the big, bucolic young man with his besotted gaze and determined chin told her that nothing short of violence could deter him. She was losing ground on every front, for out of the corner of her eye she saw Delbert Goudge bidding farewell to Squire Styles and Quentin Radcliffe. The opportunity to discover their plot had slipped through her fingers. Worse yet, Uriah's feelings for her would make him more of a hindrance than a help. And she had to get a warning to Justin, either on her own or through Philene.

Back in the pantry, Faith had noticed Honor with Uriah and asked no awkward questions. "I must go into the village," Honor announced, taking off her apron. "I'm told that strawberries are in early."

"That's why Mother and Clarity went," Faith said, up to her elbows in pastry dough. "Here they are now, loaded down with baskets."

It was true. Both women had a half dozen wicker containers hanging from each arm. The pantry air turned almost oppressively sweet as the afternoon grew warmer and Mistress Goudge cooked jam. Honor searched frantically for another reason to leave the house. Finally, after the last berry had been washed and hulled, she seized upon a worn sole as her excuse.

Mistress Goudge's beady eyes snapped, then she shrugged. "It grows nigh on to suppertime. Don't tarry. I'm saving some of these berries to serve with cream. Here," she urged Honor, displaying an unusual amount of hospitality, "taste this first batch of jam. I use a secret recipe."

While the kitchen at Creepers produced ample food adequately prepared, it always lacked some ingredient that Honor could only define as heart. Aunt Lucy's cooks had been an erratic lot, yet the congeniality of the table had added zest to many a mediocre course. At Creepers, even the most delicious morsels seemed blighted by the absence of kindness.

Mistress Goudge's strawberry jam proved the exception. The balance between sweet and tart seemed quite perfect, while the berries' flavor brought back memories of sunny June days in the meadow beneath Whitehorse Hill, plucking only the ripest fruit and giggling with her cousins. Honor let Parthenia coax her into yet another taste. At least Mistress Goudge wasn't arguing about her jaunt to the village. Perhaps she should take the little mare … it would be much faster, especially if she went all the way to Beggar's Oak … of course Smallwood was closer, but she might be seen on the Burton Road …. Honor's brain went round and round, as if she were already on her way, riding in circles. Her last conscious memory was of a jam-coated finger falling away from her mouth as she slipped slowly onto the tiled pantry floor.

IT WAS DARK WHEN SHE awoke in her room and only the half moon floating above the trees gave her any indication of the hour. Late evening, she judged, and wondered why she'd taken a nap. Rubbing her eyes and untangling her hair, she glimpsed the red stains on her hands and gasped. Mistress Goudge had tried to either poison or drug her. No wonder, she thought groggily, that so little resistance had been put up in the face of her proposed trek into Rutbury. Whatever scheme had been concocted by the Goudges and their cohorts was obviously already set in motion. Somehow, they must be planning to bring Justin to the house. Unless, of course, they were going to deceive him about her whereabouts and lure him to some other, less obvious, place. But the details weren't as important as letting him know about the proposed trap. Fearing that she might learn of their plans, the Goudges apparently had gotten her out of the way so that she could not warn Justin in time.

Even before she tried the door, Honor knew it would be locked from the outside. After vainly trying to free the latch, she called out, first to Faith, then to Clarity. An ominous silence filled the house. If something sinister were not already afoot, certainly her shouts would have raised at least one of the Goudges.

Forcing herself to stay calm, she sat down on the bed and tried to clear her confused brain. Justin must be warned. Unless the trap had already been sprung, he would still be at Beggar's Oak or, if his wound wasn't healing, at Smallwood. Perhaps it would be best to go straight into the forest; at least the other highwaymen might be there. But first she had to get out of Creepers.

Purposefully, she went to the bureau to get her pistol. Everything in the drawer was in order, but the gun was gone. "Damn and blast!" she cursed, knowing that she shouldn't be surprised. After all, the Goudges knew about the pistol, and they'd had ample time in which to search her room.

At the window, she pushed the casement open, wincing as it creaked on rusty hinges. Looking down, she saw the stout vines that had carried the highwayman into the house. In the darkness, the ground seemed very far away, but Honor had no other choice. Her skirts and petticoats were an impediment, but Justin had managed in a flowing cloak. Honor climbed over the sill and slowly began her descent.

Obviously, Justin had had far more practice than she. Her foot got tangled up almost at once. In her effort to get free, one of the vines snapped. Honor stifled a gasp and clung to the thicker one she was already holding. Fumbling for more security, she finally eased her way downward, then skirted the pantry window and landed none too neatly in the herb garden. Her hands were scratched and her dress was torn. Life in Rutbury had taken a heavy toll on her wardrobe these past few months.

But at least she was safely on the ground. Overhead, the stars glittered and the moon shone with a companionable light, yet Honor felt no reassurance. She avoided the kennel, lest the dogs sound an alarm, and took the long way around the house to get to the stables. Keeping close to the edge of the gravel drive, she was passing the abandoned lodge that had once housed the Tippers. Ordinarily, she would have gone on by without much notice, but a flicker of light from behind one of the lodge windows caught her eye. Stopping in her tracks, she peered into the gloom, but the light was gone. It was possible that the lodge was where the trap for Hood had been set. Though removed from the manor house itself, the building had the advantage of still being on Goudge property. A stranger, such as Hood, wouldn't know his way around the little building.

Except, of course, that Justin Blake knew the lodge as well as the Goudges did. The thought comforted Honor only slightly as she stood her ground and tried to figure out what to do next. Ironically, it was she who knew next to nothing about the lodge. And if she was wrong about its being part of the Goudges' plot, she was wasting valuable time. But she had to find out. It was even possible that Justin was already being held captive behind those gray stone walls.

As the light flickered again, she tiptoed up to the window. Delbert Goudge was standing just inside. A torch mounted on a wall turned his bluff features a garish orange. He wasn't alone, for Honor heard him speak to someone just beyond the range of her vision. As she flattened herself against the cold outer wall, the night seemed to come alive with menace. There was only one reason Delbert could be waiting in the lodge at such a late hour: Justin must be on his way. Honor had to try to intercept him before he got to Creepers.

"Halt!" boomed the voice of Lyndon Styles. "Who goes there?" But Honor's golden hair, gleaming in the moonlight, immediately gave her away. "Mistress Dale!" cried Styles, all but pouncing on her as he aimed his musket at her breast. "Come with me!"

Honor had to obey. Helpless, she trudged ahead of the squire, toward the lodge. When Styles pushed Honor through the door that led to the old buttery, Delbert Goudge and one of the woodhouse tenants gaped in astonishment.

"The Devil take you, whoring bitch! How did you escape?" Delbert's face turned the color of ripe grapes in the glare of the torch. "Take her back, tie her up! Where's Uriah?"

Styles's hold on Honor's arm was rough. "By the Belmot Road, with Radcliffe. Your other tenants are divided between the south field and the woodhouses."

Delbert nodded curtly. "Hood'll be here soon, I'll wager."

"Sooner than you might expect," came a casual voice from the screens passage that separated buttery and pantry from the main house. Captain Hood stepped under the torch into the light, with a dejected Uriah chivied at gunpoint in front of him. "The curate is taking an unscheduled nap," he went on, ignoring Delbert's muttered oaths, "so release Mistress Dale without a fuss or you might disturb Radcliffe's slumbers."

Delbert swore again, but it was Styles who spoke out. "A musket ball in your doxy's back would spoil your fun, Master Thief. It appears we've reached a stalemate. The hounds have treed the fox, but the fox has a plan of his own." As ever, Styles was vexingly pompous.

Only the faintest twitch of Justin's jaw revealed his dismay. "As you will. Mistress Dale is no doxy, yet Hood is ever foxy. The wedding is off, since the bridegroom will have to come with me. Your safekeeping Mistress Dale will ensure young Master Goudge's life." Still holding the pistol at Uriah's back, he sketched a courtly bow. "Good night, and keep my honor unbesmirched."

The indolent move of his body gave no hint of the sudden whirlwind of motion that yanked the torch off the wall and plunged the room into darkness. Expecting the explosion of the musket behind her, Honor opened her mouth to scream but instead heard a strangled groan from Lyndon Styles. In the gloom, she could just make out Justin grappling with Delbert, while Padge, who had sneaked in through the buttery door, wrestled the musket from the squire.

The woodhouse tenant had leaped on Justin's back. Grabbing what appeared to be an old wooden cooking mallet, Honor hammered at the man's head and shoulders. Uriah, in turn, tried to pull Honor away.

"Stop, Honor! You'll hurt poor Daggett! He's got six wee ones!"

Honor didn't care if Daggett had sired half of Rutbury, but Uriah was determined to stop her without hurting her in the process. None of them noticed the torch, which had all but flickered out before catching again in a box of dry wood chips.

For more than a decade, the wood box had sat untended. The brittle chips virtually exploded, momentarily blinding the combatants in the small room. Stunned, Honor heard Justin call her name, but it was Uriah who was clutching at her, dragging her out through the back door. The two of them all but fell against an ancient bird-bath, but Uriah didn't let go. Honor started to shriek at him, then was struck dumb by the sudden glare of light coming from the buttery. Through the window, the entire room already seemed filled with fire, including the door through which she and Uriah had just exited.

"Sweet God!" she cried, pounding on Uriah's chest with her fists. "He'll be burned alive!" So agonized was Honor that she failed to see the puzzled, then pained expression that crossed Uriah's face.

"My father is in there, too," Uriah protested. "We must do something!"

But before they could take any action, shouts from several directions broke into the night. Men were running toward the lodge, one of whom was Quentin Radcliffe. "What's happening?" demanded the curate, looking very much unlike himself in layman's garb.

Uriah fumbled his way through an explanation, at the same time losing his grip on Honor. As the timbers inside the lodge began to crackle and smoke filled the air, Honor saw that the flames had spread into the pantry and perhaps across the screens passage toward the main house. Holding a kerchief over her face to ward off the smoke, she approached the door. Before she could reach the arched portal that led to the actual entrance, she heard Delbert cursing and coughing as he made his way up the curving drive. Turning, she saw him puffing along with Lyndon Styles and the tenant called Daggett. All three men were dirty, bruised and sweating.

"Uriah!" bellowed Delbert. "Where are you?"

Honor knew but didn't bother to say so. It was Justin's whereabouts that concerned her, and she deduced that he and Padge must have fled down the screens passage and out through the front door with the others in vain pursuit.

Having failed to catch the highwayman, Delbert was now expending his efforts on stopping the fire. "Get buckets! To the well with them," he ordered as

Uriah and Lyndon Styles appeared on the run. "Get all the tenants! Villagers, too. We'll bring water from Rutbury!"

Ignored now by everyone, Honor stepped back from the smoke and heat. Nearby Mistress Goudge and the two girls huddled along with Durwood and some of the other servants. The bucket brigade was forming in a chaotic fashion between the well and the lodge. Wiping at her stinging eyes, Honor decided that the lodge was a lost cause. The entire structure was now afire, with dancing flames sprouting up from several parts of the roof. The night was distorted by the sinister red glow, though billows of black smoke kept obscuring Honor's vision. Parthenia had now unleashed her self-righteous wrath, calling on the Almighty to simultaneously put out the fire and bring down His vengeance on the perpetrators responsible for setting it. Faith seemed all atremble in the face of the frightening inferno, while Clarity wore a bedazzled expression that bordered on fascination.

Yet some order was emerging from chaos. Even as several newcomers arrived on foot and by horseback, the fire fighters' purpose became clear: Master Goudge had given orders to let the lodge burn but to spare Creepers itself at all cost. Forced by the intense heat to move closer to the female Goudges, Honor watched the tongues of bright fire ring the eaves while crimson fingers darted through the windows. The noise was now quite deafening, as timbers snapped and walls collapsed.

"It's all that demon highwayman's fault," raged Parthenia, somehow managing to make herself heard over the roaring din. " 'Just as silver, bronze, iron, lead and tin are gathered into a furnace and smelted into the flames, so I will gather you together in my furious wrath, put you in and smelt you! … Thus, you shalt know that I, the Lord, have poured out my fury on you!' Ezekiel, chapter 22, verses 20 to 22." For emphasis, Parthenia shook a fist at the fire, which was now threatening the nearby trees.

Honor found Mistress Goudge's scriptural quotations considerably less helpful than digging a trench between the lodge and Creepers. Trying to assume a meek air, she said as much, and received a stern glare of reproach for her efforts.

"The men will see to it," put in Faith, speaking through a kerchief. "They know how to deal with such matters."

"Then why haven't they done so?" Honor rejoined crossly. It was not up to her to make any suggestions to the Goudges, of course, yet it seemed the men would have to act soon. The past few days had been mostly sunny and warm and the shrubbery was dry. Should the wind, which had thus far been relatively calm, pick up from the west, the fire could easily spread toward the manor house. Not that Honor should care, she told herself, for it would serve the Goudges right if they lost their ill-got gain. But Creepers had once belonged to Justin Blake and his family. She would hate to see it destroyed. Indeed, she felt faintly wistful for the sake of the Tippers as she watched the flames now totally envelop the lodge, leaving only a few brave timbers still standing amid the relentless inferno.

Across the drive, Delbert was still ordering his men to pour their buckets onto the ground and over any of the shrubbery that stood in danger of catching fire.

Faith, who was at Honor's elbow, was striving for optimism. "You see, the flames can't go beyond the wet places. The men have ringed the lodge with water."

Even as she spoke, a huge fireball burst from the roof, scattering the men who had just arrived from Rutbury with a half dozen large casks. Faith screamed, Delbert swore, and Clarity insisted she was about to swoon. Everyone was driven back, to the very walls of Creepers. The dampened ground offered little resistance.

Aware of her impertinence, Honor pushed Clarity aside and confronted Delbert. "Why aren't you digging a trench? Nothing short of that will stop this fire!"

"A trench?" Delbert's long face went temporarily blank. "A trench!" he sputtered, eyes streaming from the smoke. "How can we dig with no tools? All but a few picks and shovels were in the lodge!"

A deep, rumbling voice seemed to hover on the smoky air without effort. "What of your tenants? Have they no tools of their own?"

Honor swerved off balance as she recognized Matthew Thorn. "Of course! Their farm implements!"

"Indeed," replied Thorn. "They would be quite safe in the woodhouses."

Though she knew he could not see her, Honor gave the schoolmaster a grateful smile, then saw that he was accompanied by a wide-eyed Jeremy Tipper. "Jeremy," she said, bending down to speak directly to the lad, "take Uriah, along with any others who will come, and bring back what's needed. Hurry, now!"

To her relief, Uriah and most of the male servants seemed only too glad to have orders to follow. They fell to eagerly behind Jeremy, who was already scampering toward the woodhouses. A shower of sparks evoked terrified screams from Faith and Clarity. All four of the women, along with the growing crowd that had been drawn by the blaze, sought sanctuary next to the house. Their safety was threatened almost immediately by a fiery timber that crashed onto the drive, barring the path of the bucket brigade. A flaming splinter broke free, catching in the ivy that crawled up the west side of the house. A collective gasp rose from the horrified onlookers as the dry old vines began to burn.

"The house!" screeched Parthenia, hands to her head. "Creepers is afire!"

The ivy had caught near a window on the second floor, at the opposite end from Honor's bedroom. Durwood or Cook resided there, but Honor wasn't sure as she had never ventured into the servants' quarters. Whoever it was apparently had felt the need to open the casement and let the night air freshen up what was probably a stuffy chamber. Pale curtains, drawn by the ominously rising wind, fluttered over the sill, as if daring the fire to come closer.

Someone was calling for a ladder. Honor thought it was Delbert, but the din was so loud she couldn't be certain. In the drive, several men tried to douse the burning timber while Lyndon Styles asserted his customary authority and supervised the bucket brigade. The last of the timbers fell inside the lodge, and with one mighty explosion, what remained of the roof caved in. Honor hid her eyes from the awful brilliance before she hurried to help the others refill their buckets from the well. Somehow, it seemed imperative to save Creepers.

Yet even as she passed one bucket after another down the line, it also occurred to her that it was even more important to save herself. And Justin. The Goudges had used her as bait once; there was every likelihood that they would try again. Glancing from right to left, Honor realized that neither of the men on either side knew her. They were villagers probably, or from neighboring farms. Everyone was concentrating on putting out the fire, which had quickly climbed up the tapestry of vines. Not even Parthenia, who was urging some of their tenants to go inside and try to beat the fire back from that direction, seemed the least bit interested in Honor's activities. Passing on another bucket, she slipped from the line, tried not to cough and attempted to melt into the crowd of spectators.

Conforming with the others, she gazed up at the window, where the flames now licked furiously. To her surprise, she saw two figures already inside, frantically trying to beat the fire out before it took over the room. It was only when a huge flame danced behind one of them that she recognized the flaxen hair of Jeremy Tipper.

"Sweet God," she murmured, racing from the crowd and snatching at the first available bucket. Her eyes were smarting and her heart was pounding as she charged through the front entrance and felt a rush of cool air touch her hot cheeks. Temporarily invigorated, Honor flew up the two flights of stairs and down the hall. To her horror, the open door had somehow sucked the fire into the bedroom. Eager flames already framed the entire threshold.

"Jeremy!" Honor called, hoping she hadn't spilled much of the water during her flight upstairs. "Jeremy, are you in there?" It was possible, of course, that he'd already taken the back stairs to safety. It was, she realized with a frightened pang, also unlikely. She called his name again, and this time she heard a faint choking response as well as a deeper voice from the same vicinity. Of course, she remembered, there had been two figures at the window. In her concern for Jeremy, she had forgotten that he was not alone.

Honor approached the flaming doorway and began splashing water onto the fire. Amid the hissing sounds and the billowing smoke, she tried to see into the room. The outline of Jeremy and his companion could be barely made out in the dense black haze, though they could be no more than ten feet from where Honor stood. Emptying her bucket, she shouted again, hoping to serve as a beacon. The room was swiftly turning into a holocaust, the fire swallowing up what was probably the dry and brittle remembrances of a lifetime. Seeing Jeremy stagger in her direction, Honor finally perceived the hooded form behind the boy.

"Master Thorn!" she cried. "Hold on to Jeremy! Take his shirt!"

With a desperate lunge, Honor felt sparks bum her hands and sputter onto her gown. She was a foot or less away from Jeremy. His hands clawed at the smoke, his feet stumbled over the trails of fire on the floor. With all her might, Honor leaned into the inferno and hauled Jeremy across the threshold. There was no one behind him.

"Master Thorn!" Honor called again, panic rising to a terrified crescendo. "Here! Please God …!"

A sharp crack, followed by a storm of glowing embers and a dull thud, shattered the night. The room was a fireball. Honor screamed again, this time mindlessly, and dragged Jeremy down the corridor to relative safety. At the head of the stairs, she cradled the boy's smudged and stricken face in her hands. "Jeremy …" she gasped, "are you …?"

But Jeremy's eyes were full of tears made bitter more by loss than by the suffocating smoke. "He tried to save me … it's my fault …."

Honor gathered him close and wept as shamelessly as the child.

Chapter Fourteen

IRONICALLY, THE LADDERS PLACED OUTSIDE the window had been mounted almost immediately and the bucket brigade had gained access to the blaze within the next few minutes. Aided by the unpredictable wind, which suddenly shifted, the fire had finally been contained. Creepers had been saved, intact except for the servants' wing, which was badly charred. The Goudges had been very lucky. They had lost the old lodge and some shrubbery, but there was nothing that couldn't be mended with money.

As for Matthew Thorn, Parthenia asserted that his death was a blessing in disguise. "How unhappy he must have been, living out his life with such a handicap. I often wondered what crime he had committed to make God punish him so harshly."

If Honor hadn't been in a state of shock when those words were uttered, she would have been moved to rip Parthenia's tongue right out of her head. But as it was, the horrors of the night had left Honor debilitated, a limp, disheveled figure huddled on the settee in the withdrawing room, where the Goudges had gathered to recuperate in the pale light of a cloudy dawn. Lyndon Styles had stayed on, somehow managing to manipulate the entire disaster into a showcase for his amazing organizational talents. The curate, in a less than affable mood following the failure to capture Hood, was trying to wrest a homily from the debacle by depicting the fire as an epic struggle between Good and Evil. As for Jeremy, Faith had shown uncommonly good sense by piling the boy into the family carriage and driving him back to Stubby Lane. Honor wished she could have gone with him. She had to escape Creepers at the earliest opportunity.

Meanwhile, she felt obligated to see that Matthew Thorn's soul was formally commended to God. Braving a sour look from Parthenia, she put the question to Quentin Radcliffe.

"Alas," he began, sniffing at the air, which was still tainted with smoke, "that's irregular, there being no … uh, body, to speak of." He made a distasteful face and glanced at the other women as if apologizing for Honor's lack of delicacy in bringing up the matter in the first place.

"You mean," pressed Honor, "there were no remains?"

Radcliffe's disconcerted gaze flitted between Honor and Delbert Goudge. "That part of the house was totally destroyed, even the floor and the ceiling," Delbert put in grumpily.

"It was only the kind face of God that spared the rest of the house," Parthenia remarked with smug piety.

Honor shot both Goudges a sharp look. "It still seems to me that Master Thorn's death should be commemorated in some way. I would pay for such services myself," she went on, turning back to Radcliffe, "but I have no money."

Quentin Radcliffe made a steeple of his fingers beneath his chin. "A pity. We must then leave Master Thorn to God's mercy."

Honor assumed that would be far greater—and less costly—than Radcliffe's. Had she been less tired, she would have said so. But as the wind picked up outside and more rain clouds blew in from the north, she wanted only to sleep.

Parthenia, however, was full of vigor, seemingly thriving on disaster. "Praise the Lord, rain is on the way to cool those devilish embers at the lodge." She glanced meaningfully at Delbert. "Shall we beat the storm?"

"Paugh," responded Delbert, his clothes changed but his face as yet unshaven. "Why rush?"

The beady eyes snapped. "You bungled, Husband. Your cheap trickery brought us loss, not gain. Uriah and Honor must wed at once." She gave her startled ward that awful, gleaming smile. "I want Mistress Dale brought into the family fold before anything can happen to spoil Uriah's fondest wish."

Honor saw Uriah redden with pleasure. For her own part, panic overtook her. She had never suspected that the trap for Justin might be real. The morning was turning into an impossible nightmare. "You can't force me," she declared, finding sufficient strength to stand. "What will Cousin Dick say when he finds out?"

Parthenia's hand flew out to grab Honor's wrist in a viselike grip. "No one cares what Dick Cromwell says anymore except his creditors. Come, we're off to Saint Barnabas."

Honor tried unsuccessfully to wrench her hand away. "I refuse! I'll charge you with abduction!"

"You can charge us with whatever you like, but you'll do it as Honor

Goudge," Parthenia retorted grimly. "If our son wants you as his wife, then that's what he'll have. Though God Almighty only knows why Uriah has chosen such a pagan Jezebel."

"Mother …" Uriah began.

But Parthenia was snapping her pudgy fingers. "Come, come, no more delays. The day moves apace."

With Delbert on one side and Radcliffe on the other, Honor was marched down the hallway to the front door. Stumbling over the threshold, she tried to think of some way to appeal to one of the Goudges. Faith was cowed by her parents, Clarity was too self-absorbed, and Uriah genuinely believed that he could make Honor happy. There wasn't a suitable ally of any sort at Creepers, as far as Honor could tell.

Outside, there was a brief delay while a half dozen woodhouse tenants and horses were brought around. The sun had been swallowed up by clouds and the first soft drops of rain had begun to fall. Honor had no shawl and the little lawn cap covered only part of her head. "I need my cape," she insisted, trying to pull free of Radcliffe. "I must go back inside. I'm not even wearing a good dress."

Uriah looped an arm around her shoulders. "You look fair as ever to me. I'm not much for fancy fripperies."

Desperately, Honor racked her brain for some other means of escape. If only they would let her ride the little black mare, she might be able to break away and plunge into the forest. But the Goudges ordered that she ride pillion behind Radcliffe while Uriah kept to their rear. Despite some confusion among the tenants, the little party finally headed out down the drive toward the Burton-Rutbury Road. The rain was falling harder now, in big, stinging drops, with the rumble of thunder low across the Dove. Wildly, Honor looked around her, seeking an opportunity for flight. But there was Uriah, a scant six feet away, and behind him the tenants, who seemed to be enjoying their early-morning jaunt immensely. One of them, Honor noted hazily, must be newly married, for he was being taunted mercilessly by his companions, and though he refused to respond to their goading, at one point he actually made as if to leave the road. If only I could do the same, Honor thought frantically.

But the horses were now trotting toward Rutbury, each hoofbeat resounding in her breast like a nail driven into a coffin. The wind soughed among the trees, the morning grew very dark, and jagged lightning flashed above the spire of Saint Barnabas. The thunder rolled again, sending a shudder along Honor's spine.

They were in the village now, passing The Lamb Without Wool, where the old innkeeper's sign creaked in the wind while rain dripped from the cottage eaves and puddles formed in Cornmill Lane. In front of them, the church loomed like a hulking beast. Honor felt sick.

They were dismounting, tying up their horses, making for the west entrance in the tower. Honor barely saw the magnificent scene of the Nativity or the handsome carvings above the door. She was only vaguely aware that Quentin Radcliffe was insisting that Vicar Busby should be summoned. "We want no questions about the legality of this ceremony, you understand," the curate explained to Delbert. "There is no marriage contract, no banns, nothing that is regular."

"A wedding's a wedding," growled Master Goudge, but offered no further resistance. Radcliffe hurried off while Faith shivered under her thin lamb's-wool shawl and Clarity complained because there hadn't been time to put her hair up on its new wire frame.

Honor was standing next to Uriah, his hand on her shoulder. The rain rolled in droplets off her nose and she was soaked to the skin. But her physical discomfiture was as nothing compared to the emotional turmoil in which she found herself. Marrying Uriah was an appalling prospect in itself, but the loss of Justin Blake such a marriage would entail was far worse. Perhaps, she thought disjointedly, it was all a ruse, yet another attempt to snare the highwayman.

But the proceedings smacked of reality. Radcliffe appeared with the vicar, who was in much disarray, his vestments askew and his untied shoes flapping about his bare ankles. "It's scarcely six o'clock," he protested, passing a hand through his wispy gray hair, which all but stood on end. "Praise God, 'tis an unseemly time for a wedding!"

"Young love won't wait," Parthenia snapped, all but shoving Uriah through the church door. "We shall be as generous as you will be hasty."

Her offer was lost on the vicar, who frowned into the rain. "Such a day. Only minutes ago I welcomed an old colleague from Sidney Sussex College at Cambridge. Or was it Trinity at Oxford?" His face creased in befuddlement as he turned to Radcliffe. "At any rate, he had the sense to come in out of the rain. He's a dean at Lincoln. Haven't seen him in nigh on thirty years. Perhaps Penrothy should join us."

Though the curate rather testily tried to discourage his superior, a veritable barrel of a man with a prominent nose and jutting chin came rolling out of the vicarage. With his clerical garb billowing around his body and his long, straight hair swinging across his face, he made an awesome impression, even on Honor. "Ho, my good Busby," the Lincoln dean rumbled from the depths of his capacious chest, "we do indeed have a wedding party! How delightful!"

Defeated, Radcliffe waved his hands. "Well and good, we shall proceed." Entering the church, he ordered the woodhouse tenants to light the candles.

Moments later the church was filled with quavering amber light while the stained glass windows rattled in the wind. Honor stood in the vestibule, unable to move another inch.

"Honor," urged Uriah, "take my arm."

Honor couldn't speak, either. She gave Uriah a helpless look, as if she had no idea who he was or why they found themselves in the aisle of Saint Barnabas Church. Averting his face, Uriah put both hands on Honor's waist and propelled her down the aisle. Quentin Radcliffe and Vicar Busby were standing close together, the younger man beaming pontifically, the older cleric still looking bewildered. Dean Penrothy hovered behind them like a great disheveled bat. It was the curate who began the service, his stentorian voice filling the all but empty church.

Honor didn't hear a word Radcliffe uttered. She was vaguely aware of Uriah, slumping beside her and swallowing frequently. When they came to the part of the ceremony that required the bride's and groom's responses, Uriah shyly took Honor's hand. His touch was clammy and her impulse was to pull away. But Uriah clung fast, and though his voice was nervous, it held a note of conviction. Honor had turned to stone.

Uriah's anxious eyes begged her to respond. Leaning down, Radcliffe whispered at her to at least nod. But still she remained mute and immobile. A flash of lightning transformed the pale amber nave into ghostly brilliance. Thunder shuddered through the church. Honor felt as if the stone floor might open up beneath her feet. Indeed, she prayed that it would.

And then the south and east doors were flung open. Incredulously, Honor turned around to see Padge and Wat poised at each of the doors with pistols drawn. Another man, the tenant who had been teased by his fellows, stood by the west entrance, also holding a gun. But as Honor stared in disbelief, she realized that although he wore the garb of a farmer, the blond hair and fresh face belonged to Nip.

Despite Parthenia's scream for Delbert to grab Honor, his reactions were too sluggish. Instead, Dean Penrothy burst between Radcliffe and Busby to push her out of reach. With a rapid move, he delved into his commodious vestments and pulled out a pair of pistols. Stunned, Honor gaped up at the clergyman and saw beneath the flyaway strands of hair and the false nose and chin that a pair of emerald eyes glinted down on his captive audience.

"I'll not be shy about firing guns in church," asserted Captain Hood, moving Honor with him toward the east door. "Enough desecration has already been done within these walls, I fear."

Delbert was cursing himself blue in the face, Parthenia seethed with fury, and Uriah stood dumbfounded. Faith clung to Clarity, who was hanging on to the squire. The five tenants from Creepers wore dazed expressions while

Quentin Radcliffe shuddered with indignation. Only Vicar Busby seemed unaffected as the highwayman guided Honor out through the door while Padge kept his weapon trained on the little gathering. "Penrothy always was a stormy petrel," Busby murmured. "I marvel that he was ever made a dean."

THE WIND, THE RAIN, THE flash of lightning and the rumble of thunder made no impression on Honor as she and Justin galloped through the forest. She had assumed they were headed for Beggar's Oak, but when she recognized Buttermilk Hill, she knew their destination must be Smallwood.

"You'll stay no more at Creepers," Justin declared, holding Honor curled against his chest, her wet hair streaming over her shoulders. "I cursed myself all last night for not succeeding in getting you out of the lodge."

"I cursed myself, as well," Honor replied, oblivious to the soaked garments that clung to her skin. "After all, I was the fool who let myself be given a sleeping potion. I should not have trusted Parthenia Goudge in a gracious mood." She paused, peering past his arm to note that they were taking the same route along which she'd followed him earlier. "But how did you know it was a trap?"

"At the lodge?" Justin guided Shandy off the road and through the poplars. "The word of your impending marriage was quickly spread. Originally, it was set for midnight. But I assumed you would not be in the lodge, as was rumored. Therefore, we approached by stealth, managing to circumvent the watchdogs posted around the house. It was, you'll admit, a stupid plan."

Stupid, yes, Honor agreed, but at least part of its aim had fooled her. "I didn't dream they actually wanted to marry me off. I can't think how Parthenia would permit it. She hates me."

"She also dotes on Uriah," Justin answered, riding past the rhododendron bushes, whose glossy leaves had already begun to lift in the rain. "Being the only son and heir, he is the one person to whose will Mistress Goudge will bend. As long, of course, as it doesn't thwart her own."

Reining up, he dismounted, then carefully lifted her from the horse. Fleetingly, he ran his hands over her hips, and she leaned against him, reveling in the warm glow his touch always brought to her. Loxley appeared virtually from out of nowhere, a surprised look on his face. Justin waved and grinned as the steward finally recognized him under the dean's disguise. "We've had a merry morning and it's not yet seven o'clock. The others will be along shortly," he went on, hustling Honor through the back entrance. "They were to leave at two-minute intervals after letting the other horses loose to deter pursuit."

Exhausted, Honor leaned against a mahogany cabinet in the withdrawing room, where Justin was rummaging. "But how did you know about the wedding?"

Justin was pouring out a tumbler of Scots whiskey. "Drink this," he urged, disturbed by her pale face. "And take off those clothes. I'll have Loxley fetch warm blankets." He went to the door and glanced into the corridor. "I doubt if Philene is up yet. My fair sister-in-law could sleep through fire, flood, and quake." Stripping off his clerical vestments, he sat down next to Honor on the settee and began unfastening the tiny buttons of her bedraggled dress. "Here, you're being a poor patient. You haven't downed your whiskey yet."

Honor took a deep breath and swallowed, then choked. "It's putrid stuff," she protested, but was distracted by Justin's touch on the bare skin of her throat. "You still didn't tell me how you found out about the wedding."

"Easy enough," he responded, peeling her bodice and shift away. "It seemed prudent to keep Nip and Padge in the vicinity, lest the night's adventures not end with the fire. Besides," he said quite seriously as he traced the outline of one breast with a lazy finger, "I couldn't abandon you to their mercy or be sure that if the fire got out of control anyone would make sure you were safe."

"Ohhh." Honor thought his explanation made perfect sense so far, or at least as much as she required when he was kissing her.

A leisurely time later, he raised his head. "When Delbert ordered his tenants to ride into Rutbury for a wedding, Nip acted swiftly, knocking out one of the men and changing clothes with him. It was such a gloomy morning that all he had to do was ride along at the rear and keep quiet. Padge, of course, had raced off to get me. I put together my dean's disguise and had arrived at the vicarage only minutes before you came along with the Goudges."

"How clever," Honor commented. Her voice was more than a little breathless, for Justin had lowered his head to her breast. She was lying back, giving herself to his embrace, when a discreet rap sounded at the door. Honor stiffened and then tried to refasten her garments, but Hood laughed and tossed the dean's vestments at her as he strode toward the door.

Philene was wearing yet another elegant black robe, but this one was lined in scarlet silk with matching ribbons, including the one that tied back her dark hair. "La," she exclaimed, assuming an appropriately shocked expression, "have we here the *déshabillée?* Should poor Philene blush for shame?"

"You could lend me a robe," Honor shot back, not entirely certain that she enjoyed being the butt of Philene's banter. "I almost died of chill between here and Creepers."

The Frenchwoman, however, had already slipped back into her more brusque attitude. *"Mais oui, ma chérie,* and food, too. Wat has arrived and recounted your history of this morning, as well as confirmed rumors of last night. Mignon is making up a room for you, the kitchen is abustle, and Loxley has gone to bring you a *robe de chambre.* As for you, Justin," she said, turning to her brother-in-law, "you seem dry enough. Those vestments under which poor Honor cowers must have lent you heavenly protection."

It was true, inasmuch as Hood's own shirt and breeches bore little evidence of their wet ride to Smallwood. He was hungry, however, and as soon as Loxley arrived with an exquisite muslin robe printed with great swatches of brightly colored flowers, other servants brought in several trays with covered dishes and a hot beverage Philene called *café*.

"It's all the rage in Paris, being brought from Turkey. Try it, Honor. Justin's quite fond of it already."

"He also likes whiskey," remarked Honor, taking a sip of the bitter brew and making a face. "Really, this is quite horrid stuff. I'd rather drink medicine."

The coddled eggs and fresh buns and spicy sausage were another matter, however. Honor ate almost as eagerly as Justin, using butter and marmalade lavishly. Philene merely nibbled from a platter of fresh fruit and cheese, though she drank at least four cups of *café*. Throughout the meal she seemed vaguely preoccupied and had to be dragged back into the conversation twice by Justin.

Finally, scooping the last bit of egg from a dainty porcelain cup, he posed a question to her. "Are you nervous about Honor staying with you?" He glanced at Honor, who suddenly looked apprehensive.

But Philene waved a graceful hand. *"Non, non, mon cher,* I am delighted to have the company of a young woman who is not a simpering ninny such as La Goudge. Nor should you worry about her safety here. Loxley will see to our protection." She hesitated, allowing the sound of the rain on the windows to beat relentlessly against the leaded panes. The thunder and lightning had passed over, however, and the morning sky had brightened a bit. "Now that Honor no longer dwells under Creepers' roof, I think it is time she knew the truth." Philene's iris eyes fixed on Justin's face. "One of us will tell her. The only question is, which one?"

He shifted uneasily in the armchair across from Honor. "Why rake up the past? The present is trouble enough."

"It's a matter of integrity," Philene asserted, rising from the velvet-covered stool on which she'd been sitting. "Or," she asked, her chin lifted in challenge, "don't you think she can face up to her own *histoire?*"

Again, he glanced at Honor. "I'm not sure she should have to. She's faced a great deal already, particularly in the past twenty-four hours."

Now it was Honor who stood up. "Stop talking about me as if I weren't here! You're both right. I've managed to grapple with life no matter what it's dealt me, and though I'm bone-weary at the moment, I'd rather hear whatever this truth is now than fret over it and not be able to sleep. Speak, one of you, or both, but pray *speak."*

Philene and Justin exchanged glances.

"I shall permit him," she said, wrapping the black robe around her body, "and leave the two of you alone." With dignity, she left the room.

"Well." Justin sat back down, a hand running through his hair. "Extraordinary woman is Philene."

"So she seems," Honor replied, not without bite. Certainly the Frenchwoman was far different from the flighty, flirtatious creature Honor had first met. But the cool, efficient, even calculating, personality that had emerged from behind the façade was almost as off-putting in a far different way.

Another silence had filled the room. The rain was letting up but water streamed from the gutter just beyond the windows. None too patiently, Honor waited for Justin to start with his story. Instead, he put a query to her.

"I must ask of your parents," he said with all the dispassion of a hanging judge. "Will you tell me?"

Honor bridled. "Why? It was you who would talk to me."

Doggedly, Justin pursued the question. "So I shall. But first, I must know what happened to them."

Vexed, Honor sighed. "Very well. They were murdered. By Royalists." Her eyes flashed; the old wounds were still raw.

"Why?" The word fell like a stone between them.

"Because the Royalists were butchering brutes. Does that amaze you?"

He fingered the hard line of his jaw. He'd had no chance to shave, and in the overcast morning light, he looked vaguely saturnine. "It hardly amazes me that soldiers, being taught to kill as a means of survival, would lose control. The Royalists are not unique in that respect, I assure you. Or have you forgotten your uncle's Irish massacres?"

She had not, nor had she obliterated from her memory Oliver Cromwell's excuse that he had fallen victim to blood lust. "War is horrid," she muttered. "I can't imagine killing people just because they had different beliefs."

"No?" His eyebrow rose. "As I recall, you once wanted to kill me."

Honor stared at him. "That was different! That was because you … that is, people like you, had killed my parents!"

Leaning back in the chair and placing one leg over the other knee, Justin inclined his head slightly. "Specious, if passionate, reasoning, that." With difficulty, he launched into the story Philene had insisted he tell. Gone was his usual glibness, the easy self-confidence, the indolent manner. He was earnest, solemn, and occasionally hesitant. At first, Honor was more arrested by his manner than his words.

"When I was eighteen, I'd already been a fatherless exile in France for several years. I was quiet, reserved. I'd loved my father deeply. My mother mourned him. Always, obsessively. Nor could I give her comfort." He stared past Honor, his mouth twisted, as if he had gone back in time and were trying to form the words that might ease his mother's heartbreak.

"On Easter Sunday—it was 1649—she died. She wasn't yet forty." The green eyes grazed Honor's face, then resumed their faraway look. "I vowed to use my wits from that day on, but only to avenge my family's tragedy. Does that sound familiar?"

Honor actually recoiled from the sudden, unexpected, piercing gaze. "I ... yes, I'm sure many people sought revenge." She was flustered, as uncomfortable as if in the presence of a stranger.

"Let me go back." He leaned forward in the chair, both feet now planted firmly on the floor. "I haven't yet told you about Adrian. His death was the final blow for my mother."

"I should imagine," Honor said weakly.

Justin didn't seem to hear her. "You know that he was married to Philene. It was a brief but passionate union, two strong-minded people of principle who could put duty before love. Adrian had to go off to war in England. Philene refused to press him to stay. They had a perfect understanding, those two. I didn't appreciate it then, I was too young, but I do now."

Honor shifted self-consciously. "They sound very selfless," she remarked, though her tone was faintly grudging. "All for the sake of war."

He lifted one shoulder. "Don't judge them. And remember that the fight was not Philene's. She was—is—a foreigner." Sunlight was filtering in through the diamond-shaped windowpanes, and only the faint dripping of the gutter broke the silence as Justin seemed to gather his rambling thoughts. "Adrian fought at Preston, in Lancashire, with the Scottish army under the Duke of Hamilton. Cromwell first met up with Langdale's van outside of the town. That's where Adrian was, and Langdale sent him to warn Hamilton. When Adrian tried to get back to Langdale's troops, he discovered that they were on the other side of the Preston-Skipton Road. He was cut off, with no choice but to go around Cromwell's army on Preston Moor.

"I'm not sure what happened next. I've pieced this story together from many sources over a number of years, but Adrian may have ended up with Hamilton's men. I do know that my brother and the Duke tried to escape by swimming across the Ribble. Cromwell had posted men to keep the Scots from fleeing north. It was raining, as it did this morning, a heavy summer storm that turns the earth to mud and swells the rivers. The fighting was fierce. But Cromwell prevailed. Hamilton and several of his followers fled south, to Cheshire. Adrian somehow eluded the sentries and went north to Yorkshire." He paused, fixing those omniscient green eyes on Honor's face.

"Adrian stopped at Ingleton, in the dales. For the most part, the north was Royalist country. I don't suppose it occurred to Adrian that he might be in as much danger there as in other parts of England. But he'd hurt his leg, either in battle or in flight, and his horse had gone lame. He came to an inn seeking refuge but was betrayed by a local squire." The green eyes seemed to be boring holes in Honor's flesh. "His name was Sir Langston Dale."

Honor expelled a strangled cry. It couldn't be possible. Of all the Royalist soldiers, of all the Roundhead supporters, how could it be that Justin's brother and her father should have fatally collided in the Yorkshire dales? *Coincidence* was too weak a word, but even so, Honor couldn't believe that "Fate" worked as insidiously as Justin contended. She had no idea how long he had to wait for her to regain her composure, but she realized distractedly that he was speaking again.

"Sir Langston," he recounted, keeping the reference to her father impersonal, "rounded up as many like-minded fellows as he could find and had Adrian hanged. I've never understood why those Roundheads weren't stopped, since the majority favored the Royalists. But it's an isolated place and no doubt the deed was swiftly done. So was the vengeance that followed."

Justin stopped speaking, rose from the chair and, without looking at Honor, sought out the whiskey decanter. "Other Royalist troops had slipped through Cromwell's net, of course. Adrian was well liked and respected. His comrades wasted no time in seeking out the man who had been his judge, jury, and executioner." He took a long drink and turned his back. "You know the rest."

For some time, Honor didn't respond. She was huddled on the settee, the brightly colored robe providing a contrast to her pale face. The clang of steel on stone echoed in her ears, but to her surprise, she could no longer conjure up the grisly picture that had haunted her for so long. At last she spoke, in a hushed, trembling voice. "It was … all … my fault. I could have … stopped them."

"Rot." Justin spoke sharply, placing the now empty whiskey tumbler on the table. "It was nobody's fault, it was everyone's. That's war. And Fate."

But Honor wasn't listening. Her body was shaking, and despite the sunlight, she felt as if she were in the grip of a winter ague. "It was my fault! I didn't save them! No wonder they won't show me their faces!"

Justin moved to her side. She was convulsed by racking sobs, but her eyes were blank, staring at some scene he could not see. "Honor! Stop it!" Shaking her roughly, he managed at last to make her acknowledge his presence.

She finally locked gazes with him, but her body still trembled and her voice was choked with tears. "I stood there, hiding, helpless, doing nothing! I might have gone for aid, I should have found a weapon, I could have taken—"

"You were ten years old." He gave her one more little shake, then pushed her away, a bare arm's length. "You felt helpless because you *were* helpless. Use your usual common sense, Honor. What could you, as a child, have done to save your parents?"

The face she turned to him was white as a shroud. "I don't know .... It always seemed as if ... I did nothing, and they died. Had I done *something*, they might have lived." Tremulously, she reached out to touch him. "Oh, Justin, why was it your brother? How you must hate me! And Philene, too!"

With a sense of relief, he let her collapse against his chest. "I don't suppose you'd believe me if I said it was Fate." He felt her head shake jerkily under his chin, then smoothed the tumbled golden tresses. "As for hating you, how could I? I didn't know you."

Exhausted by her racking sobs, Honor let his weight support her tired body. "Yet what could my father have done, seeing that Adrian was the enemy?" The words were muffled against his shirt. "Had they changed places, your brother might have hanged my sire."

Thinking back to the boisterous, kind, strong-willed young man who had been his brother, Justin couldn't quite see Adrian Blake dispensing justice in the same merciless manner as Sir Langston Dale. But it would not do to say so to Honor. At least not now.

"It was all a long time ago," he said evasively. "Almost eleven years. Not," he added, resting his chin on the top of her head, "that I'll ever forget. It didn't seem fair somehow that Adrian, who had so much to give, should have been the one to die."

His remark did much to help restore Honor's equilibrium. "What do you mean?" she demanded, looking up at him squarely. "That you have nothing to give?"

He made a rueful face. "Not as he did. Ask Philene."

Honor wiped at her wet cheeks and set her shoulders. "You're comparing a boy to a man. Ask me. I'll tell you what I think of Justin Blake."

A faint smile played at his mouth. "You didn't know Adrian. You can't compare. And your argument is no more convincing to me than mine to you. We speak now as adults, both of us, and damn our youthful selves for not acting as we would do now."

"True." Her voice had turned wistful. "Oh, Justin," she sighed, "I'm so weary." Her head was again on his shoulder. "Put me to bed, please."

He closed his arms more tightly about her. "Alone?" The small smile she offered him was as feeble as it was fond. "No. I want to wake up in your arms."

Tenderly, he picked her up and carried her from the withdrawing room. Loxley, who had just finished seeing to the three other highwaymen's needs, directed him to the bedchamber that had been prepared for Honor. Before he could get to the top of the stairs, he glanced down at her and saw that she was already fast asleep.

Chapter Fifteen

HONOR'S WISH WAS GRANTED. JUST as twilight settled in over Buttermilk Hill, she awoke in Justin's arms, her back snuggled up to his bare chest, his fingers entwined in her hair. He had not been with her the full ten hours that she had slept but had tended to a number of other pressing matters, at Smallwood and beyond. He had come to a decision, but as he felt Honor stir in his embrace, he decided to postpone telling her.

Rolling over onto her back, Honor blinked twice and frowned up into the damask canopy above her head. She was momentarily confused, never having seen the room in which she found herself. "I thought it was a pasha's harem," she said, putting an arm around Justin's neck and observing the vivid splashes of red and blue that dominated the room. "Don't tell me this was Sir Ralph's bedroom!"

"I doubt it," said Justin, who had managed to doze for the better part of an hour. "I suspect it belonged to his mother, who lived to be almost ninety and was rumored to have once gotten in the last word with Queen Elizabeth. Even so, the old dame was said to disapprove of her son's Roundhead leanings."

The political reference wiped the smile from Honor's face. She started to sit up among the pillows, realized that she was naked and pulled the satin sheet up to her neck. "Who undressed me? You, I hope?"

The green eyes sparkled with mischief. "A modest soul would insist on having the lady's maid perform that chore." Pulling himself up to sit next to her on the pillows, he put his hand in the masses of her hair and turned her head to face him. "Or have you no shame where I'm concerned?"

"That's true," she replied with total candor. "I feel as if I belong to you whether we are wed or not." She saw his eyes grow serious as he searched her face and wondered if she had revealed too much. "But I sense that in some ways, we are still strangers, if not enemies." Under the satin sheet, she could feel the warmth of his body, yet she was determined to convey the confusion in her mind. "Do you understand what I mean?"

"I understand desire," he answered slowly, "and mayhap I begin to understand love. But not knowing if tomorrow will ever come, I live for today. Your philosophy is more complex than mine."

The room was growing dark. She wished he would light a candle, but he made no move to leave the bed. "You must be more optimistic," she said, but there was scant force in her voice. "You talk of love." She put a hand to his face, tracing his profile with her finger. "Surely you have loved before, Justin."

"I think not." He bent to nip her finger with his teeth. "I dared not risk loving for fear of being loved in return. It wouldn't have been fair, as it was not for Adrian and Philene."

"I don't think Philene would agree with you."

He took her hand and kissed the palm. Previously, even a few weeks ago, he would have argued with her about Philene's feelings. But now he wasn't so sure. As the moon rose to fill the chamber with its pale silver light, her skin took on the sheen of pearls, her hair turned luminescent against the pillow. He gazed into the dark eyes with their innocent passion and knew he could discourse no longer. Nor did he wish to, at least not without admitting his own self-doubts. But Honor was too near, too enticing, too eager. He pulled her close, kissing her mouth again and again. Except for an initial hesitation, she made no attempt to free herself, but let him explore her mouth even as she submitted to his caressing hands at her breasts and surrendered to the desire in his hungry eyes.

"You're evasive," she chided, but there was no sting in her reproach.

"You're maddeningly desirable," he countered, sliding her down from the pillows and casting aside the satin sheet. Though the rainstorm had cooled off the summer countryside, it remained stuffy in the bedchamber. A breeze stirred in the poplars, and he moved swiftly to open one of the windows.

Honor's naked body felt rejuvenated as she luxuriated on the downy mattress. She stretched her arms out to welcome him back to her. "You distract me," she sighed against his ear. "Your method of argument is unfair."

"No more than it is unfair for you to make me want you so much in the first place," he said as she tipped back her head to offer him the curve of her throat. "It would be difficult to avoid any lovely lady who happened to wake up in bed beside me. With you, it's impossible."

She couldn't help but smile at his words. He was kissing the hollow that led to the valley between her breasts, his hands clasping her hips. In one deft move, he tumbled her over on top of him, leaving her breathless and giggling.

The long, shining tresses shimmered over her shoulder while thick strands caressed his face. He felt as if he were drowning in a cascade of pale gold.

"Who touched you, fair Honor? Midas or the angels?" he asked.

"I had blond forebears," she replied, never so poetically inclined as he. "Or so," she continued uncertainly, "it must have been." Even now she couldn't remember her parents' coloring. But that was in the past, and in Justin she envisioned her future. If only, she thought fleetingly, he could do the same.

Justin, however, was feasting on the present, holding her so that her breasts smothered him as he stroked her back and buttocks. His tongue, that glib weapon that served the highwayman as well as his pistols, spoke a different language as it probed Honor's most intimate secrets. As eager to please as to be pleased, she repaid him in kind, reveling in her ability to make him groan with pleasure.

While the moonlight washed over their bodies, they tantalized, provoked, enkindled, aroused, until at last neither could put off the searing moment of surrender. Each gave; each received. Their union was a spiral of delight, culminating with a rapturous crescendo. Even after they had attained the pinnacle of joy, their bodies remained entwined, as if they were no longer independent of each other but irrevocably joined together for all time.

But time being not as infinite as love, Justin finally withdrew, though he kept Honor clasped in his arms. To her surprise, he seemed unduly somber. For a brief moment she was afraid. Had she done or said something to disturb him? "You're sad, my love," she whispered, noting that the wound on his chest was healing cleanly. Brushing it lightly with her fingers, she looked up into his face. "Are you troubled?"

He shook his head. "Merely melancholy. Tomorrow, I leave Burton Old Forest."

"What!" Honor sat bolt upright, hoping she hadn't heard him correctly. But the fact that he was avoiding her gaze wasn't encouraging. "But why?"

The broad shoulders slumped a bit. "For many reasons," he replied, now looking directly at her. "The most pressing is that my presence here in Rutbury endangers the forest itself. As long as the Goudges and their ilk think they can collect that damnable reward, they'll keep hacking down the trees."

"They'll hack away in any event," she protested, remembering to draw the sheet back up over her breasts, lest she divert him from his explanation. "Reward or not, they stand to make a great profit."

"From whom?" Justin leaned back against the pillows, his hands linked behind his head. "England's government is precarious at best. Dick Cromwell hides from his creditors, Monck sits in Scotland, Lambert connives in London, and Charles waits across the Channel. These Rutburians don't own the woods—the Crown does. If the King returns soon, God help it to happen, the monies from the timber sales will go to him."

She was silent for a moment. "I didn't realize that."

"Nor, I'll wager, do they." He gave her a sardonic look. "Greed often fogs the brain."

"But they'll keep chopping down trees whether you are at Beggar's Oak or not," she argued.

"Mayhap, but I refuse to be responsible for any further arboreal carnage." His jaw hardened. Honor was tempted to run her fingers from ear to chin. "Besides," he went on, while she was still fighting off the urge to touch him, "I almost caused Creepers to burn last night. Losing the lodge was heartrending enough, but Goudges notwithstanding, I'd never forgive myself if I did anything to destroy the home my ancestors built."

Honor could understand his feelings, but they did not convince her he should go away. "You could hide out here at Smallwood and wait until Charles comes back. How long, think you? Weeks? Months?"

"I can't guess." Impatiently, he got out of bed, moving to the open window. "And no, I can't wait here. That's the coward's way."

She watched the moonlight play off his tall, muscular body and dreaded the moment when the miles would separate them. To keep from crying out to dissuade him, she busied herself by lighting a candle next to the bed and putting Philene's flowered robe back on. The hands on the Viennese clock pointed to almost ten.

"Where will you go?" she asked, unable to remain silent any longer.

He moved away from the window, gathering up his clothes from a bench at the foot of the bed. "I'm not sure," he replied.

She caught his elusiveness and gave him a sharp look. "Don't you trust me yet?"

He paused in the act of fastening his breeks. "Yes. Yes, I do."

"Then why can't you tell me your plans?" She was petulant, yet self-righteous. Surely, after all they'd been through together, she was entitled to share his thoughts.

"They're not my plans to tell." Abruptly, he pulled the lawn shirt over his head, then tried to cheer her with his smile. "Truly, I'm not certain what's to happen. I'll find out when I get where I'm going."

She was not appeased. Maybe he didn't know the details, but she was sure he knew more than he was telling her. The prospect of sitting idly at Smallwood for what might turn into forever was only slightly less dismal than staying on at Creepers. Even if King Charles came back, Justin had made no promises about their own future.

"Nip will stay here," Justin said, sitting on the bench while he pulled up his jackboots. "He broke some ribs in a tussle with a foolhardy woodhouse tenant."

Honor's sympathies didn't lie with Nip at the moment but with herself. "Fine," she said curtly, standing by the dormant fireplace with her hands up the sleeves of her robe.

"I must go back to Beggar's Oak tonight before we leave. There is still much to make ready." He came to her side, a frankly pleading expression on his face. "You're vexed. I'd not have us part in anger, even if only for a little while."

"You think you're going to be killed." She spoke in a dull voice, putting emotion aside lest her feelings give the words a life of their own.

He was tight-lipped. "It's possible. The political climate is dangerous, after all."

"You court danger. You live for risk." She made the observations in a calm voice, but when she saw his impassive face, her anger erupted once more. "Don't let it happen!" she cried. "Don't let it happen! Live, Justin, live for me, for yourself, for the future! Spit in the face of your so-called 'Fate'!"

Visibly shaken by her fervor, he caught her wrists and pulled her closer. "You embarrass me with the depth of your feelings. I'm not worthy, Honor. Even at best, I'm a penniless exile."

"So's your Charles Stuart, and if you have your way, he'll soon rule over us all." Her dark eyes burned with intensity. "Come back, Justin," she urged, now speaking in a compelling whisper. "Come back to *me*."

He loosened his grip on her wrists, then gave them a little shake before bending to brush her lips with his. "I will," he said softly.

He kissed her once more, deeply, lovingly, lingeringly, as if to carry the memory with him on the morrow. His green eyes glittered, a reflection of candlelight, of moonlight, of dark shadows and bright hopes. "I will, Honor," he repeated, reluctantly letting her go. From the doorway, he saluted her with a smile that was neither flippant nor wistful but newly confident.

"I promise," he said, and disappeared into the empty corridor.

DURING THE FIRST TWO WEEKS that Honor stayed at Smallwood, she kept close to the manor house. The Goudges were reportedly irate over what they termed her "lawless abduction," and if rumor could be believed, they were certain that she'd fled to Captain Hood's hideaway. Consequently, Honor dared not show herself in the vicinity for fear of being dragged back to Creepers.

Their privacy was at least partially assured by Lady Ferrers's announcement that she was suffering from severe headaches brought on by grief. If anyone found her sudden debility odd at such a late date after her husband's death, at least her wish to avoid company was observed.

This very absence of social activity might have contributed to Honor's safety, but it also caused the time to hang heavy on her hands. Philene was a gracious, if distant, hostess, though Honor sensed she could be much warmer. But Honor wasn't seeking friendship from Philene, only sanctuary. There was still something about the Frenchwoman that nettled Honor.

As the summer days spun out into late July, Honor's need to venture farther than the pastures of Smallwood became almost overwhelming. Finally, on an overcast morning, with the air oppressively sweet from new-mown hay and clover, she headed for the outer boundaries of the estate. After an hour, she had seen no one except a groom from the stables and felt relatively secure as she wandered along the edge of Burton Old Forest where the trees climbed halfway up Buttermilk Hill.

Turning back where the poplars began and the woods ended, she kept a sharp eye on Stubby Lane. Her watchfulness kept her from seeing the bundle that stuck out from under an outcropping of stone. Nor did she notice the long pole until she had tripped over it and barely avoided sprawling on the edge of the cornfield.

"Damn and blast!" she muttered, about to give the pole a kick in retaliation. But her foot stalled as she looked more closely at the offending object. This was no ordinary farmer's pole but a stout staff, charred in several places. Kneeling, she turned the staff in her hands, heedless of the black smudges it left on her fingers. Then she tugged at the bundle, which also bore evidence of having been burned. There was no doubt about it—the monklike robes and staff had belonged to Matthew Thorn. But that was impossible, for Thorn had perished in the fire. His singed belongings couldn't have survived unless he had, too.

The voice from the road made Honor jump. Her first reaction was to run, but an apprehensive glance over her shoulder revealed Judith Tipper, a basket of eggs over one arm. Relieved, Honor got up, still clutching the ruined robes.

"I thought you were hurt," called Mistress Tipper, coming over to the edge of the field, "or ill. I also thought you'd left Rutbury."

"I did." Honor eyed Judith a bit warily, wondering if she'd misplaced her trust.

Mistress Tipper glanced down at the crumpled garments in Honor's arms. "What is that?" She pointed to the staff. "And that? Holy heaven, are those the remains of Master Thorn?"

"So it seems," Honor replied grimly. "Can you explain it?"

Judith's blue eyes blinked in puzzlement. "Explain? Oh—I see what you mean." Her pert features frowned in the effort of concentration. "There is only one explanation. Master Thorn is alive but not dressed."

Honor caught the merriment in Mistress Tipper's eyes and had to laugh. "That's possible. But not likely. How, being blind, could he have escaped?"

That was a mystery Judith seemed unprepared to solve. "It would be miraculous, I suppose. The Good Lord knows I've shed as many tears for him as Jeremy has. For our old home in the lodge, too. Will and I had dreams of returning there someday." She gave Honor a self-deprecating smile. "Foolish, weren't we? I wish Will had stolen everything in it."

"The lodge must have been a charming place at one time," Honor said tactfully. "You knew the Blake sons. What were they like?"

Judith's glance was wary. "Good boys. Different from each other." She paused, clearly reticent. "Why do you ask?"

"Oh … I don't know," Honor temporized, picking up the staff and trying to avoid the splinters. "At Creepers sometimes I felt their presence. They must have been vital young men."

"Adrian was. He'd have made a rollicking country gentleman." Judith's blue eyes grew overbright. "Justin was quiet. His father feared he'd grow up to be a poet and spend his days in moody dissertation." She looked searchingly at Honor. "I suspect that's not what happened."

Honor hesitated. Mistress Tipper knew about Hood. She knew that Honor did, too. Still, it might do more harm than good for either of them to openly acknowledge the fact. "I suspect it isn't," Honor finally allowed. "Life pushes people in strange directions."

Judith nodded, apparently satisfied with the exchange. "It pushed Adrian into the grave." If she noticed Honor's mouth tighten at the reference, Judith gave no sign. "He married a French girl, you know. I hope she loved him as much as he deserved."

"I'm sure she did," Honor said, inadvertently glancing in the direction of Smallwood's chimneys.

Mistress Tipper followed her gaze. "Yes. I've wondered." The enigmatic remark triggered a burst of energy. She adjusted the white linen fall at her neck, cradled the basket of eggs under her arm and inspected the left sole of her shoe before turning back toward Stubby Lane. "I must be off. Will should be home by now with the pig. I hope it's one of Squire Wills's. They make the best bacon."

With her pert smile intact, Judith swung down the lane, her leaf-green skirts raising little puffs of dust behind her. Will Tipper might be a thief, but his wife was trustworthy in her fashion. Honor knew her secret was safe, not on any merits of her own, but because Judith Tipper had known and loved two young boys named Blake.

TO HONOR'S SURPRISE, PHILENE WAS furious with her. "Such folly! To walk abroad, where any spy can recount your whereabouts to the Goudges! Never, never do that again! *Jamais, écoutez-vous? Jamais!*"

Dutifully, Honor listened to Philene rant for a good five minutes. After Parthenia Goudge's tedious sermons, Philene's voluble reprimands were actually a relief. But Honor dared not mention Judith Tipper lest Philene decide that the chance meeting had somehow ruined all. When at last Philene had becalmed herself and was soothing her nerves with a plate of smoked pheasant and a glass of white wine, Honor produced Matthew Thorn's belongings. "What do you make of these?" she asked without inflection.

Philene's shrewd gaze flitted over the bundle and staff. "What do you?" she countered.

Honor had had her fill of guessing games for the morning. "Matthew Thorn didn't die in the fire," she said evenly. Boldly, she hazarded the thought that had come to her as she returned to Smallwood. "Indeed, I believe he never lived. Thorn is—was—really Justin Blake."

Philene shrugged. "*C'est vrai.* I marvel you didn't realize that sooner. It matters not now with Justin gone from Rutbury. But for a long time, Master Thorn was very useful."

It was not only what Honor perceived as Philene's proprietary attitude toward Justin that rankled, but that the Frenchwoman should be privy to so much about him that Honor didn't know. The discovery of Thorn's real identity had been something of a triumph, or so she'd thought until Philene had dismissed it with a shrug.

"You," she burst out angrily, "are insufferable with your secrets and confidences! You remind me constantly that I'm the outsider, while you and Justin are such dear, close allies and friends! You make me feel like a leper!"

"La, *ma chérie*," said Philene lightly, taking the last slice of pheasant, "you *are* an outsider. You're a Puritan, *c'est entendu*!"

Honor had been standing by the bay window while Philene reclined on her settee. Outside, Loxley was supervising two gardeners who were thinning out the earlier summer blooms. Honor scarcely saw them as she pondered Philene's words.

"I was raised a Puritan," she said slowly, with her back still to Philene, "but there is much about the religion that I find distorted. Uncle Oliver was stern, yet just. Neither he nor Aunt Elizabeth was as fanatical as the Goudges. Still," she went on, finally moving back toward the settee, "I'm troubled by what I see as so much that is negative. I don't think God is mean but merciful. Too many Puritans make Him over into their own images. It's a faith lacking in love, short on charity. I don't wonder that Aunt Lucy balked at its practice."

Bemused, Philene set down her wineglass. "Aunt Lucy, eh? She sounds wise. I like people who think for themselves." Sitting up, she tucked her feet under her body and patted the settee's damask upholstery. "Sit, Honor, be at ease. Tell me of Aunt Lucy."

Honor did, stiltedly at first, then, as Philene encouraged her with apt remarks and pertinent questions, she warmed to the subject. She even told about how she'd been brought from the Yorkshire farmer's cottage where she'd been taken in after her parents' murder. It was at this point that she grew self-conscious; Philene's animated features had suddenly grown tense.

"I'm sorry," said Honor, lowering her gaze. "This part must be painful for you. I shall omit the rest."

A small line appeared between Philene's brows. "No. I need to hear it. I've spent many years imagining." She picked up the wineglass, saw that it was empty and set it aside again. "We must face all things, no matter how cruel. Your father was too harsh, yet he acted as men do in times of war. In consequence, he—and your poor *maman*—paid a terrible price. Where no mercy is given, none is received."

A rush of disconnected memories pressed in on Honor, of her father's short barking laugh, of strict justice with the rod, of scoldings for lessons unlearned, of a smart cuff to the cheek for interrupting when adults were present. To her astonishment, she suddenly could picture her father, a blunt, balding man with deep-set eyes and an eagle's beak of a nose. And then she saw her mother, too, smiling under a jumble of ash-blond hair, a basket of summer flowers on one arm.

"Damn and blast," breathed Honor. "I think I'm going to cry."

Philene merely inclined her head. She obviously did not wish to pry, but Honor wanted to tell her about the mental images that had taken so long to conjure up out of memory. Haltingly, she poured out the story of how, from the day of their death, her parents had proved elusive in her mind's eye.

"I must have been waiting for them to forgive me, or for me to avenge them, or both," she continued, wiping at the tears that had threatened to spill down her cheeks. "But Justin helped make me see that their deaths weren't my fault. And now you have said much the same thing. Of all the people who could have reassured me, what irony it is that I'm in the debt of the man who caused my parents to be murdered. It's almost as if Adrian has spoken to you and Justin from beyond the grave."

"So he does," replied Philene, with an offhand gesture. "At least to me."

Making a final dab at her eyes with a lace-edged kerchief, Honor forced a wan smile. "I don't think I'm a Puritan anymore." She looked down at the peony-pink petticoats and lavender overskirts that she'd borrowed from Philene. Having come to Smallwood with nothing but the clothes on her back, she had had to let Philene lend her the equivalent of a full wardrobe. Only now did she realize that in discarding her plain Puritan garb, she'd also cast off the faith into which she'd been born. "I believed in Uncle Oliver, but not in everything he stood for. Now he's gone, and only a wrangling passel of soldiers and politicians remain. I feel as if I'm playing at children's games that I should have given up long ago."

Nodding her approval, Philene squeezed Honor's hand. "This English quarrel over religion never made much sense to me, but oh, how it mattered to Adrian! And Justin, too. Their consciences drove them to defend both King and Church. Oh, how mighty is the English conscience!" She shook her head at the folly of foreigners. "In your case, Honor, I sensed you lived out of habit, not conscience. I am most pleased that this dissension between you and Justin has been resolved."

Honor made a wry face. "You mean I won't try to shoot him?" She didn't wait for Philene's response. "Nay, I couldn't do that, even when I didn't know him. But I wish he'd trust me more." She gave Philene a look that was unintentionally hostile. "It's obvious that he trusts you implicitly."

"Yes." Swinging her foot over the edge of the settee, Philene got up and went to the dressing table, where she peered briefly at her image. "Give him time. Remember that you represented everything he hates most, as he did for you. With love comes trust."

"If he loves me," said Honor, who had also stood up. "I'm not sure he really does. He plays the gallant wooer as if it were a second skin."

"Zut!" Philene waved the notion away. "That is all due to the most artful grooming. Only as Captain Hood and Matthew Thorn and whatever other guise Justin puts on can he be what he is not. Tell me, *chère* Honor, who do you love, the dashing highwayman or Justin Blake?"

It was not a question Honor was prepared to answer straightaway. Certainly she'd succumbed to Hood's glib tongue, to his casual charm, to his boundless confidence. So, it seemed, had many another maid and matron. But that other side of him, the uncertain, self-deprecating, melancholy fatalist that was Justin Blake had proved more difficult to understand. As Captain Hood, he seemed invincible; as himself, he was a vulnerable man.

"Captain Hood doesn't need me," Honor said at last, while Philene waited patiently. "But Justin Blake does. He may not know it, but it's true. I suspect that's the real reason he says he's never fallen in love. No one else knew him, not as himself."

"True. Oh," Philene said with a soft laugh, "there were many sweethearts, if you will, and each was courted ardently, though briefly. But do not doubt his love for you, *ma chérie*," she continued earnestly, "for if he did not love you, he would never have let you know about Justin Blake. There is the real trust he has placed between the two of you."

Honor savored the words, and for once, was glad that the Frenchwoman shared her lover's confidences. "You have been very kind, despite my rude tongue. Can you forgive me?"

Philene put her arms around Honor and gave her a warm hug. "Of course! Do you think Philene dull witted when it comes to matters of the heart? It was I, after all, who had the task of making you jealous to find out for Justin if you really cared. How could you not hate me, at least a little?"

Honor leaned toward Philene and brushed her cheek in an affectionate gesture. "You certainly did it well. I was convinced you were a scheming viper."

Philene went to the cabinet and brought out another glass, then poured wine for them both. "I scheme, yes, but I am no vixen. For Adrian's sake I abet the Royalists. He gave his life for his King, and French or not, I owe him that much." She held up her glass. "To you, to Justin, to King Charles!"

A bit awkwardly, Honor let her glass touch Philene's. It seemed very strange to be toasting the monarch her uncle had worked so hard to keep off England's throne. Yet if all went well for Charles, then so it should go with Justin. "To all of us," she said, taking a sip of wine. "Oh, Philene, if only he comes back!"

Philene opened her mouth to speak but clamped it shut before any sound came out. Honor watched her expectantly, but when the other woman finally gave voice to her thoughts, it was in an oddly wistful manner. "Often, they do come back. But sometimes, they do not. Still, love lasts forever."

Chapter Sixteen

THE OLD FAMILY NAMES ECHOED from another era, evoking the ghosts of clerical pomp and royal rule by Divine Right: Herbert, Derby, Legg, Egerton, a roll call of staunch High Church and even Roman Catholic nobles who had fought in vain against the tide of Cromwell's Puritan Commonwealth. Yet as they gathered off the Tudor courtyard of Dunham Massey Hall near Altrincham, they were men who looked not to the past but to the future.

But among these Royalist scions were also numbered some of their former opponents. The owner of the house was George Booth, Lord Delamere, who on the face of it seemed an unlikely candidate to help foment a rebellion to unseat John Lambert's Parliamentary cabal. Not only had Delamere served in the Long Parliament that had defied Charles I, but he had been Cromwell's treasurer for the army during the Civil War.

Yet Lord Delamere had become disillusioned. Upon trying to resume his seat in Parliament, he had been rebuffed and sent back to Cheshire. Other members had been kept out as well, their lack of enthusiasm for John Lambert's high-handed attempt to take over the government marking them as newly minted rebels. When Delamere had been barred from going any further than the lobby of Parliament, he had ridden home to Dunham Massey in a state of deep thought. It had become clear to him that Lambert hadn't ousted Dick Cromwell solely on the grounds of incompetence. Lambert was an old crony of Oliver Cromwell's and was making it clear he felt that he, not Dick, should be the rightful heir to the Protectorate. John Lambert could not come to terms with General Monck and the army, and Monck's anti-Royalist feelings had visibly weakened in the face of Lambert's brazen ambition. But Delamere had gone one step beyond Monck: once back in Cheshire, he had cast his lot with the Cavaliers and had been instrumental in forming a coalition known as the New Royalists. From Lancashire, Staffordshire, and Wales they now came, eager to get on with the business of bringing the King back and ousting Lambert.

"There is no point," Delamere declared before his rapt audience in the great hall, "in replacing one form of tyranny with another. In the beginning, this country was divided between Royalist and Puritan, Roundhead and Cavalier. When we toppled King Charles from the throne and had him beheaded, we were fortunate to have the great leadership of Oliver Cromwell to fill the vacuum. But our revered captain is gone, his son, alas, is inept, and there is no outstanding commoner to assume command of the government. John Lambert has divided the army against itself. He will divide the country, as well. If General Monck refuses to act on Charles II's behalf, someone else must." His voice rose as the flames from the fire in the huge grate added fervor to his face. "England cannot afford to be patient. King Charles waits at Calais. It is up to us to bring him home!"

The hall reverberated with an enthusiastic roar, yet not every voice was raised. Lounging under the venerable arms of the Booth family, Justin Blake remained silent, the alert green eyes scanning the company. It wasn't that he distrusted the newly found Royalist sympathies of Lord Delamere but rather that he felt uneasy about this impetuous plot. No matter that the Cheshire conspiracy was just one of many being hatched across England: the old and the new Royalists were acting precipitately.

"You go too fast," he said when the clamor had died down. He had stepped out of the shadows and now stood close to the glowing hearth where Lord Delamere had delivered his impassioned speech. Though he was only known to a handful of Royalists in both his guises, most of the assembly recognized him as Justin Blake, who had spent long years in exile abroad. His story was not uncommon and his presence among them went unchallenged. "I applaud your sentiments," he continued, having gained their attention to a man, "yet you are fragmented, you have no military support."

"We have four thousand men in Cheshire alone," Will Herbert countered, his blue eyes bright with zeal.

Justin inclined his head to one side. "That's so, but like many of the previous King's adherents, they are ill-trained and ill-equipped. I suggest we wait for General Monck and his army to commit themselves."

"As they will do," asserted Lord Delamere, "once they see King Charles stepping onto English soil. They'll declare themselves then and give a hearty cheer in the process."

"Charles is being toasted openly in half the inns of England," put in an older man whose ravaged appearance gave evidence to the years of imprisonment he'd endured under Oliver Cromwell. "Likenesses of His Majesty are appearing all over London. I speak only for myself," continued the Earl of Dartmouth in his hoarse voice, "but I've already waited too long."

Justin, however, remained obdurate. "If Charles comes back now, the Presbyters will oppose him—with open conflict, if need be. They fear persecution."

"They ought to," Herbert murmured. "They are as intolerable as they are intolerant."

Most of the men nodded in agreement. Watching their faces, Justin tried to gauge the depths of their determination. Most he did not know by sight, but many were familiar by reputation. At least half of them had been imprisoned at one time or another under Cromwell. Some of them had been maimed in the Civil War. All, whether originally Roundheads or Cavaliers, had lost a father, brother, or close kinsman in battle. There were those who burned to avenge the execution of Charles I; there were others who would not rest until Charles II was back on England's throne. Justin understood all of this, for he was numbered among them by loss and loyalty. Yet he could not agree with their haste.

"You make a good point, sir," he said calmly to Dartmouth, "but therein is the problem. We have suffered through too much war. Now we should sue for peace. The Presbyters must be placated, along with the Puritans and the Catholics and the Anglicans and the Quakers and all the rest. Otherwise, it is pointless to restore the King. We will only end up shedding the rest of our blood and possibly force England into chaos. For however much many of you might have hated Oliver Cromwell," he went on, raising his voice just a notch and sounding faintly defiant, "you must admit he was able to restore order. I hope and pray that restoring Charles will do the same. But *not* yet."

Stepping back into the shadows like an actor who has delivered his lines and left the stage, he again surveyed the rest of the group. They were looking very solemn for the most part and spoke in low voices to one another in twos and threes. At least five minutes passed before Lord Delamere called for order.

"Our friend Justin makes good sense," he declared in his strong, yet pleasant, voice. "But Lambert goes too far. His opposition to Charles and his self-advocacy will ruin England. We cannot afford to sit and wait."

As a murmur of assent crept about the hall, Justin stifled a sigh. He, who had passed much of his life in waiting, either across the Channel in France or at the roadsides of England, could not convince this gathering that patience was a virtue. To a man, they believed that to wait was to fail. For Justin, it was only a matter of time. Charles's return was ordained by Fate.

But it was obvious that this foolhardy group was prepared to rush Fate. And if they did, he had no choice but to support them. They might fail, but he could not stand aloof. He thought of Honor, how she had insisted that Fate was a crock and that he must shape the future with his own hands. Perhaps, somehow, they would wrest victory from what seemed to him to be certain defeat. Justin gave a wry smile and shrugged his shoulders. He would ride with the Royalists to Chester.

THE WARM WEATHER HAD FINALLY broken over the Staffordshire plain, this time bringing heavy rains that churned up the roadway, battered the tall cornstalks and left large puddles in the newly harvested fields. In Burton Old Forest, the tree cutters were idle, covering their tools to keep them free of rust. At Creepers, the workmen halted in their task of restoring the burned bedchamber. Along the muddy road to Rutbury, ox carts stalled, coaches were mired down, and farm wagons were delayed in their delivery to the market square.

At Smallwood, Honor was forced to stay inside virtually all of the time. To pass the hours, she learned to play once forbidden card games, practiced the technique of lace insertion and acquired a working French vocabulary. Best of all, she made a new friend. Now that she was able to see her own relationship with Justin more clearly, she could also better understand the special bond between him and his late brother's wife.

One gray August afternoon, when the rain let up and the clouds lifted, Honor ventured as far as the kennels, where a litter of whippets had been born the previous week. Four of the original six pups had survived, but Philene feared for the runt. In need of fresh air, Honor took it upon herself to see how the sickly animal was doing.

Looking down at the little mound of gray fur, Honor couldn't help but feel compassion. The dark eyes seemed enormous, the tiny, pointed ears stood up like small horns, and the long, thin legs looked too spindly to support a mouse. With an unsure hand, Honor stroked the pup's back and felt it shiver at her touch. The other three whelps were nursing vigorously. "Let's see if you can manage," she said softly. "There's ample room."

But even as Honor picked the animal up, its small body went limp. "Oh, no!" she cried, then took the dog by the muzzle, noting with alarm that its eyes were open but blank. Perhaps he couldn't see yet, she told herself, but her fumbling fingers found no sign of life. Turning her back on the bitch as if to spare her maternal grief, Honor set the pup down by a small water trough. When she looked away, her startled gaze recognized Uriah Goudge, standing uncertainly at the kennel gate.

"What are you doing here?" she gasped, searching beyond his big, awkward form to see if any of the other Goudges were also present.

"I came to see you," Uriah answered, pulling nervously at his rumpled brown cloth jerkin. "Do you mind?"

"Mind?" Honor swallowed hard and approached Uriah warily. "That depends. How did you know where to find me?"

Uriah shifted uncomfortably. "I guessed. That is, I asked Clarity first."

Honor gave him a skeptical look. "How would she know?"

"Well," he replied slowly, pulling one of his square-toed shoes out of the muck, "I asked her where she'd go if she ever ran away and she said to Smallwood, because Lady Ferrers entertained so many fancy folk. Only Squire Styles told us she stopped entertaining right after you were carried off, so I wondered, mayhap she was hiding something. Such as yourself."

For all Uriah's apparent slow-wittedness, it occurred to Honor that he was the only person in Rutbury who had figured out where she had gone. "Are you going to tell the others?"

Uriah's surprise was genuine. "Why, no. They'd fetch you back and make you marry me."

Dumbfounded, Honor fretted the fringe on her shawl and reviewed his words to make sure she'd heard correctly. "I thought you *wanted* to marry me."

"Oh, I did, I do," Uriah asserted, flushing. "But it wouldn't have been a happy match. I love you too much to marry you. I wouldn't have made a good Puritan husband at all. You were right. It was most unsuitable. So now I've come to say goodbye."

"Where are you going?" Honor asked, still astounded by his confession.

Uriah jammed his hands into the pockets of his baggy black pants. "I was supposed to go last week to London with Squire and Curate to see John Lambert, but I decided to bide. I'm courting, you see," he confided shyly.

The three pups had sated themselves and were nuzzling Honor's hem. She shooed them off, then inquired after the identity of Uriah's current sweetheart.

His face grew even darker. "My parents don't approve, but then they never liked you, either. That is ..." he suddenly mumbled. Honor waved away his attempt at apology so he gained courage once again. "Laura Tipper."

Honor gasped in astonishment. "Will and Judith's daughter?" She saw Uriah nod. "Why, that's splendid! She's a bonny maid, favoring her mother, as I recall from seeing her in the village."

Uriah gave Honor a diffident smile, then sobered quickly. "If we wed, we can't live at Creepers. My parents won't permit a Tipper inside the house. I'm thinking of moving to the Massachusetts Bay Colony."

Visions of dense forest and red-skinned natives unfolded before Honor's eyes. The colonies across the ocean had always sounded unbearably primitive to her. Their lure was powerful for other Englishmen; even Uncle Oliver had almost gone there in his youth. But Honor had never felt the appeal.

"You'll find great hardship there," she said, and was immediately sorry for it. "But no doubt great happiness, as well. I wish you and Laura all God's blessings." On tiptoe, she strained to kiss Uriah's cheek.

Even Uriah's ears turned red. "We should manage, if it comes to that. My parents know a family over there named Mather. One of their sons is preaching here in England now and mayhap we'll sail back with him." He ran a finger inside his faded lawn collar. "I'd like to build my own home. I've never liked Creepers. It doesn't .... I can't say it right, it's like wearing a coat made for someone else. Do you know what I mean?" he asked plaintively.

Honor nodded. "I know. You've put it very well. You're an intelligent man, Uriah."

A strange noise that seemed to convey disbelief erupted from Uriah's throat, but the ensuing grin revealed his pleasure at Honor's compliment. "I'm not really. I try to puzzle things out, like what's right and what isn't. It takes me a lot of time to find the answers."

Overhead, the gray clouds were pressing in on them again. The pups had gone to sleep next to their mother. After so much rain, the air smelled of wet grass and rich earth. Honor pulled her shawl more closely around her and smiled up at Uriah. "You'll find what you want, Uriah. And I'll wager you'll be thankful it wasn't me."

"No." The word was matter-of-fact, yet irrefutable. "But I don't mind." He glanced down at the still body of the little whelp. "Life's like that poor pup. We have a litter full of dreams, but they can't all come true." Shyly, yet candidly, he looked back at Honor. "If I marry Laura and go to the New World, I may never see my parents again. I'm very lucky, all things considered."

As Uriah loped out of the kennel, Honor realized that for an inarticulate man, he put things very well.

THE NEW ROYALIST ARMY HAD been close to Manchester when Padge and Wat rode up like a pair of exhausted hounds to deliver their depressing news. Justin Blake met at once with Lord Delamere, Colonel Egerton, and the Earl of Derby. Thomas Middleton, who had joined them at Wrexham, was there, too, his long, handsome face sallow with frustration.

"We should keep marching for York," he insisted, adjusting the plain baldric sash that held his sword in place. "We had success at Cheshire and Chirk. What do we care if the others have made a mess of things?"

"We'll care if we find ourselves isolated between Lambert to the south and Monck in the north," said Justin, moving away from the tree he'd been leaning against. "I agree with George," he went on, gesturing at a solemn Lord Delamere, "in that we must either fend off Lambert or quit the field."

Delamere gave him a wry look. "You were right, Justin. The news your men have brought us proves you prophetic."

Justin waved the words aside. "Even I would not have guessed that the uprising would prove so feeble except for your brave men."

Middleton surveyed the trampled field behind them where the bulk of their army rested. "Our men are weary. We shan't best Lambert, I fear."

Justin, Delamere, and the others followed Middleton's gaze. Half the men were dozing, some were wounded, and a few stragglers were still wandering in from the road to Manchester. The skies had cleared, yet summer seemed to be on the wane. So, Justin thought, did the New Royalist cause. At least for now.

The fighting at Winwick Bridge outside of Northwick was brief but fierce. Lambert's fresh troops had marched only the short distance from Macclesfield that morning and had not tasted battle for some time. Fired with Republican zeal and Puritan fervor, they stormed the bridge with belching muskets and slashing swords. The New Royalists were driven back, turning the field to mud and the river to crimson. The defeated men tried to flee but many were taken prisoner. Still others surrendered outright, recognizing either the futility of their cause or the faces of recently abandoned comrades still fighting with Lambert.

For Lord Delamere, it was a dark, bitter afternoon. He had put on a brave show, refusing to give up hope until he saw that men could die in a struggle that promised neither glory nor success. At the last moment, with Lambert's troops converging on Delamere, Justin Blake had ridden straight into the fray, wielding his sword in one hand and his pistol in the other.

"Flee!" he had called to Delamere, shooting one foe's horse out from under him before he could turn swiftly to fend off the saber thrust of another man. An explosion close by had added to the confusion, allowing Justin to gallop off in Delamere's wake. Moments later, the two men were under the bridge itself, where they found a sweating, cursing Thomas Middleton.

"Are we cowards?" Middleton demanded after he'd finished his litany of oaths.

Delamere was breathing hard as he wrapped a kerchief around a cut on his left hand. "Nay, we had no choice. I'll be damned if I'll let that villain Lambert parade me back to London like a pirate's booty."

"Well said," agreed Justin, looking up as more men and horses thundered over Winwick Bridge. "I suggest we make for Scotland."

"Scotland!" Delamere spoke the word with scorn. "And crawl to General Monck with our tails between our legs? I go back home, to Dunham Massey."

"And I to Chirk Castle," said Middleton. "It's mine again, at last."

Justin had unbuckled his sword and stripped down to his shirt. "But for how long? Think you that Lambert will not march straightaway to both your ancestral homes? I'll wager he has Chester as well as Chirk back in his grip within the week."

His comrades eyed him doubtfully as the chaos above their heads finally seemed to abate. "Mayhap you're right, Justin. You were before." Delamere sighed wearily. "But not Scotland. Monck will play us like a lute."

"I think not," Justin replied, kneeling down to bathe his face in the murky river. "He must listen. His spies don't seem to be as efficient as Lambert's. I doubt that he realizes how strong the prorestoration feeling runs."

"Pah!" Middleton winced as a lone rider overhead dislodged several chunks of dirt, striking the nobleman on the head. "It's not strong enough to carry a battle," he averred, brushing himself off, "or else we wouldn't be hiding like chickens from a fox under this damnable bridge."

"I disagree, Tom," Justin said amiably. "It's not a question of strength but one of organization. We can't field a proper army because most of this country's professional soldiers are with Monck. I suggest that he is our destination, and that we take a roundabout way to get there to avoid Lambert's scouts." He was putting his shirt back on, muffling the last few words. "For safety's sake, we use disguises."

Delamere and Middleton exchanged bemused glances. "You're adroit at that, I'm told," Delamere said. "What shall we be? Shuffling yokels or country parsons?"

Justin's smile was enigmatic. "The quickness of your suggestions discourages me. Lambert will think the same." He inclined his head to one side and grinned devilishly. "Your blond curls are fetching, George, though you could do with a shave. And, Tom, a bit of powder is required to give you a fashionable complexion." He noted their puzzled expressions and made a mock curtsy, almost banging his head on the underside of the bridge. "Henceforth, you two are simple maids, bound for London to barter your virtue for a bag of gold. I will be your yokel servant."

THE ACQUISITION OF THEIR NEW wardrobes turned out to be easier than they might have hoped. Now joined by Padge and Wat, who had been hiding out upriver from the bridge, they had come upon an empty farmhouse at the edge of the field where the New Royalists had been so briefly encamped. Apparently the owner and his family had fled during the battle. The cold remains of their midday meal still sat upon a trestle table, providing sustenance for the weary foragers. Their luck held with the discovery that the farmer had not only a buxom wife but at least one equally bountiful daughter. Amid much guffawing and clumsy efforts with petticoats and kirtles, the two men outfitted themselves satisfactorily. Padge and Wat rode on ahead as lookouts, while

Justin borrowed from the farmer to produce a costume suitable for the fair maids' humble servant.

For two nights they slept under the stars, but on the third, before turning due north, they paused in Newport Pagnell at a small inn just after midnight. If their sleep-befuddled host was surprised to find two homely females and their companion at his door, he gave no sign, ushering them upstairs to one of the only two rooms in the inn. Not bothering to undress, the two supposed maids fell onto the lumpy bed and were asleep almost immediately, while their manservant stretched out to guard the door. All slept like logs, and did not stir until midmorning, when the smell of frying meat wafted up into the chamber. Justin summoned a potboy to bring breakfast and a razor.

"We won't fool anyone with these damnable beards," Delamere asserted, rubbing his chin.

Justin was looking dubious. "Since we're heading north now, we might be able to do away with the female disguises. Lambert's scouts may have given up on the roads to Scotland."

The razor arrived, but the potboy made apologies for the delay of breakfast. "A busy morn," he mumbled, backing out of the room, "with soldiers and all."

As soon as the door was closed, the three men exchanged worried glances. Justin went to the window and looked out. At least a dozen horses were tethered in front of the inn, lazily cropping at the sparse patches of grass next to the High Street.

Cursing under his breath, Justin moved away from the casement. "Padge and Wat must have missed them somehow. Or else," he added grimly, "they've been captured."

Delamere, who was trying to see his image in a polished square of tin, shrugged. "It's probably nothing to do with us. Do you really think Lambert would waste his men on an extended wild-goose chase all over the English countryside?"

Before Justin could respond, a serving wench pushed the door open, started inside with a huge tray full of food and came to an astonished halt. "Oh!" she cried, all but dropping the tray. *"Oh!"*

Justin moved quickly to block her view of Delamere with the razor in his hand. "There, girl, put those victuals down and begone. Next time, knock first."

The girl turned and ran like a rabbit. Justin shut the door behind her and made a face. "Damn all," he breathed.

Delamere flung the razor across the room, the blade sticking in the worm-scarred wall. "I should not have shaved! I've ruined it for all of us!"

"You should not have gotten caught," grumbled Middleton. "That was the Devil's own bad luck."

The sausage, bread and cheese grew cold while the three men waited. Less than five minutes passed before a knock sounded at the door. Justin responded to the call and found the innkeeper on the threshold with a trio of soldiers behind him.

"Ah!" Justin exclaimed, feigning horror. "We were about to take our leave, but I see we've been found out. Perhaps you can stay and dally with our creditors when they get this far."

The soldiers eyed the unlikely trio with suspicion. "Who are you?" demanded the tallest among them as the innkeeper nervously stepped aside.

Delamere started to reply, but Justin cut in smoothly, "Manners, Lodge and Ives, all from Northampton. We've run afoul, I fear, of a mean-minded Scot. Once we get to London, I'm sure we can straighten it all out, eh, lads … or are you still lassies?"

"We shall still be in debt, nonetheless," sighed Delamere, taking his cue. "But at least we shan't go to prison for it."

"I should hope not," averred Justin, turning to Middleton and Delamere. "Now that you pretty ones have made your toilette, shall we pay our gracious host and depart? The morning moves along."

"The sooner the better," grumbled Middleton, who had managed to get his lace-edged neck band on sideways. "I've had enough of Newport Pagnell."

Delamere was already passing out a princely sum to the innkeeper but remembered his part and groused a bit over the strain on his purse. Uncertainly, the soldiers moved out of the way, allowing the bizarre group to precede them down the stairs. They had reached the common room when the fourth soldier, who had been left behind as a security measure, looked up. "Delamere!" he cried. His hand went to his pistol, pointing it straight at the nobleman's head.

Delamere turned, but the other soldiers blocked his way back up the stairs. There was no chance for any of them to grasp their weapons. Indeed, it was all they could do to keep from falling down in a heap at the bottom of the stairwell. Cursing themselves for being taken in so readily, the three soldiers at the rear pushed roughly at their would-be prisoners.

"Damnation," cried Delamere, "I will not risk more lives to save my skin!" He held up his hands, an incongruous sight in the gray dress with his flounce of white petticoats and crochet-edged bodice. Ruefully, he glanced at Justin and Middleton. "Had I used more common sense, we should not be in this fix to begin with. My apologies, gentlemen. I've been most reckless."

"And brave," Justin remarked, brushing off one of the soldiers who tried to grab his arm. "Don't fret. We'll bide awhile in the Tower and no doubt be free by Christmas-tide."

"Don't count on it," grunted the soldier who had recognized Delamere.

"By then, Master Lambert will have all England under his thumb and the three of you will rot in prison." He paused, glaring at Justin and Middleton. "Who, aside from being foul traitors, are these others?"

Justin exchanged a swift glance with Middleton, who introduced himself. "As master of Chirk Castle, I formally protest any effort on Lambert's part to retake our ancestral home from my family. We have been deprived too long."

"Tell that to Parliament," muttered one of the other men. "And who might this eloquent bumpkin be?"

Justin assumed a self-deprecating air. "Justin Blake, once of Staffordshire, now a man of the world. I've been in France since I was fifteen."

"Should have stayed there," the man replied, heading for the door to signal the waiting troops. "Let's be on our way. It's a long ride to ...."

He stopped as two men barged into the common room, long capes swinging about their knees. "Innkeeper!" shouted Lyndon Styles, waving a beefy hand. "Don't tell me you're full up! We've a lame horse."

"They're all leaving," replied the host, who had rarely seen his inn so well populated since a blizzard three and a half years earlier.

"I hope so," murmured Quentin Radcliffe to the squire. "We are desperate for a decent dinner."

Justin drew a sharp breath, hoping that neither Styles nor Radcliffe would recognize him. Certainly they had never seen him as either Captain Hood or Justin Blake. Styles was already taking off his cloak and inquiring after the inn's provender. Radcliffe, however, was eyeing the ill-assorted group in the common room.

"May God defend us, what have we here—a masquerade or some new Papist perversion?"

Averting his face from the curate's view, Justin gestured at the soldier in command. "Let's not delay," he said, pushing his way toward the door. "Enough disturbance has already taken place within these walls, I fear."

Friends and foes alike agreed with him. But before they could cross the threshold, Radcliffe's voice cut through the common room. "God help us! That's the voice from Saint Barnabas! 'Tis Captain Hood! I knew those green eyes all along!"

The inn turned into bedlam. Justin wrestled with Radcliffe, Delamere grappled with two of the soldiers, and Middleton managed to upend the squire. The innkeeper, who had scurried to safety under a table, moaned over the fate of his establishment. Someone fired a pistol into the air, bellowing for order. As another half-dozen soldiers finally charged into the room, the prisoners were forced to face up to the futility of further resistance. Even though Radcliffe lay dazed on the floor and Styles had the wind knocked out of him, sheer numbers had won the day.

"There's a rich reward on this one," the tall soldier announced, waving a pistol at Justin. "I'll take him in myself."

"No, you won't," Styles puffed, staggering to his feet. "You'll either help us take him back to Rutbury or go to hell!"

The soldier started to make a blasphemous retort but reconsidered. "As you will. We'll provide an escort and expect recompense. You can afford it, after all."

Middleton and Delamere were being hustled out of the inn. Justin was nursing a fist, which he had grazed on Radcliffe's jaw, and musing upon the ironies of life. After so many years of eluding his would-be captors, who had numbered among them the Protector's men, several sheriffs and a host of irate Puritans, he had finally come to grief at the hands of a blustering squire and a fanatical curate. Defeat was not only bitter but ignominious, as well.

As a soldier prodded him sharply in the back, Justin threw back his head and laughed.

"What's this? What's funny?" the man demanded.

Justin's laughter died away as he glanced over his shoulder. "Life." He gave an indolent shrug. "I call it Fate, and oh, my good fellow, it's so funny that a man could almost die laughing."

Chapter Seventeen

IT WAS A PERFECT SUMMER night, filled with bright stars and a ripe quarter moon. Honor had retired early, more the result of boredom than fatigue. It had been more than a month since Justin had left, and as reports of various uprisings filtered into Rutbury, she was positive he had been involved in one of them. Since all had been quashed, she and Philene knew that he must be facing failure—if not worse. Thus, she found sleep elusive these late-August nights and often rose several times to read by candlelight or merely pace the room.

But on this Thursday eve, she was sound asleep when the knock on her door brought her out of a confused and troubled dream. Philene's maid, Mignon, requested Honor to join her ladyship in Sir Ralph's study. Visitors had arrived, the plump maid chattered on, a most disreputable-looking pair she would never have admitted to the house.

"But Steward Loxley, he welcomed them without ado! The English, they are too trusting. We shall thank the *bon Dieu* if we are not all murdered in our beds!"

In the study, a bedraggled and begrimed Padge and Wat were drinking from large tankards and stuffing themselves with a plateful of cold meat and cheese. Sitting behind her late husband's big oak desk, Philene sipped at a glass of Burgundy and looked uncharacteristically disconcerted. Nip stood behind her, by a tall narrow window that gave out onto the rose garden.

"Drink," Philene said abruptly. "Justin's been captured."

Honor sat very carefully in one of the matching Spanish armchairs, feeling for a moment as if her heart had stopped beating. "How?" she asked, her voice a dull echo of its usual sure sound.

"Satan's foul luck," grumbled Wat, his grizzled face bearing evidence of a recent melee. The graying hair hung lank over his torn collar. A man of few words, he turned to Padge. "Tell her. I've heard it enough to gag a goat."

Without enthusiasm, Padge recounted the story he'd already related to Philene and Nip. Having skirted Newport Pagnell, he and Wat had ridden north to scout the road Justin and the others would take to Scotland. Finding no sign of Lambert's men between Newport Pagnell and Olney, they had returned to report to their captain.

"We got there just as the soldiers were hauling him and his two friends away. To Stony Stratford they were headed, according to the innkeeper. Off we rode," Padge went on, taking a quick quaff of ale and ignoring the line of foam left on his upper lip, "only to learn that half the company was going to London while the others were headed for Rutbury. Delamere and—" Padge glanced at Wat "—Middleton? Aye, from Chirk, those two were carted off to the Tower while the captain was being brought back to Rutbury for the reward. We were plain puzzled until we spotted Quentin Radcliffe and Lyndon Styles in their midst. Then we knew what dirty work was afoot."

Heedless of the Ferrers's fine Persian carpet, Wag spat on the floor. "Those two demons! I'd boil 'em both in oil, if I had the chance!"

Having accepted a glass of wine from Nip, Honor was still overcoming her shock. "What were Radcliffe and Styles doing in Newport Pagnell in the first place?"

It was Philene who answered. "They'd gone to see the odious Lambert in London a fortnight ago. He wasn't there, of course, being engaged by Justin and the other rebels in Cheshire. So they waited for him, to secure permission for the sale of timber in Burton Old Forest. By chance, they stopped at this Newport Pagnell on the way back."

"You see?" exclaimed Wat. "Poxy luck! They should have taken the Oxford Road in the first place!"

It seemed to Honor that Justin and the others had indeed been unlucky. She couldn't help but blanch as the word *Fate* came to mind. "Where are they now?" she asked, trying to fight off a sense of doom.

Padge lifted his broad shoulders. "Near Rugby, I'd wager. We made a dash for their van, hoping to take hostages, but there were too many, even in the rear." He fingered a bruise under his left eye. "We got away and rode like the wind for Rutbury."

A sudden silence filled the room. Outside, the light of false dawn was breaking over the village. Philene tapped her glass and looked disturbed. Nip stared out into the rose garden, one hand clinging to the deep blue draperies. Padge and Wat each made a last, desultory pass at the plate of food, then lapsed into weary contemplation.

"Where will they take him?" Honor asked at last, setting down her half-empty glass and standing up.

Nip turned around, his fine features still warped by concern. "Criminals usually go to Burton, where there's an official jail. Rutbury's citizens have been content to use the stocks and pillory for alleged violations of local law."

"We must find out," Honor asserted, beginning to pace the room. "When we know, I'll need a pistol. The Goudges took mine."

Philene's eyebrows lifted. "*Ma chérie,* are you mad? Leave shooting to our brave men here. They are, after all, a valiant band."

But Honor wasn't to be dissuaded. "We'll need every bit of help we can get," she asserted, coming to the oak desk and slamming her fist down on the mother-of-pearl inlay. "We're up against not only Lambert's soldiers but most of Rutbury." Her dark eyes rested briefly, if urgently, on each of her listeners in turn. "I'd prefer using guile to free Justin, but if I must resort to guns, I will. Fate be damned, they will not hang him! I promise all of you that!"

THE HARDEST PART WAS WAITING. For more than a week, there was no word of Justin or his captors. At least once a day Honor became convinced that he had escaped and fled to Scotland. But Philene, whose nerves were almost as raw as Honor's, stubbornly rejected the idea.

"Where's Styles? Where's Radcliffe? And all those soldiers? We'd have heard by now if Justin had gotten away. It's more likely that his captors are haggling over the reward."

As it turned out, Philene was right. Before bringing Hood back to Rutbury, Lyndon Styles had sent word to Whitehall that he wanted the reward first. John Lambert, caught up in a fight for his political life, showed little interest in the petty affairs of a renegade highwayman, an obscure squire, and a country curate. Lambert had not offered the reward; that had been Dick Cromwell's doing. And hadn't Styles and Radcliffe just been granted a great boon by being allowed the proceeds from Burton Old Forest? John Lambert turned his back on the Rutburians and his face to the north, where General Monck still vacillated.

Undaunted, Styles and Radcliffe brought their captive into the village under cover of darkness the first week of September. Three days later, justice was meted out swiftly and mercilessly by the curate and a council of elders, which had included Delbert Goudge. Honor had heard the news upon returning from a brisk canter with Philene, their first outing since the report of Justin's capture. The next day they learned that he had been sentenced to hang the following morning.

Honor, who had remained determinedly calm and practical, finally broke down at this news. "I can't bear it," she sobbed, sinking onto Philene's settee.

"This can't be happening! I should have stopped him! We should never have let him leave Smallwood!"

Philene gave her arm a sharp shake. "We couldn't have, *ma chérie.* His mind was made up, as was Adrian's." She flinched at the comparison and shook her head in consternation.

"Maybe it's not too late," Honor said thickly. "Maybe I can talk to Uriah, beg him to influence his father."

Philene's violet gaze was fixed on Honor's flushed face. "It's possible, that. Yet it all seems to march with Radcliffe now, not the Goudges. At least not Uriah. The curate is hand in glove with the sheriff, who lies ill at Burton. Still," she reflected, trying to conceal her agitation, "it is worth a try."

"Of course it's worth it!" Honor gasped. "Send Loxley to Creepers to fetch Uriah. I'd go myself, but God alone knows what the other Goudges might do to me."

Philene was already tugging at the bell cord. "Courage," she said softly, but her silent prayers to the Virgin were almost a cry.

IF URIAH FELT UNCOMFORTABLE AT Creepers, he seemed even more out of place in Smallwood's elegant withdrawing room. Leda and the swan romped on the ceiling while carved garlands of spring flowers decorated the walls. Three large tapestries brought a century earlier from Belgium retained much of their original vivid colors. The furnishings were mainly French, too delicate for the late master's bulk and just as unsuited to the present guest's awkward frame.

Nevertheless, Uriah sat calmly enough on a gilt-edged chair while Honor sketched the situation to him. Justin was being held in the cellar at the vicarage; the scaffold was a-building in the market square. Lambert's soldiers remained outside, guarding the prisoner and waiting for their share of the reward. There was no way to storm the makeshift prison, since at least a dozen men surrounded the vicarage on all sides. Therefore, other means must be employed to secure Justin's release, the most effective of these being Delbert Goudge's intervention. Or so Honor insisted.

Uriah listened patiently, and though he already knew the facts, he was moved by Honor's distress. Even so, when she'd finally wound down, he shook his head with regret. "It's hopeless, Honor. My father would never change his mind. My mother would never let him."

She had not really expected anything else, yet her heart thudded dully in her breast. "There is one other chance," she ventured, weaving her fingers together. "It would take great cunning on your part, Uriah."

"Ah ...." He put a hand to his forehead. "That's not for me, Honor. Truly, I would if I could—"

"You can, Uriah!" She leaned closer, speaking with the utmost earnestness. "I told you, you're an intelligent man. All you need is a little subterfuge."

Uriah blinked at the word, but Honor hurried on, explaining her plan. When she was done, Uriah still looked reluctant. "'Tisn't strictly honest. And Curate is no fool."

"We'll avoid Radcliffe, if we can," Honor said, waving a hand. "As for honesty, would you condone murder? That's what this hanging amounts to."

"But Hood is a thief!" Uriah protested.

Honor gave him a hard stare. "He is also Justin Blake. Your family stole from him. Should your parents hang, as well?"

Observing the stone-cold set of Honor's face, Uriah shifted uneasily on the fragile chair. "I don't want to refuse you," he said miserably. "But my parents will disown me."

Honor sat up very straight, no longer visibly nervous but resolute. "That's not an excuse, Uriah. It's an opportunity. You said you've never been at home at Creepers. Clearly, you feel guilty. This is your chance to make amends."

Uriah was quiet for a long time. The ormolu clock ticked persistently over the marble mantelpiece. Honor's mouth tightened as she saw the filigreed hands move to four o'clock: only fifteen more hours before Justin was to die ....

Slowly, like a man in a daze, Uriah nodded.

Though the tiny cell in which Justin Blake was being held prisoner was no more than four feet wide and six feet deep, Beggar's Oak had accustomed him to cramped quarters. But nothing in life had quite prepared him for death.

The only furnishing in the cell was a lumpy straw pallet. There was no window and the smell of damp permeated the stale air. The scurrying sounds in the walls warned Justin that mice—or rats—or both—dwelled close by. A test of the iron bars that formed the cell door gained him no more than a strained muscle. The thin gruel and water that had made up his meals were brought by Radcliffe himself, always in the company of a hulking oaf whom Justin recognized as the village simpleton. The curate gloated over his fate but lamented the mercy shown by the majority of the church elders.

"God clearly works through these good people," Radcliffe said waspishly that afternoon, "in that only Divine intervention could save you from being drawn and quartered as well as hanged. You should serve as an example for other misguided spawns of Satan. I would have thought heaven would be better pleased by the spectacle of your dismemberment than a mere dangling from the gibbet."

"Heaven's whims, it seems, are unpredictable," Justin remarked coolly.

Radcliffe peered between the iron bars as the oaf loomed behind him like a homely guardian angel. "Don't blaspheme! Your soul is already in jeopardy.

Are you ready to repent?" the curate asked with expectant eyes.

Justin's initial reaction was to cut Radcliffe off entirely. But his penchant for candor prevailed. "I've numbered my sins," he said easily. "Pride and bad poetry come to mind most readily."

"Lord Jesus have mercy," murmured a flabbergasted Radcliffe. "Your sacrilege astounds me."

Justin gave him a blank look. "Which is worse, pride or bad verse?" he rhymed, turning contemplative. "Verse, probably, since it can make posterity suffer."

Radcliffe's face turned an unhealthy shade of plum. "There! You're bound for hell! You mock God!"

"No. Nor do I aspire to *be* God." Justin picked up the battered pewter bowl that contained his ration of gruel. A dead fly floated on top. "Here," he said, shoving the unappetizing concoction through the bars. "I intend to fast to redeem a particularly inept couplet." Before Radcliffe could take hold of the bowl, Justin flipped it over, sending the gruel plopping onto the curate's carefully polished shoes.

"God's eyes!" cursed Radcliffe, batting at Justin with his hand but managing instead to crack his knuckles against one of the bars. "You're the archfiend himself! I'll see you tortured yet!" His eyes glinted dangerously, then he whirled on the hulking man behind him. "Stop that smirking! And clean up this foul mess! My shoes, too."

The oaf obeyed wordlessly, doing a thorough job in the process. Radcliffe, who now had control over himself, gazed thoughtfully at his servant. "Yes, Bull, you have earned a reward. You may claim it tonight, when the good villagers are asleep." He gave Justin a malevolent look. "I wouldn't want to wake them with your cries for mercy. They'll need their rest for the fine spectacle we'll put on for them in the morning." With an arrogant swing to his shoulders, Radcliffe moved quickly away from the cell, while Bull followed him like a docile dog.

After they had gone, Justin slid slowly down the wall to sit with his head resting on his knees. There had to be a way out; he had been in too many menacing situations to think otherwise. Radcliffe didn't come into the cell at mealtimes, but if his intention was torture, either he or the man called Bull would have to open the iron door. Radcliffe would be easy enough to overcome, for despite being almost as tall as Justin, his body was flaccid. Bull was another matter. He was huge, a good three inches taller than Justin and probably four stone heavier. Justin didn't like the odds, but he might not get another chance. With a heavy sigh, he wondered what fate had befallen Padge and Wat. It was possible that they, too, had been captured. At least Nip was safe at Smallwood with Philene and Honor ....

Honor …. He rubbed his hand along the rough wool of the breeches he'd borrowed from the farmer. He remembered Honor the last time he'd seen her, wearing that brilliant robe of Philene's, the golden hair cascading down her back and the enticing curves of her body outlined under the flowing gown. She hadn't wanted him to leave; perhaps she'd sensed the terrible danger. His need for her, which he'd dared to call love, had wrung a promise to return. How ironic that for the first time in his life he wouldn't be able to keep his word, when it was the one vow that meant more to him than any he had ever made before.

Almost as galling was his failure to see Charles Stuart sit on England's throne. Lambert's star continued to rise over England like a chill winter sun, and Justin had almost started to lose his faith in the eventual restoration of his King. But it was, of course, pointless for him to worry about Lambert or Charles or the future. It was an empty landscape for him, a place where he would never tread. The world would have to go on without him. It wouldn't matter to the Puritans or the Anglicans or the Catholics or anyone else.

Except, he thought morosely, it would matter much to Honor.

"It's perfect," Honor breathed, torn between fear and excitement. "See, Philene, isn't Nip a replica of Master Thorn?"

"I only glimpsed the schoolmaster," said Philene, carefully studying the draped robes and the cowled hood that covered Nip's face, "but Justin's role was memorable. *Mais oui,* Nip is the very picture of that unique presence."

"I'm not clever at imitating voices," Nip said doubtfully from somewhere inside the hood.

Honor waved a hand at him. "Leave that to me. You may not have to say a word." Anxiously, she went to the long window that looked out toward Buttermilk Hill. "It's dark enough, but nonetheless too soon. Damn and blast, why do the hours drag so?"

The clock on the mantel showed almost ten. Honor didn't want to leave any sooner than midnight. The guards must be drowsy when they arrived at the vicarage and Quentin Radcliffe should be fogged by sleep.

"I have the potion Uriah sent," Philene said, her own nervous state evidenced by her incessant toying with the cluster of pheasant feathers in her dark curls. "You will vouch for its efficacy?"

"It worked on me," Honor reassured her. "Thank God Uriah knew where his mother keeps her vile brews."

"Très bien." Philene removed the feathers and tossed them onto her gilt-edged dressing table. "*Alors*, where is Loxley?"

The steward was readying the horses, according to Nip. Honor arranged her borrowed pistol among the folds of her riding skirt and watched the clock.

It was now after ten; another two hours to wait. Her heart was already beating too fast and her palms were moist with perspiration. Any thought of failure had to be put from her mind, lest she lose heart before she left Smallwood.

By midnight, a light drizzle had settled over the countryside. The three riders set out from the manor, while Padge, Wat and Nip delayed their departure for another quarter hour. Just outside the village, Honor and the others slowed their mounts to a cautious walk. Along the Mill Fleam, past the Cornmill, the castle ruins and The Lamb Without Wool they rode, scarcely daring to breathe. Entering the lower High Street, they glimpsed the church, its spired fastness a bulwark against the night.

The soldiers were gathered between the gibbet and the vicarage, seated around a small bonfire. The arrival of three people in the wee small hours of the night brought them to their feet. Philene was the first to dismount, cradling a linen-covered hamper and twittering anxiously as Loxley handed her onto the ground.

"Sainte Vierge!" she exclaimed, reverting to the vacuous coquette Honor had first known, "it is the vicar I must see! *Maintenant, mes amis!*"

"Speak English," growled a veteran soldier with a well-fed paunch. "Who be ye?" His rough hand took in the little band, which hung back, heads down in the face of the steady drizzle.

Philene assumed an injured air, the dark lashes fluttering. "I am Lady Ferrers, a widow twice over. Your countrymen don't last long, I fear. I came to see my brother-in-law before he, too, dies."

In the saddle, Honor winced at Philene's words but kept her face averted as the old soldier exchanged puzzled looks with two of his men. "You mean the poxy highwayman, otherwise known as Blake?"

Philene let her black cloak slip just enough to reveal a glimpse of milky-white shoulders. "Call him what you like, to me he is kin, brother to my first husband. You will permit that I see Vicar? I must ask permission to hold a vigil in the church. With me are a pious priest from Normandy and my maid," she went on, seemingly oblivious to the rain that was falling on her bare shoulders. "We have brought bread and wine to consecrate into the Body and Blood of our Savior. Vicar must approve, I understand that much."

The soldier eyed the covered hamper and shrank back a jot. "Sacrilege! You'll work no mumbo jumbo in Saint Barnabas! Vicar and Curate will have you in the stocks!"

"Zut!" Philene clutched the hamper to her bosom, in the process allowing the man a further glimpse of flesh. "But where is mercy? Where is charity? Justin is to be hung at dawn!"

Nervously, Honor peered into the drizzle, searching for a sign of Uriah. Perhaps he'd been waylaid by his parents. Maybe he'd changed his mind. It was even possible that he was confused about his instructions. With unsteady fingers, she tucked a stray blond lock back under the close-fitting cap and prayed that their efforts would not be in vain.

"Vicar's abed, Curate can't be disturbed," the soldier insisted smugly, though he was openly ogling Philene's bosom. "What, might I ask, did those husbands of yours die of?"

The hint of a smile flitted across Philene's face. "Happiness." Her iris-colored eyes fixed on the soldier's face, making an obvious impact. "A pity, too, since widowhood is such a lonely vocation." She sighed prettily, then reached inside the hamper. "If we cannot use this wine for holy sacrifice, it must not go to waste. Perhaps you would accept a bottle or two for your men? It's an excellent vintage, from my family home near the Loire."

The soldier's broad brow furrowed. "A bribe? I don't know. But it's a wet night and a miserable duty. Why not?"

Honor watched Philene hand out three bottles while the other soldiers clustered around their leader. Time was running short, the rain was growing heavier, the road that led to Creepers remained empty. Next to her, Loxley, muffled to the eyes, shifted impatiently even as he tried to quiet his restive mount. It was at that moment that Honor turned again in the saddle and saw a lone rider clip-clopping up the Lower High Street. When she recognized the sloping shoulders and the big, shambling frame, she knew her prayers had been answered. Uriah approached at a lackadaisical pace, doffing his steeple-crowned hat at the soldiers.

"Ho, Lady Ferrers, is that you?" he inquired, pulling his mount up short. "What brings you out on such a night?"

"How dare you ask, Uriah Goudge," Philene replied indignantly. "You stole my first husband's home, now you'll take his brother's life. And these cruel soldiers refuse to let me see Vicar so that I may go to church and pray for Justin's soul."

"Well, now." Uriah spoke his part stiltedly, but Honor hoped the soldiers wouldn't notice. "Come, my good fellow," he said to the veteran, sounding as if he were reading from one of Master Thorn's primers, "let Her Ladyship pass. Sir Ralph, after all, was a staunch Roundhead. I am sure that the vicar will treat her kindly."

"Young Goudge, is it?" The soldier wiped moisture from his forehead. "But they're sleeping inside."

Uriah opened his mouth to respond, apparently forgot what he was supposed to say, and had to be rescued by Philene. "*Le bon Dieu* will forgive you much for this little gesture." The lashes fluttered invitingly again. "I, too, will be grateful." Without waiting for further commentary, she beckoned to both Uriah and Honor. "Come, Master Goudge. You, too, Mignon. Our holy priest can wait until we've seen Vicar."

Moving purposefully, Philene led the way up the three stone steps to the front entrance of the vicarage. She tugged sharply at a bell cord, but there was no responding sound.

"Sleeps like a brick, does Vicar," Uriah murmured as Philene yanked the cord again. "Am I doing well?"

"Fine." Honor realized that her voice was as unsteady as her legs. There was still no response from inside the vicarage, though Honor thought she heard a noise: not footsteps, but something else; an almost human sound, yet strangely distorted.

"Should we go round back?" she asked, but knew the answer before Philene could reply. The soldiers would interfere, no doubt insist on coming, too. The carefully concocted plan would be ruined.

After the third pull, a faint shuffling noise could be heard on the other side of the door. At last it opened a scant inch, revealing the vicar with a taper in one hand and a groggy expression on his face. "God bless you," he greeted them, then opened the door another crack. "*Who* are you?"

Uriah identified himself, which caused the door to swing wide. Once inside, Honor heard the peculiar noise again, a keening sound, like an animal in pain. Even as Philene was making her request, Honor moved away to listen. With a growing sense of horror, she realized that the cry was indeed human and that it was coming from the cellar.

Honor could wait no longer for Vicar Busby's brain to clear itself. Philene had taken note of Honor's sudden alarm and was steering Busby toward his parlor while Uriah strained to sort out the unexpected development. Honor blindly searched for stairs that would lead to the cellar, paying no heed when she heard Uriah call after her. Moments later, she was hurtling down the curved stone steps, drawn to that terrible sound.

"Ahhh!" Quentin Radcliffe jumped as he saw Honor flying toward him. "What is this?"

Honor stopped just short of the curate, who was leaning against the iron bars of the cell. Inside, a candle gave an eerie glow to the ugly scene that was being enacted within. Justin dangled from the ceiling, his wrists bound by leather thongs, which had been secured around the cell's single oak beam. His feet swung free of the floor by a good three inches and his bare back was a mass of bloody stripes. Below him stood Bull, the bruises on his face indicating that Justin had not succumbed willingly to his fate.

With a scream that tore out of her throat, Honor threw herself at Radcliffe. "Stop! Stop, you vicious beast! Cut him down!"

The curate righted himself and tried to prize Honor's fingers from his night robe. "Get away, strumpet, or I'll put you in with Bull! He knows how to tame the most unrepentant soul!"

But Honor's fury had been unleashed by the sight of Bull raising a grotesque steel-studded scourge. She reached into the skirts of her riding habit, drew out her pistol and took aim at Radcliffe. "I said cut him down! Now!"

Radcliffe stared incredulously at the pistol, then smirked. "Ah, yes, I remember now, you're the whore who arms herself with manly weapons. You won't fire, of course, for if you do, I promise you that Bull will break Hood's neck." He glanced at the hulk of a man, who grinned back vacantly. "Won't you, Bull?"

Honor couldn't help but waver. She didn't doubt for a moment that the brutelike Bull would carry out Radcliffe's orders. So caught up in the ghastliness of the situation was she that she didn't realize Uriah had run up behind her.

"Christ!" he exclaimed, taking in Justin's bleeding body. "Is he alive?"

"Of course he's alive," retorted Radcliffe, straightening out his rumpled garments. "Do you think I'd cheat the hangman?"

Honor was clutching at the iron bars, calling Justin's name. He appeared to be unconscious, his head slumped onto his chest, the blood oozing out of the raw wounds. Bull was still grinning as he twirled the awful scourge in his beefy paws.

Uriah winced, then swallowed hard and turned to the curate. "I must have the key. The elders have voted to free Hood."

"Nonsense!" rejoined Radcliffe. "The elders have done no such thing!"

"Aye, they met at Creepers this very night." He glanced at Honor for encouragement, but her entire being was focused on Justin. "They … ah, want him released. Or is it that they want him brought before them?" Confused, he touched Honor's shoulder. "Which is it?" hissed Uriah. "I forget."

Honor turned a stricken face to him. "Does it matter? It's all ruined! Justin is half-dead!" Still holding the pistol, she buried her face in her arms and began to sob wildly.

"Oh, stop that, you silly slut!" ordered the curate. "You'll rouse half the village." He turned toward the cell and made a slashing gesture at Bull. "Cut the demon down for now. I've other amusements planned for him. Indeed," he went on, leering at Honor, "I've an idea that ought to give pleasure to everyone. Do you still lust after this filthy baggage, Uriah?"

Flushing, Uriah assumed as much dignity as he could muster. "Don't use such wicked words, Curate. You sound like my mother."

"Now, now," chided Radcliffe, forced to shout over Honor's cries, "remember the Commandments, exercise respect for your parents in all things." With an insidious smile, he moved closer to Uriah. "Wouldn't you enjoy the sweetness of her honey pot? Who needs holy matrimony to lie with such a pagan slut? You could have her now, here, with witnesses to your triumph."

Repelled by Radcliffe's lewd suggestion, Uriah backed away, knocking up against Honor. "You're foul," he gasped at the curate. "You're not a man of God, you're a devil!" Clumsily, he put an arm around Honor and tried to draw her away from the iron bars. She remained rooted to the spot, resisting his well-meant efforts, her sobs reduced to whimpers as Bull cut through the leather thongs and let Justin collapse onto the floor.

"Stay," Radcliffe commanded his servant. "I must escort these two misguided souls out." He gave Uriah a stern look. "You're a fool, Goudge, a pathetic dupe. Have you no pride?" He waved a long finger at Honor. "She's cast a spell over you, just like the witch we always thought her to be."

"I told you to speak with respect," Uriah warned, keeping Honor close.

"Get out," ordered the curate, standing very erect with his arms folded and his hands now tucked into the sleeves of his night robe. "There is still work to be done this night. Crawl back to Creepers like the snake that you are and take that wicked woman with you. You shame your pious parents!"

Honor felt Uriah flinch, but she was too spent to care. All her carefully laid plans had been destroyed by Radcliffe's unspeakable cruelty. She still had her gun, she could shoot him, but just as surely as the curate fell, Bull would answer with Justin's life. And even if he did not, the sound of the bullet would bring the soldiers. She made no further effort to be brave but clung to Uriah, vaguely wondering if she might be better off dead.

Stumbling back through the darkened passage with only a flickering sconce on the wall to guide them, Radcliffe was at their heels, still fulminating about the duties of a child to its parents. He didn't stop until they had reached the bottom of the winding staircase. There, in the curve of the stone steps, stood a ghostly figure in dark robes, clutching a gnarled staff.

"Who's there?" breathed Radcliffe on a sharp intake of breath.

Uriah and Honor retreated, managing to slip around Radcliffe and stand behind him. The hooded figure descended a single step and banged the staff, the sound echoing to the far end of the passageway. "It can't be!" gasped Radcliffe, clutching at his night robe with shaking hands. "He's dead! Who is this?"

The staff thudded again, the figure came down another step. Honor, whose strength seemed to return in proportion to the ebbing of Radcliffe's courage, stepped out of the circle of Uriah's arms. " 'Tis Thorn," she whispered, now at Radcliffe's elbow. "He was never properly put to rest!"

"Impossible!" cried the curate, glancing wildly in every direction.

"But is it?" Honor asked softly. "Oh, see how he comes toward us! His soul must be in torment!"

"No!" Radcliffe wheeled about even as the ghostly form reached the bottom of the staircase. The curate would have fled down the passageway but Uriah blocked his way. "Move! Run!" wailed Radcliffe, shoving at Uriah. "He means to take me to hell! Help me!"

The staff banged three times on the stone floor, signaling each step of the specter's progress. From the cavernous folds of the hood, a rasping voice made the dank cellar air tremble. "A life for a life! A soul for a soul! Follow me, Quentin, to dwell in Gehenna forever!"

"*No*!" Radcliffe threw himself against Uriah. "Save me! Help! I'm doomed!"

"Not if you agree to his bargain," Honor said, grabbing the curate by the collar of his robe. "He asks for a life, a soul. Give him Justin. Give us the key." She was so close to Radcliffe that their noses almost touched. "The key. Hand it over or we'll give you to Master Thorn!"

A strangled sound erupted from Radcliffe's throat. For a brief moment, Honor thought he had fainted. But he was fumbling in his night robe, finally extracting a small iron ring bearing several keys. "It's the longest one," he said, and struggled to right himself. But even as he shifted his weight against Uriah, the hooded figure loomed directly over him, uttering a terrible ragged growl. Radcliffe screamed, and this time he fell into a swoon at Uriah's feet.

Honor was halfway down the passage by then. To her astonishment, Bull was sitting in a corner of the cell, his head on his shoulder and his eyes closed. How he could have fallen asleep with such a commotion raging not ten yards away baffled Honor, but she had no intention of questioning her good fortune. It was only after she had gotten the stubborn key to turn in the lock that Justin lifted up his head and gave her a weak shadow of his customary grin.

"I'll be interested to hear what happened out there," he said with obvious effort as he struggled to his feet. "God's ghost, but I feel weak as a newborn foal. Stiff, too."

"Justin!" Honor snapped out of her sudden paralysis and started to fling herself at him. But remembering the painful stripes on his back she stopped in her tracks. "You're not almost dead?"

"Not quite." He straightened up and winced. "Give me your pistol. Do you have horses?"

"What?" So stunned was Honor that she couldn't remember the original plan. "Oh, yes, out the back way, with Padge and Wat. Oh, dear heaven, your poor back!"

With a glance at Bull to make sure he'd remain unconscious for at least another few minutes, Justin took the pistol from Honor and hustled her out of the cell. Nip and Uriah were already hauling Radcliffe down the passageway. After they had locked the curate and his servant inside the cell, they raced up the steps, then paused to listen for signs of further danger.

"...at a shrine with the most miraculous springs! Even Protestants are cured." Philene's awed voice floated from the parlor into the hallway. "So I think to myself, does God distinguish between religious sects? If not, why can't I say French, if not Latin, prayers in your fine church?"

There was a long silence, during which Honor, Hood, Uriah, and Nip moved stealthily down the corridor. "Well, yes, I understand your feelings," Busby responded in his vague manner. "Yet here in England, there has been much strife between believers." He paused, then spoke again. "Are you sure you don't hear those odd noises?"

"Only the beating of angel wings," said a stricken Philene. "Death hovers close by. Mayhap God doesn't dwell in Saint Barnabas ...."

Her voice faded away as Justin led the others through the back entrance. By the trees that lay between the church and the river, Padge and Wat waited with the horses. A lone soldier lay on his side under the porte cochere, snoring lustily. Parthenia Goudge's sleeping draught had again worked its magic, though certainly not on victims she would have chosen. Honor, who was overcome with relief and fatigue, could hardly climb onto her horse. But moments later, with the wind at her back and the rain now only a soft mist, she was fording the River Dove, crossing over into Derbyshire—and freedom.

Chapter Eighteen

The Earl of Derby had a cousin named Edward Stanley, who owned a modest house near the village of Tissington. Stanley was as steadfast a Royalist as his noble cousin, if also recently converted to Charles's side. Though he was astonished by the sight of the bedraggled fugitives arriving on his doorstep shortly after sunrise, he welcomed them warmly. His wife's first concern was Justin Blake, whose bloodied back threatened to fester. She ordered him straight to bed while Honor and the three highwaymen ate breakfast before also collapsing with exhaustion.

Philene had returned to Smallwood, accompanied by Loxley. The steward had gone undetected, and since she had taken no active part in the escape, Philene scoffed at any danger to her personal safety. As for Uriah, he had not returned to Creepers but to the Tipper cottage in Stubby Lane. If he was distressed at the estrangement from his parents, he hid it well.

To Honor's dismay, Justin became fevered and was confined to bed for the better part of a week. Along with Mistress Stanley, a relentlessly cheerful women with broad hips and a surprisingly small waist, Honor kept a bedside vigil. Finally, as the wounds on Justin's back began to heal, he rallied. He was back on his feet the following Sabbath, insisting that they must leave at once for the Scottish borders.

"You're still weak," Honor argued, careful not to hit her head on the low, sloping ceiling of the gabled bedchamber. "Why must you go at all? You've often said it's only a matter of time before Charles comes back now that the Cromwells are gone."

Justin tested the steaming water in the tub two Stanley servants had just brought upstairs. "The country's on the edge of a cliff. Monck broods, I'm told, afraid that Lambert is acquiring too strong an army of his own. Let's be candid, Monck is basically not a Royalist. There are few men who can rise above their own feelings for the good of their country. The longer he waits, the more entrenched Lambert becomes. I have the feeling that if Monck thinks Lambert can bring stability to England, he'll let Charles grow old in exile."

Having virtually no recollection of living under any form of government other than a republic, Honor still couldn't quite see what difference it would make to either of them. "Do you honestly think you can convince Monck to act? Surely others have tried."

"Surely." Justin ripped off his shirt and breeks, then stepped into the tub. "They've failed, it seems. I would hope to succeed."

"I don't see how," Honor said, but she was distracted from her argument by the sight of Justin's strong masculine body. "Pray sit, I'll tend to your back." She moved briskly to fetch soap and a linen cloth. "I must say, you're not healed yet. Another week of rest will do you good."

"Another week will bring October," Justin retorted, letting Honor bathe his back with gentle hands. "How long would you wait for me to make an honest woman of you?"

She moved around so that she could see his face. "I didn't know you planned on doing that at all," she said a bit testily. "Nor do I see what King and country have to do with our future."

"Much," replied Justin, catching her in the back of the knees and tumbling her into the tub. She shrieked and sputtered, flailing on top of him and trying to gain some sort of equilibrium. He was roaring with laughter, holding her so that only her feet, head, and shoulders were out of the water even as the skirts of her borrowed dress billowed about her legs like ships' sails.

"Stop, Justin!" Honor cried, but she, too, was laughing. A moment later, he was peeling away the sodden garments, casting them onto the floor and stroking the cool soft length of her hip and thigh.

"Now we can have a proper bath," he said, pressing his wet cheek against the curve of her throat. "Will you allow me?"

As she turned so that she could see his profile, Honor's eyes grew wide. "You're a devil, Justin. I'm not an honest woman yet!"

He was turning her around to face him, the grin still in place. "You're a wet one, though, which suits you. Remember our idyll in the Dove?"

"Of course," Honor replied, suddenly sober. "How could I forget? But why not marry now? You're safe, I'm well away from the Goudges, and I don't give a jot if you're poor."

"A good thing," he mused, cupping her breasts under the water. "But I refuse to come to you a penniless groom. And only King Charles can so endow me that I might be worthy of your love." He spoke lightly, yet his intent was serious. "Hence, yet another reason why I must go north."

"You've done enough for the King," Honor contended, but it was a halfhearted effort.

Justin had rescued the linen cloth and was cleansing her shoulders, her breasts, her belly with the most sensuous of strokes. With her legs wrapped around his lower torso, she leaned back against the tub, letting him drizzle fragrant, soapy water from her chin to her throat to the valley between her breasts. At last he delved between her legs, his fingers guiding the cloth into the most intimate recesses. Honor moaned softly with pleasure but remembered to be careful of his back as she wound her arms around him.

For two months, she had survived on only the memories of his touch, savoring each detail like faded petals crushed between the pages of a much-loved book. Now, with his hands cradling her buttocks and his mouth exploring hers, she was lost in a haze of desire. Slowly, cautiously, he lifted her up from the water and carried her to the trundle bed. The golden hair lay shining against her wet skin, the dark eyes were wide with the wonder of his naked flesh. Arching her hips to meet him, she trembled with delight at his first thrust, then held him fast within her. Together, they moved in blissful concert, higher and higher, further and further, into that realm where only lovers dwell.

Exultant and replete, they lay in each other's arms for a long, quiet time until Honor's thoughts finally caught up with her senses. "I love you, Justin," she said on a quavering sigh.

One hand clasped her hip, the other made a fist under her chin. He started to speak, frowned briefly, then gave her a wry smile. "I love you, too, Honor. If not yet free to marry, at least I'm free to love."

Faintly puzzled, she gazed at him questioningly. "I didn't know people decided when and whom to love. I thought it happened, of its own volition."

He rolled over onto his back, pulling her with him. "It does," he replied in a low voice. "Thank God it never happened to me until you."

They had slept for a while that morning, and when Honor was the first to awaken, she was convinced that Justin still wasn't well enough for an arduous journey, especially in what was turning into foul autumn weather. But later that day, while they were returning from the village green where they'd gone to feed the ducks in the little pond, ominous news reached Tissington. Edward Stanley met them in front of the limestone house, his face troubled.

"I detest bearing unhappy tidings," he said apologetically, "but John Lambert has discovered that you are not just a troublesome highwayman but a noble whose staunch support of King Charles can be construed only as treason. My cousin and Thomas Middleton lie in the Tower even now, awaiting trial. Lambert is after your head, as well." Stanley wrung his hands. "I *am* sorry," he repeated, "but the situation in London grows worse by the day."

Justin placed a hand on Stanley's shoulder. "Don't apologize," he said lightly. "You've been more than kind, as well as brave, to take us in. We'll be gone before sunup."

He glanced at Honor, who was still looking stunned. "I would beg you to take care of my betrothed," he said, grasping her hand and bringing her forward. "She is innocent of any crime against the Republic and has always been a devout Puritan as well as Cromwell's kin. If you and Mistress Stanley would—"

"No!" Yanking her hand away, Honor whirled around to face Justin. "This time I go with you! I'm no more of a Puritan than you are, certainly no more so than Master Stanley here or his cousin, the noble earl! But most of all, I don't trust you alone in the hands of Fate! You need me, Justin Blake, as much as I need you!"

Seeing the determination in her eyes and the set of her chin, Justin not only recognized defeat but secretly relished it. "We must get ready," he said, saluting his host. "There's no need to wait until the morrow." Briskly, he headed for the house, calling to his men. Honor watched him go, hoping that his strength was fully restored. For her own part, she would match him stride for stride, mile for mile. From now on, Justin Blake's fate was hers, as well.

THEY TRAVELED NORTH, THROUGH SHEFFIELD, Doncaster, Scanthorpe and Selby, with the damp, sharp smell of autumn in the air and the wind blowing crisp brown leaves in their path. By the end of the week, they were sloughing along on mud-clogged roads in a driving rain, but at least there was no sign of Lambert's troops. Indeed, in several of the inns where they stopped, the King's health was toasted and hopes were held high for his speedy return. As ever, the North was a fortress of tradition. Outside of York, in a tiny village called Romsby-le-Beck, they found sanctuary with Royalist supporters whose names had been known to Adrian Blake. Yet for all the openly expressed sentiments, the future remained uncertain.

Rumors ran like hungry cats through the northern shires: Lambert had been cashiered; Fleetwood had been relieved of his army duties; Lambert had turned Parliament out and barred the doors; Monck still waited in the Borders. Justin listened thoughtfully, pondering his next move. He had planned on forging ahead to Berwick and General Monck's headquarters, but when he learned that some of the Royalists were trying to bribe Lambert with offers of exalted marriages for his daughters with the Duke of York and even the King, he decided to take stock of his role in the growing crisis.

"If I went to London and somehow secured Delamere and Middleton's release," he told Honor one gloomy October night in the only inn at Romsby-le-Beck, "we might be able to rally the rest of the ousted Parliament members and put up a fight. Lambert still holds no official title of governance."

"He seems to have power enough, though," Honor mused, picking at a plump partridge leg. "Or else those skittish Royalists wouldn't be trying to make alliances with his children and the royal family."

Justin took a last bite of his apple and tossed the core in the direction of a crackling fire in the open grate. "That's what puzzles me. Do they think to bring Charles back and have him share the government with Lambert? It's an idiotic idea to which neither man could possibly agree. But why else make such offers?"

Honor had no more answers than Justin. As Padge and Nip came through the inn's door, wiping the rain from their faces, a third man followed them with his cloak still held close around his face.

"Will Herbert," whispered Padge, leaning on the table. He glanced around the room, but except for a lethargic serving wench, the place was empty.

Justin had not seen Herbert since Cheshire. Obviously, he'd managed to avoid prison. Curious, Honor watched the Catholic nobleman slip onto the bench next to Justin and give her a cursory nod.

"Our Yorkshire friends told me I'd find you here," he said in a low voice. A single-minded man in the best of times, Herbert now seemed particularly insistent. "Lambert has just been made major general. Even now he is marching north to root out those he considers his opponents. God spare us, we're faced with a new civil war."

Honor saw Justin tense. Surely after Uncle Oliver's death, Cousin Dick's flight and King Charles's growing popularity, it was impossible that such an obscure man as John Lambert should rule over all England. But there was ample evidence of the possibility in Will Herbert's drawn face and Justin's snapping eyes.

"It's not hopeless," Herbert was saying, his hands tightly clenched on the table's rough edge. "The word is out. By tomorrow, most of Yorkshire will be armed."

In an uncharacteristic gesture, Justin jumped to his feet and slammed his fist against the wall, rattling the plate rail behind him. "And beaten before they take the field! God's eyes, when will the Royalists learn that all the valor in the world isn't worth one well-primed cannon!"

Herbert was also on his feet, scowling at Justin. "You'd put up no fight at all? For shame! What, then, is your answer?"

Justin had no chance to give it. The door burst open, revealing a dozen soldiers pushing their way into the common room. "That's him!" one of them shouted, pointing at Hood. "It's Blake, from Cheshire's folly!"

Grabbing Honor with one hand and his pistol with the other, Justin toppled the table, scattering the first four men. Padge and Nip charged into the fray while Will Herbert fumbled for his sword. Amid flying fists and crashing furniture, Honor felt herself being dragged out through the kitchen while Justin kept his gun drawn on any would-be pursuers. The warning shots exploded, sending the serving wench into hysterics and the innkeeper onto the floor. A moment later, Honor felt her feet touch the damp earth while Justin ran for their horses.

The stable was small and in need of repair. No lantern showed the way inside and Justin tripped over a feed bag before he reached the stalls. Cursing, he felt for Honor's hand. Together they led the animals outside just as Wat came hurrying up, shouting that more men were coming over the stone bridge on the other side of the village.

"Damn!" Justin vaulted into the saddle, pulling Honor up behind him. Grunting with exertion, Wat clambered onto a frisky bay and yelled to Nip and Padge. There was no answer except for the chaotic noise, which now seemed to be coming from the kitchen.

Next to the road, Justin hesitated. He couldn't abandon his friends, or Will Herbert, if it came to that. Anxiously, he peered into the night, which was now half fog and half rain. The company of men could be heard rather than seen coming along Romsby-le-Beck's narrow High Street. Honor sensed his indecision and held on even more tightly, her eyes shut against the dampness. She hardly dared breathe until she suddenly felt him relax and utter an oath of relief.

"Inglesby! Streeter!" he called. "Into the inn! We've a bunch of Puritans trapped inside!"

The Royalist leaders and their men set off with a roar, thirsting for battle. There were at least thirty of them, and all seemingly well armed. For once, Justin wasn't able to disparage the odds. "I must join them," he said, trying to shake Honor off, but she dug in and refused to budge.

"Don't be a fool! They'll subdue that crew in no time! Why risk your neck for such a small reward? See," she exclaimed, gesturing with one hand toward the inn's rear entrance, "here come Padge and Nip now!"

Battered but triumphant, they both laughed as they swung into the saddle on the horses Wat held for them by the stable. "Herbert stays on," chuckled Nip, his boyish face marred by a long scratch. "He says he aims to skewer a few Presbyters before the night is out. I think it's a hobby with him."

Justin grinned, then set his horse off at a canter. "His is the easy task," he called over his shoulder. "It's up to us to steal back a crown!"

IF OLIVER CROMWELL HAD HAD the look of an ordinary man, George Monck possessed the demeanor of a king. He wasn't more than average height, yet his impressive physique gave the illusion of great size. In middle age, he retained a fair, fresh complexion, though his hair was turning gray and there was the suggestion of a paunch under his military garb. If he was uneducated, he made up for the lack by innate intelligence; if his political leanings might be deemed changeable, he compensated with prudence. It was said that he thought as well as he fought, and for a general, the compliment was rare.

To Justin's surprise, he had no trouble gaining an audience. To Monck's amazement, Justin brought Honor with him. It had been a heated argument between them, but Honor had won it by asserting that if he went to see Monck without her, she'd follow him. It was that simple; Justin had no answer for it and, with a bemused shrug, took her arm and led her into the general's headquarters at Berwick Castle.

Monck proved as obdurate as Honor but in a less voluble manner. Yes, he was alarmed at Lambert's new post as major general. Indeed, he found Lambert's military force growing at a dangerous rate. Certainly there was a threat of renewed civil war. No, he didn't think it wise for Royalist supporters to barter Charles's kingdom away with marriage to the Lambert daughters.

"The fact is," Monck said, leaning back in his ancient high-backed chair, "I believe this country is tired of fighting. If Lambert can bring peace, then the future will take care of itself, praise be to God."

Justin, who was sitting across the battered desk with Honor at his side, turned faintly sardonic. "Do you speak of God, General—or Fate?"

Monck had picked up a long clay pipe and was cleaning its bowl with a small knife. "Eh?" He inclined his head, which seemed almost too small for the wide shoulders. "God, of course, though some might call it Fate. I trust in the Almighty to guide us in all things."

Honor glanced from the general to Justin and back again. "Then the Almighty had better march across the Tweed. Lambert is driving north at this very minute."

Monck straightened up in the chair, his lower lip thrust out in surprise. "What's this? My scouts have told me nothing of the sort."

"Will Herbert told us," said Justin. "We rode like the wind to tell you. All Yorkshire is in revolt."

"I heard of disturbances there these past few days, yes." Setting the pipe down, Monck rose from his chair and came around to Justin and Honor. "But there is always trouble in the north. It's a hotbed of Royalist sentiment." His keen gray eyes looked hard at both of his visitors, though he softened slightly when Honor met his gaze head-on. "When did they leave London?"

"As far as I know," Justin answered evenly, "almost immediately after

Lambert was named major general. I'd gauge them to be only a day or two behind us, depending on the weather."

"An army!" Monck clapped his hand to his balding head. "Damn Lambert's eyes! He means to rule all! The man goes too far!" He paused, suddenly thoughtful. "Yet King Charles connives with the Papists. Where, then, is compromise?"

"There can't be any," asserted Justin, rising to face the general. "We're beyond compromise. The only solution is to bring Charles back. You must send for him now, sir, even as your forces beat back Lambert."

Monck's chest seemed to expand to immense proportions as he drew himself to the full illusion of his height. "I will not be coerced! I've not waited this long to act rashly! I tell you, there must be compromise between Royalists and Roundheads! Otherwise, England is doomed to eternal civil war!"

As Justin lifted a calming hand prior to reiterating his argument, Honor tapped him gently on the arm. "Hold, Justin, General. The compromise has already been reached."

Both men stared down at her, a small disheveled figure in the capacious Turkish chair. "What do you mean, mistress?" demanded Monck with a show of impatience. It was sufficiently unconventional that a convicted highwayman and rogue had hauled his light-o'-love along with him to the headquarters of the general of the English army, but now the little chit was daring to offer advice. Still, Monck had to admit, she was a charming creature, and well-spoken. He'd been listening to everyone else for months on end; perhaps there was no harm in hearing her out, too.

"It's quite simple, really," explained Honor, assuming her most sensible air. "Justin Blake has always been a staunch Royalist. His father and brother died for their beliefs. I was raised a Puritan, a niece to Oliver Cromwell." She paused just long enough to make sure that fact had hit home with Monck. Noting the slight lift of his bushy eyebrows, she continued. "By chance … or was it Fate?—" she slid Justin a quick glance "—my father had Justin's brother hanged. In turn, my father and mother were murdered in revenge. I escaped. Some might say it was the hand of God that spared me, and maybe it was, but when I met Justin almost ten years later, I couldn't hate him even though I tried. Nor could he hate me. We plan to marry, you see, and it strikes me that our generation is born to love, not hate. The compromise is in accepting each other for who we are, not what we are." She reached out and took Justin's hand. "I very much doubt that we are the only man and woman in England who feel that way."

"Well." Monck fingered his upper lip, seemingly lost in solemn thought. "You have a point, mistress. I'd no idea you were Cromwell's kin."

Honor shrugged. "Mall Cromwell married a Royalist noble. If she could compromise, there's no reason why the rest of us can't."

The general had gone silent again. Justin waited patiently while the heavy fog rolled past the narrow windows and the sea air crept in between the chinks in the old, weathered stone walls. Monck took a few steps around the room, his hands linked behind his back.

"Sending for Charles would go against much of what I've believed for most of my life." He saw Justin incline his head while Honor merely listened impassively. "Charles would have to make many compromises of his own, especially with regard to religion." Encouraged by Justin's firm nod, Monck continued. "He'll have to stop dealing with France and Spain. The English won't tolerate popish ways of any sort." Again, Justin nodded. "He must be merciful to his enemies, judicious with his friends and temperate in all things."

"We can but hope for the best," Justin remarked evasively. The general was describing a saint, not a sovereign, particularly not the kind of indolent, loose-living man that was Charles Stuart.

"Well, then?" Monck was tapping his booted foot on the rush-strewn floor.

Justin's mild gaze was inquisitive. "Then what, sir?"

"Will you go to the King, of course?" He gave a little impatient shrug. "You've been sending him funds, your family has been ardent in its support, you seem more determined than most to bring him back. You've even," he added, with a surprising twinkle in his eyes at Honor, "made a convert of your, ah, bride-to-be. If you will go to Charles with the conditions I've listed, then I will fight. Agreed?"

Justin stared incredulously at the general's outstretched hand. "God's ghost!" he exclaimed, grasping Monck by the forearms. "I'll go on the next tide, if need be!"

"Then go." Monck allowed himself a smile of relief as he searched through stacks of paper on his desk. "This must all be official, of course, and executed with due respect to the legalities involved. Meanwhile, I'm giving orders to secure Edinburgh, Leith, and Berwick."

Inwardly, Justin groaned. "How long will that take, sir?"

Monck had snatched up a sheet of blank paper and was now rooting about for a pen. "What?" He glanced at Hood and actually winked at Honor. "How long? Two days." Noting his listeners' astonished expression, he chuckled. "Oh, it takes me some time to make up my mind, but once I act, I do it quickly. I expect to have all England under control by New Year's. Assuming, of course," he added, with a long, hard look at Justin, "that you are right."

Justin put his arm around Honor. "I am. For once in my life, I have no doubts about the future."

* * *

AMAZINGLY, MONCK WAS AS GOOD as his word. Edinburgh and the border towns were secured within forty-eight hours, a well-nigh miraculous military achievement. John Lambert, who had marched his own army almost to the Tweed, was not merely impressed but intimidated. Still not convinced that Monck would send for King Charles, Lambert sought to negotiate. Monck, after all, had openly declared for the ousted Parliament but had made no mention of restoring the monarchy. Lambert's troops outnumbered Monck's. Surely the general could be persuaded to Lambert's way of thinking.

But like a stubborn spark that refused to ignite until it explodes into an unquenchable inferno, George Monck could not be stopped. After two days of fruitless talks, his men swooped down on Lambert and crushed the Republic's army. The Irish brigade immediately defected, joining up with the Yorkshire Royalist insurgents. Lambert's cause, along with his career, lay in shambles.

If John Lambert's vaunted ambition had been laid to rest in the most pronounced, public way, Dick Cromwell's plummet from the pinnacle of power had ended ignominiously. The late Protector's son and heir had been hounded not so much by his political opponents as his London creditors and had stolen away in secret to the Continent. No one knew exactly when he left or where he was headed, for so deep was his disgrace that he had used an assumed name in booking his passage. There were no well-wishers to see him off, not even his wife, Dorothy. There was not even an enemy on hand to mutter good riddance.

Honor and Justin had no idea that her kinsman was going abroad when they set out on their own voyage to the Continent. Had she known, Honor might have been one of the few people in England to spare a pang for Dick Cromwell. As it was, she had her own problems to confront as the first storms of winter roiled the North Sea. Never having been on a ship before, Honor spent most of the journey clinging to her bunk and being sick. Resisting an urge to remind her that she would have been better off staying back in England, Justin held her head and rubbed her back.

"You will recover," he assured her, trying not to smile. "Once you're on firm ground, you'll forget you were ever sick in the first place."

He was wrong. Upon landing at Scheveningen in Holland, Honor was just as miserable as she'd been at sea. Alarmed, Justin considered making the trip to Breda without her. Sir John Grenville, a cousin of Monck's, had accompanied them and brought along a suitable train of servants. Surely Honor would be well tended in his absence. There had already been enough delay, what with waiting for the outcome of the battles between the opposing armies, the resumption of Parliament and the drawing up of demands. Even now, the roads were icy and the canals were frozen in places. He was anxious to be off before the next storm blew in over the Low Countries.

Even as they awaited word from Breda to go ahead, a message arrived from England, saying that Parliament was eager to send for the King, assuming he would accede to their demands. Further delay could prove fatal. The mood was of change, the time was ripe. Justin refused to delude himself into thinking that everyone in England wanted King Charles on the throne. And even when he got to Breda, there was no assurance that Charles would accept the stringent conditions put forth by his future subjects. Growing restless, he prowled Scheveningen's wharves and hoped that Honor would not insist on holding him back because of her indisposition.

She, however, remained steadfast in her aim to stay at his side. "I've come this far, I intend to see the King at Breda. I just wish he'd stayed in Flanders. It would have been closer."

"He couldn't. It's under Spanish domination," Justin replied reasonably. "Monck insisted on Charles removing himself to Protestant territory. Breda belongs to the House of Orange."

Honor brightened. "How I'd love an orange right now! A whole basket of them! Would they have some in Flanders?"

"In January?" Justin eyed her curiously. "It's cheese in Breda. Tasty, too, I'm told. Wait until summer for oranges, my love."

But Honor had turned petulant. "I can't. By summer the babe can eat oranges on his own."

Stunned, Justin knelt down by the cot on which Honor was resting in the inn by the harbor. "Babe? Are we to have a babe come summer? Honor? Answer me!"

But the heavy lashes dipped onto her cheeks. "I'm sleepy. Let me doze a bit. Then I shall be refreshed to leave for Breda."

"Honor!" He shook her by the shoulders. "Tell me, now!"

Slowly, she opened her big, dark eyes. The look she gave him was both tender and insouciant. "I'm not going to tell you until we're married. I'm still not an honest woman."

Exultant, Justin gathered her up in his arms, all but crushing her against his chest. "My love! You should have told me sooner! Why didn't you say something before we left England?"

"Because you wouldn't have let me come," Honor said a bit querulously. She wriggled in his arms, trying to get her breath. "Nor was I sure until the week before we sailed." She tipped her head back, feeling his lips pressed against her throat. "Don't you dare leave me behind now! I'll feel like an abandoned woman!"

Tenderly, he kissed her ear, her temple, her nose. His hands strayed to her breasts, which were full to bursting beneath the simple muslin traveling gown. "How could I not have guessed?" he breathed, savoring the newly made ripeness of her flesh.

"You've been a bit preoccupied," she chided, but surrendered her body to his probing hands.

"And as blind as Matthew Thorn," he murmured, laying her back down on the bed and lifting her skirts. "Am I forgiven?" he asked, the green eyes glistening as he pulled away petticoats, shift, and undergarment.

"No." She tried to stifle a little sigh of pleasure but was unsuccessful. "That is, not yet. In truth, you mustn't make love to me. I'm unwell *and* unwed."

Justin stared in awe at the still flat belly, then touched the smooth flesh with reverent fingers. "Our child lives there," he said softly. "A child descended from despised enemies but conceived in mutual love. Is this our compromise, my love?"

Honor batted away his hand. "You aren't listening, Justin! I am the one who is compromised. Don't touch me until you've rectified the situation, do you hear?"

Jarred, Justin leaned back, his face a study of mixed emotions. "I'm sorry, I'm overcome .... Passion's child to us is born, the fruit of autumn's harvest morn ...."

Honor fell back among the pillows, an arm raised over her head, her body convulsed with laughter. "You dream, you rhyme, you invent your endless guises." She grew more serious and sat up, putting a hand on his cheek. "Now you've created a child," she said quietly. "Isn't that the most wonderful invention of all?"

Justin kissed her fingertips and cocked his head to one side. "It is, indeed, Honor." Tentatively, he put an arm over her hip. "Whom do I ask for your hand? Dick Cromwell has disappeared, the Goudges would pillory us both— Should I track down that worthless brother of yours?"

Honor wrinkled her nose. "For all I know, Palmer may be in Peru. Next to Tyler, he is the most self-serving man I know."

"Well, then." Justin's fingers trailed down her thigh. "My back is against the wall, with no hope of escape this time. Which will it be, marriage or love? I'm told Puritans can't have both."

"I'm not a Puritan," asserted Honor, pulling him close. "It's early yet today. We can have love in the morning if you will promise marriage by afternoon."

FOR GENERATIONS, A WEATHERED STONE chapel with a huge stork's nest on its tiled roof had served the seamen who sailed in and out of Scheveningen's harbor. It was there, on a chill winter's day, that Honor Dale and Justin Blake were joined in holy matrimony. The clergyman who united the couple spoke almost no English, but with faith that God understood all languages as well as intentions, the ceremony was duly binding. Honor cried a little, wishing that Philene could have been present. Justin had soothed her, saying that if not at the wedding, their kinswoman would stand as godmother at the christening. They celebrated with John Grenville and the rest of the entourage with supper at the inn.

Once they were alone in their tiny chamber overlooking the sea, Honor's health was miraculously restored. Indeed, she bloomed, with a new sheen to the golden hair, a touch of pink at her cheeks, a lilt in her step.

"Is it real? In Dutch or not, are we man and wife?" she asked happily, wrapping her arms around Justin's neck.

"Of course," he replied, still awed by the precipitous step they had taken that wintry afternoon. "Are you happy?"

In answer, she closed her eyes and went slack in his arms, a dreamy smile on her face. "Ecstatic."

He grinned at the delectable piquant features, then kissed her eyelids and pressed her close. "Had it not been for you, I'd be a dead man by now," he said with fervor against her ear. "I owe you much, Honor, including my life and that of our child."

"Don't talk of owing," breathed Honor, planting little kisses on his bare chest. "You saved me from the Goudges, from emptiness, from a world where I didn't belong."

With deliberate care, he removed her clothing and the rest of his own, all the while watching her with a new sense of wonder. "You have become a woman as well, I'll grant you that," he said with a shadow of his usual grin. "Your body's fruitfulness reaffirms our love."

On bare feet, Honor moved toward him, her nakedness spurning the chill winds that blew in from the sea. "It seems to me," she said dryly, "that it's the other way round."

Justin gathered her up in his arms, a precious cargo, warm and willing in his embrace. "I love you more than life, Honor. Someday I shall write a letter to Tyler Vail, thanking him for being such an ass."

She had her legs entwined around his midsection as he held her under the buttocks. Teasingly, she leaned forward so that her ripe, round breasts just touched his face. "I scarcely recall the man," she said, writhing with pleasure as he captured a budding nipple with his lips. "Honor Dale, Honor Vail, neither suited me in the least." Taking in a short little breath, she leaned back in his arms as he laid her on the bed. His lean, dark face with those glittering green eyes looked down on her with no secrets left between them. "The mask is gone," she murmured, more to herself than to him.

"What?" He looked puzzled, then lifted one broad shoulder. "That's so. Captain Hood is dead. We buried him at sea."

"Thank God," sighed Honor, opening her thighs to welcome him. "At last you can truly be Justin Blake again."

A strange expression crossed his face. "Not again, exactly. If not reborn, Justin Blake is a different man." He clasped her hips, savoring every inch of her being. "Thanks to you." The green eyes flickered, then were drowned in the sea of desire that overwhelmed them both. At last an honest woman, Honor Blake also counted herself among the happiest.

Chapter Nineteen

THE FOLLOWING DAY THEY STARTED out for Breda with Grenville and his retainers. It was not a long journey, but they traveled slowly over the frozen ground as Justin hovered at Honor's side to make sure she was not jarred along the way. In places where the canals were unclogged by ice, they boarded trekschuits, slow-moving barges used by the Dutch instead of land-bound coaches. By the end of the week they were at Breda, where the exiled King of England lived in an ancient castle that had been built with defense, not comfort, in mind.

Honor's first glimpse of Charles Stuart revealed a tall, swarthy man in shirtsleeves who was braving the winter weather to play ice hockey on a pond outside the castle walls. Almost two hours passed before Charles skated back to the frosty ground and announced his intention of supping privately with a pretty young woman swathed in furs who probably wasn't as old as Honor. Justin and Grenville were left to cool their heels with a fat, pompous man named Edward Hyde, who had recently been appointed the King's chancellor.

"I shall review the conditions and convey them to His Majesty," Hyde asserted, holding out a pudgy hand for the papers. "Here, my good fellows, let me have them. My reply—that is, the King's," he amended, his chins jiggling, "will be made in due time."

"Hold, sir," said Justin firmly. "We need more haste. This is an urgent situation. General Monck is due to arrive in London at any moment, and when he does, John Lambert will be arrested. In the meantime, Parliament has been sitting for nigh on a month. They grow impatient, I fear."

Hyde gave Justin an ironic glance. "Impatient? And what has His Majesty been all these years? A vacillating general and a tempestuous crew of politicians cannot command a king. It is now their turn—and yours—to wait."

AS IN THE PAST, IT seemed to Justin Blake that he had spent much of his life waiting. Now, as the snow fell across the flat Dutch countryside and the sharp north wind whined in the walls of the castle, he paced the cramped quarters in the tower room he shared with Honor and cursed Edward Hyde's perversity and Charles Stuart's indolence.

Honor, who no longer felt ill but was finding the few garments she owned too tight, watched her husband with sympathy. "I never dreamed I'd start my married life in a foreign country. Why can't you and Grenville go directly to the King? From what I can tell, His Majesty seems an agreeable sort."

Justin leaned against the window embrasure. "He is. It's Hyde who blocks our way. The Chancellor is very protective of Charles, believing that in the past, without his august guidance, our monarch has acted too rashly."

Putting a hand to the gentle curve of her abdomen, Honor sighed deeply. "Oh, Justin, are we ever going to go home?"

His jaw set in a hard line. "To what purpose, Honor? We have no home."

"You know what I mean," she mumbled, contrite at having reminded him of their impecunious state. If he was never allowed to see the King privately, their chances of a royal boon would evaporate. The future, which had seemed so deceptively bright just weeks earlier, now loomed barren and unsure. How ironic, Honor thought glumly, if Justin succeeded in his quest to bring King Charles home, while the two of them—and their child—ended up impoverished exiles.

IT WAS MID-MARCH WHEN HONOR decided to take a desperate gamble. Even though Hyde was said to be discussing Parliament's demands with Charles whenever the restive monarch could be pinned down, there was still no summons for Justin and Grenville. On a mild morning with the soft scent of spring in the air, Honor went in search of Charles Stuart.

It was the sound of laughter that drew her, and she found the King outdoors playing croquet with several of his courtiers, including the pretty brunette Honor had noticed her first day at Breda. Now the grass was free of snow, and the early bulbs poked sturdy green shoots out of the rich earth along the castle walkways. Overhead, the linden trees were leafing out, swallows darted among the battlements with nesting material, and the pale March sun edged out of the clouds to shine fitfully on the royal competitors.

Keeping her distance, Honor watched the merry group with a sense of inadequacy. Men and women alike were bedecked in such ribbons, laces, braid and buttons that they seemed as exotic to Honor as a clutch of brightly plumed tropical birds. In her plain, ill-fitting muslin, she felt as out of place as a hag in a harem.

For the better part of half an hour, Honor watched the King and his companions frolic around the course. Informality reigned, with Charles on the receiving end of as many gibes as he made at the others. In particular, Lady Palmer, as the lovely brunette was known, seemed on quite intimate terms with her monarch, at one point threatening him none too playfully with her mallet.

Alone and ignored, Honor waited restlessly until a redheaded young man smacked his ball with such verve that it careened off course, struck the base of a sundial and rolled to a stop a scant two feet away. The redhead and Charles raced each other for the ball, but the King stuck out a foot and tripped his loyal subject, who went sprawling near Lady Palmer's miniver-trimmed hem.

Charles roared with laughter, a diversion sufficient for Honor to reach out and kick the ball under her own drab skirts. Searching the ground in front of him, the King suddenly became aware of Honor's presence.

"Aha!" he exclaimed, still chuckling. "You must be a conjurer, mistress. Or did you not see a croquet ball roll in your direction?" He paused, pushing back the dark hair from his forehead, and scrutinized her more closely. "Such golden hair! So fair a face! And yet no reply. Are you Dutch?"

"No," replied Honor evenly. "I'm English." She attempted a little curtsy. "And, yes, I have your ball. You may ransom it, Your Majesty." An ingenuous smile played at her lips as she gave him the full benefit of her thickly lashed dark eyes.

Amused, Charles took her hand. "What price, mistress? A bauble? A kiss?" He leaned down, his homely dark face radiating a masculine charm far more powerful than ordinary good looks. "If you're English," he murmured, "why have I not met you before?"

While Honor could appreciate Charles's attraction, she was immune to it. "Chancellor Hyde has kept me hidden," she said lightly, deciding this was not quite the right moment to mention Justin or the burden with which he'd been charged. "As for the ransom of your ball, I want a house."

"A house?" Charles straightened up, the heavy dark brows raised. "What sort of house?" he inquired, giving his companions a sidelong glance.

"A purloined house called Creepers in Staffordshire." She ignored the curious, faintly scornful gazes of the others and concentrated on Charles. "It was once the property of a family named Blake. My husband is the only surviving heir. He is here at Breda awaiting an audience. Perhaps you would know him better as the highwayman, Captain Hood."

Recognition dawned on Charles Stuart. "Of course! Is this the fellow who came with Grenville?" He saw Honor nod. "The infamous Hood! He sent me funds when I desperately needed them. I was wearing threadbare hose and patched breeks a year ago last winter when I received a fine collection of jewels from him. God bless him, those cold stones warmed my heart as well as the rest of me." He beamed at Honor. "Except one, a magnificent ruby I couldn't bear to part with. Barbara," he called to the lovely Lady Palmer, "come here!"

With a swish of her satin-clad hips, Barbara Palmer glided up to the King. "Who is this baggage?" she asked under her breath, seemingly indifferent if Honor heard.

"Never mind. Just show her that fabulous ruby." Ignoring Barbara's pique, he held out her right hand, where a large square red stone caught the light and blazed to life.

Honor gasped, a hand at her breast. "That's mine!" she blurted. "Damn and blast, it's my dowry!"

Charles dropped Barbara's hand. "Zounds! Are you sure?"

"Of course I'm sure," Honor retorted heatedly. "Captain Hood stole it from me on the London-Oxford Road."

"But …." Bewildered, Charles glanced down at the ring, but Barbara Palmer had it covered with her other hand. "I thought you were married to the rogue," he said to Honor.

"I am." With effort, she tried to check her annoyance. "But I wasn't then, and somehow, I'd always thought he might have … never mind, of course he sent it to you. I was a ninny to believe otherwise."

"You must have it back, then," the King insisted, trying to haul Barbara forward. "Here, sweet Babs, give Mistress … Blake? Yes, Blake, her ruby."

"Not in a pig's arse," snapped Lady Palmer, jerking away from her monarch. "You gave me this the first night we lay together! Do you think I'm unsentimental, you royal jackass?"

If Honor was appalled at the beautiful young woman's brazen tongue, Charles merely chuckled. "Barbara's the possessive sort," he said apologetically to Honor. "I'm sure that when I've had an opportunity to reason with her, she'll be generous enough to return your jewel."

Honor couldn't resist a sharp glance at the rapacious Lady Palmer. "Let her keep the blasted thing," she insisted. "I want Creepers."

Charles tugged at his left ear and shook his head. "It seems that one of the conditions Chancellor Hyde has conveyed to me is allowing our former Roundhead enemies to retain the property they took as their spoils during the Civil War. I don't dare make such a promise." His black eyes were genuinely contrite.

Honor reflected briefly, glancing from Charles to his indignant mistress. "Very well. Then I'll take the ruby after all. And to make up for the rest of my dowry, I'd like those sapphires Lady Palmer has around her neck, as well."

Barbara actually emitted a strangled shriek, then fled across the grass toward a side entrance into the castle. Charles made as if to go after her, thought better of it and turned back to Honor with a sheepish grin. "She's a bit touchy when it comes to her baubles." With a heavy sigh, he put a hand on Honor's shoulder. "Creepers, did you say?" His dark eyes had the ability to make his audience feel quite special. "I suppose I could make an exception. But," he added, bending down and whispering in her ear, "don't tell a soul!"

It was a perfect May morning, the sea as smooth as satin, the sun smiling down from a cloudless blue sky. England's flagship had been launched as *the Naseby,* but rechristened t*he Royal Charles.* On its deck stood His Majesty, in as affable a mood as anyone had ever seen him, recounting those harrowing episodes of his youth as he fled from Cromwell's men at home and later, from poverty abroad.

As they cast off from the harbor at Scheveningen, cannons roared and the huge crowd of well-wishers waved the fleet out onto the tide. More volleys came from the Dutch ships that lay to starboard, cheering the exiles home. At the rail, overlooking a cluster of mingled Dutch and English flags, Justin Blake squeezed his wife's arm.

"I'd almost despaired that this day would ever come," he said, shielding Honor from being jostled by a group of particularly rowdy courtiers. "Thank God for Edward Hyde!"

Giggling, Honor brushed her head against Justin's shoulder. "To think you once cursed him! But, like Monck, when he set his mind to his task, he carried it through to the letter."

"Almost." Justin's green eyes scrutinized Honor. "You're forgetting King Charles's one exception." A puzzled look had crossed Justin's face. "I still can't believe he'll restore Creepers to us. It's like a miracle."

The sails were filling out as the wind picked up; the flagship rolled gently on the waves. Getting the feel of the deck beneath her feet, Honor realized that not only didn't she feel sick, she was invigorated. "Oh, I don't know. I'm sure His Majesty will reward other loyal servants, even at the detriment of a few Roundheads." She spoke without apparent guile, but Justin frowned.

"Perhaps, yet it still strikes me as strange," he insisted.

Puffs of smoke were drifting out over the harbor from the belching cannons onshore. The crowd noise grew fainter, the spire of the chapel where Justin and Honor had been married began to recede into the distance, the sea opened up between them and Holland. Honor said nothing. Not for all the world would she ever let her husband discover how she'd finagled Creepers out of King Charles. There were some things that men didn't need to know.

"The King is a good man," she finally allowed, watching Charles gesture his way through yet another anecdote.

Bemused, Justin pulled Honor closer as the breeze caught her golden hair and the salt spray tingled against her cheeks. "True," he agreed, caressing the mound of her belly. "Indeed, I always felt that somehow Fate would bring me back to Creepers."

Honor shot him a sidelong glance. "Fate?" She gave a little shrug and nestled contentedly in his embrace. "I suppose," she said, looking straight ahead to the open sea, "that's as good a word for it as any."

SEATTLE NATIVE **MARY RICHARDSON DAHEIM** lives three miles from the house where she was raised. From her dining nook she can see the maple tree in front of her childhood home. Mary isn't one for change when it comes to geography. Upon getting her journalism degree from the University of Washington (she can see the campus from the dining nook, too), she went to work for a newspaper in Anacortes, Washington. Then, after her marriage to David Daheim, his first college teaching post was in Port Angeles where she became a reporter for the local daily. Both tours of small-town duty gave her the background for the Alpine/Emma Lord series.

Mary spent much of her non-fiction career in public relations (some would say PR is fiction, too). But ever since she learned how to read and write, Mary wanted to tell stories that could be put between book covers (e-readers were far into the future and if she hadn't seen her daughter's iPad, she might not know they exist). Thus, she began her publishing career with the first of seven historical romances before switching to mysteries in 1991. If Mary could do the math, she'd know how many books she's published. Since she can't, she estimates the total is at least 55. Or something. See below—count 'em if you can.

At the time of her husband and mentor's death in February 2010, David and Mary had been married for more than 43 years. They have three daughters, Barbara, Katherine and Magdalen, and two granddaughters, Maisy and Clara. They all live in Seattle, too. Those apples don't move far from the tree … literally.

For more information, go to: www.marydaheimauthor.com.

If you enjoyed this book, check out Camel Press's other reprints of Mary Daheim's historical romances:

Serena Farrar dreams of being a journalist in Massachusetts. First she must obey her family and marry sea captain Brant Parnell. Her coldness drives him back to sea, so when an ugly scandal erupts, Serena has no choice but to flee to her sister in New Bern, NC. Brant arrives as conflict engulfs the city. Serena is not only a Yankee in enemy territory, but also a woman at war with her heart.

In the time of Mary, Queen of Scots, a young girl left destitute by her father's death meets a pirate in the service of the Queen. They make a bargain: he will marry her, giving her security, and she will not reveal his profession or curtail his freedom. By the time love begins to blossom, it may be too late. First they must survive the turmoil plaguing the court of their Queen.

THE SEQUEL TO THE ROYAL MILE

1585: at Gosford's End in the Scottish Highlands. 17-year-old Sorcha Fraser is impatient for life to begin. Graced with beauty and spirit, she doesn't have long to wait. While out riding, Sorcha meets a young man in priestly robes. From henceforth, as they negotiate the intrigues of the Scottish court, their lives will be intrinsically linked, though fate continues to tear them apart.

In the court of England's King Henry VIII, Morgan Todd, the niece of Sir Thomas Cromwell, is a lady-in-waiting to the queen. An exotic beauty, she is mistaken for a willing servant and deflowered by Francis, the brother of the husband her uncle has chosen for her. Motherhood, war, and intrigue will come between them, but Morgan will never forget Francis, an honorable man in a land of schemers.

COMING IN 2016:

Improbable Eden

Gypsy Baron

Made in the USA
Middletown, DE
16 February 2016